SUNBURNER

Claire Luana

To Zane and Sandy,
Burn bright!

To Mom and Dad.

This book wouldn't have been possible without your love, support, and willingness to drive me to the library about three million times as a kid.

Misty Forest
Seishen Island City
Churitsu Plain
Ushai Shoen
Little Tottori Oasis
Tottori Desert
Kistana
Lost City of Yoshai
LAND OF KITA
Shima Islands

Akashi Mountains
Citadel
Kyuden
Hozuchi River
LAND
OF
MIINA
N
W
E
S

PROLOGUE

The days and nights blended together in this place of darkness. Her captors slid food through the slot at the base of the door from time to time. The prisoner suspected from the deep gnawing hunger in her belly that it was not every day. Her body was wasting away, eating itself from the inside out.

At least they didn't hurt her. She supposed she should be grateful for that. Overall, this captivity was far more pleasant than her last. This time, they seemed content to let her slowly waste away, forgotten and alone.

But she hadn't resigned herself to death. And so yet again, she prepared to perform the ritual that should summon the goddess. She didn't have light and she didn't have a sacrifice. She only had the words, her will, and her own blood. She didn't have a weapon; they weren't foolish enough to leave her in here with a means to end her life. So she scratched ragged marks across her inner arm with her fingernail, bringing warm blood welling to the surface. She couldn't see in the darkness, but she could smell the metallic tang of the blood as it mingled with the smells of her filth, feel its slick wetness against her skin. And she could feel the scabs up and down her arms bearing witness to her previous failed attempts to summon the goddess.

This time, though, this time she had something different. A bone, picked from the measly scrap of oily meat that had been her latest meal. Maybe the blood and the bone together would come close enough to the little creatures she used to sacrifice to summon her.

The prisoner dipped the bone in the blood coating her forearm and chanted the words she had said so many times. *Please*, she thought. She willed it to work. *Please*.

For the first time in many weeks, something happened. A breeze tickled her skin, and static crackled in the air, raising the hairs on the back of her neck.

The goddess appeared, radiant in gray light.

The prisoner closed her eyes and cowered from the being, the sudden brightness burning her retinas. As she opened her eyes, letting them adjust to the light, the goddess's figure became clear, its black gown billowing as if in a storm. It filled the space of the small filthy cell, towering over the cringing prisoner.

"Why have you summoned me to this place?" The goddess's voice was low but harsh, the strange sound grating to the prisoner's ears.

"I have been jailed," the prisoner said, trying to still her quaking body. "They mean to let me die in this cell. Please free me so I can continue your work."

"Why should I?" the goddess hissed. "You failed. The moon and sunburners are at peace. The centuries of hatred and war that we have worked for threaten to be for nothing. Without the discord and death, we are wasting away."

The irony of that statement was not lost on the prisoner as she looked down at her own emaciated form, dimly lit by the goddess's glow, for the first time in months. She fought down the urge to laugh. It came out as a deranged hiccup.

"There must be some way I can be of use to you," the prisoner pleaded, her mind racing. "The burners believe me a traitor. Think of what pain it will cause them if I escape and assist in their downfall. They will fight amongst themselves, blaming each other."

The goddess seemed to consider her, though it was hard to tell through the blurry nothingness where its face should have been. "Perhaps you may be of use to me yet," the goddess said at last.

"How?" the woman asked eagerly, latching on to the goddess's statement like a lifeline. "Let me help you. I'll do anything."

"Anything? You do not even know the task I might ask of you."

The question was a test. She had no true choice here. She had made her choice two decades before in the dark dank of another cell. "The task doesn't matter. I will serve," the prisoner said, bowing her head once again.

The goddess seemed satisfied. "The era of the burners is coming to an end. They have stood in our way long enough. We will destroy their power so they are left with nothing but the bitter memory of their former glory. We will remake this world so it serves us."

"I don't understand," the prisoner admitted, afraid to voice the words, but more afraid to misunderstand her mission. "Burning needs the sun and the moon. How could you destroy that power?"

"That is not your concern," the goddess said sternly. "Your only concern should be whether you will do your part to bring about the end of this world and usher in a new one. A world of darkness."

The prisoner already lived in a world of darkness. The darkness of her cell was only a shadow of the blackness that lived in her soul, what she had been twisted into. She had left the light a long time ago. "Tell me what to do," she said.

CHAPTER 1

The stag was nothing but skin and bones. It moved warily through the sparse pine trees, its hooves crunching the dusty leaves and needles that coated the forest floor.

Kai notched an arrow to the string of her bow, her sweaty fingers struggling to find purchase. She squinted at her quarry, hesitating.

A horse jangled its halter some ways behind her, startling the stag. It darted away, disappearing into the brown camouflage of the trees.

She lowered her bow, relieved. At least she could help one creature today. She turned her horse to the noise and spotted Quitsu, her silver fox seishen companion, perched on a tree behind her.

"Not a word out of you," she said.

"You always were too soft-hearted," he said.

Kai made her way to join the other riders who had come into the clearing. The hunt had been one of her mother's lunatic ideas. Strengthen her ties with the noble families by taking them out into the royal game preserve for a hunt. Nothing brought people together like killing.

But despite Kai's protests, her mother had gotten her way, as she most often did. So Kai found herself in the middle of the dry forest underneath the sweltering heat of the sun looking for game to kill. At least her companions were not entirely unpleasant. Though the men and their wives came from Miina's royal houses, they did not seem as vapid as some of the nobles she had encountered. They were flanked by two master moonburner bodyguards, wearing navy blue uniforms and vigilant expressions.

Her friend Emi sat on a leggy gray mare a stone's throw from them, her fine-featured profile illuminated by the sun. From this angle, Kai couldn't see the extensive burns that covered one half of Emi's face, a permanent reminder of last year's sunburner attack on the citadel. She could see Emi's set jaw and hunched shoulders, her haunted dark eyes. Emi hadn't been herself since their friend Maaya had died in what had become known as the Battle at the Gate.

Kai turned in her saddle and watched as Hiro approached, stopping his horse next to hers. She reached a hand out and he grasped it, closing her hand in his warm calloused fingers.

"She'll come back to herself eventually," Hiro said, following Kai's line of sight to where it had rested on Emi. "She needs time."

"It's been over a year," Kai said. "I miss Maaya too, but I...I've moved on."

"You've had a kingdom to run. You've hardly had time to wallow in grief."

That was true. But as she looked at Hiro, the golden sun shadowing his rugged jaw and highlighting his hair like a halo, she knew that her duties as queen were not all that had helped her cope with losing her friend.

"Maybe she needs a romance," Kai mused.

Hiro raised an eyebrow. "Do you have someone in mind?"

"No," she said. "Not like there are a lot of eligible men around the citadel."

"Maybe one of those fancy nobles." Hiro nodded towards the nobles riding ahead of them, clothed in colorful linens and silks. They were like preening peacocks in a field of brown—colorful, decorative, and useless.

Kai rolled her eyes. "I meant eligible *and* worthy."

"You're right. Emi'd eat those fellows for breakfast."

"Maybe I should bring Leilu and Stela back from Kistana," Kai suggested. "They might be able to lift her spirits."

Their friends Leilu and Stela were serving as ambassadors to King Ozora in the Kitan capital city, which was an important post. But she missed them. She'd be happy to have them back as well.

"You sound as meddlesome as your mother," Hiro remarked.

Kai laughed and held up her hands. "All right, I'll let it go. For now."

"Speaking of letting things go," Hiro said, turning to her with a twinkle in his eye. "Ryu said he smelled a stag in the clearing up there."

She blushed. "Tell him to get his nose checked." She tapped her horse's flanks with her heels and trotted back towards the citadel.

The sun loomed large and red over the brown farmland as the hunting party made their way out of the forest. Cooler autumn weather should have settled over Miina a month ago, but sweltering summer hung on with a vengeance. Kai had dressed for the heat in a loose white wrapped top and light brown trousers, her silver hair knotted in a bun under a wide-brimmed hat. Nothing helped. She could have been naked, and it would still have felt as if she were riding through an oven.

The farmland around them served as a testament to the stark devastation of the drought. Fields that should have been filled with green crops ready for harvest instead sat brown and dusty under the oppressive heat. While the hunt was an opportunity for her to bond with her subjects, it also served a practical purpose. The citadel would need all the resources it could get to survive the coming winter without the crops and plenty it normally relied on. Every little bit helped. Kai thought briefly of the stag she had let go, but then banished it from her mind. The bony creature would do little to stave off the hard season they faced ahead. She was glad she had let it live.

It was as if their world itself was rebelling against them. Last winter had been bitter, cold, and long, and then the land had skipped spring entirely, roaring straight into a sweltering summer. It hadn't rained in months. Crops hadn't stood a chance. Her people couldn't feed their families. Frightened whispers of a new disease, a spotted fever, was sweeping through both nations. It was supposedly highly contagious—skin-to-skin contact was enough to spread the disease. Only a few cases of the fever had been reported so far—on the outskirts of Miina—but those cases had been fatal. These new enemies she faced were not flesh and bone. How could she fight them?

Kai had heard whispers already. Her mother and advisors had tried to keep them from her, but she wasn't blind. Her people were saying that the gods were displeased with Kai's ascension to the throne and the peace between Kita and Miina. Word of the Oracle's prophecy, spoken the night of her coronation, had spread.

"And in the reign of Kailani Shigetsu, daughter of Azura, there will be a great war. A war of gods and men. For Tsuki and Taiyo are displeased with the lands of Kita and Miina, and only one side will remain standing when it comes to the end."

People were whispering that the only way to break the unnatural weather cycle was to return to war with Kita. Kai wasn't sure what would happen to her in that scenario, but she didn't think it would be pleasant.

Emi slowed her mare down to match Kai's pace. "You wear your worry plainly, Your Majesty," Emi said softly. "Best to not let them see it." She nodded towards the nobles.

"A good reminder, Emi; thank you," Kai said. "And speaking of reminders, how many times have I asked you to call me 'Kai,' not 'Your Majesty'?"

"You think just because you're queen, I'll listen to you?" Emi said, a ghost of a smile passing across her face.

"I wouldn't dream of it," Kai said.

"This will pass," Emi said, growing serious. "It has to pass. Soon we'll stand in the rain and laugh about how worried we all were."

"I hope you're right."

Emi gave Kai a sympathetic smile and nudged her horse's flanks, rejoining the other moonburner guards, who were riding ahead with the nobles.

Kai rode alone for a while, Quitsu silently trotting at her side. It was how it was to be queen, she realized. To be surrounded by people yet always alone. She shot a furtive glance back at Hiro, who was bringing up the rear of their column, chatting with Ryu, his lion seishen. Maybe not alone. If anyone understood the demands of ruling, Hiro did, as crown prince of Kita. If anyone could love her as queen and as herself, it would be him.

They neared the farming settlements that dotted the land outside the city of Kyuden. To her left was a stout house, the wood of its walls faded and shrunken with age. The house was surrounded by a dusty farmyard, vacant but for one sorry-looking chicken. *It's much like the house I grew up in,* she thought wistfully. Solid and functional.

"Get off the road," a high-pitched male voice called from ahead.

"Please," said a sobbing female voice, hardly coherent. "My husband."

Kai urged her horse towards the commotion. There was a woman in the middle of the road sitting on her knees. Her dirty face was tear-streaked and wreathed in greasy black hair. A threadbare dress that once might have been pink hung from her thin frame, tied tight with an apron. The nobles' horses danced back from the woman, no doubt picking up on their riders' unease at being so close to a commoner.

Emi had dismounted and was trying to help the woman stand.

Kai swung off her horse and strode to join Emi, taking the woman's other arm. "We have to get you off the road. Then we can talk about your husband."

The woman nodded and stood shakily with their assistance. "He's sick. He's so sick." She was near hysteria, her eyes darting to and fro. "I thought you could heal him. With your moonburning. You have to help him."

Emi and Kai sat the woman down on a bit of brown grass at the side of the road, leaning her against a fence post.

"I have medical training," Kai said. "I will look at your husband, and we will send a healer for him if we can help." If the man was truly ill, there wasn't much she would be able to do without supplies or herbs. But at least she could evaluate his condition and give the healer she assigned her diagnosis.

"Thank you," the woman said, gripping Kai's hands tightly.

Kai wriggled from the woman's grasp, standing.

"Your Majesty." One of her master moonburner guards approached, an older woman with thick silver eyebrows. "I have to advise against this. We don't know what his condition is. You should not risk yourself."

The peasant woman's eyes widened as she realized who Kai was.

"Thank you for your suggestion, but I did not ask for your permission," Kai said.

"I must insist," the woman continued. "It is our job to keep you safe."

Hiro approached from behind her, putting a broad arm around Kai's shoulder. "You should know by now that the queen will not be dissuaded when she has decided upon a course of action. I will accompany her. She will be safe."

The moonburner guard's thick brow furrowed, but she nodded her acquiescence.

Kai ground her teeth in frustration. How was it that Hiro commanded more obedience from her own guards than she did? She knew he meant well, but she would have to talk to him later about undermining her authority. He was not in charge here. She was. And she didn't need him to protect her...

She was getting worked up now, and there was a sick man to see. She shook off her annoyance and smiled at Hiro. "I would welcome your company. Let's see if we can help him."

The smell of disease struck her like a stiff wind as they walked into the farmhouse. Hiro placed an arm over his mouth, breathing through his shirtsleeve.

"Open the windows," Kai instructed. "Let's get some airflow in here. Fetch some clean water. And the wife. I need to know his symptoms."

Hiro handed her the water flask that hung on his belt and saw to her other orders.

Kai sat gingerly on the edge of the bed next to the man. He rolled about in the tangled sheets, deep in his delirium. He was thin but wiry with salt-and-pepper hair and a face deeply lined from a lifetime of sun and hard work. His ragged trousers and worn shirt stuck to him, soaked through with sweat.

Kai felt his forehead and let out a gasp. He had a raging fever. Despite this, his color was pallid and his lips were almost blue, as if he were chilled to the bone.

Hiro returned with the man's wife.

"How long has he been like this?" Kai asked.

"Two days, Your Majesty," the woman said.

"Was he exposed to anything?"

"No, I don't think so," the woman said, desperation in her voice.

"Did he receive an injury? A wound or a bite? Could it be an infection?"

"No," the woman said. "But he does have some strange marks."

"Show me," Kai commanded.

The woman knelt next to the bed and unbuttoned her husband's shirt.

Kai hissed and stood up, backing away from the man into Hiro.

"What is it?" Hiro asked.

The man had red-ringed marks covering his chest and stomach.

"We're leaving," Kai said. "We will send a moonburner healer for your husband as soon as we return to the citadel," she told the woman.

"Keep him well hydrated and as cool as you can until she arrives."

"Thank you," the woman said, still on her knees. She tried to grasp Kai's hands, but Kai jerked back involuntarily.

Kai swallowed a lump in her throat and nodded, striding from the farmhouse.

"Mount up," Kai called to the hunting party, who had dismounted and were fanning themselves by the side of the road. "We head back to Kyuden."

Kai swung onto her mount and trotted off, leaving the rest to follow. Her heart was pounding in her chest. She willed it to slow.

Quitsu leaped from the ground onto the saddle in front of her. This was a common enough occurrence that it didn't startle her horse anymore. "What's wrong?" he asked.

Hiro approached from the other side. He had put the pieces together. "That was the spotted fever, wasn't it," he said, his voice low. "I didn't know it had spread this far."

Kai nodded, refusing to look at him. "Neither did I." Her voice sounded hollow. "The only reported cases came from the outskirts of Miina."

"We'll figure it out," Hiro said. "We'll find a cure before it infects too many."

"We'd better," Kai said. "I touched him."

CHAPTER 2

The hunting party reached the citadel an hour later. Kai felt fine, despite being worn out from the hunt and the heat of the day.

"We don't know for certain that I'll get it," Kai had said, more to reassure herself than Hiro. She couldn't afford to fall ill with Miina in such a precarious position.

Hiro had opened his mouth, no doubt with a concerned but nevertheless patronizing lecture about taking unnecessary risks. Thankfully, he had shut it. "We'll figure it out," he had said. "Whatever happens."

Gratitude had welled in her. There was no criticism he could have leveled that she wasn't already berating herself with tenfold. It *had* been a foolish risk to tend to the man herself. But the only other reported cases of the fever had been hundreds of leagues from here. She had only wanted to help.

Kai stifled a sigh as she dismounted and handed her horse to a servant.

"I'm going to give the news to my council," Kai said to Hiro. "I'll see you later?"

He nodded, concern etched across his tanned face. "I'll come check on you."

Kai blew him a sorry little kiss and turned to Emi. "Will you find a servant to gather my council? We have work to do."

The queen's council met in a long rectangular room lined with parallel rows of high windows. It housed a polished wooden table flanked by high, stiff-backed chairs, and the whitewashed walls were decorated with tapestries bearing scenes of grisly battles plucked from the annals of burner history and lore. Kai sometimes glanced at those tapestries to remind herself of the cost of a wrong decision. Or even a right one.

Kai stood in the corner of the room near her usual chair to put more space between herself and her advisors. One by one they filed in.

Her mother, Hanae, formerly Azura, arrived first, her graying hair pulled into an elegant bun that complimented her neatly-tailored lavender gown. She took the seat to Kai's left.

Next came Nanase, headmistress and armsmistress of the Citadel, known reverently by students as the Eclipse. Her stern face was covered in a sheen of sweat. Judging by the leather armor she was removing and depositing on the floor next to her chair, she had been summoned in the middle of a sparring round. Her silver eagle seishen, Iska, flew through the doors after her and perched on a bookshelf in the corner of the room as Nanase dropped into the chair next to Kai's mother, blowing out a deep breath.

Nanase was soon followed by Quitsu and Master Vita, Quitsu moving slowly to match Master Vita's shuffling steps. Master Vita's bright white hair looked even more disheveled than usual. He struggled to pull the big chair out from the table and lowered himself into it gingerly, leaning his cane against the table. He was still weak from his near-death fight with consumption, but he had been nursed back to some semblance of health by Hanae's skilled hands.

The last member of their council came in a few seconds later proceeded by her silver raccoon dog seishen. Chiya and Tanu padded to the final chair at the table. Chiya straightened her navy uniform and sat down, tossing the end of her silver ponytail over her shoulder. Tanu curled up at her feet. Chiya had healed from the bolt of lightning Queen Airi had struck her with at the now infamous Battle at the Gate, though she had lost the baby she had been carrying. Kai had appointed Chiya to a teaching position at the citadel and to her council. Despite their former animosity, Chiya seemed committed to the citadel and to serving her queen. More importantly, Chiya would not hesitate to call Kai out if she failed in the least bit to act like the ruler that Miina deserved. She needed that sort of honesty.

"Should we see if we can get General Ipan in the bowl?" Nanase asked, nodding her head towards the silver basin of water that sat quietly in the middle of the long table. The enchanted bowl allowed the council to communicate with whoever possessed its twin, which happened to be General Ipan, head of King Ozora's sunburner forces. He participated in many of their regular council meetings, keeping them apprised of the situation in Kita. He had provided valuable intelligence and sage advice thus far.

Kai shook her head. "What I have to say is not for his ears."

Nanase shrugged, fixing her hawklike gaze on Kai. "What's going on?"

"There is no easy way to say this. We saw a man on our way home from the hunt today with spotted fever. The disease appeared to be advanced. We need to send a team of moonburners to keep him and his wife quarantined and to try to keep them from infecting any of the neighboring villagers."

Her council looked at her, stunned. "So close?" Master Vita asked. "I can't believe it has spread so quickly."

"That's not the worst of it," Kai admitted. "I touched him. I might be infected."

For a moment, four sets of unblinking eyes stared at her, words temporarily stolen by the shock of Kai's statement. Then they all started talking at once.

Kai held up her hands to quiet them and they grudgingly obliged.

"We don't know that I'm infected. But to be safe, I'll need to be quarantined. We can't risk anyone touching me until we know whether or not I have it."

"We must find a cure," Nanase said. "I will charge our best healers with this task."

"I agree," Kai said. "Unfortunately, despite our other issues with the famine, we need to make this a top priority. If the disease reaches the city, people will start to panic. Start with the man and woman I found today."

"We will have to keep your quarantine a secret," Hanae said. "You normally do your weekly ride through the city. We can say you are praying and consulting with experts to discover a way to end the drought."

"Is that really necessary?"

"Hanae's right. We can't let this get out," Chiya said. "The people's confidence in your rule is already at an all-time low."

Kai winced.

"I'm sorry, Your Majesty," Chiya said with grudging respect. "But it's true. There have been demonstrations in Kyuden, people in the squares saying that the drought and the fever are punishment from the gods for your peace with the sunburners. There are rumors that those who would see us return to war are rallying."

"That's insane," Kai protested. "Have the people forgotten so quickly what the war was like? Sons drafted and sent to the front lines like fodder, crops requisitioned for the crown, villages indiscriminately attacked and burned?"

"People can be shortsighted," Hanae said. "Their lives are a struggle to get from one day to the next. It's hard to look at the bigger picture when you don't know where your next meal is coming from."

Kai massaged her temples. "You're right, of course. I just wish we could make them see sense."

"You can't fight this kind of superstition with reason," Nanase said.

Master Vita spoke softly. "Perhaps it is time for us to address the leviathan in the room. Is it superstition? Or are the gods targeting us? Are these natural disasters their doing?"

Everyone shifted uncomfortably in their chairs.

Chiya spoke first. "The Oracle's prophecy is hard to ignore. She said there would be a war between us. She was right about the eclipse before the Battle at the Gate. Why would she be wrong about this?"

"Perhaps it is just figurative. We will be battling the forces of nature and such," Hanae said.

"What does Roweni say?" Master Vita asked, referring to the moonburner Oracle by her given name. He looked pointedly at Kai.

"She says that she sees real…gods. A battle. She doesn't think it's figurative." Kai spoke reluctantly. She knew the reason for that look. For the thousandth time since Kai had heard those prophetic words, she thought about telling the rest of her advisors what she had seen. General Geisa and Queen Airi had used a blood sacrifice to summon the goddess Tsuki, but not the benevolent goddess they all worshipped—a dark twisted form of Tsuki intent on suffering and destruction. Kai had no problem believing that the creature she had seen would try to destroy the burners—or to incite a war so the sun and moonburners destroyed each other. Master Vita had seen this dark Tsuki's destructive appetites firsthand. But Kai wasn't ready to tell the rest of them yet. Because telling them meant actually considering a return to war. And so she had sworn Master Vita to silence. They would continue to bear this burden alone.

"Your Majesty…"

Kai had stopped listening, intent on her own thoughts. She sorted through the discussion she had half heard. Master Vita had asked what they should do. Another pointed look. Perhaps…she could exploit her knowledge without having to share it. The situation was growing more dire by the day, and if she was infected…

"I don't want to face the possibility of the gods turning against us, but I don't think we can ignore it anymore," Kai said. "Master Vita, find every book in the library that tells you anything about Tsuki, Taiyo, the formation of the world, the origin of the burners, or anything even close to those topics. Bring me the most interesting to keep me busy until this quarantine business blows over. Look through the rest. Enlist the help of some novices if you must; I'm sure Nanase can spare them. Let's educate ourselves as much as we can and consider all possibilities."

This seemed to please her council. They all settled back in their chairs, relaxing slightly.

"That's all for now," Kai said. "Everyone has their orders. Unless anyone has an issue to raise?"

"I do," Chiya said, almost apologetically.

"What?" Kai asked, her mouth turning dry. Chiya? Apologetic?

"What is the succession plan if you…pass away…of spotted fever?"

Hanae tsked, crossing her arms with a huff.

Chiya's words hit her like a punch in the gut. It wasn't a tactful question, but it was a fair one. Kai hadn't invited Chiya to join the council for her tact. A ruler needed brutal honesty sometimes.

"I don't know," Kai admitted. "There is no heir to the Shigetsu line. I don't know who would be next in line for the throne."

"I can look into the lineage to see if there is a cousin or aunt somewhere who could serve," Master Vita said.

"Please," Kai said. "And what happens if we can't find that person?"

"I don't think there is a protocol for that. If…the worst were to happen," Hanae said, glaring at Chiya, "the best chance of avoiding a fight over the throne would be for you to announce your successor and make sure your choice has the backing of the citadel and as many others as we could muster."

"Bring me candidates then," Kai said. "To the next meeting."

Her council nodded grimly in agreement.

Nothing like planning your own funeral, Kai thought.

Kai strode from the council chamber to the hospital ward, Quitsu flanking her like a silver shadow. They took the back way, trying to avoid any of her friends or subjects. As she exited an alley across from the hospital ward, her vision swam for a moment, and the earth seemed to tilt sideways. She placed a steadying hand against the stone of the building. The feeling passed.

"Quitsu," Kai said. "I don't feel so good."

Her seishen was standing stock still, all four paws planted firmly on the ground, staring at the cobblestones below him. "I don't either."

"You can get sick?" Kai asked.

"I didn't think so," he admitted.

"Hospital ward. Now."

Kai's heart raced and her vision blurred as she continued across the cobblestoned courtyard. A wave of heat rushed through her body, a flush of fever that left her panting. She staggered against the door of the hospital ward, opening it and nearly falling inside. The blood was rushing to her ears, a raging ocean inside her head.

The nurses hurried to her side but she shooed them away.

"Don't touch me," she said, her voice sounding strange and hoarse. "Spotted fever. Quarantine."

CHAPTER 3

Hiro sat in an oversized velvet armchair in front of the empty fireplace. It was too hot for a fire. Hiro's room at the citadel faced the east, so while he was greeted by the sun's golden rays each morning, the room heated up like a greenhouse, too hot by midday to continue to sleep. The thick curtains that hung to black out the sun helped a little, but he had never fully adjusted to the upside-down Miinan schedule, where day was night and night was day. He was perpetually groggy.

Hiro turned a ring over and over, worrying it with his fingers. It was made of two bands of silver and gold, twined together and studded with tiny diamonds.

"You keep playing with that ring and you'll wear it down to nothing," said his seishen, Ryu, in a deep baritone rumble. Ryu sprawled on the floor, his pink tongue lolling out of his golden lion muzzle.

Hiro leaned forward, resting his head in his hands. "Why did she have to go into that house? Why did I let her? She worries about everyone's safety but her own," he said. "And the timing! The timing could not be worse."

Hiro peeled himself off the chair, stalking to the window, unable to contain the nervous energy pinging about inside him. "I had just firmed up my arrangement with the biwa player... The florist was all prepped to decorate the barge tomorrow, and the chef... It would have been the best food either of us had ever tasted. It would have been perfect."

He looked at the ring in his hand, curling his fist around it. "She's been so worried lately, so busy...She deserved something special when I asked her to marry me."

Ryu sat up from his position on the floor, peering at Hiro with imperious golden eyes.

"What?" Hiro said. "Do you think I'm being an ass because Kai is probably dying and I'm complaining about how my proposal got ruined?"

Ryu just blinked.

Hiro threw up his hands. "I know! I am being an ass. No need for you to rub it in. But Kai practically slammed the door to her council chamber in my face and there's nothing for me to do but sit here and worry."

"So you'd rather act like an ass," Ryu said.

"It does occupy the mind," Hiro said wryly. "And another thing. Now if I propose, she'll think I did it because I'm afraid she's going to die! What's romantic about that?"

"She's not going to die," Ryu said softly.

Panic seized him, wrapping his chest in a vise grip. "What if she does?" Hiro thumped down into the chair, his face ashen. "I can't lose her."

"You won't," Ryu said. "You don't even know if she was infected."

Images of Kai flashed through Hiro's mind. There were bright brilliant memories there. Dancing under the flickering sparkbugs at the Longest Night Festival. The rice pudding fight that had gotten them banned from the kitchens for a week. Standing shivering and wet under the waterfall below the citadel, his limbs freezing, but his core warmed by the heat of Kai's kiss.

There weren't enough happy memories though, not nearly enough. Not as many as Kai deserved. There were too many memories of her face lined with weariness as some servant reported the next piece of bad news, dark smudges under her eyes from the worry and bad dreams that kept her awake. Kai poring through piles of books in the library, desperately searching for a way to fix the latest disaster. Pretending not to notice her quickly-brushed-aside tears after some cruel Miinan shouted obscenities at her while she passed by. The sorrow Kai had seen since he had known her far outstripped the happy times, yet still she bristled with optimism, wore it like armor. There had to be more happiness, more joy, more love in store for her. For them. Anything else wasn't right. Surely, the gods wouldn't be so cruel.

"She won't die," Hiro whispered. "She's the strongest woman I know. This will pass by and we'll look back and laugh at how worried we were. And then I'll ask her to marry me the right way."

A knock sounded on his door and Hiro flew to his feet. "Come in," he said.

The door opened to reveal Hanae. The look on her face was grave. "You had better come with me."

Hiro watched helplessly as Kai thrashed in her bed. Her sheets were drenched with sweat, and she looked as pale as a corpse. She twitched, moaning and holding her hands up to fend off some invisible foe. "No…Tsuki…stop." The words wrenched from Kai's lips were laced with terror.

Kai had been moaning and screaming Tsuki's name for hours now, unnerving everyone in the room.

Quitsu lay on a bed next to Kai, limp and quiet. Though no one would admit it, the fact that the disease was harming Quitsu was almost more worrisome than its impact on Kai. No one had heard of a seishen getting sick, even if its burner did. Certainly, the burner and seishen were linked, but even the most experienced moonburner healers hadn't seen anything like this before. It was a disturbing omen.

Hiro had sat by Kai's bedside for the last day and night, watching the woman he loved grow sicker and sicker. The healers had tried everything. Herbs, tonics, poultices. Every form of healing the citadel moonburners knew. Master Vita was poring over his tomes, searching for any evidence of a previous outbreak of this type, grasping desperately for a clue to a cure. They had consulted the best of Kita's healers through Nanase and General Ipan's bowls. They had mobilized every resource they had to help Kai. Nothing had worked. Hiro had never felt so helpless.

Hiro sat with Hanae on one side, Ryu on the other. Hiro stroked the thick fur of Ryu's golden mane absentmindedly, his seishen's solid presence comforting him. Hanae had matched Hiro's vigil at Kai's side with her own, refusing to leave her daughter. She had seemed annoyed by Hiro's presence at first but had grudgingly come to accept that he had as much a claim to Kai's bedside as she.

"Have you tried praying?" Hanae asked softly, startling him. She hadn't spoken in hours. He thought she might have dozed off.

"Yes," he admitted. "Though I don't think I have enough faith in Taiyo to make much of a difference."

"Isn't that the rub," Hanae said. "You have to have faith in your faith. Hard thing sometimes."

"Have you prayed?" he asked.

"I've thought about it a hundred times, but somehow it doesn't feel right. She keeps screaming about Tsuki... It's like she's being tortured by her. Maybe it's superstitious, but I don't want to attract any more divine attention."

Kai whimpered again, moaning Tsuki's name.

"Whatever she's dreaming, it doesn't seem pleasant," he admitted. "Is it always this bad?"

Kai had admitted to him that she often had trouble sleeping, even had nightmares on occasion, but she had brushed it off as stress and worry.

"No," Hanae said, frowning. "At least, I don't think so."

"Do you really think...the gods caused this? That Tsuki is trying to destroy our alliance?"

Hanae looked at him thoughtfully, her perfectly-smooth doll's face disguising her age and wisdom. "Yes," she finally said.

"Yes?" he repeated, his heart sinking.

"I think it's time we face it. This summer is not natural. Neither is this disease. The sooner we face reality, the sooner we can figure out how to fight."

"How do we fight a war against the gods?" Hiro wondered, more to himself than Hanae.

"I don't know," Hanae admitted. "But we'd better figure out fast. Because the opening blows have been thrown. And they're not holding back."

It was as if the goddess herself heard Hanae's words.

Kai spasmed in her bed, beginning to shake and convulse. A nurse with thick gloves hurried to Kai's side, trying to hold her down against the worst of her convulsions.

Hiro and Hanae stood, watching helplessly. Hiro grasped the ring in his pocket, squeezing it so tightly that he thought he might crush the metal.

Quitsu too started to shake, his furry body twitching angrily.

Hiro and Hanae looked at each other sharply. That was new.

Hiro grasped desperately for a solution in his mind. *Think. Think.* Kai would have known what to do. She would have figured it out. She didn't give a damn about protecting herself, but she would never forgive him if he let anything happen to Quitsu. He thought of her face on the battlefield after Quitsu had been struck by lightning. Wild and fearsome, like an animal. She had saved Quitsu though, had brought the spark of life back into his body after it had gone.

"Idiot!" he hissed, smacking himself on the forehead. "Why didn't I think of it before?"

"What?" Hanae asked, startled by his outburst.

"Just keep her alive! I have to go get something!"

Hiro sprinted through the corridors and courtyards of the citadel, out the hospital ward and across to the queen's tower. How could he have been so blind? When Quitsu had lay dying, he and Kai had used the solar crown to blend their moon and sunburning into something new, a white-hot power unlike any he had experienced. Maybe the same could save Kai. Since that day, they had tested the power a few times, explored the bounds of their link. They couldn't burn the white light just by linking the two of them. They needed some sort of conduit, like the crown.

He dashed into the queen's tower and around a corner, screeching to a halt to head up the stairs to Kai's chamber. He almost ran headfirst into Emi coming out of another room in the hallway.

"Get to the hospital ward," he instructed Emi, grasping her by the shoulders.

"What? Why?" she asked, her dark eyes wide against the scarred half of her face.

"No time to explain," he said. "Hurry!" He dashed past her, taking the stairs up to Kai's chamber two by two. He burst through the door and skidded to a stop before Kai's armoire. He threw open the dark wood double doors and opened the drawer that he knew contained the lunar crown. Kai had given the solar crown back to his father, King Ozora, as a sign of good faith after their peace accord had been signed. But the lunar crown had the same mysterious ability to access both sun and moonlight. It should work.

Crown in hand, Hiro ran back to the hospital ward, trying not to think of what a long shot this plan was. He hoped the crown was charged… Kai had explained that it needed a full day and night outside to fill with sun and moonlight. *She must have charged it,* he thought. Kai was practical like that, methodical. She thought of details he never would.

As he made it back through the doors of the hospital ward, Hanae turned to meet his gaze, her bottom lip quivering. Emi's face was ashen and her eyes brimmed with tears.

Kai's convulsions had grown more violent. Sweat poured down her face, drenching her clothing and her silver hair. She looked possessed.

"They say she isn't going to make it," Emi said.

"Not if I have anything to say about it," Hiro said, grabbing Emi's hand and pulling her forward.

Hiro held up the crown to Emi. "We're going to link and make the white light. Like Kai and I did at the Battle at the Gate. She saved Quitsu with it. Maybe…maybe we can recreate its healing effect."

Emi nodded, grasping one side of the crown with both hands. "It's worth a try."

Hiro opened his qi, that part of his spirit that connected him to the sunlight and allowed him to burn its power into heat and light. He pulled in sunlight that was pooling through the hospital ward windows, filling his qi with it. Through the power of the crown, he linked with Emi, connecting his qi to her own. Yes. It was working in the same way it had for him and Kai so many months ago. Through his link with Emi, he could see the quicksilver moonlight stored in the crown beckoning him, pooling in a doorway opened by Emi's spirit.

Hiro wasn't a strong healer, but he knew how burner healers worked. He had learned the rudiments of the art, how healers used heat to destroy infection, to mend wounds, to encourage the body's own healing process. Hiro began to explore Kai's physical body with tendrils of magic, looking for the sickness within her. Though her body was fevered, he couldn't pinpoint the disease. Was he missing it? Where was the illness?

But Hiro knew that there was more to a person, to a burner, than the physical body. He looked at Quitsu, Kai's spirit animal, sick and dying beside her. Perhaps the illness wasn't just physical.

Hiro directed his and Emi's energy to join with Kai's own, to explore her qi, to lend it their strength. As soon as his energy touched Kai's, he recoiled in shock. He and Emi exchanged a wide-eyed look. Kai's qi was much changed from the silvery fresh spirit he would have expected, that he had felt when he had linked with her in the past. Now, it was a mottled, withered, dry thing that he hardly recognized. No wonder they were losing her. Losing Quitsu. Would the white light be able to fix such a disease of the spirit? He didn't know.

Hiro pushed these thoughts aside and turned to the task at hand, weaving his sunlight through the crown's moonlight. The energy combined in an explosion of pure white light, arcing from Hiro, Emi, and the crown to Kai. He squinted against the glare, ignoring the brilliance, instead focusing his efforts on pushing heat and energy into Kai's qi, willing it to heal.

And it did.

Through their link, he could feel Emi's elation mirroring his own. Wherever the white light touched, Kai's spirit seemed to regenerate, cleansed and new. Her thrashing died down until she lay still on the bed.

Hiro and Emi continued as long as they could, bathing Kai's body and spirit in the radiant light. Finally, there was no more to give; the crown had run out of moonlight. They broke their link and Emi sighed heavily, stumbling slightly against his shoulder. He put his arm around her to hold her up. His own legs felt like rubber, and his head pounded. But Kai looked as good as new. Her color had returned, and her breathing was deep and even.

"We did it," he said.

"Thank the goddess," Emi said.

No sooner had the words left Emi's lips than Kai began quivering again. Her skin, having returned to a normal even tan color, began to fade, turning a sickly shade of gray once again. She spasmed like a rag doll and then fell still.

"No!" Hiro exclaimed, running to Kai's bedside. Quarantine be damned. He hovered his ear over her mouth, feeling for a whisper of breath. There was none.

"She's not breathing," he choked out.

"No!" Hanae cried. "Try the crown again!"

"It's empty," he said, the words sticking in his throat.

Hanae rushed in, pushing Hiro out of the way. His body felt like lead, but he stood to give her access to Kai.

Hanae checked Kai's vitals and began pumping on her chest with gloved hands, trying to send air back into her lungs.

Hiro couldn't tear his eyes away from Kai's still form, lying limp on the sweat-soaked sheets. Just twenty-four hours ago she had been filled with life, her hazel eyes sparkling as she teased him about his aim with a bow. And now they were losing her. This couldn't be.

CHAPTER 4

T his dream was new.

At first, Kai's dreams had been filled with feverish nightmares. Sometimes she had found herself walking through the spirit world with its unnatural night and bright full moon, crossing paths with strange seishen and oddly-dressed burners. They looked at her with frowns and suspicion, as if she did not belong, and she shrank from them, fleeing into the dark.

Other times she had been stalked by dark shadows, twisted remnants of animals and men, and she had shamelessly hidden, praying that those swiveling ears, those slavering snouts, did not register her presence.

In the worst dreams, she had seen Tsuki—the strange unnaturally large figure that Queen Airi and General Geisa had summoned in the citadel temple. Her voice, deep enough to drown in and sharp as the headsman's axe, echoed through Kai's mind. Tsuki was everywhere. She'd come through Kai's window, she'd come through a ray of moonlight pooling in a citadel courtyard, she'd risen through the still water of the lake in the Akashi Mountains where Kai once had seen her mother.

There was no hiding from Tsuki when she came, no cowering in the bushes. Kai had tried. Tsuki saw her, despite that strange blur where a face should be. Always, she said the same thing.

"This world belongs to us. The time of the burners is at an end."

And then she would devour Kai. She would grow huge and unhinge her jaw and Kai could only sit, frozen, and let it happen. Down, down, down into a suffocating darkness that she could not escape. A blackness that melted her into nothingness. And somehow Kai knew that this dream was more than a dream, that it was a vision of what was to come.

Now, that void seemed but a memory. Kai squinted into bright sunlight as her eyes adjusted. She sat at a small table atop a castle built of warm sandstone. The castle continued below the crenellated walls that cradled the courtyard in which she sat, descending in ornate levels filled with fountains and gardens, cheerful squares, and sturdy structures. Beyond the outer castle walls stretched a vast city—a patchwork of homes and businesses decorated with colorful awnings and sparkling stained glass windows. In the far distance a lush green landscape bowed to the thin shining line of the sea.

Here, there was only serenity—the feel of the sun on her face and the breeze tousling her hair, the fragrance of the flowering vine climbing the wall behind her, its blossoms buzzing with honeybees. Her tense muscles relaxed. She could be safe here for a while.

"This is my favorite view in the whole world," the man sitting next to her said.

She looked at him, surprised by his presence, but also not. He had been there all along, hadn't he?

The man was perhaps forty years old with a pleasant profile—his honest brow and straight nose led to a neatly-trimmed beard, an unusual fashion in Miina. When he turned to her, his eyes puddled with the deep brown of loamy soil. Quitsu sat in his lap, curled up as unabashedly as a housecat. That sight jarred her back into reality.

"Where are we?" she asked.

"Yoshai," the man replied, gazing into distance. He stroked Quitsu's silver fur. "Or I should say, its shadow."

She furrowed her brow, studying the man. He wore simple but well-made clothes—green pants, white shirt. His feet were bare on the warm stones of the courtyard. He seemed harmless enough, but yet…

"Its shadow?" Kai asked. "What do you mean? And where is Yoshai? I've never heard of it."

He pursed his lips. "You mortals always ask so many questions. I only came because my light was so strong in you. I've never known a mortal to wield it before. And with you passing through… I was curious to meet you."

Kai blew a lock of hair off her forehead in frustration. *His light? Passing through? What in the seishen's name was he talking about?* "Let's start at the beginning. Where am I?"

He heaved a sigh. "This city is called Yoshai. It is my holy city. But we're in its shadow. I think you mortals call it...the spirit realm."

Kai's mouth fell open in slack disbelief. Her head swiveled, surveying the city in new appreciation. The spirit world. *How did she get here? Was she asleep? And what had he said...'my holy city'?*

"Who are you?" Kai asked carefully.

"I am all of this." He swept a hand across the view before them. "That butterfly," he pointed at a brilliant indigo creature flapping by on lazy wings. "You. That ocean. Or should I say, all of this is me."

"You're...a god?" Kai asked, awe filling her. "The god of the earth? Like Tsuki and Taiyo are the gods of the moon and sun?"

He stroked his chestnut beard as he considered that. "No, I don't like that word. It's not quite right. Tsuki and Taiyo are my creations as well."

"You created the sun and moon? The earth?" Her mind was struggling to take it all in.

He looked at her proudly, like a child holding up a painting to its parent. "Yes, I created it. Beautiful, isn't it? I really outdid myself."

Kai couldn't help but smile at his enthusiasm. "You did," she agreed, turning her gaze back to the tapestry of color before her illuminated in buttery sunlight. "But why am I here? Not that I'm not pleased to meet you...but...what do you mean that I'm passing through?"

"Oh," he said, scratching Quitsu's head, not meeting her gaze. "I thought you knew. You're dying. Passing through...passing over. Beyond."

An icy chill snaked through Kai's body despite the warmth of the morning. She remembered. The spotted fever. The dreams. Flashes of her mother and Hiro's worried faces, Nanase, the citadel nurses. Pain, and fear...and for a moment, a warm glow bathing her in light and love.

Hiro had used the crown. The lunar crown.

"Your light. Are you talking about the white light? When sun and moonlight combine? That's your power?"

"It's the raw stuff of creation. Like I said, I've never known a mortal to wield it. It should be too much for your limited heart and mind to behold, to understand."

She shook her head, too distracted to be offended. "They tried to save me with it. But it didn't work. I'm dying anyway."

"That spotted fever is a nasty business. Corrupts your ties to me. It wouldn't be enough for them to heal you with it. To eradicate the fever. You'd have to wield it—purify yourself from the inside."

"And I was too weak to," Kai said. She was dying. Would die. The faces of her family, her subjects, flashed before her. What would happen to Miina? To her kingdom? Tears pricked her eyes. She wasn't ready to go yet. To give up. To let darkness fall over the land.

As despair filled her, she looked at the creator with an appraising eye. Surely, he could fix what was wrong with Miina. Perhaps she could give her kingdom one last gift before she went.

"If you created the world," Kai asked, "you must know what's going wrong with it. The seasons, famine, and now this spotted fever is spreading. Could you fix it?"

"No," he said wistfully. "I don't intervene directly like that. Not anymore. It's one of the rules of creation. It was up to my guardians to find the way to fix things, and I fear they have failed."

"Whose rules?" Kai asked.

"The universe," he gestured widely. "Something had to create me."

She took his hand, pleading with him. It was warm and calloused, like her father's hands. Like someone who worked the land. "Even if you can't intervene directly, can you tell me how to fix things? I could get a message to my subjects before I go. Who are these guardians?" Kai said.

He shook his head. "It's admirable that you care so deeply. But it's not your problem anymore. It's time for you to find your peace."

"I can't," Kai said "I can't go yet. Not with Miina in shambles."

"People live and people die. That is what it is to be mortal. You will move on to a better place." He motioned around him. "A place of beauty and peace. You needn't worry anymore. Miina is no longer your responsibility."

"I understand why you say that," Kai said, "but respectfully, you're wrong. I made an oath when I became queen. To my country, but to myself as well. I would leave Miina a better place than I found it." Her face flushed as she voiced the secret promise she had made to herself, her vow to be better than Airi, to somehow find a way to be the queen

Miina deserved. She had so far yet to travel down that road.

"You mortals are such unusual creatures," he said, his brown eyes warm. "And I think you are a very unusual mortal, Kailani Shigetsu. Even though I created the burners, I'm still often surprised by your nobility."

"Isn't there anything you can do?" Kai pleaded. "Show me how to help fix things. Otherwise, this beautiful world you created will be lost to the darkness."

"It does pain me to see the corruption that has infected my world," he said.

Kai held her breath, not daring to hope that he would help her somehow, give her some piece of magic or information that would allow her to fix things.

He stood, picking Quitsu up off his lap and handing him to Kai. He walked to the side of the courtyard, nodding for her to follow.

They stood along the crenellated wall in silence for a moment, the soft breeze slipping by her like a warm embrace.

The creator turned to her. "The rules are firm. Once I set a world in motion, I cannot interfere. I am more sorry than you know."

Kai nodded, crestfallen at his words. So she would walk into whatever lay beyond this world, leaving her promises unfinished and her kingdom abandoned. It was a bitter pill to swallow.

"But," he went on, "my creations are capable of deep wisdom, and my guardians still stand bravely against the forces of darkness in this world." He scratched Quitsu's chin and then looked her square in the eye, pinning her with the strength of his gaze. "Though I can't interfere"—he raised his eyebrows, punctuating the last two words with a strong inflection—"if you look deep within your heart, you may find the power you need to be victorious."

Kai wrinkled her brow, exchanging a look of confusion with Quitsu. *Was he...*

"Do you understand?" he asked. "Look within your heart." He placed the palm of his hand flat against her chest over where her heart beat its last mortal beats. His skin—warm against hers—began to burn.

Kai cried out as sharp pain lanced through her, at the smell of burning flesh filling her nostrils. She wrenched back from him, her eyes stinging from the pain and betrayal. Her heels hit the wall edging the courtyard and she careened back, toppling over the edge, Quitsu in her arms.

She reached out in panic—her mind, her spirit straining to grasp at moonlight, at anything. Brilliant white light was waiting, just beyond her reach.

As the air whistled past, she reached for it... and blackness closed in.

INTERLUDE

The man cowered before the god, his forehead pressed against the cool tiles of the empty temple. If he was being precise—which he always was—it wasn't a god. Perhaps the opposite of that. But it had been masquerading as Taiyo for so long that it had become habit to think of it as a god. To call it Taiyo. When he didn't, it grew angry. So it was Taiyo. At least to its face.

"Rise," false Taiyo said, and the man did as he was instructed.

The false Taiyo towered over him—at least ten feet tall. It wore fine robes of dark gray, and from its navy obi sash a broadsword hung, as long as the man was tall. All in all, the creature cut quite an intimidating figure, even if the man didn't look at its face. The face was chilling, strange and distorted as if peering through a thick block of ice. It made the man feel sick to look directly at it, filling him with a clamminess that leeched the heat from his body. And so he fixed his eyes firmly on the mosaic pattern of the tiles before him.

The man hated sniveling before this false Taiyo, but he had worn this face of meek subservience for so many years that it had grown comfortable. Like a pair of boots that pinched and chaffed at first but molded to its owner over years of wear. He needed the creature's help to secure the final destruction of the burners and their wretched seishen. For that prize, he could tolerate a bit of bowing.

"Our plan is progressing," false Taiyo said. "With the suffering caused by the drought and the spotted fever, we are growing strong enough to break through the barrier into the mortal world. We tire of being trapped in the prison of the spirit world. We have waited long enough."

"Soon, you will be free," the man said. *Their plan is progressing. Pah. His plan!* This "god" couldn't think its way out of a ricepaper box on its own. It had been his idea to initiate the natural disasters after that meddlesome queen had unceremoniously ended the war that had been bolstering his master and mistress for so many years.

"What update do you have for me on your mission?" false Taiyo inquired.

The man grimaced. "I have located where the god Taiyo has been hidden from us, suspended in sleep these several centuries."

The hairs on the back of the man's neck stood as false Taiyo growled, a rumbling sound emanating from low in its throat.

"The burners and their guardians thought they were clever, hiding the god and goddess from us. But I will have the last laugh when I plunge my sword into their chests and all light bleeds from this world," false Taiyo said.

And I will use the power you have given me to rule that dark world without your tiresome interference, the man thought with a grim smile.

"Our victory is not assured yet," the man said. "I was unable to wake…the original Taiyo from his supernatural sleep. I had with me a vial of the blood of the heir, which I believed would open the tomb where Taiyo sleeps. But it was not sufficient."

"It did not open?" The false Taiyo's fist clenched.

"Do you see the god before you?" the man snapped and then schooled himself, tamping down his annoyance. "There was an inscription on the tomb. It must be the heir's blood, freely given."

"So hold a knife to the heir's throat and encourage him to give freely," false Taiyo said.

"I'm not sure that will satisfy the enchantment," the man said.

The creature paced the room in agitation, its head nearly striking the tall wooden beams crossing the ceiling.

"But I have an idea," the man said hastily, backing out of the way of the giant scabbard as it haphazardly swooped by his head.

"Always another idea. I grow tired of your ideas!" false Taiyo said.

Without my ideas, you'd still be mewing in the spirit world, complaining about your lot in life, the man thought.

"We near our goal," the man said. "But there is a bit more deception to be had. I mean to convince the heirs to open the tomb freely."

"How will you accomplish this?"

"You just leave that to me," the man said, a smile spreading across his face.

CHAPTER 5

I t was an uneasy feeling, like she was a stranger in her own body. Kai's chest burned, and her muscles and joints ached. The lights in the hospital ward shone harshly in her vision. As she squinted across the room, her eyes traced the flecks and cracks in the gray stone, the dust motes dancing in the ray of sunlight pouring across the neighboring bed.

Quitsu roused in the bed next to her, but he was forgotten as she turned to face the rest of the room and her mother fell on her, wrapping her in a crushing embrace.

"You came back to us," Hanae said, tears pouring down her face. "Thank the goddess. I couldn't outlive all of you."

What was going on? The last she remembered, she had been infected with spotted fever. She had collapsed in the hospital ward. There had been dreams...so many dreams. She tried to remember them, but their substance eluded her; like a slick fish, they slipped from her grasp. She knew she had seen Tsuki, had felt terror at her presence. The rest were dark.

As her mother loosened her grip and sat up, Kai saw Hiro and Emi, hands clasped and eyes wet with tears. Kai's small smile seemed to release Hiro from some invisible hold, and he crossed the distance between them in two strides, wrapping her in his arms.

She closed her eyes and melted into him, letting the warm feel and musky smell of him fill her senses. And then they were all around her, smothering her with arms, fur, kisses, cold wet noses. Kai laughed and took it all in stride. "All right, all right, I need some air."

"Get back, get back," the head nurse said. "Let me check her."

Her friends and family reluctantly backed away while the nurse pulled down the collar of Kai's shirt to check her heartbeat.

The woman's face paled. "What is that?" she whispered.

Kai looked down and saw that while her spots were gone, something else had taken their place. A handprint, puckering the smooth skin of her chest like it had been burned into her, shiny and white with scar tissue.

"I...I don't know," Kai said.

Kai wolfed down a piping hot plate of sweet porridge and a cup of steaming lemongrass tea while a servant gathered the rest of Kai's council. It turned out that almost dying made a person hungry.

After the initial unsettling revelation of the handprint, those in the room seemed to reach an unspoken agreement that the strange mark would not be spoken of. It was enough that Kai had almost died and through some miracle now lived, healthy and strong. There would be time to unravel the mystery later.

The head nurse refused to discharge Kai from the hospital ward yet, but there was work to be done. Her time of delirium and nightmares had cemented one dreadful certainty in her mind. They *were* at war with the gods. And they were losing.

Hiro hadn't left her side since Kai had awoken. He sat on her bed, a solid presence tucked against the pillow behind her, content to let her eat and drink in silence.

Kai relished his presence, tension unraveling at his nearness. Even before this wretched business with the fever, they had been so busy. Hiro frequently traveled back and forth from Kyuden to Kistana and she had an increasingly needy country to run. There had been little time for romance, or even fun. It felt good to just sit together.

"Thank you for what you did," Kai finally said. "With the crown. It was genius."

"It didn't work." He shook his head, his thick brows twisted in confusion. "I mean it did—until it didn't. I wish we knew...how you were healed. But I suppose I should just be grateful for the miracle."

"I'll remember in time. I hope. But somehow I feel like what you and Emi did with the crown...that it was important." Kai's memories of her illness were foggy and dark. The harder she tried to remember, the further away they seemed. She shoved down her frustration. Her mind was tired and her body was weak from illness. Berating herself for not remembering wasn't going to help anyone.

"I still can't believe it. After we came so close..." He trailed off. He ran his hand over his golden hair, which shone dully in the light of the moon orbs. He looked as if the color had been drained from him.

Kai squeezed his hand with her own. "I'm not going anywhere."

Hiro didn't speak while Kai finished her breakfast, but his weary face still bore such a look of mixed fear and relief that she realized the depth of what her fever had put her family through. They'd thought her a dead woman; her crypt was reflected in their eyes. She fought down a pang of guilt. She hadn't meant for this to happen.

Kai wiped her mouth and moved the plate from her bedside. She looked down at herself and winced. Her clothes were stiff with dried sweat and smelled sickly. Her hair was a mess. She sighed.

"Nurse," she called, "please have a servant draw me a bath and get me a fresh uniform."

She didn't wear her moonburner uniform very often anymore, but somehow it seemed appropriate. They were going to war.

☾

Her council gathered in the hospital ward, drawing chairs around her bedside. Kai asked Hiro to stay. The kingdom of Kita would have a role to play in the things to come as well.

"I think it is time we addressed the Oracle's prophecy," Kai began. "We had hoped it would prove to be false, to have some other meaning than the obvious. But it is time we...time *I* face the facts. And it is time that I share something with you that I have concealed for some time."

Her council shifted forward, curious.

"I have seen Tsuki," Kai said. A roiling set of images flashed before her eyes, nightmares blending with images of the past into a terrifying portrait of Tsuki. "When I was fairly new at the citadel, I was in Tsuki's chapel, and I saw something that I wasn't supposed to see. Queen Airi and General Geisa slit open a koumidi and used its blood to summon Tsuki. Or something that professed to be her."

Kai described all she had seen to the stunned faces of those around her.

"She wanted blood. And suffering. And another sacrifice. And before the eclipse…" Kai faltered, swallowing her own shame. How could she tell them that she had seen a man murdered just steps away from her and had done nothing?

Master Vita came to her rescue. "Airi and Geisa sacrificed one of the sunburner prisoners. She came when they called her. Kai speaks the truth."

"How can this be?" Hanae asked. "All the ancient stories tell of Tsuki as a healer, an extension of the moon and the oceans. She is a benevolent force that is part of the earth. Part of its lifecycle."

"Part of the lifecycle is death," Chiya said. "Maybe she grew tired of being good."

"She just woke up one divine day and decided to become evil? That doesn't make sense," Hiro said.

"Chiya is right," Master Vita said. "She's on to something anyway. When the burner wars started, something changed. As much as the histories make it sound like the burners have always hated each other, that isn't true. They lived together for many hundreds of years. It wasn't until the division of Kita and Miina when the animosity truly started."

"So you're saying something about the gods changed? And started the war?" Kai asked.

"Lovers' quarrel?" Hiro mused.

"That's the legend," Kai said, "but that can't be true. Can it?"

Master Vita wiped his half-moon spectacles with a white cloth and put them back on. "I don't know. We do know that the world is not as it should be. It has been declining for many years, slowly, but now it gains speed. We can ignore it no longer."

"I agree," Hanae said. "I think something has gone desperately wrong with our god and goddess. There's a reason they've abandoned their holy charge to keep balance and light in this world. If we have any hope of setting things right, we must discover the cause."

"How do we do that?" Kai asked, more to herself than the council.

"It's a shame we can't ask Airi or Geisa how to summon Tsuki," Chiya mused. "Maybe we could find out what she wants."

"Besides suffering and death?" Kai said flatly.

Chiya ducked her head. "Besides that. All I mean is, perhaps there is some other way to appease them that we could discover."

Kai's mood blackened as she thought of the cruel facility Airi and Geisa had built under the floors of the citadel, a twisted place where they had forced innocent moonburners to bear burner children for the queen's army. It was a black mark on the moonburners' already bloody history.

"I'm afraid the secret of summoning Tsuki may have died with Geisa and Airi. Perhaps it's for the best," Master Vita said.

"That's not...entirely true." Nanase spoke for the first time. She was leaning against the hard stone wall of the hospital ward, examining the end of one of her braids. She had been silent throughout the exchange.

"What? Which part?" Kai asked.

"Geisa isn't dead."

"Excuse me?" Kai said. "Geisa isn't dead?"

Nanase sighed, thunking down hard into a chair like a block of stone. "I was going to tell you...eventually."

"Eventually?" Kai's voice rose an octave. "How is this possible?"

"After the Battle at the Gate, after I...killed Queen Airi." Nanase mumbled through the words as if it was a bad dream she wished she could forget. "I went down to the facility to collect Maaya's body."

Kai remembered that moment when her carefully-laid plan to sneak them out of the facility without bloodshed had come crashing down. When her best friend, the sweetest, most innocent moonburner of all, had betrayed them. When she had fallen, crimson blood staining her white servant's uniform.

Hiro squeezed Kai's hand.

Nanase continued. "I found Geisa near death, but still alive. I had a lot to deal with, what with the casualties from the battle, your new reign, and the sunburners on Kyuden soil, so I had her thrown into a cell. I assumed she would just bleed out in the next few hours and die. Perhaps I should have put her out of her misery, but frankly, I didn't think I owed her the courtesy."

"I went in the next day to collect her body, but she was still alive. She was crumpled into herself, babbling about the sunburners and King Ozora. The loss of blood had made her delusional. I decided that Geisa didn't deserve a clean death. She deserved to suffer. So I had her stitched and cleaned up and gave her food and water. I planned to keep her in that cell one day for every day she'd imprisoned one of our sisters in that facility. I figured we could execute her then."

Chiya had turned white at the mention of the facility but seemed emboldened by Nanase's statement. She nodded her approval.

Kai shook her head with disbelief. "How could you keep this from me? You unilaterally sentenced a moonburner without my consent or knowledge." Anger flared to life within her. "Nanase, you have served me faithfully, but this…this borders on treason."

Nanase slid to her knees before Kai's bed, bowing her head. "I accept full responsibility for the wrong I have done you, and I will accept whatever punishment you deem appropriate. I know it's no consolation, but I had hoped…to spare you. The knowledge that she still lived. The pain it might have caused you. The decision that would need to be made. I know it was wrong, but that is why I did it."

Kai's council was still and silent around her, their collective breaths held at the scene.

Kai's anger dimmed. "Get up, Nanase," she said wearily.

Nanase rose in a lithe movement, her head still bowed in deference.

"Each of you hear me. No one makes critical decisions without consulting me, and no one keeps information from me, no matter how benevolent your reasons." Kai's voice was hard as she looked from face to face.

They nodded, and Kai saw in Nanase's dark eyes that she understood. They were her friends, her family, but she was their queen, too. They needed to see her as such.

"I can't condone you keeping Geisa alive behind my back, but I suppose it's good that you did." Kai stood. "Anyone else have any secret prisoners they're hiding from me?"

Her question was met by silence. Master Vita shook his head.

"Very well," Kai said, steeling herself for what was to come. "Let's interrogate a prisoner."

CHAPTER 6

Kai and Nanase descended the stone steps into the citadel's dungeon. The twisting staircase was dimly lit by moon orbs. Kai's cheeks were hot with anger at Nanase, but a secret part of her felt relief as well. What would she have done if Nanase had brought this information to her in her first week as queen? She would have been paralyzed with indecision about how to deal with Geisa. Public execution? Kill her quietly? Keep her prisoner? Each of the choices left a bitter taste in Kai's mouth—even now.

The dungeons were empty but for one cell. Nanase nodded her head to the guard, who unlocked the door. The stench hit Kai like a physical thing. She looked crossly at Nanase, who set her jaw and crossed her arms before her.

The woman inside was hardly recognizable as human. She shied away from the light, her eyes covered by stringy hair that appeared more brown than silver. She was gaunt, barely more than skin and bones. The tattered dress she wore hung from her frame, and goosebumps pebbled her flesh. It was a miracle she hadn't frozen to death down here with nothing to protect her from the seeping cold of the stone floor and walls. Her forearms were covered with ragged gashes, some more healed than others.

"What happened to her arms?" Kai murmured.

"Self-inflicted," Nanase said. "We thought maybe she was slowly succumbing to madness. The gashes weren't deep enough to kill her. But now, hearing your tale, I can't help but think she was trying to summon divine help."

Kai shivered, and not from the cold.

"Guard, move her to a clean cell where we can interrogate her," Kai ordered, moving back into the stairwell, where the smell wasn't so pungent.

"You know we don't mistreat prisoners here," Kai said to Nanase in a low tone. "I wouldn't have thought it of you."

Nanase looked at the ground, two parts contrite and one part defiant. "I wouldn't have thought it of myself. But every time I started bettering her conditions, I thought about what she and Airi did—right under our noses. How she abused the students and women that I had sworn to train and protect. And I would get so furious that I wanted to storm down those stairs and kill her with my bare hands. She's lucky neglect is all she got. She didn't treat her own prisoners with such courtesy."

They both watched as the guard half-carried Geisa from the cell, moving down the hallway. The woman was too weak to walk on her own and leaned against the guard for support. Kai couldn't condone torture or neglect, but...thinking of what Geisa had done to Chiya and the others made Kai's blood boil even now. She laid a hand on Nanase's shoulder. "I understand. But the mistreatment ends now. And no more secrets."

"Agreed. I don't regret what I did, except that. Keeping it from you. It wasn't right."

The guard poked her head into the hallway. "She's ready for you."

Kai straightened her uniform and nodded.

The room where Geisa now sat was clean and well-lit with oil-lanterns— a vast improvement over the overwhelming filth and stench of the burner's former habitat.

Kai sat down in a sturdy wooden chair across a table from Geisa. The woman's wrists and ankles were chained in heavy iron manacles attached to each other through a ring in the table. Nanase stood behind Kai with her lean arms crossed, her stern face a still mask.

Kai examined the woman across from her. Geisa was painfully thin— her eyes hollow and sunken in dark rings. Yet she did not seem weak. Hatred coiled in the woman, waiting patiently for its time to strike. Geisa had not been broken.

"Did she come?" Kai asked. Kai had decided to try the direct route in the hopes that she could trick Geisa into thinking Kai knew more than she did. She prayed it would work. She didn't have the stomach for torture, even of a woman like Geisa.

"Who?" Geisa asked, her voice soft and hoarse, as if she had not used it in many months.

"Tsuki," Kai said, motioning to the ragged cuts on Geisa's arms, still angry red and puffy. "Did she come?"

Geisa met Kai's eyes, searching, evaluating. Kai stilled her heartbeat and stared back, unflinching.

"Yes," Geisa finally said, a knowing smile growing on her face. "She did come."

"I understand that you will not give us all of your mistress's secrets freely," Kai said, "but if you provide us with some information, we can make your time here more...comfortable." She motioned to the room around her. "Otherwise, I can put you back in Nanase's capable hands."

Geisa flinched slightly at that, her eyes flicking to Nanase and back. "Ask your questions."

"What does she want?" Kai asked. "What is her endgame?"

Geisa chuckled quietly. "They want you to die. All of the burners. They plan to remake this world, to usher in an era of blood and darkness where they reign supreme. Those who follow them will be rewarded. And those who oppose them will be crushed."

"Oh, is that all?" Kai looked back at Nanase, who rolled her eyes. "Who are they? Tsuki and Taiyo?"

"My mistress and her lover."

"How do they plan to bring about this era of blood and darkness, etc.?" Kai willed her voice to remain disinterested, though inside she was chilled to the bone.

"Even I don't know that. Free me, and I might be able to find out," Geisa suggested.

"I'll pass, thank you," Kai said. "It doesn't make sense. Taiyo and Tsuki created the burners. Why do they want to destroy them now?"

"Maybe they tire of you and your endless questions." Geisa said.

Kai looked at her, pursing her lips. Geisa was toying with her.

"I won't tolerate my time being wasted," Kai slapped the table.

"Answer truthfully or I will send you back to your cell and let you waste away to nothing."

Kai kept her eyes locked on Geisa's. They glittered dangerously. If it was a battle of wills the woman wanted, Kai was here to play.

"Tsuki and Taiyo rule the sun and moon. Why would they want to usher in an era of darkness?"

"Simple Kai," Geisa said. "Always a step behind."

"That's your queen you speak to," Nanase growled behind Kai's shoulder. "One more comment like that and you'll never see moonlight again."

Geisa sighed, like she was speaking with a small child. "Tsuki and Taiyo wouldn't want such a world."

"What?" Kai asked, frustration welling in her. "You just said that was your mistress's plan."

All of a sudden, realization dawned on Kai. She remembered joking with Quitsu about how the fearsome spirit they had seen seemed more like Tsuki's evil sister than the goddess herself.

"Your mistress calls herself Tsuki, but she isn't really her, is she?"

Geisa's face split into a grin and she released a wild, raucous laugh. "How bittersweet it must be to finally understand, only to find out you are too late."

"Where is Tsuki?" Kai asked.

"Tsuki is dead!" Geisa said through peals of hysterical laughter.

Kai stood up, backing away from Geisa, knocking her chair back. She clasped her hands to keep them from shaking. "Back in her cell," Kai growled, storming from the room.

Kai hurried back up the stairs, her need to feel the open night air around her overpowering any worries about maintaining an aura of queenly serenity. Despite the darkness, the heat still permeated, hanging over the citadel like a thick blanket. It felt just as suffocating as the low stone ceiling of the citadel dungeons.

Kai leaned against the wall, willing her breathing to return to normal. Tsuki could not be dead. Gods and goddesses didn't die. They were divine. Immortal. That was the whole point.

Nanase joined her, her face full of questions.

"I believe that the being I saw, the being Geisa worships, is something other than Tsuki. It would make perfect sense," Kai said. "But I can't believe Tsuki is dead. I won't. Not without proof."

"What do you want to do?" Nanase asked.

"I don't know," she admitted. "We need to know more about this creature Geisa worships. What she is. Get the others on it."

Nanase nodded.

"Don't tell them what Geisa said about the real Tsuki being dead," Kai said after a moment of indecision.

"Shouldn't the council be working with all the facts?"

"Normally, I would agree," Kai said crossly. "But this would be incredibly demoralizing news, and it may be a ploy by Geisa. We keep this between us—at least for now. Am I understood?"

"Of course, Your Majesty," Nanase said.

"In the meantime, life needs to carry on. Word may have traveled that I was ill. We need to assure the people that I am healthy and strong. Tomorrow I will do my ride through the city."

As Nanase nodded her assent, three dark shapes swooped through the night sky. They were but shadows against the stars and the lights of the citadel, but Kai could tell from the shape of their wings that they were eagles, not koumori.

Nanase's sharp eyes had caught the same. "Are we expecting anyone from Kita?" she asked.

"Not that I know of," Kai said. "Let's go see."

As they arrived at the koumori landing field, a large figure dismounted from one of the eagles and strode towards them, a cloak billowing behind him.

"General Ipan?" Kai asked.

He gave them a courtly bow, flourishing his cloak.

"I hear you gave everyone quite a scare, Majesty," General Ipan said in his deep baritone. "Don't you go dying and leaving the hard work to the rest of us."

"I wouldn't dream of it," Kai said. She was overcome by a sudden urge to give the sunburner general a hug. He had a comforting presence and an easy way with people.

"Headmistress." General Ipan nodded to Nanase.

"To what do we owe this pleasure?" Kai asked.

"To cut right to it, I am here to deliver good news and bad news. Which do you want first?"

"Bad news?" Kai's stomach lurched. She didn't think she could handle more bad news.

"Very well," the general said, stepping his huge girth aside to reveal a scowling figure striding towards them. "The bad news."

A hiss escaped her lips. Kai couldn't think of anyone, save perhaps evil-Tsuki herself, who she dreaded seeing more. It was Daarco.

CHAPTER 7

I t took all of Kai's self-restraint to not pull her knife from its sheath.

"What. Is. He. Doing. Here?" Kai asked, not taking her eyes from his face.

Daarco stood next to General Ipan, his muscled arms behind his back. They wore matching red sunburner uniforms tailored in gold thread, General Ipan's straining a bit in the middle.

Though he was trying to keep his face impassive, Daarco's perpetual scowl crept back into place. She supposed an impartial observer could find him handsome with his close-cropped golden hair and heavy brows. Perhaps his crooked nose could be endearing in the right setting. But not to her. She knew the venom that lay beneath that exterior.

"He is here to learn and serve at your pleasure."

Kai ground her teeth. "It would serve my pleasure to see him get back on his eagle and return to Kistana."

"I don't want to be here any more than you want me here," Daarco hissed.

General Ipan held up his hand and Daarco fell silent, his eyes dropping to the ground.

"A few of our officers, Daarco chief among them, are having trouble…embracing our new alliance. Overcoming old ways of thinking."

"You mean old prejudices," Kai said.

General Ipan ignored her quip and went on. "King Ozora thought that it would be best to send some of these individuals—not too many at a time of course—to Miina to get to know who the moonburners really are. He is confident that once they spend time with you and your subjects, they will come to see you with the same respect that the rest of us do."

It wasn't a terrible idea in the abstract. She had a few moonburners who could use a month in Kistana to humanize the sunburners in their eyes. But it was a risk and a distraction she could little afford right now.

"It's an unnecessary security risk," Kai said. "Daarco tried to kill me. Twice. I don't have the manpower to watch him while he's here."

Daarco crossed his arms but kept his eyes to the ground and said nothing. He must have gotten some lecture from the king before being shipped off to Kyuden.

"I can assure you, Daarco will behave like a perfect gentleman while he is here. Hiro will oversee his behavior himself."

Kai recoiled slightly. "Hiro has agreed to his?" How could Hiro not have told her that he was bringing a monster on a frayed leash into her very sitting room?

"Well, he hasn't agreed…so much. But his father was sure he would be willing."

"Ah," Kai said, her temper cooling slightly. She was familiar with the whims of meddling parents who thought they knew best. "I suppose I needn't remind you that Daarco was under Hiro's watchful eye the two times he tried to kill me."

"I know Daarco regrets his actions very much," Ipan said. "Respectfully, circumstances have changed, Your Majesty. The burners are allies now. Daarco will present no danger to you. I stake my life on it."

She sighed. This wasn't a battle she could fight right now. "He may stay, *under guard*, until I can take this up with Hiro. But this isn't decided. Nanase, please find Daarco and General Ipan quarters while they are here."

Nanase nodded imperceptibly.

"And Daarco," Kai said, taking a step towards him and fixing him with her gaze. "General Ipan is right. Circumstances have changed. I am queen of Miina now. If you step even a toe out of line while you are here, you will be punished to the full extent of Miinan law."

Daarco's lip twisted slightly as he said two words through gritted teeth: "I understand."

"Well," Ipan said, clapping his hands, "now that the pleasantries have been exchanged...we can't forget the good news."

Kai grumbled. "I hope it's very good."

"You can be the judge of that. Ah, here he comes."

"He?"

"He's not a very strong flier," General Ipan whispered conspiratorially. "He needed a minute or two to get his legs back under him."

A man approached from the landing ground and bowed low before her. A bulging leather satchel slipped from his shoulder to the ground with a thud.

"Queen Kailani, meet Jurou, King Ozora's chief historian."

Jurou had a long nose with a slight hook, a narrow mouth, and oversized glasses. His shabby clothing was faded and too big for his thin frame. The only thing remarkable about the man was his hair. It was golden and thinning slightly. So he was a sunburner. She hadn't known they came in this scholarly variety.

"It's a pleasure to meet you Jurou. Welcome to the Lunar Citadel. Though I did not hear that you were coming..." She looked to General Ipan and back again.

Jurou spoke first. "It was I who asked to come. Forgive my impertinence for inviting myself into your house, so to speak."

"Not at all," Kai said. "But I am curious why you made the trip."

"We live in quite remarkable times, as you no doubt realize. I have been poring over the libraries of Kistana seeking an understanding of the events of the last few months."

"The drought?"

"Yes, the drought, the sickness, the gods' apparent distaste for the burners, whom they once held dear. The trail of my research has gone cold in Kistana, and I thought I might pick it up here. I know the citadel has an extensive library with many volumes Kita does not have."

"You seek the cause of the gods' anger at us?" Kai said.

"Yes, and hopefully a remedy."

A measure of hope bloomed in Kai's chest for the first time in several weeks. "Then you are very welcome indeed. Master Vita, our librarian, has had little luck finding answers, but perhaps you two can combine efforts."

"Excellent," Jurou said. "I have several theories, you see. Some scholars believe that worlds like ours have lifecycles, and perhaps ours is nearing the end of its life. Hopefully, it would be reborn, of course, though that wouldn't help any of us."

"Ah," Kai said politely.

"Now it could also be a result of the secularization of our great nations. Perhaps a return to more zealous worship is what is needed to soothe the gods' anger."

"Both excellent theories," Kai said. "We will owe you a great debt if you can find a solution."

"Now I have several other theories—"

"Jurou," General Ipan cut in, "I'm sure the queen has many tasks to attend to. Perhaps we could arrange another time where you could present your most promising theories after comparing notes with Master Vita."

"Of course," Jurou said, rubbing his hands nervously. "My apologies, Your Majesty. I have a tendency to get carried away sometimes."

"No apology necessary," Kai said.

"I would like to head to the library now if you don't mind."

"Absolutely. I'm sure Master Vita will make you feel right at home. Nanase, please have Jurou escorted to the library. I will be in my chambers."

Jurou retrieved his satchel, heaving it over his narrow shoulder and heading after Nanase.

Thank you, Kai mouthed to General Ipan behind Jurou's retreating figure.

He winked.

☾

Once Kai was around the corner from Daarco and the others, she picked up her pace and jogged to her chamber. She hadn't had a minute to herself since she had awoken. It turned out that queens didn't get much time alone. Almost none, in fact.

When she entered the carved wooden door, Quitsu was laying on the thick coverlet. He hadn't wanted to see Geisa, and Kai didn't blame him.

She flopped on the bed next to him and gave his head a scratch.

She still hadn't gotten used to this life. Perhaps she never would. Her chambers were large and sprawling, taking up the entire floor of the tower. The bedroom, which connected to the sitting room on one end and the washroom on the other, was lined with tall windows swathed in thick velvet drapes. The floors were covered in lush white carpets that were just about the most impractical things in the world.

The bed dominated the room, a huge monster four-post affair with more pillows than a whole family would have back in Ushai shoen. The coverlet was made of soft silk trimmed with silver fringe that she toyed with when she couldn't sleep. There were a lot of nights when she couldn't sleep.

Quitsu had been unusually silent the past few minutes.

"What's wrong, furball? No witty jabs today?"

He rolled so his back was to her, hitting her in the face with his long fluffy tail.

She sat up, rolling him back over so he was looking at her. His snout was set in a thin line and his pointed silver ears were laid back on his head. Though adorable as ever, he looked...angry.

"Are you mad at me?" Kai asked with incredulity.

"You almost got us killed," he exclaimed, jumping to his feet. "You didn't even think before you burst into that house to help that man. How could you be so careless? Don't you see that we all depend on you? Everything depends on you!"

She recoiled as if he had struck her. "You're the last person I need this from. You know I never asked for any of this! I never wanted to be queen."

"But you are, whether you like it or not."

"I know that," she said defensively.

"Do you?" he peered at her, his ebony eyes cutting through her defenses.

She looked away. "I guess," she muttered.

"If you're truly embracing being queen, why have you kept Hiro at arm's length? A child could see you're hopelessly in love with him. Why haven't you even discussed an engagement with him?"

Her cheeks reddened. "There's been so much going wrong. The time never seemed right..."

"Things haven't always been this bad. That's not the reason, and you know it."

Kai's face was burning now. Her lip quivered. *Don't cry.* "I don't deserve him," she said quietly.

"I can't hear you," Quitsu said.

"I don't deserve him!" Kai shouted. "I don't deserve any of this. I'm no one. I keep thinking he will wake up one day and realize that I'm plain and boring and he deserves someone better. Or that someone is going to march in here and say they made a mistake making me queen and throw me out on my backside! I don't know what I am doing! I don't know how to be queen! I don't know how to fight a god and goddess! Or a…whatever that thing is. I can't do any of this." Kai took a pillow and threw it at the stone wall with all her might. It exploded, raining a shower of goose down feathers over the bed. She blinked, looking at the mess through the refraction of tears in her eyes.

"Feel better?" Quitsu said. His signature grin was back on his face.

A smile quirked at the corner of Kai's mouth. It spread and she grabbed the other pillow, smacking Quitsu with it.

He yowled in mock pain, darting around the bed until she pulled him towards her chest with a sniffle.

"I'm sorry I put you at risk," Kai said. "I didn't know he had spotted fever."

"I know. It was an accident. But you have to be more careful. Tsuki would welcome any opportunity to take you out."

She closed her eyes briefly. "It would have been a lot simpler if I'd just died of spotted fever."

"For you maybe! What about the rest of us?" Quitsu said. "Well, not me, I would have been dead too."

"It would have been very selfish of me to die," she said, cracking a smile.

"Exactly. You're queen now. It wasn't a mistake. You're exactly where you're supposed to be. You need to embrace it until you feel it in every fiber of your being," Quitsu said.

She buried her face in his fur. It was as soft as silk under her hand, and she could smell the scent of him, fresh as new-fallen snow. The handprint on her chest thrummed at his nearness.

"Do you feel…different since we awoke?" she asked. She stood and went to the mirror, pulling the collar of her shirt aside to reveal the mysterious handprint.

"Yes," Quitsu whispered, jumping up on the table to examine the mark. "I feel more...alive somehow."

"Me too," Kai said.

"Do you remember any of what happened?" Quitsu asked.

She shook her head. "You?"

"I remember...feeling frightened. And then feeling safe. That's all," he said.

She brushed the scarred skin of her chest with her fingertips. "We should have died, Quitsu. But somehow, we didn't. We need to remember how. Why. It's important. I can feel it."

CHAPTER 8

Ryu seemed to know things in that strange seishen way. When Hiro was coming of age, Ryu would tell Hiro which courtiers were interested in him only for his crown. Which turned out to be all of them, much to his younger self's frustration. Ryu's talents were useful in all sorts of situations—card games, politics, managing his Kitan estates. Hiro owed much to the insights Ryu shared with him.

Nevertheless, Hiro was still startled when Ryu told him that General Ipan had landed at the citadel with Jurou and Daarco over an hour ago.

They would be housed in the west quarters—the wing was filled with rooms kept open for visitors and dignitaries. Hiro's rooms were located in the same wing, though he hardly felt like a visitor anymore. He fingered the ring nestled in the pocket of his jacket. Not a visitor, but not quite at home, either. Not yet anyway.

"Why in Taiyo's name did my father send Daarco?" Hiro muttered under his breath as he rounded a corner, searching for the sunburner visitors' quarters. Kai already had enough to worry about; she wouldn't be happy about this development.

"You could ask him," Ryu said. "He would know better than I."

"Maybe I will." He could ask Nanase to borrow the bowl she used to communicate with the sunburners in Kita. But in truth, he didn't want to talk to his father. Their correspondence as of late had been growing more and more unsettling, leaving Hiro with the feeling that he was going to soon end up between a rock and a hard place—namely his father and Kai.

A moonburner guard was posted at the door, but she stepped aside as Hiro and Ryu approached. Muffled voices argued from within the room.

Hiro let himself in.

The scene inside gave Hiro a sense of déjà vu. Daarco was draped over a lounge chair in front of the empty fireplace, a glass of sun whiskey in his hand. He hardly looked up when Hiro entered.

Jurou was standing by a table, flipping through a leather-bound tome he had apparently brought with him. The man was a true bookworm, but also whip-smart and politically-savvy. He played a critical role on Hiro's father's council. Hiro trusted the man implicitly, as did his father. That he was here was a very bad sign indeed.

"Planning an invasion?" Hiro half-joked, shaking Jurou's hand.

"This is probably the most sunburners the citadel has housed since its inception," Jurou said. "Well, that's not true. At least six came before the Flare War with Ozora's delegation, and then there was King Oxalta's envoy one-hundred and forty years ago, give or take—"

"It's a sign of changing times," Hiro said. He had long since given up feeling guilty interrupting the man. Jurou could go on for hours if left unchecked. "We are allied now. It's a sign of growing trust."

Daarco snorted and Hiro shot him a pointed look.

"Perhaps," Jurou said. "Troubled times."

"What are you doing here?" Hiro tried to ask the question gently.

"I have two purposes. What I am about to tell you, I trust you will not share with the queen. I understand you two have grown close, but your true allegiance lies with Kita, does it not?"

Hiro furrowed his brow. "I didn't know the two were mutually exclusive. Tell me why you are here, and I can assure you that I will keep it quiet if I believe it to be in the best interest of Kita. That will have to suffice."

Jurou looked at him for a moment with his piercing blue eyes.

"Your father is concerned about the Oracle's prophecy. It's coming true. Since the peace treaty between Kita and Miina, strange things have been happening. The drought, the spotted fever, but more than that. Things you have not heard about yet. Things we have been trying to keep quiet. A horde of locusts descended on some farms in Western Kita. But they didn't just eat the crops. They were flesh-eating. They destroyed the cattle, the livestock—even people who were unfortunate enough to be caught outside."

Hiro's stomach turned.

"There is more than I can even recount. We cannot ignore that these horrors may be caused by the gods' anger."

"You can't believe that superstition," Hiro protested.

"We can't afford not to," Jurou retorted. "Of course, I am looking into alternative explanations. But often the simplest explanation is the right one."

Hiro nodded reluctantly. "We have reached the same conclusion here. We have to be open to the possibility that the disasters are caused by the gods. But that brings us no closer to a solution."

"My first mission is to see what I can find in Miina's library. Maybe there are texts that reveal more about Tsuki and Taiyo's proclivities and how to placate them."

Relief flooded him. Jurou was here to help. Then Hiro remembered the man had said *first* mission.

"Your second purpose for being here?"

"Yes. The secret one. I am to evaluate the citadel's leadership and defensive capabilities. If worse comes to worst… your father is willing to break the alliance."

"What?" Hiro exploded. "How could that be on the table? It's the first time we've had peace in hundreds of years. We finally sent our soldiers home to their families. Now you want to call them back?"

"The king is being practical, examining all options. War is preferable to starvation. These gods know how to hit us where it hurts."

"It's not natural," Daarco said from his chair, still looking into the fireplace. "Peace between sun and moonburners. It's not natural."

Hiro rolled his eyes. "Your mother was a moonburner. None of us would have been here if not for a moonburner and a sunburner getting along, at least for a short while. Just because you don't like it doesn't mean it's not natural."

Daarco stood, setting his empty glass down. From his red-rimmed eyes, it hadn't been his first drink. "Moonburners killed my father. I saw his body, burned and blackened by their evil. I vowed that day to make them all pay. So you're sure as hell right that I don't like it."

Hiro massaged the bridge of his nose, holding his frustration in check. He hardly recognized Daarco anymore. "Jurou, I will keep your orders to myself...for now. But I trust you will do everything in your power to ensure that you find a solution in the library. That is the only type of solution I will accept, understand?"

"Understood, Prince Hiro."

"Daarco, I'd like to talk to you in the hall for a moment."

"Yes, Your Highness," Daarco said with a mocking half-bow.

They closed the door to Jurou's chamber, and Hiro pulled Daarco by the arm down the hallway.

"We'll be less than one hundred paces away," Hiro said to the guard as she moved to follow them. As soon as they turned the corner, Hiro rounded on Daarco, slamming him into the wall. "Why are you here?" he hissed.

Daarco seemed taken aback, sobering up for a moment. "Your father sent me. To teach me....tolerance," he mumbled.

"How is that going?" Hiro asked. "It seems to me that so far you've managed to get drunk and continue to hate moonburners."

Daarco glared at him.

Hiro softened, taking his hands from his friend's shirt collar. "Everyone lost someone in the war. I know it stings, but...it was war. My father's decree resulted in Kai's father's death, and she has found a way to forgive."

Daarco opened his mouth to say something, but Hiro held up a finger to silence him.

"Despite what Jurou says, our future is peace with the moonburners. If you want to be a part of that future, you have to find a way to get past your hatred." Hiro looked at his friend, seeing the small boy he knew as a child grieving over the loss of his father. "You have hated for so long. It drains you. Try to lay it down. Or you can't stay."

Daarco nodded, averting his eyes from Hiro's. "I'll try. That's all."

"That's all I ask," Hiro said. Hiro didn't need Ryu's abilities to see that his friend had been drowning his sorrows in sun whiskey. Daarco's warrior's physique had softened and he had put on weight around his middle and under his chin. His eyes were bloodshot and his skin was blotchy.

Hiro felt a stab of guilt. He had been away too long. He had left his friend to his own devices and this is what had happened. Daarco's hatred of the moonburners was slowly killing him.

But now that Daarco was here, Hiro would do his damnedest to make it right. He would drag Daarco into this new era—kicking and screaming if he had to.

"You should have something to do while you're here," Hiro said, racking his brain. How could he keep Daarco occupied? Who could put up with him?

A brilliant idea dawned on him. Someone just as tough as Daarco who wouldn't take any flack.

"Would you consider helping in the armory? Assisting with teaching weaponry and tactics and such?"

"Fine," Daarco said, apparently defeated for the time being.

"You'll help Chiya," Hiro said. "That'll be perfect."

CHAPTER 9

The next night fell quickly, and Kai could have sworn that there was a crisp of autumn in the air. Perhaps she was imagining it, but she felt hopeful nonetheless. She had slept the full day, spared from the worried tossing and turning that had filled her nights as of late. Her steps were light as she and Quitsu made their way to the stables for her weekly ride into the city.

Her mood was further buoyed when she encountered Hiro in the stables, saddling his tall chocolate stallion.

"Going somewhere?" she asked, straightening the buttons of the fitted leather vest he wore.

"I was hoping I could accompany you this evening. If you'll have me," he said, gazing down at her.

Kai examined the ceiling, pretending to consider. "I suppose, since you did help save my life yesterday, I could bear your presence for one ride."

"I didn't do anything," he said, his voice filling with emotion. "You saved yourself without any help from me."

"Nonsense," she said. "Emi told me how you went for the crown and worked with her to try to save me. It was inspired."

"It didn't work," he said.

"You don't always have to be the one to save me," she said softly.

"It's my job," he said. "If I can't protect you, what am I good for?"

"Plenty," Kai said. "I don't need another bodyguard. I need someone who will make me laugh when I'm in one of my moods."

"I suppose I have some practice at that…There have been enough moods," he said.

"And encourage me go for morning runs about the citadel when I'd rather loaf under the covers."

"Your endurance is getting much better. Though I'm not categorically opposed to loafing."

"And I need someone to explain the finer points of Kitan military strategy to me."

"Master Vita could do that."

"But Master Vita doesn't make my heart race when he explains the famous Phoenix Flanking Maneuver," Kai said, running her thumb across Hiro's rough palm.

"I would hope not," he chuckled. "I wouldn't stand a chance with that type of competition."

"I'm serious. I need someone who knew me before all of this madness. A friend. And…" Her tongue always tied itself in knots when the subject tilted towards the physical. "And a lover?" The statement came out like a question.

Hiro looked at her for a moment, his green eyes smoldering, seeming to bare her down to the soul. He pulled her into a tight embrace, burying his nose in her neck.

Kai melted into him, relishing the moment of tenderness. With his very presence, Hiro had a way of making her feel like everything would be all right. He pulled back and his mouth found hers, his tongue gently searching, parting her lips with sweet insistence. And then she stopped thinking of how he made her feel and just felt it, her mind drifting into a bliss empty of worry about gods and droughts and fevers. He invaded her senses and left her reeling. The musky scent of him, the feel of his hard muscles pressed against her body. Her body ached for him.

But, as he always did, he pulled away, leaving her breathless and quivering. Though they had spent months together and had shared countless passionate kisses, he seemed unwilling to cross some invisible line. She'd almost begged him to continue a dozen different times, but her pride had killed the words on her tongue.

A cleared throat sounded behind them and Kai whirled around, her face red. Ryu and Quitsu stood in the hallway, bland expressions on their furry faces.

"Let's get my horse saddled," Kai said, smoothing her hair and heading to the next stall. She risked a glance back at Hiro and was rewarded by a stormy look of longing on his face. Though it stirred her own emotions once again, she felt a touch of satisfaction. *Good. Let him stew.*

☾

Kai and her retinue made their way out the big oaken citadel gates and into the city proper. Though Nanase insisted on Kai having at least two master moonburners and four other guards with her, it still was preferable to remaining cooped up in the citadel.

Kai held court once a month, during which her subjects could come to her to present a problem or complaint, but she had taken to riding through the city at least once a week to let the people see her. Sometimes she visited Tsuki's temple or the merchant's guild headquarters. Other times she'd go to a school or library. Last week, she had visited a boarding house Emi had set up, where vulnerable women could learn a real trade and escape a life of prostitution. That visit seemed like a lifetime ago.

Tonight, having Hiro at her side was a welcome addition. With Quitsu and Ryu trotting along beside them, they drew quite a few stares from Kyuden's citizens. Often her passage was met with cheers and hollers, but this ride was different. The faces she saw were withdrawn, guarded. Hungry.

They made their way through the well-kept streets that bordered the citadel into the Meadows, the rundown neighborhood where Kyuden's poorest citizens lived. Kai had made efforts to better the situation for those who lived in this area, opening an orphanage and kitchen paid for with royal funds. It was a start, but there was very far to go.

Tonight they were headed to the city's granaries situated on the docks of the Nozuchi River. Kai had read reports about the sorry state of Kyuden's food stores, but she'd had to see it for herself. Hanae had arranged an appointment and tour with the dockmaster.

Kai glanced over at Hiro, who seemed lost in thought. He worried at the reins with his hands, his attention far away.

"What's on your mind?" she asked him.

He started, as if he had forgotten she was there. "Daarco," he admitted.

"About that," Kai said sharply. "I don't want him here. We have enough to worry about as it is."

"He won't try anything," Hiro said. "He knows he has to behave or he will be stripped of his rank and discharged."

"The man tried to kill me," Kai said. "I don't trust him."

"I don't blame you. I wouldn't either if I were you. But at the time, he was doing what he thought was best for the sunburners. I have made it very clear that what is best for the sunburners now is peace. Our alliance."

"Will that be enough?" Kai asked.

Hiro sighed. "Daarco wasn't always like this. Once, he was like a brother to me. Now...I'm losing him. This hatred is consuming him, and if I don't try to bring him back from the edge..."

"You'll lose him forever," Kai finished.

"I know I have no right to ask you to let him stay, especially with all that is going on. But just give me two weeks. To get through to him. If there's no improvement...we'll send him home."

"Two weeks?"

"Two weeks."

She blew out a breath, fluttering her silver hair. "I can't refuse you anything."

"You are a most magnanimous queen," Hiro said with a chuckle. He took her hand and kissed it. "Thank you. Besides, I gave him to Chiya to look after. I figure if those two don't tear each other apart, she'll whip him into shape."

Kai laughed. "I'm impressed. They'll probably glare at each other until one of them goes cross-eyed."

"Indeed. We can just sit back and watch."

Kai's smile grew wistful. "I wish everyone believed it as strongly as we do."

"What?" Hiro said.

"That what we're doing is right. The alliance. I know it in my bones. But how to show people?"

"We will," Hiro said, squeezing her hand.

As they crested a hill, the view of the city stretched out beneath them. The lights below punctuated the inky darkness of the evening, and the stars above them seemed a mirror, reflecting the beauty of her city. A split in the road veered to the right, ending at a small grassy park designed to take in the view.

"Let's stop for a moment," Hiro said. He had a strange gleam in his eye. Kai considered rejecting the idea, but he had already swung down from the saddle, handing the reins to one of the guards. *A short break can't hurt,* she thought. The park, despite the warm evening, was deserted.

Kai dismounted, landing on the cobblestones of the road. She wore fitted black trousers and a violet silken tunic with a high neck. She was still more comfortable in pants than anything else.

Hiro took her hand and led her into the park, where he looked into the distance for a moment.

"Gives Kistana a run for its money," he said, referring to the Kitan capital where he had grown up.

"Kyuden beats Kistana hands down," Kai said.

"You've never even been to Kistana!" Hiro retorted.

"I don't have to," Kai said. "I know that Kyuden is the most beautiful city in the world."

"Agree to disagree," Hiro said, turning to her. "Neither of them hold a candle to the most beautiful sight I've ever seen."

"And what might that be?" Kai asked, arching an eyebrow.

"You," he said.

She chuckled, playfully swatting at him, but the intensity of his expression stilled her.

"I mean it," he said. "Inside and out. I can't imagine my life without you. I don't want to have to." He pulled something out of his pocket.

"Kailani Shigetsu, Queen of Miina. Will you marry me?" He held up a ring that glittered in the starlight. It was simple, formed of interwoven bands of silver and gold, studded with tiny winking diamonds. It was perfectly lovely, unlike the gaudy gems that were all the rage among the nobles. Somehow he had known that this would be exactly what she would want.

Kai's breath caught in her throat, her mind racing with excitement. A life with Hiro was a dream that she had hardly dared dream, for fear that thinking of it would cause it to slip away. She loved him with force that she felt like a physical thing.

But a flicker of guilt flitted through her mind. War was coming. The very earth was rebelling against them. How could she play the happy bride when her people were starving? Dying?

Hiro seemed to understand the doubt in her face. "I know the timing seems strange. The truth is, I've been carrying this ring in my pocket for months, trying to find the perfect time. But there is no perfect time. You almost died yesterday. When I thought I had lost you, I kept thinking what a fool I had been, that I hadn't told you how I felt. That I had missed my chance. I'm not going to miss my chance again. I love you, Kai. Even if Taiyo scorches the earth tomorrow, I want to spend today with you."

"I love you too," she whispered, her thoughts tumbling inside her. She wanted it too. To marry Hiro. To have one piece of happiness to hold on to while the world crumbled around her.

So she threw her arms around Hiro and kissed him, deep and long, giving him her answer without a word passing her lips. When she pulled back, both of their faces were wet with tears.

"Yes," she said.

He slipped the ring on her finger.

CHAPTER 10

Ryu and Quitsu plowed into Hiro and Kai with bounds of happiness, nearly knocking them off their feet. Ryu had his paws on Hiro's shoulders and Quitsu sat on Kai's head and they laughed and shooed at their seishen with happy tears shining in their eyes.

"Don't tell me we're stuck with the fox," Ryu rumbled as he dropped back to all fours.

"You would be so lucky," Quitsu said with mock affront. "You have the sense of humor of a bale of hay, and the look of one too! I could teach you a thing or two!"

"Now, kids, don't fight," Kai said with a laugh, her gaze meeting Hiro's with the sudden joy of possibility. He could see it too. Children. A family. A life to build.

Hiro circled behind her and wrapped his arms around her, resting his chin on her silver-topped head. They looked over the sparkling lights of Kyuden, reveling in the moment. His spirit soared. She had said yes.

Kai wasn't one to play games, and Hiro had thought he'd known what her answer would be. But a small part of him had been terrified. He wasn't used to feeling so exposed.

Now, holding her in his arms, Hiro felt silly for doubting their love. They had been through so much together already.

"I never thought I'd get to marry for love," he said.

"You assume your father will approve?" she joked.

"You know he respects you," Hiro said. "He thinks you'll keep me in line."

"He's not wrong," she said.

"If I married at all, I was resigned to a marriage that would only serve Kita's political needs. I thought I'd be fortunate to end up with a wife who didn't despise me."

"I'm afraid you'll have to suffer through a marriage with a wife who adores you," she said.

Hiro kissed the smooth indent at the side of Kai's neck, and she shivered lightly under his touch, turning in his arms for another kiss. Her lips tasted of honey. When she pulled back, he drank in the sight of her: the sprinkling of freckles that dotted the bridge of her nose and cheeks, her warm hazel eyes that revealed such intelligence and wit. He felt like they could see to the heart of him, and for once, the exposure didn't frighten him.

"I wish I could stay here forever," Kai murmured, pulling back slightly.

"But…"

"But I have a meeting with the dockmaster to walk through the granaries," Kai said. "I shouldn't miss it."

"Duty calls," he said, unable to keep from smiling. He thought he might never stop smiling.

They mounted once again and made their way down the hill to the maze of warehouses, docks, and ships that made up Kyuden's port.

Hiro had never been to this part of the city, and he took it all in with interest. A spiderweb of rickety wooden docks splayed over the meandering Nozuchi River, creating a bustling city all its own. They passed a floating market full of merchants in long wooden boats hawking their wares—spices, cloth, dried meat, little black shellfish that cracked open to reveal gooey flesh inside. There were human wares too, women with high hemlines and low necklines, watching him hungrily as they passed. Young girls and boys who should be in school peering around corners with haunted eyes. Kai saw all of these things, her mouth set in disapproval. He could see her mind working, whirling through strategies and initiatives that might help these people.

They rode through many docks and stalls before they arrived at the first of four identical warehouses. The warehouses were huge, set on large platforms built half on the riverbank and half over the river. It didn't seem like the best location for a granary, but it was close to where the flat barges of grain came into port from farms upriver. Perhaps it was just a temporary storage area. Armed guards patrolled the fenced perimeter of the warehouses. With no crops this year, the grain in these buildings was more precious than gold. It was a wise precaution.

A tall older man strode out of the granary to greet them. His salt and pepper hair curled about his head in a wild fashion, bobbing as he walked. His angular face was framed by pronounced cheekbones and held discerning blue eyes that seemed too fine for the rest of him.

"Gooday," the man said with a drawl, shaking Hiro's hand with a surprisingly firm grip after he'd dismounted. The man's other hand grasped a tall wooden staff smoothed by years of handling. The man was Hiro's equal in height and build, well-muscled under his suede trousers and faded linen shirt.

The man turned to Kai, taking her in with an appraising look before bowing low before her and kissing her hand. "I am at your service, Your Majesty," he murmured.

Hiro furrowed his brow. What kind of merchant was this man?

"I am a trader, a merchant, and an entrepreneur," the man said to Hiro, as if reading his mind. "If you can name it, I've done a bit of it in my time."

"What kind of entrepreneur?" Hiro asked.

"Antiquities, mostly," he said unabashedly.

"Antiquities," Kai said with suspicion, retrieving her hand like a handkerchief someone had sneezed into.

There were many who smuggled artifacts out of historic sites in Kita or Miina to sell on the black market. The rich adored displaying trinkets from long-lost dynasties in their sitting rooms. But it was a dangerous business. There was more to this man than met the eye.

"Merchant Silvie, as an…entrepreneur who trades in antiquities, how did you come to serve as my dockmaster?" Kai asked.

"I'm not your dockmaster," the man said airily. "He's a snivley little man with a ledger twice his size. Somewhere in the back." He pointed a thumb back at the warehouse.

"What?" Kai exclaimed.

Hiro drew his sword.

"Who are you then?" Kai asked.

"Why, I'm Colum, at your service." He twirled his staff before slapping the end to the dock. "I wanted to get a look at you. I heard you'd be visiting this part of town."

Before Hiro could respond, a great rumble sounded. It echoed across the docks and the river, drawing little ripples on the water.

"What was that?" Kai asked, her eyes widening in alarm.

Ryu yowled and Quitsu cried out with a screech, their voices blending in an animal cacophony that stood Hiro's hair on end.

As their voices died out, the world hung perfectly still for a moment, as if taking a deep breath. A sense of overwhelming wrongness flooded through his bond with Ryu.

"That, I suspect, is what Tsuki has planned for you next," Colum said.

And then the wrongness exploded, seeming to rip the very fabric of the world itself. The dock bucked beneath them in great galloping strides, the ground shuddering in an earthquake. Hiro's feet lost contact with the dock as the ground lurched up to meet him. He hit the dock hard, pain exploding up his tailbone and spine. He clung to the boards, forcing his fingers between the tightly-packed wood, seeking desperately for purchase. It did little good—the rolling of the dock flung him into the air like a leaf on the autumn wind.

Kai and the others were doing no better. Kai was flattened on her stomach clinging to one of Quitsu's legs as the dock heaved beneath her. Ryu had dug his claws into the wood of the dock and appeared to be holding firm. The weathered man was on his backside, bouncing about like he was breaking in a yearling in the stableyard. He had a mad smile on his face and...was he laughing?

As suddenly as it had begun, the shaking ended.

People poured out of the granaries and warehouses down the length of the docks. Guards and merchants, laborers and nobles all scrambled over each other in headlong flight towards the shore. The mass of humanity seemed united in one goal: get to safety.

Hiro pulled Kai to her feet. "Are you all right?"

"Yes," she said, drawing in a shaky breath. Blood dribbled from a split in her lip. "But I'm getting awfully tired of the gods playing dirty."

"They haven't played all their cards," Colum said. "Let's get out of here."

No sooner had the words left his mouth than the earth let out another ominous groan.

"More?" Kai said, the dismay plain in her voice.

They joined the crowd of people fleeing the warehouses and docks running towards land. There were people all around them—a woman carrying her baby in a sling, a huge burly warehouse guard who overtook them easily, an old bookkeeper who was falling behind.

The shaking grew more violent as the earth not only undulated in waves, but also tossed them side to side like rag dolls. The mass of docks began to list to the side, leaning precariously towards the river.

"The docks are collapsing!" Hiro said, grabbing Kai's hand. "Run!" He knew Ryu and Quitsu followed somewhere behind, but he only had eyes for Kai. He had to keep her safe.

The world lurched beneath him in the most violent jolt yet. Kai's hand was ripped from his as the dock let out a colossal boom and the boards snapped in two. Hiro was tossed towards the land, while Kai was thrown towards the raging middle of the river.

Hiro hit the surface of the river like a ton of bricks, taking in a mouthful of cold dirty water. He flailed about in blind panic for a moment before orienting himself and kicking to the surface, spluttering and coughing. The dark water around him roiled with people, wood and waves.

Hiro scanned the churning surface of the river, trying to locate Kai. Where was she? His fear for her pulled at him like an anchor. He caught a flash of silver out of the corner of his eye and spun to see Quitsu pressed beneath the waves by two men barreling towards the shore.

Adrenaline exploded through Hiro's body and he crossed the choppy water with all the speed he could muster, quickly closing the distance between himself and Quitsu. Ryu could swim, but he didn't know about Quitsu.

About halfway to Quitsu, he crossed paths with a panicked woman flailing and moaning in the dark water. Without encouragement, she clung to him, pushing him under the surface with her desperate efforts. Hiro kicked with his legs, freeing himself from the pull of her grasping hands and heavy skirts.

As he surfaced, he threw an arm around her waist, pulling her hard against himself. "Stop struggling," he managed to gasp, taking in a mouthful of foul water. He kicked towards a large piece of wood and heaved her on top of it. "Hold on," he gasped.

The spot where he had seen Quitsu struggling was now empty. He swam towards it with powerful strokes, praying that he wasn't too late. He reached it and peered through the water for Quitsu. Nothing.

He took a deep breath and dove, searching the blackness with his hands. There. He felt fur brushing softly against his skin under the water. He grabbed Quitsu's tail and heaved the seishen towards him, struggling against the river's greedy pull. Quitsu would never let him hear the end of this.

Hiro grabbed under Quitsu's chest as he surfaced and swam towards the shore, pushing beams and debris out of his way. The river was a mess of people and wood, a layer of grain floating over the surface of it all. Kyuden's faint hope for surviving the winter was quickly becoming a drowned memory.

His feet struck the muddy bottom of the river and he scrambled onto the riverbank. Quitsu's body was limp and heavy in his arms and blood poured from a gash over the seishen's eye. Hiro resolutely ignored the worry that was seeping through his mind like a poison. It wasn't too late for Quitsu. He wouldn't allow it.

Once on dry land, Hiro fell to his knees on shaky legs and gently laid Quitsu down. Quitsu wasn't breathing. Hiro, remembering his medical training, began rhythmically pounding on Quitsu's chest, willing the seishen to breathe.

It wasn't working. He knew the other piece of the medical treatment, but had been hoping it wouldn't be necessary. He lifted Quitsu's snout, cupping it so none of the air could escape. He blew into Quitsu's mouth and then returned to his pounding. He did this again, and again. The third time, Quitsu shuddered and with a lurching cough, water exploded out of Quitsu's mouth right into Hiro's own.

Hiro spluttered and spit, wiping the regurgitated water off his lips.

Quitsu opened his eyes. "Sorry, Prince," he rasped, "but you're not my type."

Hiro blinked with surprise and then started laughing. He swept Quitsu up into his arms, giving him a backbreaking hug. "Thank Taiyo you are all right."

"Where's Kai?"

Hiro looked over the dark river full of people who still struggled and cried for help. "I don't know," he admitted, his worry like a dark storm in the pit of his stomach. "I haven't seen Ryu either, though I know he's a strong swimmer. He'll be all right. I guess we should help these people and see if we can find her."

It was the right thing to do, and he couldn't go back to the citadel without Kai.

Hiro heaved himself up and waded back into the river.

CHAPTER 11

The collapsing dock flung Kai high into the air. She enjoyed a feeling of strange lightness before she hit the water with a teeth-rattling crash. The river spun her around until she didn't know which way was up or down. She tried to draw in moonlight to burn, but she didn't know what to do, how to help herself. It felt raw and strange to her. She was in a foreign world that she couldn't translate.

As she contemplated her predicament in a strangely detached way, a strong hand gripped her wrist and pulled. *Hiro,* she thought with relief.

She breached the surface with a gasping cough, forcing the water from her lungs. She treaded water, taking several shuddering breaths that burned her raw throat.

She looked around for her rescuer. It was not Hiro. Even in the darkness and sliver of a moon, she knew every outline of Hiro's profile. Her rescuer had curly hair, illuminated like an eerie halo by the moon.

"Colum?" she rasped.

"Aye, Queenie," he said. "Let's get to the shore and get dry before we exchange pleasantries." He set off towards the far shore with a determined stroke.

She looked back towards the port with its roiling mass of flotsam and debris. From the far side, they could follow along the river and cross over one of the bridges back to the other side.

She swam after him.

By the time they reached the riverbank, Kai's muscles were burning with fatigue. She collapsed onto the sticky mud, catching her breath. The high stone of the riverwall loomed behind her.

"Looks like you need a bit more adventuring and a bit less cushy palace life, 'eh, Queenie?" Colum said, sitting next to her with his elbows resting on his knees. He didn't even seem winded from the swim.

"Don't call me 'Queenie,'" Kai said, glaring at the man.

"As you wish," he said. "Queenie," he added under his breath.

She growled softly but dropped it, climbing shakily to her feet. She had bigger problems.

"The citadel is this way," she said, setting off along the riverbank.

He paused for a moment and then followed, his staff making sucking noises in the mud. Somehow he had managed to hold on to it through the whole ideal.

"Your name sounds familiar," she remarked. It was on the tip of her brain. Where had she heard it before?

"I used to work at the citadel. Maybe you've heard stories of my impressive...deeds from some of the moonburners." He raised an eyebrow in a lascivious manner.

She snorted. "Don't flatter yourself. No legends of that type around the citadel. But maybe it is from someone you worked with...Would anyone you knew still be there?"

"Mariko was the headmistress of the citadel..."

Kai shook her head.

"Gypsil was chief servant..."

Another head shake.

"Master Vita was the head of the libraries."

"Yes!" Kai cried. "Master Vita! That's where I remember your name. You built the dirty song into the floor of the treasury!"

He laughed. "You bet your balls I did. I forgot about that. Though how could I? The late queen ran me out on my heel when she found out."

Kai smiled despite herself. His wide grin and square white teeth reminded her of her father. She found herself relaxing slightly in his presence, despite his sudden appearance on the docks. "So why were you looking for me? Why are you in Kyuden?"

"I want to help you."

Kai glanced sideways at him. "Help me?"

"Do so few people offer help that you aren't familiar with the term?"

She chuckled ruefully. "I'll admit, I haven't had a lot of turns of luck lately."

"Then you're due for some good news."

"And you're here to help me, what, out of the kindness of your heart? Your sense of patriotism?"

"No, Queenie. For money. I'll help you for money." He whipped a great golden coin out of his pocket and twirled it expertly through his fingers before it disappeared again.

"What makes you think that I have need of you? Or that there's money in it for you?"

"I'm a bettin' man, you see. No one wants to bet on the lame horse. But if you do…and win…" He rubbed his hands together. "That's quite a jackpot indeed."

Kai furrowed her brow. "Am I the lame horse in this analogy?"

"You are," he said cheerfully.

Kai knew she should feel offended, but somehow she felt more heartened by the fact that he thought she had a chance of winning the race.

He went on. "I pulled you out of a river after your entire granary collapsed in an earthquake. And I have a feeling that's not the worst disaster that'll happen this month. You can't afford not to hire me."

Kai gritted her teeth. She wished he wasn't right. That it wasn't so obvious. But she couldn't let her pride get in her way. She did need help. But could she trust this man? Who knew what ulterior motives he might have. She would have to talk to Master Vita, get his read on the man, before making any decisions.

Kai's heart twisted as they summited a set of stairs that deposited them back in the city streets. Her city looked as if a spoiled boy had upturned his toybox onto the floor, scattering building blocks and miniature figures. Fires raged in the distance, and the sounds of wailing and crying mingled with the dust and smoke.

Tears pricked her eyes as she turned from the chaos and began walking towards the citadel. She could do more good with the moonburners and citadel resources at her disposal than by pulling people out of buildings singlehandedly. And she had learned days ago, there was risk that came from blindly rushing into an unknown situation.

Colum paced her silently, his unassailable good mood temporarily dampened.

When they reached the main courtyard of the citadel, Kai's heart sank further. Several of the buildings had crumbled. Tsuki's temple, which had been burned in last year's sunburner attack, had totally collapsed. One half of the koumori rookery had given way, and rubble littered the ground. Koumori swooped through the sky, clicking with upset.

"Nanase!" Kai called as she saw the woman across the courtyard directing moonburners and servants.

Nanase turned and her face sagged with relief when she saw Kai. "Thank the goddess. We feared for what happened in town."

"We were on the docks; they collapsed. The granaries are destroyed."

Nanase's mouth thinned to a tight-lipped line at this news.

"I might not have made it if not for Colum."

"Who?" Nanase blinked.

Colum stepped from behind Kai and waved, his curly hair bobbing.

"I'll explain later," Kai said. "If we can spare one, send a koumori to the docks in town to retrieve Hiro, Ryu and Quitsu. We were separated." Kai had been shoving down her trepidation over what had happened to Hiro and their seishen when the dock collapsed. At least she knew Quitsu was all right. She would have felt it if something had happened to him.

"Consider it done." Nanase said.

"What's the damage?" Kai asked.

"Tsuki's temple, which is ironic. Part of the rookery, the kitchens and cellars are totally collapsed."

Kai couldn't keep the dismay off her face.

"Our god and goddess are trying to starve us out. But we'll make do. We'll dig out and salvage what we can."

Kai nodded, trying to fight her growing sense of despair. "Casualties?"

"A few. We're still digging."

"Thank you. Keep me posted."

"Oh," Nanase said, a flash of guilt crossing her face. "I heard your mother was taken to the hospital ward."

"What?" Kai exclaimed.

Nanase's next words were lost on the hot breeze, as Kai was already running across the courtyard.

Kai burst into the hospital ward. "My mother," she asked a nurse, who was busy wrapping gauze around a young woman's arm. The nurse nodded towards the back of the hospital ward, not looking up from her work.

Kai scanned the room, past the injured and those busily tending them. There she was! At the end standing over a cot.

Kai ran up to her breathlessly. "I could kill Nanase," Kai said. "She told me you were here. I thought you'd been injured."

Hanae clucked her tongue. "Don't be too hard on her. She might not have known. Will you help me turn her? I want to get a look at her back, see if there is any bruising."

Kai looked down at the patient her mother was tending and sighed. "Oh, Chiya," Kai said, rounding the cot to help her mother. "Is she all right?"

"She should be fine. She was in the armory when it happened; she's lucky she wasn't impaled by a dozen different weapons. A shelf collapsed on her."

"Why is she unconscious?"

"I sedated her," Hanae said, pursing her lips. "I wanted to make sure she didn't have internal bleeding, but she refused to sit still to be looked at. I did what I had to."

Together, Kai and her mother lifted Chiya's shoulder and back, rolling her onto her side. Kai knelt by the cot, holding Chiya's body while her mother lifted the woman's shirt, probing her back with deft fingers.

Watching her mother work, Kai noticed that Chiya had a tan birthmark in the shape of a perfect heart on her spine. "I bet she hates that," Kai said, pointing, a half-smile crossing her face. "Doesn't fit her tough girl reputation."

Hanae's hands stopped moving.

"Mother?" Kai asked. Hanae's face had turned pale. Kai nudged her with her shoulder. "Mother."

Hanae started, as if realizing where she was. She pulled Chiya's shirt down. "You can set her down."

Kai carefully returned the full weight of Chiya's unconscious body to the bed and stood, stretching her knees.

Hanae had stepped back and stood staring at Chiya, one hand to her chest.

"What is it? You look like you've seen a ghost," Kai said.

"Do you know anything about Chiya's background?" Hanae asked faintly.

"Her background? Like her family?" Kai frowned, trying to remember what she had heard. "She was raised in the citadel. She was one of the babies who were rescued from the Tottori Desert after King Ozora started the Gleaming. I don't think they know who her parents were."

"How old is she?"

"A few years older than me, I think? I'm not sure. Why?"

Hanae had not moved. A tear trickled down her face. "I think Chiya is your sister."

Her mother's words froze Kai in place. Sister. She had known her parents had had a child before she'd been born, and that the little baby's power had been exposed in the Gleaming, the terrible sunburner tradition of testing and then leaving babies with moonburning ability in the Tottori Desert to die.

But...alive? And...Chiya?

"How...do you know?"

Hanae's face was radiant through her tears. "Your sister, Saeko... She had a birthmark just like Chiya's. A heart on her back."

"And Saeko was left in the desert?"

"Yes," Hanae said. "We didn't live in Ushai shoen then; we lived closer to the Chiritsu plain."

"They told me that the Oracle would see visions about where the babies were dropped. The moonburners would retrieve them."

"Maybe she will remember the details of Chiya's rescue," Hanae said.

Kai shook her head to clear it. "Perhaps. I know this is important, but it can't be a priority right now until we evaluate the damage to the citadel. Can we deal with this tomorrow?" She stood to leave.

Hanae grimaced but nodded. "Kai..."

"What?"

"Chiya is older than you. If this is true...by rights..."

The realization hit her like a gale force wind. Chiya was older. If Chiya was really her sister, she was the rightful heir to the throne.

Hanae's gray eyes were sympathetic, pleading. "We'll figure it out. It won't change anything."

Kai nodded numbly. They both knew that wasn't true. This would change everything.

Kai had never wanted to be queen and had always thought she would hand over the reins gladly if another qualified candidate came along. But when faced with the actual prospect of giving it up…the thought twisted at her like a knife.

A sparkle on her hand caught the light and Kai choked back a laugh.

"What, my daughter?"

"Hiro and I got engaged today," Kai said, holding her hand up with a rueful smile. "I wonder if he'll still want me when he finds out the truth."

"Hiro loves you for who you are."

"I hope you're right. Can we…" Kai closed her eyes, partially disbelieving that she was asking this. "Can we keep this between us until we know more?"

"Of course," Hanae whispered.

CHAPTER 12

Kai exited the hospital ward as if in a dream. She felt strangely removed from the chaos around her. In the year since she had been crowned queen, she had come to see this citadel as hers. Her responsibility, her calling. She had made a difference, changed things for the better. But perhaps it had been a lie. Maybe it should have been Chiya, continuing the war with the sunburners, appeasing the gods' desire for blood. Maybe this earthquake wouldn't have happened.

But no. There was more to the burners than war. In the last year, she had seen marvels. Advancements in medicine, learning, improvements in the condition of her people. If it weren't for these damn natural disasters, her reign would already be sung about by the bards.

Kai watched the citadel's inhabitants work together to clear debris from the kitchens, tossing wood and stones into a pile. A neat line of bodies, covered with sheets, lay against the building. Nine so far, and many were still missing. Kai tightened her fists. She was still queen, and she wouldn't stop fighting.

Kai started towards her council chamber. She needed a report on the damage. And they needed a plan. Maybe Jurou and Master Vita had come up with something. She would go over what they had learned from Geisa...

Kai froze. Geisa.

Kai broke into a run towards the dungeons, bursting through the front door and down the stairs. The guards had abandoned their posts—not that she blamed them. She wouldn't have wanted to stay in the dungeons during an earthquake, either. Bricks had fallen from the ceiling, leaving piles of dust and mortar on the ground. But the structure appeared sound.

Kai skidded to a stop at the bottom of the stairs. A figure stood ahead of her, a shadow just out of reach of the light of the moon orbs.

The figure turned.

Daarco's face was menacing in the darkness. Had he come here to free Geisa, an enemy of the moonburners? How had he known she was here?

"Daarco?" Kai asked. "What are you doing here?"

"Chiya told me to check on her," Daarco said defensively. "I took Chiya to the hospital ward after the earthquake. She told me to make sure the prisoner hadn't broken out."

"Do you know who is in that cell?" Kai asked carefully.

"I think so," he said. The white light of the moon orb glinted in his eyes.

"She is a traitor to all burners. She imprisoned and tortured your brothers as well. She cannot escape."

"I understand," he said. "Her cell is secure."

Kai shook her head. "She must never leave that cell."

"Well, it's locked up tight," he replied gruffly.

Kai paced past him to the door, and pulled on the iron handle. It was as he said—locked.

☾

Daarco followed her sullenly back into the courtyard. No sooner had they exited the building than Kai was bowled into by a flash of silver.

"Quitsu!" she cried, wrapping her arms around his warm furry body and hugging him to her chest. Some of the tension coiled through her body loosened. He was safe.

She looked up from the embrace and saw Hiro striding across the courtyard with Ryu at his side. His golden hair, normally pulled back, was loose and damp about his shoulders. His haggard face was smeared with dirt. Kai's heart stirred at the sight of him.

She placed Quitsu down and ran to him, hurdling her body against his and throwing her arms around him. She didn't care who saw.

He took her face in his hands and looked into her eyes, seeming to drink in the sight of her. "I feared for you," he said.

"I'm all right," she said, drawing back and bending down to hug Ryu's thick mane. "Everyone's all right."

"Kai!" Emi said, jogging across the courtyard, drawing to a stop before Kai. "I mean…Your Majesty."

"What is it?"

"Master Vita and Sunburner Jurou. They found something in the library. They beg your presence."

"Lead the way," Kai said, shaking off her weariness. She desperately wanted to fall into her bed and drift into an exhausted sleep. But there was no time to rest. She had a feeling there wouldn't be time to rest for a long time to come.

The library looked like a war zone. Thousands of books lay in heaps on the floor—a jumble of pages and covers that would take weeks to organize. Two of the tall shelves had tipped over into the far wall of the library. That had been a stroke of luck. If they had fallen the other way, they would have sent a wave of destruction through the whole library.

"This way," Emi said, practically running in her haste.

Kai followed her friend to the far corner of the library, where Master Vita and Jurou were talking excitedly in front of a yawning stone fireplace. Bricks had crumbled from the mantle, revealing a small recess in the stone. It was empty.

"Emi said you discovered something," Kai said, coming to a stop. "What have you found?"

Jurou stepped forward, holding his hands out reverentially. "This," he said.

It was a scroll. The rolled surface was thick, made of finely-tanned animal hide. Its two wooden ends were ornately carved in the shapes of the moon and sun.

"What is it?" Kai asked.

"Something extraordinary," Master Vita said.

They hurried to a nearby table, and Jurou wiped the dust and mortar from the surface with a quick swipe of his shirtsleeve.

With a bit more drama than was strictly necessary, Master Vita and Jurou unrolled the scroll before them. Kai smothered a grin, despite the destruction around her. The two men were like bookends, bearing matching expressions of excitement and anticipation. They were clearly getting along well.

When the scroll lay flat, it reached end to end on the massive table in front of them. Hiro had accompanied her in from the courtyard, and everyone crowded around the table to get a closer look.

"It's magnificent," Emi said.

Jurou was grinning like a proud father.

Emi was right. The scroll was covered in a series of images, intricately rendered in bright colors with gold and silver leaf. The scroll seemed untouched by time, as if the pictures had been painted yesterday. Beneath each picture was tiny text, painstakingly lettered in ink.

"It's written in both Miinan and Kitan," Jurou said. "The script is hard to read but recognizable."

"What does it say?" Kai asked.

"It's an illustrated story. It starts with Tsuki and Taiyo on their celestial thrones in the spirit realm. They created the first burners to be their special link to the our world and its inhabitants. To be their emissaries and rulers in the mortal world."

"But Tsuki and Taiyo were not without enemies. In the demon realm were hungry demons called tengu. They reveled in destruction and havoc and fed on human suffering. The tengu's plans were often thwarted by the gods and the burners, who kept peace and balance in the world. Two tengu rose above the rest—a hiei demon, a creature of ice, and a yukina, a fire demon. These two concocted a plan to capture Taiyo and Tsuki and weaken the burners in order to secure free reign over the lands."

Kai looked over Jurou's shoulder at the picture that accompanied the text. Her blood ran cold. It was the tall supernatural woman she had seen in the temple and the Oracle's tower. There was no mistaking the flowing robes, the eerie blur where a face should be.

"I've seen that creature," Kai whispered. "That's her."

Jurou raised a quizzical eyebrow, but she motioned him to continue. She could explain later.

"The tengu tricked Tsuki and Taiyo and trapped them at the far ends of the world, where their burners would never find them. Then they masqueraded as the gods and took their places. They knew that the only things standing between them and total dominion over the mortal world were the burners. At that time, the burners were still united and were ruled from was a great city… It appears to be where the Tottori Desert is now," Jurou said, pointing to the crude depiction of the Akashi Mountains and Churitsu Plain.

"Fascinating," Master Vita said, crowding in for a closer look.

"The tengu were not without allies. They had humans who served them, men and women who masqueraded as holy people, but who worshipped the tengu in secret. The burner king and queen died mysteriously without any heirs, and these followers sowed seeds of discord between the moon and sunburners until they turned against each other."

Jurou's mesmerizing voice came to a stop, his words hanging in the air.

"This has the ring of truth," Master Vita said. "The true origin of the Burning War."

Kai's heart pounded as her eyes roved over the intricate images. This scroll was likely the most important discovery of her lifetime. It explained so much…yet left so many details unsaid. Even as she processed the information revealed, questions surfaced in her mind like bubbles in a sparkling sake glass.

"So by allying ourselves with Kita and ending the war, we have angered these…tengu?" Kai asked.

"They've been masquerading as Tsuki and Taiyo this whole time," Master Vita said.

"Without war and suffering…they go hungry," Hiro said. "So they are starving us out in return."

"And leading us back towards a war," Kai said. Despite the sobering news, a sort of relief flooded her. She knew the alliance had been the right thing. It felt good to be vindicated.

"The scroll doesn't tell us how to kill them," Hiro said.

"Or *if* they can be killed," Emi said.

"As least we know what they are now," Kai said. "That's more than we knew before. Master Vita and Jurou can use this to look for more clues about the tengu and their weaknesses."

"Certainly. The texts of Aldera and the twelve dynastic epochs might have more information…Or Master Vita, do you have a copy of the Celestial Codex in the library? Or the histories of Saguzo—"

"You could discuss the specifics later—" Hiro began, but Jurou cut him off excitedly.

"Wait! Perhaps we don't have to fight them!" Jurou said.

Kai frowned. "What do you suggest?"

"They had to trap the real Tsuki and Taiyo before they could wreak the havoc they wanted. Presumably because the real gods would have stopped them."

"I think I see where Jurou is going with this," Master Vita chimed in excitedly. "If we free the real Tsuki and Taiyo..."

Emi completed his sentence. "Then you release two furious gods who have been trapped for centuries. If I were them, first thing I'd want is a little demon revenge."

"It's a genius idea, Jurou," Kai said. "But we have no idea where they were trapped, or how. The scroll only says 'the ends of the world.' It could take us another few centuries to find them."

"Yes, that is a conundrum," Jurou said.

"It's still worth exploring," Kai said. "We have to consider all avenues. But I have no idea where to look for a trapped god. Jurou? Master Vita? Any ideas?"

Jurou shook his head, his brow furrowed behind his thick glasses. "I'm sure we can discover the location now that we know what we're looking for. It'll just take time." He hadn't taken his fingers off the scroll; he stroked the hide absentmindedly with his long fingernails.

"I'm not sure we have time," Kai said.

"Perhaps we should ask our very own tengu acolyte," Master Vita said.

"What? Who?" Jurou asked.

"Geisa," Kai breathed. "After all these centuries, the tengu still have humans who help them."

"Forgive me," Jurou said. "But wasn't General Geisa killed before the Battle at the Gate?"

"She was wounded but not killed," Kai said, shaking her head. "I'm not ready to clue her in to our new knowledge yet. But she might have information about the tengu's weaknesses. Perhaps we can get that out of her."

"That still won't help uncover where Tsuki and Taiyo are trapped," Emi asked. "Where do we even start looking?"

A new voice sounded from deeper in the library. "Simple. Ask someone who was there."

CHAPTER 13

Everyone in the group jumped. Hiro had his sword halfway out of his scabbard before Kai recognized the mop of curly hair on the interloper's head.

"Stand down," Kai said. "It's…" She struggled to articulate who Colum was. She wasn't sure herself. "Well, I know him."

"At your service," Colum said, striding to the table and slapping Master Vita on the shoulder hard enough to knock the spectacles halfway down the librarian's nose. "Master Vita, good to see you again, you old dog."

Master Vita looked like he had seen a ghost. "Colum?" he said, adjusting his glasses. "It is you! I would recognize those curls anywhere! My, you're well preserved."

"Good stock," Colum said, clapping himself on his broad chest before sprawling down in a chair, tossing his leg over one arm. "You've gotta keep moving. It keeps the years from settlin.'"

Fingering his own snow-white hair, Master Vita continued to shake his head as if he couldn't believe his eyes.

Hiro wore a scowl of such displeasure that Kai had to stifle a chuckle. Men and their egos. Perhaps the only constant in the universe.

"Everyone, this is Colum. Colum, everyone," Kai said.

"He-llo, everyone," Colum said, turning about in the chair when he caught sight of Emi.

He started to rise, drawn to her like a magnet, but Kai shoved him back into the chair.

"Colum is newly returned to Kyuden. We met...before the earthquake. Now, what do you mean about asking someone who was there? This was hundreds of years ago. Everyone is dead."

"No. Not everyone," Colum said, flashing Emi a wolfish smile.

Kai crossed her arms before her, waiting for Colum to explain. The man was clearly enjoying the theatricality of the moment.

"For gods' sake, man," Jurou said. "Tell us what you mean."

"You have to find a god," he said.

"Are there more walking around?" Kai asked, raising an eyebrow.

"Well, perhaps 'god' is the wrong word. Spirit."

"Go to the spirit world?" Kai recalled her time in the spirit world with unease. She knew she had hardly scratched the surface the night she had encountered her mother in that strange place.

"No, you don't even have to leave the comfort and safety of your own mortal realm. There's a spirit who resides here all the time. An ancient spirit who has the knowledge and wisdom of millennia. No one? No one?"

Kai scowled.

"The seishen elder," Ryu growled from behind them, where he had been laying in front of the empty fireplace.

Quitsu nodded from his perch on the table beside Kai.

"A winner! Big scary lion seishen wins a prize," Colum said.

"His name is Ryu," Hiro growled, his voice almost as low as Ryu's.

Kai pondered the idea. It had merit. Here was a plan, a real plan. Quitsu had said that the seishen elder cared for the seishen until it was time for them to journey to find their burners. It was real. It lived in the Misty Forest.

"Ryu, Quitsu, could you help us find it?" Kai asked.

"Do you one better," Colum said. "I'll take you there myself."

"It's risky," Jurou said, removing his glasses. "We have no way of knowing what kind of creature the seishen elder is. I'm sure there's another way we could discover where the gods are hidden."

Kai looked to Ryu and Quitsu, who had silently observed the reading of the scroll. "What do you think?" she asked. "Would it know something that could help us?"

"Perhaps," Ryu growled. "The elder is ancient. It is connected to both the earth and the spirit realm. If anyone knows where the gods are trapped, it would be the elder."

"Agreed," Quitsu said. "But you might not like the answers you get. It is notoriously opaque."

Ryu chuckled. "This is true."

"It's the best lead we have," Kai said. "I'm going."

At her statement, the crowd gathered around the table exploded with objections.

"It's too dangerous," Master Vita said.

"You're needed here," Emi protested.

"It should be someone else," said Hiro.

Quitsu stood and shushed them, silencing their protests. "Kai must go. She would risk offending the elder if she sent someone else in her place."

Kai could have kissed Quitsu. This journey was exactly what she needed. To take action to help her country, rather than sitting around and fretting.

"Well, I'm going," Colum said, still leaning nonchalantly. "I know the way."

"I'm going too," Hiro said. "After all, we're engaged now. I should be there to protect you."

Murmurs of congratulations rolled in from around the table and Kai put on a smile, trying to quash her annoyance. Did he have to turn the announcement of their engagement into a condescending statement about the weakness of women?

Calm down, Kai, she said to herself, taking a deep breath. He didn't mean it like that. And truth be told, she wanted Hiro with her. She would welcome the chance to spend a few days with him. She'd talk to him about his comment later.

"Fine, Hiro comes," Kai said.

"I'm coming too," Emi said. "You need someone to watch your back while you and Hiro are gazing lovingly into each other's eyes."

Kai rolled her eyes. "We don't do that."

"If you have any chance of Nanase letting you out the citadel gates," Master Vita said, "Emi should accompany you. And a group of three is not enough. You don't know what you'll face out there."

"In case any of you have forgotten, I'm the queen," Kai said, grinding her teeth. "No one has to 'let' me do anything."

"I should come as well," Jurou said. "It would be good to have another sunburner for defensive purposes."

Kai eyed his bony form, not wanting to insult him with her doubt.

Hiro saved her. "You're needed here, Jurou. No one can comb this library better than you and Master Vita together. If the seishen elder can't help us, we need you to find us a miracle here."

"I'm sure Master Vita is perfectly capable of doing the research himself—" Jurou said, but Master Vita cut him off.

"It would be helpful to have two sets of eyes. It *is* a large library. Besides, best we leave the adventuring to the young, eh?"

Jurou opened his mouth to protest, but Hiro continued. "Besides, there is another sunburner available to go with us. Daarco."

"No," Kai said. "Not Daarco." She didn't have to pretend that she liked the man. Or trusted him.

Hiro took Kai by the elbow and drew her aside between two rows of books. He turned and took her hands, squeezing them in his own. As much as she wanted to keep her back up for a fight, some of the tension left her involuntarily at his touch.

"I'll keep him in line. I swear it to you. And it might be better to have him where we can keep an eye on him. I think a journey like this could be good for him. Redirect his energy."

Kai thought about the man having free reign of the citadel while she was gone. Hiro was right; it wasn't a good idea. But she didn't want him with them either, brooding and looking down his crooked nose at her. Curse Ozora for sending him here!

She finally nodded. "Fine, he comes. But if anything goes wrong— *anything*—he's gone. No more mission, no more citadel."

"Agreed," Hiro said.

"The five of us will go, and Ryu and Quitsu," Kai said, rejoining the group. "Anyone else? The cook? Your best friend's dog?"

The group around the table was silent, though Master Vita coughed to disguise a chuckle.

Jurou crossed his arms, not happy with the decision. Well, that was the least of her worries.

"Then it's settled. We leave tomorrow."

Preparations for their journey to the Misty Forest were made quickly. Though Nanase and Hanae argued about the wisdom of the trip, and how many extra guards Kai should take, Kai got her way. Hiro made himself scarce, gathering his own few belongings for the journey.

They would make the several-hour flight to the edge of the Misty Forest on koumori and golden eagles. Though the animals were nervous around each other, they didn't have enough eagles to fly all of them, and Ryu was too big for a koumori. Hiro's eagle was used to the special harness the Kitan beastmaster had rigged up for Ryu.

The group would set off at night to avoid the still paralyzing heat of the lingering summer. They had arranged to meet in the rookery just before sunset.

Hiro walked the familiar path from his room to the rookery, Ryu at his side. The whitewashed stone of the citadel with its black tile roofs had once seemed stark and clinical compared to the warm red sandstone and copper tiles of the Sun Palace, but it had grown comfortable.

Hiro arrived a few minutes early and rifled through the provisions laid out. The kitchen staff had packed each of them satchels full of hard bread and cheese, dried meat and fruit. They would each bear two waterskins. Hiro packed his supplies onto the backs of one of the golden eagles, strapping it tightly. He tested each of the straps of Ryu's harness, giving a quiet grunt of satisfaction when he found it sturdy. He was ready.

"I hear congratulations are in order."

Hiro turned to find Hanae standing behind him, a smile on her face.

"She said yes," Hiro said with a rueful shrug. "I'll be honest; I'm relieved the asking is done."

"It's not love if you don't leap off the cliff at least once," she said. "And you know it's true love if there is someone to catch you."

Hiro chuckled, imagining falling into Kai's arms. "I'll try not to squish her," he said.

"You're good for each other, that's plain to see. I know you'll make her happy," Hanae said. "But marriage isn't for the faint of heart. You've had it easy so far. "

Hiro furrowed his brow. "Easy? You think the last year has been easy?"

"Perhaps not externally, but your and Kai's interests have been aligned. You haven't faced any true tests of your relationship."

"What do you mean?"

"Where do you plan to live after you get married?"

Hiro frowned. He had always assumed that once they married, he would be able to convince Kai to move the seat of their rule to Kistana. But if he really thought about it, he wasn't so sure she would agree. She wouldn't want to leave Kyuden. And after his father died and Hiro became king, he wouldn't want to live away from Kistana. How would they rule two countries?

"I'm not sure," he said slowly. "Wherever Kai is feels like home to me. But once I become king, I will have other duties. I suppose we'll have to work out some sort of traveling arrangement."

Hanae nodded. "And what will you do if the interests of Kita and Miina diverge?"

"Then Kai and I will find away to align them again. Together," he said, pushing down his annoyance. It was too early in the evening for a grilling from his future mother-in-law.

Hanae had always been friendly but distant. He couldn't help but worry that she held his father's actions against him. If it weren't for Ozora, her husband, Raiden, would still be alive, and Kai would never have had to suffer exile in the Tottori Desert.

As if she sensed his annoyance, she relented, crossing to stand by his golden eagle. She stroked its feathered flank.

"I look forward to you becoming a part of our family, and I know you love her. I saw how you fought for Kai when we were losing her to the spotted fever," Hanae said. "Just promise me one thing."

"What?" Hiro said warily.

"Don't force her to choose."

"Choose? I'm not sure I follow," Hiro said.

"Kai has another great love…every good queen must."

"Miina," he said, realization dawning on him.

"Kai is a good queen and this country needs her. There might come a time where she has to choose…between her duty…and you. If that day comes, don't ask her to choose."

"But it would be her choice."

"Young love is powerful, maybe the most powerful thing in the world," Hanae said. "But it lacks a rational side." As she spoke, her gray eyes were sad, deep pools reflecting the ghosts of love lost.

"Ah," he said, finally understanding. "You chose love. And you regret that choice."

"Yes. And no," Hanae said, her tone light. "I'm glad to see you're not just a pretty face."

Hiro considered her request. If it came down to Kita or Kai, what choice would he make? If he was only giving up being a prince, being a king one day, he knew he would choose Kai. But what if that choice led to tragedy, to hardship for his people? Was his happiness worth the suffering of hundreds? Thousands?

"I see the wisdom in your request," Hiro admitted. "But I cannot agree to it. If I've learned anything about Kai, it's that she chooses her own path. She would flay me for just having this conversation with you."

Hanae was silent.

"But," he continued, "I will make you this promise. If someday she must choose Miina, I will not stand in her way."

Hanae smiled, her smooth face lighting up. "I suppose that's the best I can hope for."

"What are we hoping for?" Kai chose that moment to walk through the rookery door, her slender figure sporting soft gray trousers and a sky-blue shirt. For the first time in weeks, she looked well-rested, and her cheeks were flushed with color.

"Safe travels for you, my daughter," Hanae said, kissing her on the cheek. "Be careful. Take care of each other."

"We will. Hopefully we'll come back with new wisdom about how to defeat these enemies."

"I will pray for that," Hanae said before nodding to Hiro and slipping out the door.

"You seem chipper," Hiro said, snaking an arm around Kai's waist and pulling her close.

"I am," she admitted.

"Excited to get away from the citadel?" he asked.

"Is it that obvious?"

"No," he said.

"You're lying," she laughed, tapping the black pendant that hung on a silver chain about her neck. It had the magical ability to detect lies, and it grew warm to the touch in the presence of untruth. Hiro wouldn't have believed such a thing existed if Kai had not let him test it himself.

"You caught me once again," Hiro admitted, nuzzling the curve of her neck with his nose. Her faint smell of pear and lemongrass stirred his senses.

"All right, lovebirds, that's enough of that!" Colum cried as he barged into the rookery, a pile of weapons slung over his shoulder. "I didn't sign up to babysit a doe-eyed couple here. We're on business, eh? Saving the world business."

Kai stepped away from Hiro, suitably chastised.

Hiro glowered. It was going to be a long journey with this strange man guiding their way.

INTERLUDE

The man wrinkled his nose at the smell. Rotting trash, raw sewage, unwashed bodies—all mingled together in a potpourri of mankind's suffering. They were truly a disgusting species.

He stepped over piles of fallen brick and timber, discarded furniture, bodies of unfortunate souls who had been at the wrong place at the wrong time during the earthquake. He had to give it to the tengu. The devastation was impressive. A real work of art. Far more than was necessary to shake a few stones loose and "reveal" the scroll planted in the library. As much as his master griped and complained about the current state of affairs, the man could tell the demon was enjoying itself.

Two weary citizens of Kyuden approached and he instinctively pulled up the hood of his cloak, ensuring its deep cowl cast a shadow over his face. It was an unnecessary precaution. The haunted eyes of the gaunt couple never even looked up from the ground, never questioned why a passerby would be wearing a dark cloak in the sweltering heat of the day. These people were broken. Their era had come to an end.

The man idly pulled raging torrents of sunlight into his qi as he walked. He liked to hold sunlight, to feel its liquid fire swirl through his spirit like a connoisseur might taste a fine wine. He would miss sunlight the most when this was all said and done.

He pondered the recent turn of events, his nimble mind whirring and spinning, considering and discarding myriad plans and possibilities. The queen's decision to visit the seishen elder was an unknown variable. Would the elder know the truth behind Tsuki and Taiyo's long sleep, and caution them against reawakening the gods? But if it did, it might also know where Tsuki was located, a piece of information the man desperately needed. It was a risk he must take.

He idly tugged at a hangnail, letting go of the sweet sunlight. This visit to the elder was too important a piece of the puzzle to be out of his control. The man let out a frustrated hiss, startling a grimy street boy out of his path. At the lad's presence, an idea came to the man like a gust of a cool wind. He needed a distraction. A treat.

He pulled back his hood, rearranging his features into a friendly expression. "Hello there! I'm sorry. I didn't mean to startle you."

The boy froze, peering at him through a curtain of stringy black hair. A mangy brindle dog bounded out of a nearby alley, scooting to an alert stop in front of the boy. The dog came up to the boy's waist, and though its ribs protruded painfully, it still managed to look threatening. It was a miracle it hadn't been captured and eaten by Kyuden's citizens. The man had heard such things were happening.

The man raised his hands in a gesture of surrender. "I'm sorry if I scared you or your friend. I've come from the citadel. I've been sent to provide relief for the earthquake victims."

The boy continued to regard him with suspicion. The dog growled. The man burned a tendril of sunlight, sending it into the pleasure center of the dog's brain. He had spent years studying human and animal anatomy, learning exactly where to put heat and pressure to invoke different reactions. Pleasure. Pain. Terror.

The dog's tongue lolled in its mouth and its eyes glazed. The man stepped forward, his hand stretched towards the creature's snout.

"Careful," the boy said. "He don't like people much."

The dog, floating in a fog of bliss, let the man pet its wiry head.

"Wow," the boy said. "He don't let most folks get near 'im."

The man smiled warmly. "I have a way with animals. I am staying in a building near here. I could get you some food, some clean water to wash up in. Would you like that?"

The boy eyed the man, scrunching up his dirty face in contemplation. He looked at his dog, who continued to wag its tail in lazy arcs.

"I *am* hungry."

"Let's fix that," the man said.

The man led the boy through the maze of rubble towards the empty warehouse building that served as his base of operations outside the citadel.

"What kinda food ya got?" the boy asked.

"Some apples, some rice, pickled fish. Nothing fancy."

But from the widening of the boy's eyes, the man knew this sounded very fancy indeed. "In here," he said, pushing aside a door hanging on one iron hinge.

The inside of the warehouse was dark; it took a moment for the man's eyes to adjust to the dim light.

The boy looked around at the empty interior. He turned back to the man. "Where's—"

The boy fell silent when he saw the dagger in the man's hand, its ebony hilt inlaid with a pastoral scene of ivory. In a flash, the man slit the boy's throat, catching his body as it slumped, lowering it to the floor.

The boy's eyes held a look of betrayal as his lifeblood pumped out of his arteries, mingling hot and metallic with the dust of the warehouse floor.

"You should be thanking me," the man said. "It's only going to get worse."

The dog had shaken off its pleasure-induced fog and snarled at him, baring its sharp white canines. Its hackles stood along the ridge of its skinny back.

"I have plans for you as well, my friend." The man smiled gleefully, his spirits buoyed by the afternoon's events. He dipped his fingers in the boy's blood and began chanting, pulling on the dark twisted magic of the tengu. He directed it at the dog, wrapping it around the creature in cords of blackest evil.

The dog's ferocious barks turned to whimpers as the magic sunk into its flesh, immobilizing it, beginning to twist it into something new.

The man took the blood on his fingers and smeared it on the dog's forehead, drawing the symbol his master had taught him, completing the dog's transformation from mortal beast to demon.

He stood with a satisfied smile, admiring his creation. The dog had quadrupled in size, its limbs growing into long distended arms with curving claws. Its skin blackened and cracked, its brindle coat hanging off it in patches. The head was truly monstrous, filled with yellowed fangs and bulbous dead eyes.

The man licked the rest of the boy's blood off his fingers. Yes, this would do just fine. He may need the heirs to free Tsuki and Taiyo, but their companions were expendable. Might as well make their trip a bit more eventful.

He grinned.

CHAPTER 14

The group flew silently in a loose formation. Colum flew in front on one of the golden eagles borrowed from the sunburners. Hiro and Daarco followed, and Kai and Emi brought up the rear, their koumori giving the eagles a wide berth. The night was warm and cloying, the unnatural heat a reminder of the importance of their mission.

"Are you excited to go home?" Kai asked Quitsu while leaning forward in the koumori saddle so her voice wouldn't be carried away by the wind.

"Nervous," he said. "But excited." Quitsu, strapped into the harness before her, had learned to tolerate flying. Barely.

"Why nervous?"

"The seishen elder is the wisest creature I've ever encountered," Quitsu called back. "But also the most enigmatic. After being alive for several millennia, it doesn't have patience for trivial matters."

"How could two tengu trying to destroy the burners be a trivial matter? It's tied to the burners through the seishen. Without burners, there would be no seishen. It'd be...out of a job, right?"

"Maybe it's ready for retirement," Quitsu quipped. "I hope I'm wrong. It may want to help us. All I am saying is it's old. And..."

"Unpredictable?" she said.

"Unpredictable," he agreed. "Be ready to convince it that it has to help us."

Kai swallowed. *Convince the thousand-year-old ornery seishen to see things her way. No problem.*

After several hours, the Misty Forest came into view below them, a deep swath of green frosted with soft white clouds.

Colum's eagle banked to the left along the edge of the mist, losing altitude until it landed in a wide clearing with a flourish of wings. The rest followed, landing about the clearing. The koumori and eagles couldn't navigate in the mist, so they would continue on foot.

The air was cooler here, almost crisp, and Kai drank it in deeply. The forest felt alive, buzzing with energy. Perhaps the false gods' stranglehold on the world wasn't as strong here.

Trees stretched above them like green sentinels, tall hemlock and cypress, broad-leafed oaks and maples. The scent of pine colored the air, mingling with the loamy smell of soil. Kai sat still for a moment listening to the sounds of birds, the swishing of insect wings—simply enjoying the presence of the forest around her.

"Kai and Emi, I'd fly your koumori into the neighboring clearing to the east of here. The eagles and koumori won't want to stick around each other, so if we separate them, we're more likely to find them where we left them when we get back," Colum said.

Quitsu, eager to be unstrapped from the harness, let out an audible groan. But Colum's suggestion made sense.

Emi raised an eyebrow to Kai, a silent question.

Kai nodded. "We'll rendezvous here."

Kai and Emi quickly found a suitable clearing within a few minutes' walking distance of where the eagles had landed. Their koumori dropped onto the forest floor and Kai let Quitsu loose. He hopped to the ground and danced around like a pup, bucking and stretching wildly.

Kai and Emi laughed, unbuckling the harnesses and saddles from the koumori. The animals would have to roam free for a few days, and so it wasn't fair to make them wear the harnesses.

They stacked the equipment neatly under the swooping emerald boughs of a large tree, covering the pile of leather with dead branches and leaves. Hopefully, that would keep the harnesses out of the rain and free from the eyes of roving thieves. Not that Kai thought that this forest would have any of either. It hadn't rained in months, and from what she knew of the Misty Forest, it had few inhabitants. The forest was a wild place that still belonged to the earth.

They shouldered their packs and strapped their weapons on. Kai had brought her jade-pommeled knife (a gift from Nanase) and a short sword. Emi had two wicked-looking knives peeking out of her boots and a portable rimankyu bow slung through her pack.

"Colum," Emi said as they set off towards the others, ducking around branches and tree trunks. "You trust him?"

"For now," Kai said. "I asked Master Vita about him before we left. Whether we could trust him. He seemed to think we could."

"Based on what?"

"Colum used to work for the citadel. Master Vita said he didn't like the man at first; apparently, he was just as offensive back then as he is now. Perhaps more so."

"Hard to imagine," Emi muttered.

"But Master Vita said he won him over. He was widely traveled and had a keen mind. He quickly worked his way up under Queen Isia's reign. My grandmother."

"All that proves is that he's crafty and ambitious. Which doesn't tell us he can be trusted on this mission. Or in general," Emi pointed out.

"He said he wants to help us," Kai said. "He wasn't lying. My necklace would have told me. And Master Vita told me that before King Ozora started the Gleaming to test all female babies, Colum led covert missions into Kita to rescue girls with moonburning ability before they were found by the sunburners. He's rough around the edges...but I think he means well."

Emi was silent, her dark eyes thoughtful.

"You can still keep an eye on him," Kai said.

"Good," Emi said quietly. Kai eyed her friend sideways. Emi's burns had healed well, though the left side of her face remained scarred. A portion of her ear was missing, and her eyebrow was gone, never to regrow. These blemishes did little to dull Emi's beauty, however, her buoyant silver hair, her voluptuous figure—curvy despite hard angles of muscle. What Kai missed, though, was her friend's indomitable spirit and wit; that had felt so dim since Maaya had died. Maybe Emi needed this mission, too.

"What about Daarco? Do you think it's a smart idea to have him along?" Emi asked.

Quitsu, trotting along between them, chuffed a dark laugh. "What could go wrong?"

"I don't trust him," Kai admitted. "But Hiro begged me to give him one last chance."

"Give him a chance to do what, stab us in the back while we're sleeping and defenseless?"

"Exactly," Kai said. "Though he seems more like the stab-you-in-the-front type so he can gloat about his revenge."

"Even better."

"Maybe we can give him to the seishen elder as an offering," Kai suggested with a wry grin.

"Like the elder would take him!" Emi said. "We couldn't pay someone to take him."

Kai sighed. "We shouldn't make fun. The man is emotionally damaged."

Emi snorted. "Cry me a river. We're all emotionally damaged. Name me one person who doesn't have a parent who died in the war and I'll do a dance for you."

"I can't think of anyone," Kai said. "Which is a shame because I would love to see you dance in the middle of the forest."

"You're missing out," Emi said. "I've got moves." She made a lewd motion with her hips.

Kai laughed out loud, the noise echoing throughout the forest. "I wasn't talking about that kind of dancing."

"Speaking of," Emi dropped her voice conspiratorially, moving closer to Kai. "Hiro? How are...things?" She waggled her eyebrows. "Eh?"

Kai's face colored. "Uh..."

"Ahem." Someone cleared their throat in front of them. Kai started, pulling up short.

Hiro stood in front of them, his thick arms crossed.

Kai's already-red face turned scarlet. How much had he heard?

"You two are making such a racket, the whole forest can hear. Not to mention you were so busy gossiping that I could have murdered you and you wouldn't have noticed!"

"Sorry, Dad," Emi said, strolling past Hiro and bumping him with her hip.

Kai bit her lip, trying to hold back a smile but failing. "We'll be more careful," she said, linking her arm with his and pulling him towards the clearing where the others waited.

"You two ready to move?" Colum asked, leaning on his staff.

"Where are we headed?" Hiro asked, surveying the uniform green of the forest around them.

"The seishen elder lives in an island city in the middle of the Misty Forest," Colum said. "As long as we take a straight path at a good pace, we should be there in two to three days' walk." He slung his pack over his shoulders.

"I should hope we take a straight path," Kai said, raising her eyebrow. "I thought you knew the way." Though the hazy tangle of trees and the blanket of ferns and underbrush did look identical whatever direction she looked. She could hardly identify the clearing she and Emi had just emerged from. How would they ever find the koumori again? She sighed. One problem at a time.

"I do know the way, and Quitsu and Ryu can help, too. But the forest..." He hesitated. "The forest is old. It doesn't like visitors."

Daarco scoffed and took a pull from a flask that appeared from his pocket. "Forests don't have opinions."

"Be careful, sunburner," Colum said. "This one does. I'd show it the proper respect, or it'll put ya in your place. This forest is filled with mysteries and dangers. Lose focus for a moment, and the ground will open up beneath you, swallowing you whole. Or the trees will move, obscuring your path until you lose all sense of where you are and go mad trying to find your way out. Or malicious spirits will take the form of your loved ones and lure you to a grisly death. The forest is as devious as it is old."

"Superstitious nonsense," Daarco muttered.

"Let's get moving in whatever direction you think is right," Kai interrupted, trying to ignore Colum's chilling warnings. "We're losing moonlight."

☪

Colum set a quick pace, moving through the forest like water down a riverbed. Where he silently flowed through the trees, the rest of them tangled with dense underbrush and errant branches. He had seemed unflappable in Kyuden, but here, Kai saw—with more than a little envy—he was truly at ease.

The mist was thick, curling around branches and tree trunks like smoke from a bonfire. Emi threw up two bright orbs of moonlight, maintaining them while they walked. The moonlight cast strange shadows on the trees closest to them, failing to penetrate any deeper into the forest.

Emi and Daarco fell into an uneasy alliance over their mutual dislike of the woods, serenading their group with increasingly-creative expletives whenever a limb or stray spiderweb confounded one of them.

"Is all this fresh air troubling you?" Kai teased Emi.

"It's not natural, all these trees," Emi said, starting and swatting at a beetle that buzzed past her face in a wild arc.

"It's completely natural," Kai said. "That's kind of the point."

"Give me a hot bath and a cold sake any day," Emi said. "Over dirt and deer crap."

Kai laughed. "Nature has more to offer than dirt. But a cold sake does sound pretty good right now."

And though she put on a lighthearted face, Kai didn't blame them. This was no ordinary forest. Time and again, she could have sworn that she caught glimpses of movement in the corner of her eye. But it seemed that whenever she whirled her head to see what moved in the mist, it was gone.

☾

The day dawned, visible only by a lightening of the mist above them and a warming of the air. They couldn't see the sky or the sun, though Kai knew it was there. Hiro and Daarco took turns lighting their path, burning miniature suns above them.

Colum called a halt at what seemed like midmorning.

"Might as well make camp here," he said. "Get some shut-eye."

The novelty of the trip had long since worn off. Everything hurt, but most of all, her feet ached. New boots had not been a good idea.

Kai sat down on the soft ground and unlaced her right boot, pulling it off. She winced as she pulled her sock from her foot and it came away bloody at the heel.

Colum and Hiro both approached, Hiro looking concerned, Colum looking amused.

"New boots?" Colum said, examining the one she had removed.

"I know, I know," she said.

"I have something to cover it," Colum said, standing and heading back to his pack.

"I'm not much of a healer," Hiro said, "but I can cauterize it."

She grimaced but nodded her assent. He scrunched his brow, her foot in his hands. She felt a warmth and hissed as it grew into a sharp heat. But thankfully, it was over quickly.

Colum returned with some soft cloth that was tacky on one side. Kai dressed her wound and put her sock and boot back on. It would work.

"Now that that crisis is over, can we eat?" Daarco said, scowling. His eyes were red-rimmed and his words were slurred.

Kai suppressed her irritation but nodded.

They arrayed themselves in a loose circle on the ground and munched on hard cheese and dried meat.

"Are we on track?" Daarco asked Colum.

"Anxious to reach our destination?" Colum asked.

"Anxious to get this ridiculous field trip over with," Daarco muttered.

"Worried you will run out of whatever you keep in that flask?" Emi asked with mock sweetness.

"It's the only way I can stand your company, burner," he retorted.

"We'd need something a lot stronger than that to stand your company, burner," Emi spat back.

Daarco growled.

Kai sighed. Daarco would run out of sun whiskey at some point on the trip. She wasn't sure whether that would make him more or less pleasant. Perhaps keeping him drunk *was* the best option.

"So," Hiro said, rubbing his hands together, trying to break the tension. "Colum, how did you find yourself visiting the seishen elder last time?"

"It was many years ago," Colum said. "I was a young entrepreneu— "

"I don't think that word means what you think it means," Emi muttered.

Colum continued, unfazed. "I heard rumors of an ancient city floating in a lake. Sounded like a great opportunity for a profit."

"You went to rob the seishen's city?" Kai asked, incredulous.

"I didn't know it belonged to the seishen," Colum said. "The fellow who told me about it was hazy on the details. Thought it was deserted. And what good would ancient treasure do sitting 'round in an old city? It would do me much more good." He flashed his white teeth in a grin.

Hiro shook his head. "How did you get out alive?"

"There was some bargaining...a riddle, I think. Promises never to return on punishment of death, and such." Colum waved a hand dismissively. "'Twas a few years back."

"This would have been an important fact to share when you volunteered to guide us," Kai said, pursing her lips. "If the seishen elder has a grudge against you, we can't risk being guilty by association. This is too important!"

"I didn't plan on accompanying you...into the city," Colum said. "I thought I would just lead you there and... wait outside."

Kai ground her teeth. "Very heroic."

"And I thought Daarco would be the one to get us killed," Emi snapped.

"Quitsu, Ryu, do you think the elder will hold our association with Colum against us, even if he doesn't come all the way to the island with us?" Kai asked.

"It is difficult to say," Ryu said.

"He's still our best chance of finding the elder quickly," Quitsu said. "I won't be able to pinpoint his location until we get closer. I don't see how this changes anything."

Kai met Hiro's eyes. Her concern was mirrored on his rugged face. What had she gotten them into?

But Quitsu was right. They still needed to get there. "Very well," Kai said. "We continue."

CHAPTER 15

That night, sleep fell over Kai fast and strong. When she awoke, night had fallen, or whatever passed for night in this strange, misty world. She stood, stretching her stiff muscles, feeling the pops and groans as she bent forward. It had been a while since she had slept on the ground.

As she surveyed the others, a chill fluttered through her, raising the hairs on the back of her neck. She stood still, opening her senses to the unnatural stillness of the forest, the bright white sheen of the moon, the smells of the forest. But there were no smells. No sounds.

Kai stepped forward hesitantly, peering into the darkness between the trees, unable to shake the sense of unease growing in the pit of her stomach.

The otherness of the forest struck her suddenly, and she realized where she was. "The spirit world," Kai said out loud. She had been here once before, after she had passed her test to become a master moonburner. The night she had met her mother and discovered that Hanae still lived.

Kai crouched and drew a sword from its resting place beneath her pack. She didn't know what manner of creatures prowled the spirit world, but she didn't want to find out without a weapon in her hand. Did her burning even work here? She opened her qi to the moonlight, trying to pull it within her spirit. It felt distant and faint. Her mouth went dry. She couldn't burn.

"You will need more than a sword to stop what is coming for you," an alto voice said behind her.

Kai whirled to face the speaker, her sword before her in a fighting stance. When she saw the speaker, she straightened. She was still wary, but less so.

The woman was a moonburner. She wore an elaborate wrapped dress of green silk, layers upon layers decorated with a pattern of leaves caught in a breeze. Her silver hair was twisted up into a bun high on her head and was caught with a clip shaped like a fan. She stood demurely, her hands clasped before her.

"Who are you?" Kai asked. "Are you a spirit?"

"I am Hamaio," she said. "I was once queen of the moonburners, as you are." The woman approached Kai, taking her by the arm and drawing her underneath the protection of a large tree before turning and surveying the clearing.

Hamaio was quite lovely with soulful brown eyes and dimples that revealed themselves when she grimaced. And young, Kai realized. Perhaps no more than a year or two older than herself. Had she died so young?

"You are mad to come here," Hamaio said. "Why would you risk yourself?"

"I don't know why I'm here," Kai said. "I didn't come here on purpose. I'm just…dreaming."

Hamaio furrowed her brow as she scrutinized Kai, considering. She reached out a hand and drew the collar of Kai's shirt to one side, baring a section of Kai's chest.

"You are marked by the creator," Hamaio said, a note of awe in her voice.

Kai looked down and realized the handprint scar was glowing silver in the moonlight.

"The creator? How do you know?" Kai said.

"His work is evident," Hamaio said. "Tell me how you came by this scar."

"I don't remember," Kai said. "I almost died, and when I woke up, I had it."

Hamaio frowned. "I do not understand this thing. Perhaps in your brush with death, you encountered him. Such a thing would be unusual…unheard of. But…if it was so, perhaps it would explain why you have been pulled into the spirit world. He is strongest here."

Kai shook her head, trying to comprehend the new information Hamaio was telling her.

Hamaio continued. "You must leave. It is not safe for you here."

"But…I was sick…days ago. Why is this the first time I'm here?"

Hamaio considered this. "Have you been in the Misty Forest each of these days?"

"No, I was at the citadel."

"The citadel is warded with powerful enchantments to protect creatures of the spirit world or beyond from traveling into the mortal realm. I cast some of these wards myself during my reign. They must prevent you from inadvertently traveling to this realm. You must return to the citadel at once."

"I can't," Kai said. "We're traveling to see the seishen elder. I have to talk to him."

"You will never make it if you linger here," Hamaio said.

"You said you cast enchantments over the citadel. Can't you teach me how to keep myself from entering the spirit world?"

She looked up, thoughtful. "Actually, yes. I believe so. Bind together a sprig of ash leaves and a lock of your hair. Sprinkle it with dust from the earth and water from a fresh spring. This should bind you to this world until you return to the safety of the citadel."

Kai almost laughed at the suggestion, but seeing the seriousness on the woman's face, suppressed the urge.

"Thank you. I will. But I still don't understand why I can't be here. It seems…fine."

"There has not been such a concentration of tengu in this realm since my time."

"You know of the tengu?" Kai asked eagerly. "What happened in your time?"

Hamaio gestured to herself impatiently. "You don't think I died peacefully of old age, do you?"

"What can you tell me of them?" Kai said.

"They come from a different realm, a realm of darkness and death. Over thousands of years, they broke down the border between their realm and the spirit world, claiming this realm for their own as well. That border is totally disintegrated; they can pass at will. The border between the spirit realm and the mortal realm is deteriorating quickly, its eventual destruction hastened by the help of their followers."

"I know of these followers. I have one in my dungeons."

"Every time they summon a tengu through the border between realms, that border weakens. They will make a full-scale assault soon, as they did in my time."

"But you stopped them?" Kai asked hopefully. "How?"

"It was a patchwork magic, and a force that we could never recreate. And our seal was only a partial fix. They broke through once again." Hamaio opened her mouth to continue but then froze.

"What?" Kai whispered, her hackles rising. A tree creaked in the distance.

"You must go!" Hamaio said. "Leave this place! They are coming!"

"I don't know how," Kai said, lamenting the depth of her ineptitude. This was a world she didn't understand.

"You must wake!" Hamaio said. "Wake!" She pushed Kai's shoulders, forcing her to stumble back.

Hamaio seemed to grow, the sleeves of her gown billowing, her eyes glowing bright with moonlight.

"Leave!" She pushed Kai again, and Kai shuffled back. "Wake!"

Kai's head whipped to the right as a crashing of leaves and limbs burst through the trees on the far edge of the clearing.

Hamaio shoved Kai once again, and her scrambling heels snagged a tree root. She fell backwards and hit the ground hard.

Kai awoke with a gasp, sitting bolt upright.

Colum sat against a tree a few paces away, watching her. He puffed on a thin horn pipe, its sweet-smelling smoke tickling her nose.

"Nightmares?" he asked, his voice low. "Been rollin' around like a badger in a rice sack."

Kai felt for her sword where it rested under her bedroll. It hadn't moved. She shook her head to clear it. "I don't think it was a dream."

"Howdya figure?"

Kai recounted the tale of her encounter with Hamaio in the spirit world, the tengu attack. She didn't mention that the scar on her chest glowed white. She wasn't sure what to make of that yet.

Colum listened with rapt attention. "This Hamaio sounds quite compelling. Maybe next time you can take me with you. I love me a strong woman." His grin was roguish.

Kai rolled her eyes. "Have you ever met a woman you didn't want to sleep with?"

Colum rubbed his chin, pondering. "Sure. The very elderly. Relatives—"

She tossed an apple from her pack at him, but he ducked, causing it to hit Hiro's sleeping back.

"Ow," Hiro said, rolling over on the apple as Kai and Colum snickered.

"What's life for if not appreciating the beauty of creation?" Colum said, waving his hand at the mist around them. "And let me tell you, women are my favorite part of creation."

"I'm confident the feeling is not mutual."

"It's too early for Colum's warped philosophy," Hiro grumbled from his bedroll, trying to pull the blanket farther over his head.

"It's about time to be gettin' up, actually," Colum said, standing and stretching. "Good luck wakin' that one up without a bucket of cold water." He motioned to Daarco. "He sleeps like he drained a tavern dry."

"That's because he probably did," she muttered.

Colum clapped his hands. "Up and at 'em," he said. "Time to get a move on."

The group grumpily peeled themselves out of their bedrolls, brushing leaves off their clothes, running fingers through hair. There wasn't much to do to break camp; they hadn't brought tents.

As soon as they scarfed down a bit of food, they were back on the march. The night was eerily quiet, and Kai's sense of unease grew as they walked deeper into the mist. The forest seemed to be watching them. As they passed through the trees, Kai pulled a sprig of ash from a nearby tree, beginning to make the charm Hamaio had spoken of. She hoped it would work. She wasn't anxious to find herself in the spirit world again anytime soon.

She approached Colum, curious to find out more about this strange man who had appeared so suddenly in their lives. She hoped Master Vita was right in his assessment that they could trust him.

"You're not from Miina, are you?" she asked.

"Could ya tell?" he joked. "No. I'm from the south, past where the land meets the ocean. There's a chain of islands. King Ozora claims the islands as part of Kita, but we haven't seen a tax collector in a hundred years. We reckon we're free."

"I guess he's been too busy fighting moonburners to worry about the far corners," Kai said. "What are the islands called?"

"Shima," he said.

"Do they have burners there?" she asked.

"Aye. Mostly healers, village elders and such."

"They don't go to the citadel or Kistana for training?" Kai asked.

"No," he said. "Nothing but fighting and death waiting for 'em. The elders train the youngsters when their hair starts to change."

"Wow," Kai said. "I can hardly imagine a place where burners are just...people. Not soldiers or warriors."

"Best place in the world," Colum said, a faraway look in his eye.

"Why did you leave? Why become an entrepreneur? Or adventurer? Or whatever you consider yourself."

"Why does anyone do anything?" he asked. "For love."

"You? Love?" Kai asked.

"Aye! A tender heart beats beneath this ruggedly handsome exterior!"

"If you say so," Kai said.

"I was young then. I fell in love with a girl from my village. Mesilla and I grew up together, were like brother and sister. Until we got older...and then we weren't. Her hair started turning silver, and her seishen arrived, and we knew that she was a moonburner. For a time, life was good. We played at being adults. Vowed to love each other forever, to marry. She was so beautiful," he said, his eyes wistful. "I used to lay on the toasted sand of the beach and watch her and her seishen swim in the waves. There was never a more perfect sight. Their silver hair, flashing in the turquoise water."

He fell silent, and Kai gave him a moment. But she was curious now. "What happened?"

"She was smart and ambitious. Wanted to see the world. She wasn't content to be trained by the burners on the island. She wanted to learn at the citadel in Kyuden. So I vowed to escort her. I wanted to travel too, to have adventures like in the stories. But most of all, I wanted to be near her. One day, in Kita, we were attacked on the road. Men took her and her seishen and left me for dead."

"That's awful!" Kai said.

"I was young and stupid, thinking I could protect her."

"You didn't know…" Kai trailed off. She had felt that same naiveté herself. It was easy to think you could conquer anything when your world stayed small.

"I traveled to every corner of every land looking for her. I went to the citadel, hoping she'd escaped and made her way there. She hadn't. I stayed for a few years, working for the queen, hoping she'd come ridin' through the gates one day. I eventually had to face the reality. She never would. And by then, after all those years, I was more at home on the road. Staying in one place…being too close to people…grated on my soul. I'm not made for that anymore."

"I'm sorry you never found her," Kai said quietly. What would she do if someone took Hiro from her? She shuddered at the thought.

"Now don't you go feelin' sorry for me," he said. "I've lived a full life, seen things some people have never dreamed of."

"Have you been back home?" Kai asked.

"No," he said. "It wasn't home without her."

They continued in silence, Kai contemplating the surprising nature of Colum's tale. Her mind raced with worry, flitting from thoughts of Hamaio and the spirit world to the tengu to Chiya and what Kai would face when she returned to Kyuden.

After a stretch of hours, Colum called for a break.

Kai groaned, dropping her pack to the ground and rolling her tight shoulders.

Quitsu looked at her with mock disapproval, clicking his tongue. "We've only been moving for a few hours."

Kai groaned. "Last thing I need is a lecture from a supernatural spirit who doesn't get tired."

"I'm going to take a piss," Daarco said, marching into the underbrush.

"Charming," Emi called to his retreating form.

He hadn't uttered anything but grunts over the course of the night, though he was keeping up an impressive drinking regimen.

"Is that an enchanted flask or something?" Kai muttered.

Emi snorted. "If it is, I gotta get me one."

Hiro approached Kai, rubbing her shoulders. "How you holding up?"

She closed her eyes, groaning in pleasure at his ministrations. "When did I get so soft?"

"It's palace life," he chuckled. "You have to fight it."

"Daily runs when I get back," she said. "No matter what excuse I give."

"Ha!" Hiro said. "You must think me far more persuasive than I am. I'd just as likely get Ryu to walk a tightrope as get you to go on daily runs if you don't want to."

"Leave me out of this," Ryu grumbled. "Perhaps the fox will perform like a trained circus animal."

"You wanna piece of me, fluffy?" Quitsu said, puffing his chest up and swaggering towards Ryu's kneecap.

"Enough." Kai laughed. "No one's doing anything they don't want to do." She turned her attention back to Hiro, turning and lacing her arms around his waist. "You just haven't learned the art of subtle motivation."

"Oh?" He arched a golden eyebrow, tracing his hands up and down her arms, drawing a shiver from her. "Perhaps another form of exercise would be more palatable?

She opened her mouth to respond, but her comment was cut off by a resounding scream of terror from the forest just beyond the fog line.

They looked at each other with alarm.

"Daarco!"

CHAPTER 16

Kai and Hiro drew their swords and dashed into the forest, Ryu and Quitsu on their heels.

"Daarco," Hiro cried. "Where are you?"

Colum and Emi were beside them in a flash, Emi with her two knife blades drawn, Colum with his tall wooden staff.

"Over here," a hoarse voice called, desperate and muffled. Followed by another strangled scream.

"This way," Ryu said, dashing ahead, the thick underbrush catching in his dense golden mane.

They burst through the treeline into a clearing barely visible in the thick mist.

"Where is he?" Hiro said, his chest heaving.

Ryu and Quitsu sniffed around the forest floor, their noses quivering.

Kai scanned the clearing, peering through the whiteness of the fog, looking for movement. And then she saw something unbelievable. A flash of gold buried under the roots of an ancient oak tree. But the roots...were moving. Retracting. The forest was...taking him.

"Oh my gods," she said, and launched into action, dashing across the clearing. She took her sword and reached for moonlight to burn down the blade. But the moonlight...she couldn't grasp it. It was a slippery fish, undulating out of her mental grip. *She couldn't moonburn.*

Kai shoved down the panic that was rising in her throat and threatening to choke her. Daarco had only seconds. She hacked at one of the thick roots with her sword, praying she didn't split Daarco's skull in the process.

The roots shied back at her blow, revealing more of Daarco's head.

He lifted it from the debris of the forest floor, gasping in a rattling breath. "Help...me..." he croaked.

Movement exploded around her. The forest came alive, branches whipping and grabbing at her clothes, her arms, her hair.

Emi reached Kai's side and burned, sending bolts of fire into the oak tree.

Kai continued to hack with her blade. The tree hissed and screamed as its bark burned, an unearthly sound that reverberated painfully in Kai's ears. Daarco's arm came free as the tree recoiled from her strikes.

All the trees in the clearing had come alive now, furiously pounding at them with limbs and sharp needles. She could hear the trees' buzzing, angry voices calling in a language she didn't understand.

"Try to hold them off and give us some room," Kai called breathlessly. "We're getting him free." Even while her body moved, her mind was scrambling and fumbling for moonlight. It had to be there. If she just reached far enough...

Hiro and Colum tightened the defensive circle around them, hacking at the branches, trying to keep them from interfering with Emi and Kai's desperate rescue attempt.

Quitsu and Ryu snarled and snapped at the branches, but with no weapons but their fangs and claws, they weren't much help.

Emi had locked arms with Daarco now and was pulling him free of the tree's clutches inch by inch, all the while sending gouts of flames into its roots. The fire was spreading quickly, lapping with an insatiable thirst up the roots that held Daarco.

The heat of the fire poured over Kai and pops of pitch exploded, splattering her with hot sap.

"Hurry," Kai gasped, redoubling her efforts. They didn't have much time.

"Don't let me go," Daarco gasped to Emi, clinging to her and the ground, fighting the crushing grip of the tree.

"I won't," she groaned.

Kai chopped with her sword again and at last made a final cut through the root.

The tree wailed a keening, angry sound and smashed Kai flat across the chest with a huge limb. She flew across the clearing, smacking into another tree and crumpling to the ground.

Time seemed to slow as she looked up from the forest floor, gasping for the breath that had abandoned her. The scene was grim. Emi and Daarco lay on the ground, tree branches pummeling them while Emi projected a roiling dome of fire above them as a shield. Colum whacked the limbs that came at him with his whirling staff, but sweat poured from him, and his movements were slowing. And Hiro—a tall tree had Hiro by his ankle and was swinging him, smashing him to the ground in violent thwacks. Ryu snarled at a tangle of vines that had wrapped around his hindquarters, bearing him to the ground.

Kai's breath came back in a rush of pain. She coughed and moaned in shivering breaths, sure her ribs were crushed beyond all hope. The roiling voices of the trees washed through her mind, filling her head with indecipherable cries that blended into the swirling mass of her terror. She couldn't moonburn.

Her friends still fought furiously, but she could see that the forest was winning.

No, she thought. *Not like this.* There had to be something she could do.

She closed her eyes and reached farther with her spirit, deeper, into spaces she had never dreamed to go. There was something there. Not the cool quicksilver of moonlight, but something else. She reached for it. As she did, the voices of the trees intensified, pulsing through her head with such force that the pain left her temporarily breathless. The words were foreign, but the tone was clear. The trees were telling them to leave. That the forest was sacred. They were unwelcome intruders.

Seizing on her momentary distraction, a tendril of ivy snaked out and pulled her feet from under her, wrapping up her legs in a split second. She slammed against the ground. *No!*

As her agonized thought burst free, the trees paused for a moment.

Kai felt their power thrumming through her, their voices and anger like her own heartbeat. The life of the forest, as if it were her own. Pulsing, primal energy, just out of her reach. But she could feel it. *No!* she thought. *This has to stop!*

The trees shuddered again, hesitating briefly, but it wasn't enough.

Abandoning all reason, Kai rallied her will and plunged it into the unknown power. The handprint on her chest flared to life, emanating a bright white light. She was through, she had done it, and now her qi grappled with a raging torrent of elemental power. An underground aquifer of life-giving energy that powered the rise of the sun, the wane of the moon, the sudden burst of a spring rain, the first heartbeat of a new calf. This—this was the stuff of creation. She struggled with the wildness of it; pulling it into her qi was like trying to fill a cup from a waterfall. But drop by drop, she collected it, and it filled her with a power that she had never known.

"Stop!" she cried to the forest, and pure white light burst from the scar, ripped from her like her heart torn from her chest.

The white hot fire swept past her friends, striking the trees, sending them to a shuddering stop. Their leafy foes recoiled branches and vines, unwinding from her battered companions, until in a flutter of leaves, they stilled.

Kai felt the power slip away and the bright light dimmed and died, leaving only the white of the fog and the washed out image of the forest.

Kai let herself slump back to the ground, drained and hollow. They were safe. For now.

Emi had her arms wrapped tightly around Daarco, who was partially collapsed on top of her. They seemed content to stay that way for a minute.

"You just had to…take a piss in this clearing," Emi managed, dropping her head to the ground.

Hiro started to laugh, a wheezing hacking sound that betrayed the pain he was in.

Laughter filled the clearing as their relief and exhaustion mingled into macabre humor.

Kai laid back, clutching her aching ribs as tears leaked from the corners of her eyes. She couldn't feel the moonlight. *What had she become?*

☾

Hiro couldn't identify a part of his body that *didn't* ache. His head pounded like a taiko drum and his neck felt like it was being stabbed with a hot poker. He had been thrown around by that damn tree like a rag doll. He prodded a tooth with his tongue and grimaced when it wiggled precariously. At least it was still attached. For now.

The rest of their group didn't look much better.

Kai clutched her ribs and moved gingerly as they limped back to camp. The strange handprint on her chest glistened dully on her skin, only scar tissue once again. Daarco had his arm around Emi and was leaning on her for support as his legs had been badly bruised by the vice-like tree roots. Emi herself had blood dribbling from a dozen cuts and was covered in dirt and soot. Colum and the seishen were the only ones that seemed to have come through relatively unscathed.

As soon as they reached the cluster of trees where they had left their packs, they collapsed into the dirt.

"Is it safe to stay here?" Kai asked, her voice breathy with pain.

"Aye. I think you took care of those trees with your light explosion," Colum said.

"Do you think they have...friends?" Emi asked.

Hiro let out a wheezing laugh despite himself. The thought of trees forming ranks like a gang of street thugs seemed ridiculous. Though the idea of trees attacking in the first place would have seemed ridiculous just ten minutes prior. So perhaps he shouldn't have discounted the possibility.

"I think we're safe for now," Colum said. "Let's rest and...regroup"—he motioned to their various wounds—"but we set a watch tonight."

"We can watch," Quitsu said. "Ryu and I. We don't really sleep."

"Good," Emi said. "I don't think I'd be good for much right now." Her skin was sallow and she had deep blue smudges under her eyes. She had burned a lot of moonlight defending against the trees.

"You should eat, Emi," Hiro told her, tossing her a package of dried meat from his pack before collapsing on his bedroll. "Replenish your strength."

Kai fished in her pack for the small medical kit she had brought, herbs and wraps and a needle and gut. She was quiet and her eyes were wide and glassy, as if she was staring beyond whatever was before her. But her healer's training took over, and she tended to the group's wounds efficiently. She saw to Emi first, giving her friend leaves to chew to dull the pain, and then stitching the worst of Emi's gashes with quick, neat stitches.

Hiro watched Kai as she worked, his chest tight with worry. Questions swirled in his mind. Whose handprint was that? And what in the gods' names was that white light? Why was Kai moving like a sleepwalker, drifting through the motions? What had she seen?

Kai smeared some salve on Emi's cut and then turned to Daarco.

"No moonburner magic for me," Daarco said, his voice gravely from screaming. He scooted away from Kai, wincing at the movement.

"Daarco, you can hardly move," Hiro began, but Emi cut him off with a look. Apparently, she had taken on Daarco as her charge. She stood and towered over him, hands on her hips. She nudged his leg with the toe of her boot and he hissed.

"Kai is one of the best healers in Miina, or Kita for that matter," Emi said. "You would be so lucky. You could have Hiro bumble over you once the sun comes up, but he has the healing ability of a boulder. You can hardly walk right now, and we aren't going to leave your sorry ass here, as much as we'd like to. Let Kai look at you."

Daarco glared at her fiercely but finally nodded, giving his assent.

Hiro watched Daarco's face as Kai tended to him, feeling the bruises along his legs, wrapping one of his ankles. Eventually, Daarco closed his eyes, his face almost serene in its exhaustion. Hiro had worried for many years that his friend was beyond saving, too caught up in the maze of his own hatred to ever find his way back to his old self. Hiro thought of those times now, desperate to distract himself from the questions he wanted to shout at Kai.

Hiro remembered how they used to play Burning Wars, fighting an epic battle all around the castle, stopping and picking it up again day by day. Daarco played the moonburner, insisting that Hiro, as prince, had to be a sunburner. Being the moonburner was more fun, anyway, little Daarco had said, because you got to be unpredictable.

Daarco's father, Ashtan, or "Ash" to his close friends and family, had laughed at his son, ruffling his hair. "The only thing predictable about your strategy should be its unpredictability," he had said. "Be creative."

And so Daarco had been. He'd set ambushes for Hiro when he'd left his lessons, falling upon him from above after training, or springing out from under the dining room table. They had giggled until they fell over every time Daarco had managed to get one over on Hiro. Which was fairly often. There was nowhere in the castle that Hiro had been safe. And he wouldn't have had it any other way.

Hiro thought wistfully of the afternoons he had shared with Ashtan and Daarco, when Ashtan taught them to fish and hunt. He had never minded Hiro sharing their private father-son moments, seeming to recognize that if not for sharing theirs, Hiro would have no such moments himself.

And Hiro remembered when Ashtan came home for the last time, the day he lost his surrogate father and his friend in an instant. General Geisa's moonburners had raided the camp and command center for the sunburner forces, pummeling the camp with endless streams of fire and lightning. Ashtan had died in his command tent, trying to scramble a defense from his sleepy soldiers. The men who were left had delivered the news, together with Ashtan's body wrapped in a red cloak.

Hiro would never forget the burnt flesh of Ashtan's face, barely recognizable after the fire had taken its toll. But even more so, he remembered the sound that Daarco had made. A keening, inhuman wail that chilled Hiro to the bone. When Daarco had been pulled from his father's body, he'd seemed a stranger. His eyes had been cold and his face had been angry.

They had been eleven years old—but Daarco's childhood had ended that day. He'd never ambushed Hiro again. He'd thrown himself into training, making himself a living weapon. Bent on one purpose. To destroy moonburners. Ryu had found Hiro just a month later, softening the terrible loneliness that had been left in the wake of his friend's transformation.

Ryu looked at him and then Daarco. There was understanding in his amber eyes.

"Maybe there's hope," Hiro murmured, burying his hand in Ryu's thick golden mane.

"There is always hope," Ryu said.

CHAPTER 17

H iro didn't realize he had fallen asleep until Colum kicked his boot. "You've been sleepin' for two hours. We should get movin.'"

A groan escaped Hiro's lips as he got to his feet. The brief reprieve had only given his aches time to settle in. But despite the pain, Hiro was eager to move on. The clearing where the forest had come alive was too close for comfort. Though it had lain still the last few hours, Hiro couldn't help but wonder what magic lingered there. It was best to keep moving.

Kai walked as stiffly as Hiro did, her thoughts clearly fixed on some distant worry. Or perhaps her worries were closer than he realized.

"Kai," he said softly, falling into step beside her, "are you all right?"

She let out a harsh laugh. "No, I don't think I am."

He risked putting a hand on her shoulder, though this Kai seemed as unpredictable as a wild horse.

She finally turned to look at him, and tears shone in her hazel eyes. "I can't moonburn," she whispered.

Hiro missed a step, stumbling. "What?" he hissed.

Kai bit her lip, looking at Emi and Daarco, who walked a few paces ahead of them. She lowered her voice. "I think it's been...since I was sick. With everything going on, I hadn't tried moonburning. Until last night—when I was in the spirit world."

"The spirit world?"

Kai shared her tale of Hamaio and the tengu who had overtaken the spirit world, as well as Hamaio's musings about the cause of the handprint.

"This keeps getting stranger and stranger," Hiro said.

"I thought it was the spirit world that was keeping me from accessing moonlight. But when the trees attacked, I couldn't...I couldn't reach it."

The anguish in Kai's voice twisted his heart. He imagined being blocked from burning sunlight, its sweet honeyed flames that soothed and inflamed his soul in turn. He couldn't stop himself from shuddering. Who would he be if he weren't a sunburner?

"You were able to burn that white light though," Hiro said. "It's more powerful than moonlight, isn't it? It's like the power that is released when we combine our sun and moonlight."

Kai nodded. "I can feel it even now. I'm standing on a raging riverbank. Trying to pull some of its water...It's hard not to be swept away."

"But you can pull from it?"

Kai nodded. "Yes. I couldn't figure out how to at first, but now that I have... I think I have free access to it."

"And this has something to do with the handprint?"

"Yes. No. I don't know!" Kai moaned. "What's happening to me?"

"Hey," Hiro said, pulling her to a stop and taking her smooth face in his hands. The freckles sprinkled across her nose like a dusting of spices stood out in the eerie half-light of the forest. "We'll figure this out— together. We'll find out what's happened to you, and you will moonburn again. But in the meantime, perhaps this extra power is a gift."

"A gift?" she asked, her voice small.

"We face powerful enemies. We don't know what the tengu are capable of. But now, you have gained an incredible new power. With this white light, you are a greater threat than ten moonburners put together."

A small smile appeared at that. "A gift," she mused.

"Come on." He released her. "We shouldn't fall too far behind."

The mood was somber and quiet when they stopped hours later. The strangeness of the forest seemed to settle over them like a weight with its monochrome grays and greens, its unnatural stillness where there should be birds and squirrels and insects.

Despite his exhaustion, Hiro tossed and turned in his bedroll, unable to find a position where his ribs didn't ache against the hard ground.

Hiro found himself watching Kai, tracing the contours of her angelic sleeping form with his eyes. Quitsu was curled into her chest and she had her body wrapped around him protectively. A lock of her silver hair had fallen across her smooth face. *What was happening to her?*

In the corner of his eye, he caught movement in the mist. He blinked and focused on the whiteness curling above her. Was it a trick of his imagination? But no...there was...a hand. A dark hand with long, sinister fingers and wicked curving nails. A hand that was curling over Kai's shoulder.

Hiro reached for his sword slowly, trying not to betray himself with his movement.

The mist revealed a bony, unnatural limb attached to the hand connected to a grotesque body by flaps of black membranous flesh. Even this preview didn't prepare Hiro for the rest of what he saw. A face of nightmares, of horrors, emerged from this mist. Its hollow eye sockets were dark caverns over a gaping, wide maw filled with razor-sharp teeth.

As Hiro stared in shock and horror, it went for Kai's exposed throat.

Hiro scrambled from his cloak, unsheathing his sword with a ring of steel. He would be too late!

But Colum was there in an instant, slashing at the beast with a curved blade. It reared back with an unearthly hiss.

Their camp was up in an instant, Kai scrambling away, dagger clenched in her fist, Ryu and Quitsu snarling, Emi and Daarco on their feet, weapons in hand. The creature retreated, eyes wary, knowing that it was outnumbered.

But then another dropped from the trees, raking its claws down Emi's back, bearing her to the ground.

She let out an anguished scream.

Daarco roared with anger, burning a river of fire towards the creature, tossing it back from Emi. It scrambled to its feet and launched itself at him, jaws wide, teeth flashing.

The other creature took advantage of the distraction and attacked Kai and Colum.

With a powerful pounce, Ryu knocked the second creature off Daarco and ripped its throat out. Hiro surged forward and stabbed the creature's heart...or at least where its heart should have been. Did it have a heart? Black liquid oozed and bubbled from the wounds as it screamed in pain.

The creature fell to the ground, where it twitched and jerked before laying still.

Daarco was helping Emi into a seated position, crouched protectively over her.

Just steps away, Colum slashed the other creature across the chest, causing it to fall backwards. Kai, who had retrieved her sword, bore down on its neck, severing its head half off. With a rush of brilliant white, she hacked through the rest of the flesh, and its head toppled to the ground.

She caught Hiro's gaze, sword in both hands, panting heavily, relief evident on her face. Her eyes widened. "Look out," she cried, sending another bolt of white over his shoulder.

Hiro spun and leaped backwards, just missing a vicious swipe of the other creature's claws. Kai's strike had slowed it, but it was still coming. It was half-charred, its throat was open and ragged, and ooze poured from the wound on its chest. But it was *still moving.*

"You have to behead it," Colum called.

As if the creature had heard him, it grabbed Hiro's sword in its bare talons before he had a chance to strike. Hiro grappled with it, trying to extricate his sword as it drew him in close. Hiro gagged at the sight and the smell of it so close to him, its foul breath like flesh rotting on a battlefield. A mark on its forehead was barely visible in the dim light—a mark that looked like it was etched in blood.

But then, the creature froze, going stock still. Its head leaned forward towards Hiro and toppled off its body, rolling through his arms before coming to rest on the ground.

Hiro shivered with disgust as the body collapsed to the ground, wrenching his sword from his hands in its still-locked grip.

Hiro saw Daarco standing behind the creature, his chest heaving. He had sliced through the creature's neck with a thin band of sunlight, cauterizing the wound so no black blood flowed. *Why didn't I think of that?*

"Emi," Kai called, rushing to her friend's side.

Emi's skin was pallid and her body shook. Her eyes were distant.

"Oh gods," Kai breathed. "I think the creature had some sort of venom on its claws."

They gathered around Emi, looking at the wounds marring her back. Hiro and Daarco exchanged a look of horror. The flesh around the marks was already beginning to blacken, the wounds themselves bubbling sickly white.

"Get me my pack," Kai said, and Hiro ran to retrieve it.

Kai pulled out some herbs, sprinkling them in the wounds on Emi's back. Emi's thrashing grew stronger.

"It's calendula," Kai explained, placing a bandage over the wounds. "It will fight the poison, but it won't last long. This venom is powerful. Let me see if I can do anything to slow it."

"She can sunburn now?" Daarco asked.

In the madness of the attack, Hiro hadn't even realized. It was daytime. If Kai's new power had anything to do with moonlight, she shouldn't have been able to use it now.

"It's not exactly sunburning," Hiro managed, watching Kai hover over Emi, her eyes closed. He wasn't sure exactly *what* it was.

Kai hissed in frustration, opening her eyes. "It's bad," she said, not taking her eyes from Emi. "I think I was able to cool the wound and slow the blood flow to the area so it won't spread as quickly, but this is beyond my skills. Even if I did know how to use...whatever this white stuff is."

"Colum, what were those things?" Hiro asked. "Have you ever seen them before?"

"They're tengu," he said. "Lesser tengu, but dangerous nonetheless."

"They were sent by Tsuki or Taiyo to slow us down?" Hiro asked.

"I presume so," Colum said. "They must be wise to your plans. We have to assume from now on that we'll be hunted."

"We're in no shape to put up a fight," Kai said with frustration. "Or even travel. Do you know how far from the seishen elder we are?"

"I think less than a day."

"Would he be able to heal Emi?" Kai asked, looking from Quitsu to Ryu and back.

"Perhaps," Ryu grumbled.

"He's our best shot." Daarco said. "We have to move." He hoisted

Emi into his arms and her head lolled against his shoulder, her eyelids fluttering.

Hiro raised an eyebrow slightly at Daarco's sudden protectiveness of Emi, and Daarco stared back a challenge, as if daring him to comment.

Hiro declined the invitation. Perhaps Daarco was starting to...no. He didn't want to curse it by even thinking it.

"Daarco's right," Kai said, shoving her medical supplies back in her pack and shouldering it. "Every second counts now."

They jogged through the forest, Daarco bringing up the rear. Hiro's wounds were forgotten. Adrenaline surged through his veins and his senses were alive with the possibility of threats. The white fog of the forest made it nearly impossible to see more than a few feet ahead, so he listened for twigs snapping, for rustling, for anything beyond the staccato sound of his own breathing. Anything could lay in wait just steps from them.

He increased his pace to match Colum, who had taken the lead.

"What can you tell us about these enemies?" Hiro asked.

"Not much," Colum said. Despite his quick pace, he wasn't winded at all. "These ones were low-level tengu. They were testing us, our weaknesses, our defenses. They'll send something worse next time."

"How do we kill them?"

"Beheading is really the only way. They don't like fire, but it can't kill them."

"Where do they come from?"

"Most tengu are from the demon realm. But these ones...I'm not so sure."

"What do you mean?" Hiro asked.

Colum hesitated.

"No holding back on us," Hiro said. "Any piece of information could be the difference between life and death."

"The marks on their foreheads, they looked like they were written in blood. Did you see them?"

"Yes," Hiro said, imagining the creature's foul breath in his face once again and shuddering, closing his eyes. He immediately tripped over a root and barely caught himself. *Okay, eyes open.*

"Those marks were placed on them. By someone. These weren't

tengu from the demon world. They were manufactured."

Hiro's mind reeled with this information. "Made? By who?"

"Someone who put their money on the other side of this war."

CHAPTER 18

K ai could see Hiro and Colum jogging ahead of them, conversing in low tones. Hiro occasionally looked back over his shoulder at her. She couldn't muster the energy to care what they were talking about.

She was bone tired, every inch of her body hurt, and now her muscles screamed from the hours of extra exertion she had forced them through. Her burning had betrayed her, abandoning her when she needed it the most, leaving her with some foreign power that frightened her. But mostly she worried about Emi. She couldn't lose another friend. She wouldn't. It would break her.

Her mind flashed to the moment on the cold stone floor of the facility when Maaya's lifeblood leaked out onto her white servant's uniform.

She shook her head to clear the memory. No. Emi would live. The elder would help them. It had to.

Her mind instead filled in the memory from a few moments ago: waking up to hollow eyes and putrid breath bearing down upon her like the kiss of death. The image wouldn't clear. When had her mind become a place of horrors?

"Kai," a soft voice said.

"What?" she called to Hiro.

He looked back with a puzzled glance. "I didn't say anything."

She turned back to Daarco, who had fallen behind, bearing the excess weight of an unconscious Emi in his arms. He was oblivious, his face set in a look of strained determination.

"We need to take a quick break," Kai said. Daarco looked dead on his feet.

"I'm fine," he called.

"Just for a sip of water," Kai said. "You can stretch your arms."

He relented and the group came together as he lay Emi softly on the trail. Her face was a deathly white contrasted with the red of her burn marks.

"Kai," a voice said again.

She whirled around, peering through the thick mist. "Did any of you just say my name?"

The men shook their heads, confusion on their faces.

"Did you hear…?"

"Kai."

"There!" she said. "Did you hear that? Someone said my name."

Daarco stood still, listening. "Nothing."

"Kai," the voice said again, with more urgency this time. She spun yet again and peered into the mist. And then she grew very still. What she saw…It was impossible.

"Father?" she said, her voice wavering. Though partially shrouded by mist, he was unmistakable. A face she had prayed to see again hundreds of times. Square jaw, thick brown hair, a big smile that revealed even, fine, white teeth.

"Kai," he said, extending his hand to her. "Come here, my daughter. I've missed you."

She knew it was madness, but it was a madness that she wanted to fall into headfirst. And if she could meet an ancient queen in the spirit world, who was to say she couldn't see her father? She took a step forward, tentative at first. And then she broke into a run, arms extended to pull him into a hug.

When she wrapped her arms around him, he was gone. She looked up with confusion. There he was. Right beyond her arms' reach.

"Come here, my little fox," he said.

A whimper escaped her. She started running, but again, he seemed just past her grasp. Hiro and Colum called out for her, but she ignored their alarmed cries. They were flies buzzing in her ears. She only had eyes for him.

"You're in danger," he said. "The path before you is so narrow. You mustn't stray."

"I'm so sorry," she said. "I was too late…" She stopped right in front of him. "I went in the building. They never would have found you if I hadn't gone in to save Sora. And then after they sentenced you…I would have come, but I didn't know how to save you. I didn't know how to burn…I did nothing and it killed you."

Her tears were flowing freely now, but when she tried to grasp him, he moved once again.

"It's not your fault, my daughter. You're here now. And I need your help," he said, the lines at the corners of his brown eyes crinkling with his smile, a smile she hadn't realized how much she'd longed for.

"I miss you so much," she said.

"I'm right here. You just have to reach me. Try, Kai, try to reach me."

Kai ran forward, determined, stumbling over roots, her vision blurred with tears.

She burst through a line of trees into a clearing where his ephemeral form stood. The world tilted slightly and she threw her arms out for balance. Her feet were stuck. She had sunk to her knees in mud.

"Father…" she said, twisted with misery and sorrow. "Help me! Why did you bring me here? Why do you keep running?"

Her father drew near, floating, she realized, not walking. And as she struggled with the squelching muck that held her captive, he smiled.

Her blood grew cold. The smile on her father's face grew unnaturally wide, his teeth now filed points. His eyes shone inky black without a sliver of white.

"Who…what are you?"

"Foolish girl." The creature spoke in a sing-song voice, no longer her father's velvety deep tones. "So quick to run, so quick to believe. I have not seen a mortal in many years. Are they all as foolish as you?"

"What do you want?" Kai whispered. She struggled but only sank deeper in the mud. It passed her knees and lapped at her thighs.

The creature laughed, an oily bubble that set her teeth on edge. "I want you to die!" With its words, the creature transformed into a spirit of the forest, a malevolent sprite with spindly limbs, wisps of thin hair, and a squat face that was all black eyes and flashing teeth. It rose on the wind and spun around her in a mad dash before it was gone.

Hiro couldn't believe it. Kai had run into the woods, abandoning Emi and the rest of them.

Quitsu, who seemed equally surprised, recovered faster than he did and bounded after her into the mist.

Hiro took off after Quitsu a split second later to the angry shouts of Daarco and Colum. He didn't care. These woods weren't safe for anyone alone, even Kai.

Quitsu's silver form disappeared into the mist like a ghost. Hiro stopped and searched the ground in front of him for signs of Kai's passage. It was damned near impossible to track anything in this fog.

Ryu emerged out of the mist behind him.

"Do you feel Quitsu?" Hiro asked. "Where did they go?"

Ryu swung his shaggy mane twice. "No. It's as if they vanished into the mist."

Hiro wanted to scream with frustration. He pulled his sword from its scabbard, starting in one direction, then stopping, looking over his shoulder, and changing tacks.

"I have to find her," he said, doubting his direction.

"She's in the Misty Forest now. Finding her would be like finding a raindrop in the ocean. Unless it wants her to be found."

"Ryu, this was your home. You know this place. Surely, there is some way to…bargain with it. Get it to show her again."

"Our best chance is to seek the aid of the seishen elder. This forest is his; it bends to his will."

"I'm not going to leave her out here alone!"

Ryu puffed up his mane, stalking towards Hiro with a snarl on his face. Hiro inadvertently backed up a step. Sometimes he forgot how big Ryu really was. His head was level with Hiro's chest, even standing on all four legs.

"Put that sword away before you poke my eye out spinning about like a top. Kai is capable and Quitsu is with her. She clearly has a new ability that is protecting her as well, as we saw when the trees attacked. Whereas we have her friend's life in our hands. How would Kai feel if you let Emi die on a fruitless search for her?"

"Fine," Hiro bellowed, sheathing his sword. "Let's go. But if anything happens to Kai, I will never forgive you."

"Then you will never forgive yourself."

"Exactly," Hiro muttered, jogging back towards the rest of the group.

"Find her?" Colum asked.

Hiro shook his head.

"We've wasted enough time on your runaway girlfriend," Daarco said. "Emi is getting worse. If Kai's foolishness means Emi doesn't make it, I'll gut her myself."

Hiro descended on Daarco in a tidal wave of anger. "Don't you ever threaten Kai. You think because you and Emi exchanged a friendly look five minutes ago that you have the monopoly on worry? That she's more important than Kai? Don't forget you're here by my good graces! I could have you shipped back to Kistana so fast, it would make your head spin!"

"I forgot, perfect Hiro can do everything himself. You're a regular one-man army. You never would have made it this far without me!"

"All you've done is drink and almost get us killed by a bunch of trees!"

"MATES—" Colum sidled between them, as they were almost nose to nose now. "This is not the time. The lady is fading and we have tengu on our tail."

"We do?" Daarco surveyed the mist behind them.

"Well, if we didn't before, your two-man band is sure as hell bringin' them from all corners. Now, Hiro, take the girl."

"I can carry her," Daarco said, sticking his chin out stubbornly.

"You've been carrying her for hours. I don't care how manly your arms are. You're fatigued. Speed is what Emi needs, not a pecker-measuring contest."

The two golden-haired men glowered at each other, but Daarco finally relented. Hiro lifted Emi gently from the ground. As she settled into his arms, he was alarmed by the chill, clammy feel of her skin on his own. She was fading. Colum was right.

They resumed their jog through the endless lines of gray bark interspersed with white mist. *It's enough to make a man go mad.*

After what seemed like an eternity, the texture of the mist began to change. No longer was it a swirling, oppressive force—it felt lighter, more open.

"Is the mist lessening?" Hiro asked between ragged breaths.

"Yes," Colum said. "We're almost there."

Colum and Daarco looked back at Hiro, who was lagging behind. Hiro's arms were on fire, past the point of aching from Emi's weight.

"I'll take her again," Daarco said, though his face was haggard and dripping sweat.

"No," Colum said. "Give her to me; I'll take a turn."

As Hiro transferred Emi's unconscious body to Colum's arms, a rustle sounded in the trees beyond their view. The rustle turned into a snarl.

"Run!" Colum said, dashing off into the trees.

CHAPTER 19

Hiro, Daarco and Ryu sprinted after Colum as a glimpse of a dark shape flickered through the trees. Tengu.

Hiro risked a glance over his shoulder as a tengu burst onto the trail behind them. Hiro pumped his legs even faster, desperately asking his body to dig deeper, to find some hidden reserve to draw from. The tengu's snout was covered in slather and hung open, revealing sharp, inch-long fangs and a lolling tongue.

It was gaining. A sound crashed through the trees to their right. Another one. Hiro grasped desperately for sunlight, but it was beyond his grasp. The sun hovered below the horizon, a few minutes from rising.

Daarco slowed and stopped, drawing his sword.

"Daarco, no!" Hiro cried, slowing.

"Go," Daarco shouted. "Protect Colum and Emi! I'll hold them off as long as I can!"

With a last tortured glance over his shoulder, Hiro saw the tengu crash into Daarco, who stood braced with his sword in hand. Daarco was a good fighter, and they still had the other tengu to contend with. Glimpsed through the trees, the one to their right was gaining.

Ryu slowed so he was running alongside Hiro, cutting off to the right.

"No," Hiro panted. Ryu aimed to take on the other tengu. But it would be pointless; he could hear at least two more flanking them. They would only get torn apart by those. Hiro's heart was beating in his throat, ready to explode with exertion. He could go no farther.

"Together," he gasped with ragged breath. They would make their stand, and Colum could continue on with Emi. It wasn't yet dawn, so he couldn't burn. But he still had his sword. He wouldn't go down without a fight.

As Hiro prepared to turn and face the nightmare creatures, he burst from the edge of the forest out of the mist.

Before him lay a grassy bank and a pristine lake, dark and serene. Across the lake was a temple—no, a city nestled on a green island. The towers of the city rose high in the air, squat square structures stacked with circular towers, tapering to delicate spires reaching towards the sky. The sky lightened in the east, painted in shades from yellow to velvety navy. If he had any breath left, the scene would have stolen it from him.

Colum had made it to the edge of the lake, where a small, reed boat rested.

Hiro started to head towards them but whirled back towards the forest as snarls sounded close behind. Four of the black-skinned tengu crouched before him in a semi-circle. These tengu were canine in form with hunched, hulking backs and four clawed feet churning up the earth beneath them. Their yellow eyes watched him with hunter's savvy, and their horn-like hackles were raised, ready for the attack.

"Hurry," Colum called.

Hiro started to back up as the first tengu sprang for him. But Ryu, like a golden blur, crashed into the tengu with a roar, toppling it to the ground mid-leap.

"Run," Ryu cried, and the other tengu leaped onto him.

Hiro lunged forward at the tengu on Ryu's back, who was struggling to sink its teeth into Ryu's neck. He slashed with his sword, opening up a slit in the creature's side. It screamed and fell to the ground, clawed feet scrambling for purchase.

"Hiro!" Colum cried urgently.

"Go," Ryu snarled at him while shaking another tengu off himself. "Save her!"

Hiro ran for the boat, cursing himself for leaving Ryu behind. He grabbed the sides of the boat and pushed, launching himself into it while pushing off the shore. The boat rocked dangerously but stayed upright as he settled into it, whirling around to watch Ryu's desperate fight.

134

Ryu was running towards the lake now, dragging a tengu that clung to him with talons buried in Ryu's powerful hindquarters. The others harried him, close on his heels.

Hiro's anger flared red hot as he watched the unholy creatures struggle to take down his best friend.

Colum continued rowing as the first ray of sunlight crested the far hillside and temple. Hiro smiled grimly and burned, sending three bolts of white hot lightning into the tengu flanking Ryu.

They snarled and writhed on the ground, stunned by the blasts. Ryu used the confusion to dislodge the last beast and leap towards the lake, splashing into the water. He began swimming towards them, his blood leaving a crimson wake.

The tengu that had almost taken down Ryu scrambled to its feet and galloped towards the lake's edge. Hiro pulled in more sunlight, ready to strike again.

But as soon as the tengu touched the water, it screamed in pain and steam rose from the surface of the lake. The tengu backed out quickly, whining and snuffling at its feet. The four animals paced along the lakeside, loudly protesting the loss of their prey.

For some reason, the tengu couldn't go in the lake.

Hiro breathed a heavy sigh of relief. They were safe.

Safe. Hiro looked about the remnants of their group. Emi near death. Ryu bloody and laboring to swim alongside their boat. Kai and Daarco, missing somewhere in that mad forest—if not dead already.

No, they weren't even close to safe.

Kai tried not to panic. Think. She could get out of this.

She tried to take a step back towards what she thought was solid ground, but the sticky mud refused to release its captive. She half fell forward, burying her hands in the mud as well. She was able to extricate these and wiped the gooey substance on her pants with distaste.

"Got yourself in quite a pickle, didn't you?" Quitsu said. He sat on a low branch of one of the nearby trees. The silver of his fur blended into the mist, transforming him into a disembodied set of black pinprick eyes.

"Yes." She sighed, relieved at the sight of him.

"I almost think you're lucky you got stuck in that mud," Quitsu said. "Or you would have followed your father's ghost over a cliff."

Kai cringed, trying to suppress the hot embarrassment seeping through her body. She didn't know what had come over her. She had acted like a crazed fool, rushing off without any thought to her friends. Were they still headed to the seishen elder? What was Emi's condition?

"I don't know what I was thinking," she said miserably. "When I saw him… Never mind. Just help me get out of here."

"Do you have any rope?" Quitsu asked.

Kai let out an exasperated sigh. Her pack was long gone. Clearly she didn't. "Do *you* have any rope?" she shot back.

Quitsu's ears flicked in annoyance. "If you're going to be like that, I'll just leave you to sink to a muddy demise. Serves you right."

She blew out a breath, fluttering her silver hair out of her face. Sometimes her seishen was infuriating. "I am sorry, Quitsu," she said with exaggerated penitence. "Any other ideas beside a rope?"

"We need some sort of tree limb," he said. "Or something you can grab to pull yourself out. Can you burn that white stuff?"

Kai opened herself up to the pure power, wrestling with its force and pulling a small bit into her qi. She eyed the tree Quitsu was perched on. If she knocked the tree over right next to her, she could use its solid trunk to climb out of the mud. If she didn't squish herself completely.

"I can burn it," she said. "Stand back. I'm going to try something."

Kai began burning the light across the trunk, making a precise cut that she prayed would topple the tree close, but not too close, to her. The power wanted to envelop the tree, to burn it, to heat its sap until it exploded in a cosmic fire.

"Careful…" Quitsu said.

She shushed him, concentrating, sweat breaking out on her brow from the strain of it. The tree groaned and creaked, leaning over the mud pit she stood in. She was almost there.

It was enough. A crack of splintering bark sounded as the tree split through. The tree toppled and hit the ground with a slap against the surface of the mud. The mud recoiled against the force, splattering her from head to already-mud-covered toe.

Quitsu started laughing, his signature chuffing sound growing until he was rolling on the forest floor with peals of laughter.

Kai wiped what mud she could from her eyes with all the dignity she could muster. She glared at him but couldn't hold her annoyance for long. She was coated from head to toe in chocolate mud. She must have looked ridiculous. A smile cracked at the corner of her face, and soon she was joining him, laughing at the absurdity of her plight. If she didn't laugh, she thought she might cry.

When her laughter subsided, Kai gripped the top of the tree trunk, grabbing hold of a branch sticking out of the other side. She hauled herself up onto the trunk, which sank only slightly into the muck.

She stood and balanced, carefully placing one foot in front of the other until she was standing once again on solid ground.

She immediately picked Quitsu up and hugged him tightly, smearing the mud from her face and neck onto his soft fur.

"Ack!" he cried, trying to squirm out of her grasp.

"Thank you for rescuing me, brave seishen," she said, finally releasing him and setting him down.

He shook until his fur stuck out in muddy spikes. "I won't make that mistake again."

She kicked some dirt at him and looked around, trying to get her bearings. Beside the mud pit that she knew to avoid, the mist around them was entirely uniform. She had no idea which direction to go.

"Do you know which way leads to the elder's island?" she asked.

Quitsu sat down, licking his matted fur. "Hmm?" he said. "I can't hear you through the mud in my ears."

"You know that was a joke," she said. "But be serious. I'm worried about Emi. Not to mention if one of those tengu things finds us. I only have one knife left." She fingered the jade-pommeled knife strapped to her arm, comforted by its presence. Her new power was strong but unpredictable. She would rather not rely on it in a fight, at least until she knew how to use it.

Quitsu stood, his fur still askew. "We're close enough that I can sense the way. Follow me."

☾

They moved quickly and silently through the misty woods. Kai scanned the trees nervously, keeping her senses attuned to the forest. It was still and silent but for the rustling of their feet and her mud-caked clothing.

The adrenaline of her escape from the muck died away, and she was left with only her very human sensations. Hunger, pain, fear.

"'Go on a journey,' they said. 'See the seishen elder,' they said,"

Quitsu muttered under his breath as he walked beside her. Kai smiled. She had been thinking the same thing. He knew her so well, sometimes she forgot what it felt like to see her very soul personified outside her body. It was comforting, yet unsettling.

After what felt like hours, the mist began to lift.

"Are we here?" Kai asked with a hope that she tried to swallow. She couldn't take a disappointment. If they hadn't yet arrived, she thought she might sit down and never get up.

"We're here," Quitsu said.

They had reached the edge of the forest. A grassy hill stretched down to a pristine azure lake. A gentle breeze blew across the water, its crisp scent tousling her dirty hair in its caress. The island behind it, dotted with temple towers and steeples, was perhaps the most beautiful thing she had ever seen.

"You grew up here?" she asked. "I imagined you running around in a forest. This is much more...grand."

"Tsuki and Taiyo blessed us with this place when they created the land. The seishen elder said it is the birthplace of the world."

"I believe it," Kai said. "Now we just have to see if Tsuki and Taiyo abandoned it for good."

"Get down," Quitsu hissed, dropping to his belly in the lush grass.

Trusting him instinctually, Kai followed suit, trying to camouflage herself amongst the green blades. "What is it?" she whispered.

"Tengu," he said. "Pacing the edge of the water."

Kai raised her head slightly. The demons' cracked hides looked even more unnatural under the bright light of day. They harried the water's edge, clearly upset, letting out whines and groans of frustration.

"I don't think they can go in the water," Quitsu said. "Watch how they stay back from the edge."

"But they dearly want something in the water," Kai said, hope welling in her. "Do you think the others made it across the lake?"

"I hope so," Quitsu said. "But it's the only way for us to go either way."

"How do we get to the island?" Kai asked. "I don't see any boat on the shore."

"I think we'll have to swim," Quitsu grumbled. "I'll give the elder hell for this."

Kai stifled a smile. Quitsu hated water and found swimming to be beneath his dignity. But she didn't blame him entirely. She eyed the distance from the shore to the lake. It would strain her swimming abilities on a good day. And this was not a good day. Her muscles were shaky from exhaustion and hunger.

She looked back to the edge of the forest, where mist curled and floated, and then towards the tengu circling to her right. She sighed. Nowhere to go but forward.

"Make a run for it?" she asked.

"Only honorable thing," Quitsu said.

"Screw honor," Kai said. "Let's just stay alive."

And so they stood and ran.

CHAPTER 20

Their little boat ran aground on the sugary sand of the island's shore. Colum jumped out and pulled the boat out of the water while Hiro hoisted Emi into his leaden arms.

Ryu dragged himself onto the bank and collapsed, his labored breath disturbing puffs of soft sand. The venom from the tengu's talons was mixing with Ryu's blood, coating his golden hindquarters with pink-tinged foam.

Hiro looked down at Emi, whose face matched the color of her silver hair. Her breath was shallow and halting. She looked worse than death. Soon, Ryu would share the same fate.

They needed to find the seishen elder.

"Lead the way," Hiro said, hoisting Emi a bit higher and adjusting his grip.

Colum hesitated, rubbing the stubble on his jaw. "I wasn't supposed to come back," he said. "Maybe I'll wait here while you go ahead."

"Show me the way or I will boil your blood where you stand," Hiro said, his voice like iron. He didn't have time for this nonsense. "However angry the seishen elder was with you before, it will seem a small thing compared to his wrath after you let one of his seishen die on his shores."

Colum glared at Hiro, his knuckles white on his staff. Finally, his shoulders sagged slightly and he started up from the water's edge.

"Ryu, can you walk?" Hiro asked, seeing the fatigue and pain in his friend's eyes.

"I will make it," Ryu rumbled.

A narrow set of stairs snaked up from the lake towards the temple buildings, the stones worn in the middle from the tread of a thousand footsteps. The sight was incongruous, as Hiro somehow felt like he and Colum were the only two men who had ever set foot on this island. The stairway eventually led them through a stone archway and into a wide courtyard. Hiro couldn't help but gasp at the scene around him. Winding vines and plants covered the walls and towers surrounding them, their tendrils finding purchase in the nooks of ancient-looking carvings and lettering. Hiro wished he had a moment to take it all in, but Emi's heavy weight in his arms reminded him that they were already on borrowed time.

Colum looked at his open mouth and smirked. "You can see why I was drawn to this place as a young adventurer."

Hiro stopped suddenly, breathing in the scents of fresh grass and jasmine. Before them, at the top of another staircase, was a seishen. A silver stag, small and delicate, surveying them with sharp eyes.

"You are expected," he said. "Follow me."

Hiro had never seen a seishen without its burner before. This one's burner must still be too young for her abilities to have developed. So her seishen waited—here—until it was time.

They followed the seishen, who kept up a quick pace, despite his small legs. They reached an imposing double door of dark wood carved with inlays of silver and gold. The doors opened inward, and Hiro's breath caught in his throat.

The crown jewel of the scene was clearly the tree. It rose into the air proud and strong, higher than even the tops of the temple spires surrounding it. Its white trunk was so large that Hiro guessed it would take ten men to reach around it with arms outstretched. Its silver and gold leaves fluttered in the breeze, catching the rays of the rich morning sun in a dazzling light show.

Before the tree was a still pond of sapphire blue fed by a glistening stream from the tree's base. On the stone steps and fragrant grass around the courtyard sat seishen, their silver and gold fur glistening in the morning sun. Plumed birds, big cats, nimble squirrels, and hunched wolves all rested together on the bed of green.

But none of these extraordinary sights prepared Hiro for the seishen elder. It descended from the tree on eagle's wings broader than a man is tall. Its fur and feathers were white, a white so pure that it hurt his eyes to look at it. It was a creature unlike any he had ever seen. It had a lion's body—but with the head and wings of an eagle. Its front legs bore eagle's talons, but its back had claws like Ryu's. Hiro hardly came up to the elder's chest.

It landed on the ground before them, the backbeats from its wings stirring dust into his eyes.

"I thought I told you never to return here, thief," the elder said to Colum in a deep baritone, taking a menacing step towards him.

Colum, who had the wherewithal to look apologetic, bowed low, his salt-and-pepper curls falling over his weathered forehead.

"He was our guide," Hiro said, stepping forward. "I made him cross the lake. Our friend is dying. We had no time."

The seishen elder looked at Hiro, sizing him up with sharp eyes the color of blood. Hiro wanted to look away from the strange creature but held its gaze, feeling his worth being measured.

"What makes you think I care about the plight of one dying moonburner?"

"You tend the seishen—you and they are tied to the burners. And this dying moonburner is one of the bravest warriors I know. She is fighting to save this world from an unspeakable evil." Hiro's voice grew hard. He knew he should be falling on his face to worship this ancient creature, but he was exhausted, sore, and worried sick about Kai and Emi. He didn't have time for philosophizing. "If you deny us help, if you let this burner die, you're handing a victory to the tengu."

The elder's eyes hardened, and a crest of feathers rose above its head and down its back. "Are you so young and hot-blooded that you seek to goad me with talk of those abominations? I was here when this world was formed from nothing! And I will be here when those creatures are cast back into their demon hell!"

Colum bowed low and shook his head at Hiro with a look of blind panic in his eyes.

"My apologies," Hiro said, stilling his racing temper. "We have been through many ordeals on our way to find you. We seek a way to send the false Tsuki and Taiyo back to this demon hell you speak of and return the proper balance to this world. But we can't do this if our friend dies, or if my seishen dies. Please help us." He bowed as low as he could while bearing Emi's dead weight in his arms, matching Colum's posture.

The elder's hackles settled back and it clacked its beak in what almost sounded like laughter.

"So you do have some humility in you," it said. "This is a place of birth and life, not death. I will help your friend, and your seishen, of course. Give her to me."

The elder wrapped its wings before it and Hiro transferred Emi to their feathered embrace. She had started to shiver and convulse. She didn't have much life left in her.

The elder began to walk towards the lake. "Come, Ryu," it said. "It is good to see you again, my child."

Ryu limped forward, and together, the strange white seishen and Ryu walked into the crystal waters of the lake. Steam rose from Emi and Ryu as they touched the water.

The elder dipped Emi under the surface briefly, and when he lifted her up again, she gasped and tried to sit up.

The seishen elder carefully stood her on her feet in the lake.

"Woah," she said, her eyes wide, taking in the incredible sight before her.

"Woah," Hiro said, as he took in her form.

The wounds on her back were completely gone, though the old scars on her face remained. The lake had healed her, bringing new life and vibrancy to her cheeks.

Her hands explored the clean, pink skin of her back. "I remember...the tengu attack. I was injured." She turned to the elder. "How is this possible?"

"These waters are sacred. Healing. It is said that the creator pulled the first sparks of life from these pristine waters."

Emi nodded and swallowed, wading back towards the shore.

"Where's Kai?" she asked, looking around. "And Daarco?"

A look of guilt flashed across Hiro's face. He felt responsible for failing to keep their group together. He should have been able to protect them all.

"We don't know," Hiro said. "Kai ran off into the forest. We lost them in the mist."

"You lost her?" she shrieked. "How could you lose her?"

Hiro stepped back defensively. "Magic lured her away. And you were dying; I couldn't leave you to go after them. And the tengu attacked... Daarco made a stand so we could make it to the lake. We did what we had to."

"Did Daarco make it?" Emi asked, her voice small.

"I...don't know," Hiro said.

Emi closed her eyes briefly and took a deep breath. "You should have let me die," Emi said. "If you had to. Kai is everything. What do you think will happen to all of us...the alliance...fighting the tengu...if she dies?"

"You don't think I know that?" he asked, angry now. "You don't think I'm terrified of what's happening to her out in those woods?" His heart twisted. *If I lost Kai...* He shoved the thought aside. It was unthinkable. *No.* He refused to consider it.

Emi softened. "Of course you're worried. I'm sorry. But we have to go find her."

"Lay your fears to rest," the elder said. "My children are telling me that your Kai approaches from the west. She is with her seishen and is safe."

Emi and Hiro breathed a collective sigh of relief.

"Daarco?" Hiro asked. "Our other friend?"

"He is blocked from my sight. Still in the mist. He is on his own."

CHAPTER 21

K ai and Quitsu collapsed on the bank of the island, panting. She rolled over on her back, exhausted from their swim. At least she wasn't covered in mud anymore.

"I...hate...swimming," Quitsu said.

"I know," she said, patting his damp fur. "But it's better than facing those tengu."

She closed her eyes, letting the warmth of the sun leech the water from her clothes.

"We need to get up at some point," Quitsu said.

"Yes," she said. Her body was tired, hungry, and sore. Her mind was tired of forcing her body forward. "At some point."

"Ahem," a small voice said behind them.

Kai rolled over on her belly and looked up at the speaker. It was a small silver seishen. A stag.

"Hello," Kai said, dragging herself to her knees. "We are here to see the seishen elder."

"It is expecting you," the seishen said. "Please follow me."

They followed the stag up the bank of the island and into the temple grounds. Kai gaped at the effortless beauty of the island.

"Quitsu, this is..."

"Amazing?" he said, a smirk on his face.

"Why didn't you tell me?"

"It's one of those things you have to see for yourself."

The island seemed untouched by the drought Kita and Miina had been suffering from for the last year. Kai's spirit felt buoyed, light. Here in this quiet place, Kai found herself believing that they could unlock a centuries-old secret, that they could truly find a way to defeat the tengu.

The strange power she had begun to access sang to her here, as if it was stronger in this place, closer to the surface of reality. She almost reached out to touch it with her mind, to draw the sweet white nectar into her qi, but she hesitated. She still didn't understand it, and that scared her. Perhaps the elder could help her find answers.

The little stag led them into a large room with a tall vaulted ceiling. High along the walls were open archways that let in streams of molten sunlight, trailing vines and flitting birds. In the center of the room was a low wooden table surrounded by cushions, out of proportion with the cavernous space.

"The elder will be here in a moment."

"Thank you," Kai said.

The stag turned to leave.

"We were traveling with some others. Sun and moonburners. A lion seishen. Did they make it here safely?"

"They are here," the deer said simply and left them.

A tremendous tension left Kai, and the tight knots in her stomach uncoiled. Hiro…Emi… They were all right.

The walls were rough-hewn stone, flattened to uniformity in regular intervals, forming panels throughout the room. The panels bore images of humans and seishen painted in silver and gold. As they waited, Kai examined them, marveling at the intricate detail.

The first panel bore a man and woman, beautiful, sitting on thrones in the starry night sky. Like constellations, looking over a small world below them. They wore crowns on their heads, and when Kai looked carefully, she gasped.

"Another long-lost relative?" Quitsu asked, joining her in front of the panel.

She shot him a look and shoved down the worry about Chiya that bubbled to the surface. What would Kai do if Chiya really was her sister? She shook off the thought. One problem at a time.

"Look at the crowns on their heads," Kai said. Quitsu jumped into her arms and they both peered at the picture.

"They're the solar and lunar crowns," Quitsu said. "I thought the tale about their origin was just a myth."

"Many myths are based in truth," a smooth voice said behind them.

Kai whirled, and Quitsu jumped from her arms, taking a defensive position in front of her.

What she saw stunned her. A great beast of the purest pearly white with a body both—lion?—and bird. And his eyes. Red eyes that seemed to pierce to her very soul. But more than that was the power that emanated from the creature. The pure white light that she had tapped before—it seemed as if this seishen was filled with it, infused with it.

Before she could ponder this strange phenomenon, her friends emerged from behind the creature. Hiro, Emi, Ryu—even Colum.

Hiro crashed into Kai, his hug rib-crushingly tight. "Don't ever scare me like that again," he whispered, his sweet breath tickling her ear.

"I'm sorry," she said, melting into his arms.

She saw Emi next, whose grave wounds had been miraculously healed. "I'm so glad you're all right," Kai said, grabbing Emi tightly in a hug.

Kai next knelt down and embraced Ryu, rubbing his shaggy golden head. "Thanks for looking after him," she whispered.

Colum stood back from their group, set apart, observing their reunion with some discomfort. His bright blue eyes were unreadable, his weathered face blank.

She went to him and embraced him, and he first started with surprise, but then returned the hug, patting her back awkwardly.

"Thank you for taking care of my friends," she said. "For seeing them here safely."

"You're welcome, my lady," he said into her ear. Before he pulled away, he whispered, "We still haven't talked price. Two words, Queenie: hazard pay."

Kai smiled at him, suddenly sure that she had caught a glimpse into his lonely soul. The bravado, the talk of money and treasure and caring for only profit—it was an act. At least in part.

"Where's Daarco?" Quitsu asked. Kai flinched at her oversight. She hadn't even noticed his absence in her excitement at the reunion.

"I don't know if he made it," Hiro said. "He sacrificed himself so we could make it here."

"My guests," the giant white creature said. The elder, Kai realized. "You must be hungry from your journey. We have prepared a meal for you, and then we can discuss why you have come."

They sat on the cushions around the table, except the elder, who rested on its haunches at the head of the table like the patriarch at a family feast.

Two golden seishen, a giant rabbit and a well-muscled boar, rolled in a cart with food. The rabbit managed to totter in on two legs, while the boar simply pushed the cart along with his snout.

"We have not had visitors in several centuries, and as we do not derive sustenance as you do, we gathered what we could for you."

Emi sprang up and went to unload the plates from the cart onto the table.

The first plates were laden with bananas, apples, and some strange oblong fruit with a spiky skin. Another plate bore nuts and a third was filled with fresh greens. Emi finished by unloading cups of a sweet milky liquid.

"This is very generous," Kai said as she grabbed food from the plates with her hands. Propriety be damned. "We had a difficult journey."

"I don't make this place easy to find," the elder said. "None have been here since Colum last darkened our doorstep—almost twenty years ago now."

"About that," Colum said around a mouthful of banana. "I am still very, very sorry."

"You were told never to return here upon punishment of death," the elder said. "Yet here you are."

"I'm here because the fate of the world depends upon this girl finding out everything you know about the tengu masquerading as Tsuki and Taiyo," Colum said. "I didn't think your vendetta against me was more important than the fate of the world...but maybe I misjudged you."

"Please," Kai said, glaring sidelong at Colum. "I begged him to come. He knew he wasn't welcome, yet he risked his life to get us here. We need your help to free the real Tsuki and Taiyo so they can help us defeat the tengu. They are trying to destroy us."

"And what makes you think Tsuki and Taiyo would save you?" the seishen elder asked. "Are you so certain you are worth saving?"

Kai paled. But Quitsu had said that the elder would challenge her. That she would have to convince him of the rightness of her cause.

"I don't know whether I am or not," she admitted. "But I doubt the gods designed a world of beauty only to see it returned to the fires and overrun by demons. The burners aren't perfect, but we have managed for the first time in hundreds of years to overcome our differences and find peace. Despite the false Taiyo and Tsuki doing everything in their power to keep us at war. We are moving towards a future of enlightenment, prosperity, and mutual respect. That clearly terrifies the demons. And I would think anything that terrifies the tengu is something Tsuki and Taiyo would fight for. Unless they gave up and abandoned us by choice."

The elder looked at her with its unsettling eyes, tapping one taloned finger on the stone floor.

"You talk of the peace you have achieved, yet even now, thoughts of war ring loudly in your minds." He nodded towards Hiro.

Kai turned to Hiro, watching a look of guilt play across his handsome face. "Not me," he said heavily. "But yes, my father. If the natural disasters continue, he will restart the war."

Kai felt the sting of betrayal and her mind reeled. How could Hiro have known and not told her?

The elder did not seem surprised. "I suppose you deserve some leniency. There is so much you do not know. The tengu have done everything in their power to destroy the true history of what happened and to plant falsehoods to sow seeds of discontent between you."

"Please," Kai said. "Anything you can tell us... There is so much we don't understand."

"Come," it said, rising on its huge haunches and walking to the painting Kai had been examining. The rest of their group rose and followed it.

"These panels tell the story of the formation of the world, but also the fall of it. When the creator made the world, he banished the dark to the edges with light from the sun and the moon. Taiyo and Tsuki were the personification of that light. But this angered the creatures of darkness, who resided in the vast darkness of the universe."

"The tengu," Kai said. This tale was sounding familiar to the scroll they had found in the library.

"Yes. The tengu are an abomination to this world. They are the opposite of its incarnation. And this world—and its inhabitants—is an abomination to them. When the creator banished the darkness and set up this world for its inhabitants, he divided the universe into three realms. The mortal realm, where we now stand. The demon realm, a realm of darkness and death, and between them the spirit realm, a plane that is a mirror of this one, where creatures of spirit and magic live. Gods like Tsuki and Taiyo. And me and my seishen. The spirit realm is also where your human spirits go when you first die—a place of transition. Sometimes spirits linger there longer."

It was strange hearing the elder speak as truth what she had only heard in children's stories. He went on.

"But you're in this world now," Emi said. "Why?"

The elder puffed its wings slightly, and Emi fell silent. They walked to the next panels as the elder told its tale. "The creator created the seishen as the guardians of the spirit and mortal realms. Originally, our home was in the spirit realm."

At the word "guardians," something stirred in Kai's memory. Where had she heard that before? But the thought eluded her, and she turned her attention back to the seishen's story.

"The creator set up strong walls and seals between these worlds to keep them apart. But over the millennia, the tengu were set on one goal: to break out of their dark prison and destroy the new world the creator had made. To return the world to a place where they had free reign over darkness and death. Eventually, the unthinkable happened, and the seals between the demon and spirit realm failed. Powerful tengu began to cross over, free now to travel back and forth. They were intent on killing Tsuki and Taiyo and plunging the world back into darkness. They were breaking down the walls to the mortal world as well and beginning to cross over. "

"We saw a similar story in a scroll we found in our library," Kai said. "The tengu trapped Tsuki and Taiyo in prisons so they could have free reign over the mortal realm."

"This part of the story is hidden from me," said the elder. "I was in the spirit realm at the time with my seishen, and we were under a full siege from the tengu. It was clear to me that they were intent upon destroying every last one of us. As a final desperate move, I fled through the seal to the mortal realm with my charges and established this sanctuary, building strong walls to keep the tengu out. We cannot return to the spirit world. It is overrun with tengu."

Kai thought back to her conversation with Hamaio, looking over her shoulder and pushing her forcefully out of the realm before something attacked. She shuddered.

The elder went on. "By the time the dust settled, Tsuki and Taiyo had disappeared into the mortal realm. I know there was a great battle, and the burners and the gods were able to push the tengu back into the spirit realm and at least partially seal the barrier between the worlds. But perhaps in the process, Tsuki and Taiyo were trapped as well."

"We need their help now," Kai said. "The tengu are obviously breaking their way into this world again. Tsuki and Taiyo must know how to reseal the borders between the realms. Do you know where they are trapped? How to find them?"

"No," it said.

Kai couldn't keep the look of disappointment off her face.

"But I have something that might help."

CHAPTER 22

I t was a wooden box. Its dark surface bore crude carvings, as if it had been hastily made.

The elder had sent one of his seishen to retrieve the thing, and now he held it in his taloned hand.

"What is it?" Colum asked, leaning forward to get a closer look. Clearly, the prospect of some valuable antiquity was enough to stir him from his silent musings at the back of the room.

"I don't know exactly what it is, except that it came with a message," the elder said. "When my seishen and I fled from the spirit world to the Misty Forest, the tengu were engaged in a two-pronged assault. On the seishen in the spirit world, and on the burners and gods in the mortal world. A messenger from the burners arrived on our shore after the battle was over. He was near death and only lived long enough to tell me that the tengu had been driven back for a time, but at great cost. The burner king and queen were killed and the gods were gone. He said that this box was key to finding Tsuki and Taiyo."

"May I see it?" Kai asked.

The elder handed it to her, and she turned it over in her hand. It was weighty and warm to the touch.

She looked up and found the elder's keen eagle eyes watching her. "What?" she asked, suddenly self-conscious.

"The messenger told me one more thing," it said. "That the box will only open to the heirs. I must admit, I was curious if it would open at your touch."

"Which heirs?" Hiro asked, holding out his hand for the box.

"The true heirs to the throne of Miina and Kita. The moon and sunburners."

The moment Kai handed the box to Hiro, light exploded from within.

It was like standing in a dream. Images emanated from the box, projecting on the stucco ceiling.

They all stared in slack-jawed awe as they tried to comprehend what they were seeing.

"What kind of magic is this?" Emi asked, her voice reverential.

"It's like scrying for a person...but...they managed to capture it somehow," Kai said.

Hiro peered at the image, narrowing his eyes. He turned the box slowly, and the image rotated. It came into focus.

"I see it!" Kai said. The light portrayed a narrow mountain pass covered with ice and snow. The image showed a treacherous path between two craggy peaks. Above the jagged peaks stretched a starry sky, but it was unlike any sky she had ever seen. Across the blackness stretched a band of vertical green lines dancing and undulating. Like someone had taken a paintbrush and dashed it across the heavens.

"It's beautiful," said Emi.

"What is this place?" Hiro asked.

"I do not know," the elder said. "The box has never opened for me. But I believe it may be where you can find Taiyo. You are his true heir."

The elder took the box from Hiro and the image abruptly winked out. They all stood blinking and shaking their heads, a little unsure if it had been real.

The seishen elder handed the box to Kai again. She took it, examining it, trying to ignore the sinking feeling in the pit of her stomach.

"You are not Tsuki's true heir," the elder said, not unkindly.

"That's preposterous," Emi said, stepping up next to Kai. "Kai is the daughter of Azura. She is the true queen of Miina."

Kai put her hand on Emi's shoulder to quiet her friend. A sad smile stretched across her lips.

"No, I'm not." Kai said.

"Not what?" Emi and Hiro said together.

"I'm the daughter of Azura, but I'm not the true queen of Miina. Or Tsuki's heir."

The truth didn't set her free. Not this time. Seeing the shocked and hurt looks on her friends' faces made Kai want to crawl inside herself and never come out.

"Let us sit down as we hear this tale," the seishen elder said. Was there a touch of...sympathy in its voice? Maybe it felt bad that it had outed her secret.

"I only found out a few days ago," she began, sinking gratefully to a cushion. "The day of the earthquake. You may not know this, but I was not my parents' first child. They had another daughter, Saeko. She failed the Gleaming and was left in the desert to die."

A thunderous look passed over Hiro's face. He hated hearing about the pain his father had caused to so many families through the Gleaming, the cruel test his father had used to expose moonburners just days after birth.

Kai continued. "They thought she had died, and that was the end of it. But after the earthquake, my mother was treating a moonburner and discovered she bore a birthmark identical to one my sister had had. My mother told me her suspicions. We hadn't yet confirmed it." She looked to the chief seishen. "Until now."

"Who is it?" Emi asked quietly.

"Chiya."

"Chiya!" Emi exploded. "That would be a disaster! I know what you must be thinking, but you cannot hand over control of Miina to Chiya."

"But she's the rightful heir," Kai said.

"Emi's right," Hiro said. "Chiya's come a long way, but she would use the smallest affront as an excuse to resume hostilities with the sunburners. And besides. You're the queen. You've been crowned."

"Only because no one knew about her," Kai said. She struggled to hold back tears. She had never wanted to be queen, never wanted the responsibility. But now, the idea of handing it all over to someone else, to trust them with Miina's fate... It twisted her inside.

"There's no telling if anyone would support her now," Hiro said. "If you tried to hand over the throne, it could start a civil war. A monarch needs more than just a birthright to rule. She would need allies in the burners and the noble classes, support of the people."

"That's kind of you to say," Kai said, "but I've read the reports. The people hate me right now. They think the natural disasters are my fault! The drought...the earthquake... They'd relish the chance for a new leader."

Colum cleared his throat. "Not that anyone asked me, but as I see it, you've got bigger fish to fry. You're gonna need all the burners you've got to have any shot at defeating the tengu. You hand Miina's reins over to this Chiya woman, and you may as well hand humanity over to the tengu."

They all looked at Colum in surprise.

"What? I have thoughts."

"As much as I hate to admit it," Hiro said, looking sideways at Colum, "I agree with Colum. If you want to tell Chiya about this, even though I think it's a bad idea, fine. But do it after we free Tsuki and Taiyo. We have enough problems as it is without Miina and Kita going to war. We don't know that Chiya would honor the alliance. Or, frankly, my father. He trusts you, but I don't know if he would feel bound to the alliance if Chiya is on the throne."

Kai looked at the seishen elder, expecting him to object and insist upon the truth. He said nothing.

"But...we need Chiya. The box should open for her and show us where Tsuki is."

"So we give her a half-truth," Emi said. "Tell her we need her because of who her parents are but don't tell her exactly who. Say we're still trying to figure it out. Prophecy and magic and all that. Tell her it's all very confusing."

"I don't like it." Kai shook her head. "It doesn't feel right."

"Kai," Emi said, taking her hands. "Doing what you know is right isn't always the easy path. When you had to defeat Airi, that was technically treason. But you knew it had to be done."

"Yes, but that was to defeat a tyrant who refused to relinquish power. This feels like...I'm becoming one."

"You're nothing like Airi," Hiro said. "Don't you see? The fact that we're even having this conversation proves it. What the people need is you. Not Chiya."

Kai hesitated. She felt ripped in two. Could she really live with herself if she lied to Chiya? If she kept from her that she had a mother who loved her, a sister who was a short walk away? But could she truly abandon Miina to Chiya? Kai felt in her gut that Chiya wasn't the queen Miina needed. At least not now.

"What do you think?" she asked the elder.

"The ebbs and flows of the burner monarchy are of little concern to me," it said. "But I can tell you with certainty that you will never defeat the tengu unless you are united. You are greater than the sum of your parts."

Kai nodded, praying her mother would agree to keep the secret a while longer. "I will finish this with the tengu. But as soon as it's over..." Kai pointed at all of them, meeting each of their eyes in turn. "I will tell her. And let her decide whether she wants to rule or abdicate to me. If she wants to rule, I will throw my support behind her."

The others breathed a sigh of relief.

Quitsu looked at her with a proud nod. She had made the right decision. For now.

"So it's settled," Kai said. "We'll take the box, Chiya will open the other side, and we'll find Tsuki and Taiyo and free them."

The others nodded.

"I do not know if I should let you take it," the elder said. "The box cannot fall into the wrong hands. The burner who delivered it here gave his life to keep it from the tengu and their followers. They must not have it. It is safer here than anywhere in this realm. This island is protected from the tengu by the most powerful magic in the mortal realm."

"We need it," Kai argued. "We need to know where Tsuki is. To free her."

"I doubt the wisdom of freeing Tsuki and Taiyo. They fled the spirit world into the mortal world when the tengu attacked, and though they are trapped, at least they are safe. If you free them, who knows what the consequences will be."

Kai blew out a frustrated breath, fluttering her hair before her. "That may be true, but if we don't free them, we know what will happen. The tengu will win. I'll take an uncertain chance of success over a sure chance of failure any day."

"And that is your choice. But I do not know if the box should leave this place. Bring this Chiya here if you must."

"We don't have time for that," Hiro said. "Things are getting worse.

The earthquakes, the fever… We barely made it here as it is. If we wait, who knows if there will be any people left to save."

"Please," Quitsu said, bowing his furry silver body low before the elder. "We will protect it with our lives. But we must take it. Or all may be lost."

The elder peered at the little fox with its eerie red eyes. "I could never say no to my seishen. Fine. Take it. But you must take every precaution. You will face many obstacles on your path. The tengu and their followers will do everything in their power to stop you from reaching your destination."

"Their followers?" Emi asked.

Hiro nodded. "Colum told me that the tengu that came after us in the woods were…created."

Kai grimaced in dismay. "Created by who?"

"Since the time of the first split between burners, the Order of the Deshi has lurked in the shadows, sowing seeds of discord on the tengu's behalf. They have waxed and waned in numbers over the years, but they never disappeared completely," the elder said. "They have powerful blood magic at their disposal. You will need to be careful."

"Feathers here is right," Colum said. "I tussled with this Order many years ago and almost didn't survive."

"So we have crazed demon-worshipers to contend with too?" Emi said. "That's great. How are we supposed to know who to trust?"

Kai's eyes widened. "Geisa."

"Obviously we can't trust her," Emi said.

"No, Geisa must be part of the Order. Airi was too," Kai said. "This is great!"

"Maybe you forgot the definition of 'great'…" Emi began.

Kai waved her quiet. "No, we have Geisa in custody. She can tell us who the other members are, and then we can take them down before they have a chance to raise more tengu or interfere with us finding Tsuki and Taiyo."

"If we can get her to talk," Hiro said. "But it's better than nothing."

Kai smiled. They had a plan.

CHAPTER 23

Dusk fell and her friends filed outside to sleep on the sweet-smelling grass under the great silver-and-gold tree.

"I need to talk to you," Kai said softly to Hiro, catching his arm before he slipped out the door of the paneled room where they had eaten. With knowing looks, Ryu and Quitsu disappeared into the warm night air, leaving them alone.

"I need to talk to you too," Hiro said. "Who should go first?"

"Why don't you?" Kai said, crossing her arms and leaning against the wall.

Hiro straightened, seeming to brace himself. "You were reckless today. You ran off alone. You could have died. Just like when you ran into the farmhouse with the spotted fever. How I am supposed to keep you alive if you barrel ahead with no concern for your safety?"

Kai sucked in a breath and blew it out slowly. Yes, this. It was past time that they talked about this. "Two points. First, yes, I made a mistake today, and when I went in the farmhouse. I need to do a better job of taking the measure of a situation before I get in too deep. So thank you, as my betrothed and friend, for keeping me honest, and I expect you to continue to challenge me in that regard. Second, the more important point. You are not my bodyguard. You are not my father. Your job is not to keep me safe. If I have to spend my married life with you coddling me like a nursemaid afraid I might skin my knee, we will not last the year!"

"Well, if you weren't almost dying every other day, maybe I wouldn't have to keep saving you!"

"I am just as capable of protecting myself as you are, Hiro," Kai said, pulling the raging white light into her qi and swirling it in an arc around her head. It was a flashy but pointless display, but it set her blood singing and her heart pounding. "You have to stop treating me like a child. Like your ward. It undermines my authority and it drives me crazy."

"What am I even here for then?" Hiro hissed. "You don't need me to watch your back, and you certainly don't need me to confide in, since you didn't think to mention that you had a long-lost sister who was the rightful heir to the Miinan throne!"

"You, lecturing me on keeping secrets?" Kai scoffed. "That's rich. Coming from the man who is secretly making plans to invade my country."

"That's out of line. Jurou mentioned to me that my father was considering it *as a last resort*. I defended you and told them I would never agree to it."

"You still should have told me," Kai said, her voice growing quiet. Hot tears pricked in her eyes.

"And you should have told me," Hiro said. "If we start keeping secrets from each other, our marriage will be over before it starts. We need to be a team."

"I'm on Miina's team," Kai said. "And I thought you were too. But maybe that was foolish of me. How could I ask you to choose Miina over Kita? Me over your people?

"I don't have to choose," Hiro said. "It's not you or them. It's both. We want the same thing. Destruction of the tengu. Prosperity for our people. Peace."

"It's naive to think that there will never be a conflict. That we'll never have to choose."

"So what, you want to throw away what we have as a preemptive move against some future challenge that may never come?"

"No. I don't know," Kai said, biting her lip. "But I don't see how we can marry each other if we can't trust each other."

"Then I guess we're at an impasse," Hiro said, a thundercloud of emotions playing across his face.

The tears fell now, leaving slick trails down Kai's cheeks and neck. "I guess so," she whispered.

Hiro turned on his heel and walked out without another word.

Kai sank down against the stone wall and wept.

☾

Kai awoke a little before sunrise. She had fallen asleep against the wall, and she stood and stretched, trying to work out the worst of the kinks.

She poked her head outside. Her friends' prone forms rested quietly on the grass under the great tree. Was Hiro there too, or had he gone somewhere else to find some solitude? Her heart twisted at the thought of him, of their fight.

She did need him; he did have a place in her life. And though he drove her crazy with his overbearing protectiveness, she knew she could trust him if it really came down to it. They could work through whatever maze of political and romantic challenges came with their marriage. That is, if she hadn't ruined everything.

Her eyes were puffy and sore and her throat was raw from crying. The water of the lake shimmered enticingly, like molten silver in the moonlight. She crossed the grass and sat down next to the crystal pond, leaning forward to scoop some of the water into her cupped hands.

"Do not," a voice said.

Kai froze.

"That water is not for you." The seishen elder approached, wings tucked against its back. It settled onto the grass next to her, its strange mix of eagle talons and lion paws flexing into the loamy depths of the soil.

"Why not?" Kai asked, leaning back.

"There is something unusual about you," it rumbled. "I do not know how it will react with the water."

"Something unusual?" Kai asked.

"Yes, it reminds me of…the creator. You smell of him."

"I smell of him?" Kai asked, wrinkling her nose. "That doesn't sound good."

"To the contrary," the elder said. "It is an old smell. Like the smell of rain hanging heavy in the air before a storm. A smell of promise. Of things to come."

"She said I was touched by him," Kai said, unconsciously fingering the smooth scar on her chest.

"Who?"

"Strange things have been happening to me," Kai confessed. "In the forest...I did something. To the trees. I don't know what. And one night I woke up in the spirit world and spoke to an ancient Miinan queen. At least I think I did. And I can't feel the moonlight anymore. I feel something else. Something raw and powerful and old." She chuckled ruefully. "Or maybe I'm crazy."

"No," the elder said. "Though something *is* happening to you. Something that stretches the bounds of what a burner's mind can handle. And if stretched too far, things break."

She laid her hand across the handprint on her chest.

"May I?" the elder said, its long, creamy wingtip curling around to hover over the scar.

She removed her hand. "All right."

The tip of its wing touched her, the feathers a soft tickle against her skin. But that touch was enough. Kai gasped as the scar flared to life in a pulsing throb of white light. Images flashed through her mind, broken bits. Sitting on a sun-drenched patio with a handsome brown-haired stranger. Talk of guardians. A powerful hand connecting with her chest. Falling...falling.

She sprang up as emotions flooded her, breaking the connection between them. "I remember. I talked to him!" Her breath came in ragged bursts, her heart racing at the newly-discovered memories. "He...said he couldn't help us."

"He is ancient," the seishen said. "More ancient than me. In some ways I think he is our world itself. I don't know if he could interfere if he wanted to. It is like an infection. Once it catches hold, the patient is helpless to influence the outcome. The forces in the body will either fight and live, or succumb and die."

"So he is going to let his world die?"

"Your defeat is not unavoidable." It pointed at her scar. "Perhaps he has already helped you."

"With this?" she asked. "I don't even know what it is."

"Think of it as...the light of life. Moonlight and sunlight together mimic it, but it is something more. We are all made of it in small doses. It fuels us. The burners. The seishen. It is the stuff of spirits."

"This place, it's stronger here. And you…you're full of it," Kai said, letting her senses explore the landscape around her.

"Yes, I was formed by the creator himself, and he made this place. There is more of his power in me, and in this island—its healing waters. The power also made Tsuki and Taiyo, though the gods were formed of specific elements of the creator's power, so they cannot wield the whole spectrum themselves. Neither can any burner. Except you."

"I don't know how to use it though. Or not very well. It's so strong. I can hardly control it. Can you help me?"

It shook its head. "This is a journey I cannot walk for you."

She suppressed her frustration and paced the soft grass, its cool blades tickling her bare feet. "The guardians then," she said. "He said something about guardians. Can you help me find them?"

"You are the guardians. And us. The burners and the seishen."

"But we're not enough," Kai said, sinking back onto the grass in despair. "Maybe back then we were. They were able to push the tengu back into the spirit world. But now? I don't have the first idea where to start. I couldn't even make one of those fancy boxes they made! Do you know how to stop the tengu?"

It shook its head. "I do not. I lived in the spirit world while the burners lived in the mortal one. I saw a shadow of such things, but I do not have this type of magic."

"Can you help us? Fight with us?"

"I will not leave this place," it said. "My duty is to protect my seishen. And I will not fail."

"What good will your seishen be if their burners die? We are linked. If the tengu break the rest of the bonds between the worlds, will you sit behind your walls and let them disappear one by one?"

The seishen elder rose to its feet and its wings shot out behind it in a billow of white feathers. "Do you call me a coward for carrying out the sacred duty the creator left to me? I welcomed you into our home, fed you, healed your friend, shared what knowledge I had. Do not think you are entitled to more, whatever precious gift the creator thought to give you. He may have thought you worthy, but I am not convinced."

Kai shrank back from the elder, knowing she had gone too far. Quitsu streaked in front of her and drew himself up before the giant creature, his silver paws solidly planted, his hackles raised.

"That's enough," he said to the elder, tiny but fierce before the immense white seishen.

"Quitsu, my little foxling," the elder said, settling back onto the ground, folding its wings once more. "Your mouth always was three times bigger than any other part of you. Except perhaps your heart. Now I see where you get it."

"We're going to take that as a compliment," Quitsu said, backing down and sitting on Kai's feet. "Let's not forget we're all on the same side."

"I'm sorry," Kai said. "I was hoping…you could give us more help."

"You are touched by the creator. Trust that he will guide your path," the elder said. "And I will do what I can. But I cannot abandon my post."

"I understand," Kai said.

Kai, Quitsu, and the elder joined the rest of their group around the low table and ate a simple breakfast.

Kai sat by Emi, not ready to speak with Hiro after their argument the night before. Hiro seemed similarly content to pass the morning avoiding eye contact. He was currently absorbed in the banana he was peeling.

Well, that was just fine with her. She wasn't ready to apologize.

"We must be on our way soon," Kai said. "I'm anxious to return to Kyuden and the citadel."

"I can provide you mounts to aid your journey home," the elder said, and Kai nodded in gratitude. They would have to send moonburners back to the Misty Forest to try to retrieve the mounts they had left behind.

"Am I the only one who remembers that we're leaving Daarco lost somewhere in the Misty Forest? If he's even alive?" Emi asked. "I mean, he's not my favorite person…but it seems a bit callous."

Kai bit her lip. If Daarco had eluded the tengu, how would they ever find him in the forest? They were likely to get themselves killed trying to locate him.

"Your friend has left the forest," the elder said. "He is again within my sight. He has returned to your citadel."

They all let out a breath of relief. Kai couldn't help a twinge of annoyance. So Daarco had no trouble leaving them all for dead and heading back to the citadel?

But as soon as the thought entered her head, she chided herself. What other choice did he have? Wander the forest hoping to bump into them? He must have rejected that path, just as she so recently had.

"Then it's settled," Kai said. "We return to the citadel."

As they walked outside to the lakeshore, Kai fell into step next to Colum. "What did you take from the seishen elder to make it so angry at you?" she asked, her voice low.

"A cute bunny rabbit," Colum said. "I took a shine to 'im while I was here."

"That doesn't sound so bad..." Kai frowned.

Colum looked straight ahead. "He was a golden bunny rabbit..."

Kai's eyes flew open in shock. "You stole a seishen?" Her voice raised an octave.

"I returned him," Colum said. "Eventually."

"You're lucky you weren't skinned alive!" Kai said.

"It's not too late," the elder said from ahead of them without turning.

"No, no," Kai said, glaring sideways at Colum. "I think we still need him."

INTERLUDE

G eisa sat in darkness. Since the queen had come, the conditions of her imprisonment had dramatically improved. *The queen,* Geisa thought with a sneer. That girl was in far deeper trouble than she could even conceive. She didn't have half the presence and fortitude Airi had had.

She sighed, as she always did when she thought of Airi. Though the careful shepherding of Airi towards her mistress's purpose had been a duty assigned to her, they had spent almost twenty years together. While Geisa had kept Airi in the dark about her true task and purpose for coming to Kyuden, it didn't stop Geisa from growing fond of Airi. From caring about her. She had deserved better than an unceremonial death at the hand of her supposedly loyal followers.

Geisa's stomach rumbled. It was past time for her dinner. At least they fed her now. Her frame was still painfully thin, but she wasn't crippled by the weakness that had plagued her when they had fed her only a few times a week. She supposed she should be grateful. Though if she was to spend the rest of her life rotting in this cell, food only extended things unnecessarily.

No. She wouldn't spend her life in this cell. She fingered the skin on her forearm where she had used her fingernails to draw blood to summon Tsuki. Or rather, the tengu that masqueraded as Tsuki. Yukina. It had been ten years of service before her mistress had deemed her worthy to know its true name. Geisa touched the scab on her arm again. The scab was almost gone, but it was a comforting reminder. Geisa would be free again, and she would enjoy her revenge against the petty insects of this citadel. She would watch their precious world burn.

Noise sounded outside the thick cell door, and she smoothed her hair. Since the queen had come, she had tried to regain her old sense of self, at least when she had visitors. She pasted a disdainful expression on her face. She wouldn't show weakness.

The dim light from the hallway blinded her as the door opened. She closed her eyes and turned her face, blinking slowly to adjust her pupils. The silhouette at the door was different than her normal guard, thin and slightly stooped. Male. His face was bathed in shadow, backlit against the hallway light.

And then he did a peculiar thing. He stepped inside the cell and closed the door, cloaking the cell in utter darkness once again.

"Does the dark still bother you?" he asked.

His smooth voice froze the blood in her veins. She inhaled sharply.

"I suppose it does," he said. "Those traits we pick up in our youth follow us through life."

Geisa's breathing grew frantic as she tried to pick out where he was in the darkness. Was he approaching? Drawing near? Was he going to touch her?

"The dark is a funny thing," he said. "We have five senses, but we only ever use our eyes. Take away a person's eyes, and suddenly they feel very vulnerable indeed."

Geisa drew her knees against her chest, becoming as small and tightly wrapped as she could. She began counting in her head to soothe herself. It was a trick she had learned in the sunburner prison. It calmed her but allowed her to still listen to his instructions. Allowed her to detach from her body. From what he was doing to it.

"Remember all the fun we used to have? With the blindfold? You never knew what was coming next. So satisfying."

In the darkness, the man's hand gripped her chin and raised her face to look into his own. She could imagine the face, the twisted sneer, in the darkness.

She whimpered, her memory flashing through the ways he had degraded her, body and soul. How he had stripped her down, piece by piece, until there was nothing left that she recognized. Until she would do anything to make the pain stop.

"It's too bad we don't have time for fun today," he said, releasing her chin. "But I have much to do to clean up your mess here. You did your job well for many years, but it all fell apart. You failed them."

"The goddess said I could have a second chance," Geisa said. He couldn't destroy her. The goddess still needed her. "It came here...it told me."

"Yes." The man tsked. "I would not have been so forgiving, but it is not for me to question their judgment. I will free you and give you one more chance to prove your worth."

"I will not fail again," she said, hating the eagerness in her own voice.

"Your task is a critical one. Within days, the queen and Ozora's whelp will journey to discover the locations where Tsuki and Taiyo are held captive. If they find where they are hidden, they will undertake an effort to free them."

"Free them?" Geisa said. "It cannot be allowed. I will stop them at all costs."

"Foolish woman," he scolded. "So small-minded. I suppose I could not expect more from a woman, but even so, it's disappointing to have such inferior allies."

She cringed away from his displeasure, not daring to speak.

The man continued. "You must harry them, so they believe they are being opposed, but not stop them."

"Why don't I kill them?" Geisa asked, salivating slightly at the thought.

"Because we need them. The prisons containing Tsuki and Taiyo will only open to the blood of their heirs."

"If we kill them, we will have their blood," Geisa said. "Why the charade?"

"The resting places will only open to the blood of the true heir freely given," he said, as if explaining to a small child.

"Why do we seek to free Tsuki and Taiyo?" Geisa asked softly. "I thought our master and mistress wanted the gods out of the way."

"They do," the man said, kneeling down before her. She could smell the stale odor of decay on his breath. "Out of the way for good. Once Tsuki and Taiyo are free, our lord and lady will kill them and plunge this world into darkness."

Geisa shivered, but not at the thought of the coming darkness. At his closeness.

"I'm ready," she said.

CHAPTER 24

Kai breathed a sigh of relief when they landed in the citadel's central courtyard. The seishen elder's transportation had turned out to be several white eagles as large as oxen. Riding on one of their feathered backs without the security of a flying harness or saddle had left her with frayed nerves and tense muscles.

Viewing the deadly effects of the earthquake as they descended had twisted her heart. Buildings crumbled like sandcastles along the riverbed, tents of homeless citizens sprung across squares and alleys, smoke wafting from still-smoldering embers.

It was late afternoon, and the hot sun beat down mercilessly on the stones and whitewashed walls of the citadel, painting the destruction of her own palace in harsh oranges and reds.

"Thank you," she said to her eagle after she dismounted and helped Quitsu down to the ground.

It nodded to her once and took off into the sky, sending her back a step with the force of its wings.

"Thank the goddess," Hanae said, and Kai whirled around to meet her. Kai's mother wore a colorful silk robe, her silky tresses corralled in a haphazard bun. It was still "nighttime" here.

Hanae wrinkled her nose as she pulled Kai into a hug. "You need a bath."

Kai let out a tired laugh. "It was a tougher voyage than we expected."

"We feared the worst," Hanae said. "When Daarco came back. He told us...about the attacks. He thought you had been lost in the forest."

"How is Daarco?" Emi asked as she approached, trying uselessly to dust off her uniform.

Hanae hesitated, an unreadable look flashing across her face. "He's...being held in his quarters."

"What?" Hiro asked, joining them. "Why?"

"Shortly after he returned...something happened."

"What?" Kai asked in alarm.

"Geisa escaped."

"What?" Kai shrieked.

"Someone helped her escape," Hanae said. "Daarco knew she was there and is no friend of the moonburners. He's the logical suspect."

"How could he do this?" Kai fumed. "I thought...I thought we were making progress."

"No," Emi said. "It wasn't Daarco."

"And you base that on what, your extensive knowledge of him?" Kai snapped. "He tried to kill me twice. Come on, Hiro, you know he could be capable of this."

Hiro hesitated, stroking his square jaw. "I...I don't think so," he said, shaking his head. "Why would he free Geisa? It doesn't make sense."

"But he could do it, you know that," Kai insisted. "He's capable of it." *If not Daarco, who?* She could hardly articulate the thought, let alone voice it out loud. If not Daarco...then they had another traitor in their midst. And she couldn't face that.

"I'd like to talk to him," Hiro said. "Before I make any judgments."

"Of course," Hanae said.

Kai closed her eyes, taking a deep breath. "I need a hot meal and a hot bath. Please gather the council at nightfall. We have things to discuss."

Kai lingered in her steaming bath until the water grew tepid, relishing the brief moment of stillness. After her bath, she dug into a fragrant meal of sweet glazed chicken, vegetables, and fluffy rice, further delaying the unpleasantness that she knew she would face at her council meeting. But eventually, after she pulled on a light dress of chartreuse linen and secured her wet hair in a bun, she knew she could delay no longer.

The others had already gathered in the council chamber when she arrived—Nanase, Hanae, Master Vita, and Chiya.

Kai settled into the chair at the head of the table. "Report?"

Her councilmembers exchanged glances, each hesitant to go first.

Nanase broke the silence, her face stormy. "You heard that Geisa has escaped."

"Yes," Kai said. "How?"

"The guards were overpowered and knocked unconscious yesterday during the day. One woman was stripped of her uniform. We believe the perpetrator dressed Geisa in a moonburner uniform and smuggled her out of the citadel. A koumori is gone. Just one."

Just one. Meaning the perpetrator could still be at the citadel.

"This happened during sunlight hours?" Kai asked. It didn't look good for Daarco. It would be the perfect time for a sunburner to aid an escape.

Nanase nodded grimly. "I apologize, Your Majesty. I am personally handling the moonburner guards' discipline. I am also looking into why no one at the rookery was alerted to an unauthorized use of a koumori. It was an unacceptable oversight in security, and I take full responsibility."

"Very well," Kai said. She knew Nanase would punish herself more harshly for the breach than anything Kai could impose on her. No need to rub salt in the wound. "And Daarco has been questioned?"

"He has been questioned and denies involvement," Hanae said. "But we have not used true interrogation tactics for fear of harming diplomatic relations with Kita."

"He's a lying rat," Chiya said under her breath.

Kai stifled a sigh. Chiya's prejudices could be tiresome. She examined the other woman, considering her round face, silver ponytail, heavily-muscled arms, strong hands. Those were her father's hands—she could see him in them, gentle enough to bottlefeed a newborn foal, strong enough to wrench a stray fencepost back into place. Gods, she missed those hands.

"Kai?" Hanae said, concern written on her face.

Kai started. They were all looking at her, no doubt waiting for some response. "Daarco," she said. "I will question him with Hiro. See if we can get to the bottom of this." Her necklace should reveal any lies—

should tell her whether he was truly to blame. "Have we considered who it could be if it's not him?"

"We're looking into alternatives," Nanase said. "No leads yet."

"Keep looking," Kai said. "Gods, I don't want it to be Daarco, but I don't want it not to be Daarco." She blew a wisp of hair out of her eyes. "But we will deal with what comes. What other news? More bad, I assume."

"I'm afraid so," Master Vita said. "The food situation is only growing worse. The earthquake ruined many of the stores we had, and very few crops have been harvested. Now, we are hearing news of livestock sickness."

Kai couldn't keep the dismay off her face. "Treatable?"

Hanae shook her head. "It's not something we've seen before. And it's highly contagious. We are instructing people to slaughter all of the sick animals and burn them."

"The meat can't be salvaged?"

"We don't think it's safe to eat," Master Vita said, wiping his half-moon spectacles with his handkerchief.

"That's not all," Hanae said. "The spotted fever has made it to the city. We've had to quarantine sections of the Meadow, as well as the Coin, by the docks. We're just short of a widespread epidemic."

Kai wanted to scream. These tengu thought they could starve them and sicken them and kill them? She tightened her fists. Not under her reign.

"Anything else?" Kai asked, afraid of the answer.

"Uprisings," Chiya said. "We're hearing reports of rioting in the streets. Looting near the quarantine zones. The city is near the boiling point."

Kai took a deep breath, sorting through the parade of horribles in her mind to identify something, anything, she could help. "We need to set up a hospital outside of the city. The sick can be boated down from the quarantine point out of the city. We need to get those people outside the city before the bodies start piling up. I want all the moonburners, healers and nurses we can spare to get to work on caring for those people or trying to find a cure for the livestock ailment, and the rest of the moonburners in the city need to be giving out what food we can spare. Let's see if we can release some pressure."

"And then what?" Chiya said, as tactless as ever. "All those solutions are temporary. They won't even get us through the winter."

"And then," Kai said, setting her jaw, "we free Tsuki and Taiyo, kill some tengu, and take back our world."

Kai's council listened with rapt attention as Kai detailed the journey to the Misty Forest.

"Now we need to travel to where Tsuki and Taiyo are trapped and release them. We hope they will be able to fight the tengu and show the world that these horrible events were not divine will after all."

"Did the seishen elder tell you where Tsuki and Taiyo can be found?" Master Vita asked.

"No." Kai hesitated. This part was delicate. She needed to convince Chiya that she held the secret to finding Tsuki without her understanding why. "The seishen elder did give us something to help reveal the locations."

Kai produced the wooden box and handed it to Chiya, who sat next to her. "Will you do the honors?"

Chiya looked at it in confusion, but the confusion didn't last long. As it touched her hand, the box erupted with light, just as it had in the seishen temple. But this time, the image was different.

The faces in the room turned towards the light in rapt attention, taking in the details of the scene projected by the box. The viewer was on a beach covered in fine white sand. A cluster of palm trees stood tall to the right of the scene, the green fronds fluttering in an ephemeral breeze. In the distance, a smaller island crouched in the crystalline water. As they examined the image, it began to move.

"We're moving!" Master Vita exclaimed.

"What are you doing?" Kai asked.

"I don't know. Nothing," Chiya said.

They watched in rapt attention as the image transformed. A long, thin rowboat came into view, its turquoise paint peeling in the afternoon sun. They seemed to get into the boat and begin rowing towards the next island as the sun's tangerine light slipped over the horizon to their right. Twilight blanketed the landscape and a few stars appeared. As the oars dipped into the water at the edge of the image, they left a faint trail of light in the dark of the water.

The image winked out in Chiya's hand. Chiya stared at the deceptively mundane-looking box with wide eyes.

"It must be finished," Kai said. "That's all it will show us."

"So Tsuki is on an island in the south?" Master Vita said, running his hands through his snowy hair.

"Do you know where that is?" Kai asked.

"That light in the water," Master Vita said. "I've heard of such a thing."

"What is it?"

"It's called phosphorescence," Master Vita explained. "Tiny creatures in the water that light up when disturbed. One of the burner scientists of old studied them, thinking that they might be linked to the moonburners."

"It would be an ideal place for Tsuki to be hidden then," Kai said.

"The scientist ultimately concluded that a chemical reaction caused the light, not magic. But there are only a few places where the phenomenon occurs. The Adesta Islands southwest of Kita are one of few such places. They're tiny, practically too small to be on the map. That must be where this is."

"We'll have to split up," Kai said. "The other scene is in the mountains. Snowy, somewhere in the north of the Akashi. We don't have time with what's going on to try to free one, then the other. Master Vita, can you work with Hiro to try to identify the other scene?"

"Of course," Master Vita said, his eyes sparkling with the challenge. "I'll have Jurou assist me."

"Did the elder say how to free Tsuki and Taiyo?" Nanase asked. "Or what happens after? Will the gods help us defeat the tengu?"

"One thing at a time," Kai said. "We don't know yet. We'll have to get there and evaluate. Hopefully, we can open the cages or prisons they're being held in."

"That's an awfully thin plan," Chiya said.

"I'm aware," Kai snapped. "But the elder wasn't there when the gods were trapped. He could only speculate about how to open the tombs. This box was the only piece of the puzzle he had. As for what happens after…your guess is as good as mine. Personally, I bet Tsuki and Taiyo will be angry about what's been done in their absence." She ignored the seishen elder's warnings resounding in the back of her mind.

Chiya's words dripped with sarcasm. "Release two trapped, angry gods and let them take their revenge against two powerful demons impersonating them. And hope we don't get…what, squished in the middle?"

Kai tried to let Chiya's words pass over her, but they sunk in anyway. The plan *was* risky. They had no idea what they were unleashing with Tsuki and Taiyo.

"I'm open to an alternate plan if anyone has one," Kai said.

Her advisors looked down at the table. Nanase examined the end of a braid; Chiya scowled at her fingernails.

"Hearing none, we will continue forward with the only plan we've got," Kai said. "And pray we don't get squished in the middle."

After the meeting concluded, Nanase and Master Vita filed out. Chiya reached for the box, as if to touch it again. She stopped herself just before her fingers brushed its smooth surface.

"Why did you give it to me?" Chiya asked.

Kai had spent the whole flight back strategizing what she would say. They said the best lies were half-truths. "The elder thought you might have some connection to it. His knowledge of your seishen, Tanu, gave him some clue. Something about your heritage…your parents."

"My parents?" Chiya said, her voice quiet.

"I'm sorry, I don't know any more. Perhaps we'll learn more when we find Tsuki."

Chiya narrowed her eyes, looking at Kai.

Kai kept her face neutral, open. Inside, her stomach twisted. She felt wretched. But her friends had been right. This wasn't the time.

"As you wish, Your Majesty," Chiya finally said.

"Can you get supplies ready for our journey?" Kai asked. "We'll need to leave in the next day or two."

Chiya nodded her head and made her exit. Her seishen Tanu trailed after her, his striped silver-and-white tail bobbing.

Hanae sat still as statue, her stare fixed on Kai.

Kai straightened her obi and sat back down, examining the swirling grains of the wooden table. "Say it," Kai said softly.

"It's because she's her, isn't it?" Hanae asked, her voice strangled. "She's my daughter."

Kai nodded, unable to meet her mother's eyes. "The box seems to respond to the true heir of Tsuki and Taiyo. It opened to Hiro. But…not to me. I'm not the true heir."

Hanae deflated, sitting back in her chair and closing her eyes for a moment.

"I'm not going to tell her," Kai said. "Not until this madness is all over."

Hanae's eyes flew open, but Kai pressed on. "I know you think it's wrong, and part of me thinks it's wrong too, but the last thing the country needs right now is a change in leadership. To have any chance of freeing the gods and defeating the tengu, we need Kita and Miina united. I can't trust Chiya with the alliance. She's too…hot-headed." Kai put her head in her hands, drawing in a shuddering sigh. "As nice as it would be to turn this whole mess over to someone else, I can't. I need to see this through."

"I don't think it's wrong. I mean…it is. But it's the right decision for right now. Sometimes you only have wrong choices, and you choose the one that's less wrong."

"You don't think…" Kai hesitated, afraid to voice her fear. "That it makes me like Airi?"

"No," Hanae said, taking Kai's hand in her own. "If I thought for one second that you made this decision for yourself, I would fight against it. But I know you do not. You make this decision for all of us. And that makes you nothing like Airi."

"I was so quick to condemn her, to call her evil. But I never knew what it was like to rule a country. To feel pressed upon by enemies at every turn. Maybe she was doing the best she could," Kai said softly.

"I never thought my sister was evil the way others did. But she isolated herself from everyone who could have guided her, helped her see right from wrong, see outside her own fears and prejudices. She was adrift in a sea of her own morality with Geisa's twisted agenda as her only compass. You will not become her. As long as you listen to the wisdom of those around you and seek aid from varied and diverse viewpoints that challenge your own, you will stay true."

Kai nodded, pondering her mother's words.

"It might matter little in the end," Kai whispered. "What if we can't free them? What if we fail?"

"Then we keep fighting. Until we can't fight anymore."

CHAPTER 25

Hiro sat on the floor eating a mealy pear with one hand, stroking Ryu's golden mane with the other.

His mind played over the journey in the forest a hundred different ways as he ate the sorry little fruit, trying to figure out what he could have done differently. To keep Kai from running off. To prevent Emi from being clawed by the tengu. To keep Daarco with them. A hundred decisions, split-second moments that spelled life or death. Luck had gotten them out of the forest alive. But they may not be so lucky next time.

And then there was the fight with Kai, their angry words, striking each other as surely as sword-blows. He knew he should have told Kai about his father's contingency plan, but he hadn't wanted to heap more trouble on her already-full plate. Now, it looked like he had been keeping it from her purposefully, which he would never have done. He prided himself on his honesty, and the fact that she thought he was capable of duplicitous double-dealing... Maybe she didn't know him. But perhaps he didn't really know her, if he had truly been driving her crazy when he was simply trying to protect her and watch her back—

"You will pet me bald," Ryu rumbled, though the tilt of his head showed he was still enjoying it.

Hiro let out a half-chuckle and withdrew his hand. He had come too close to losing Ryu to the tengu on the shore of the lake.

"I can't help but feel that I failed in the Misty Forest."

"Because you couldn't keep her safe," Ryu said.

"I know Kai wants to do everything herself, but what good will I be as a husband or a king if I can't keep her or the people she loves from being harmed?"

A female voice sounded from the doorway to his room. "If that's all you think a husband is good for, you're in for a very boring life indeed."

Hiro whirled and stood. Emi leaned against the doorjamb, bathed and dressed in a fresh uniform. Her skin glowed with health from the healing waters of the lake.

"Kai didn't pick you so you could protect her," Emi continued. "If you haven't noticed, she can look out for herself."

Hiro's face burned as he thought of his failure in the forest. "She shouldn't have to look out for herself. I should be there for her."

Emi cocked her head, examining him. "You really don't understand, do you?"

Hiro bristled. "No, as Kai was quick to inform me, I don't. Please enlighten me."

"Kai picked you to be her partner. Her equal. Don't protect her like some weak porcelain doll or put her on some pedestal to be worshipped. Stand beside her. Fight beside her. That's what she wants."

He did see Kai as an equal. He had never met a woman as fearless and inspiring as she was. But wasn't it the husband's duty to provide and protect?

"Forget whatever you're thinking," Emi said. "Whatever lessons you learned from your father, or the generals, or while bounced on your Kitan nanny's lap. You and Kai are making a new story. A new path. Equals." She held her index fingers up next to each other for effect.

A smile quirked on his face. "I pity the man who ever tries to tame you."

"A moonburner is not a horse to be broken." A feral smile played on her lips. "Nor is any woman, for that matter."

Hiro held up his hands in surrender. "Very well. Equals. I will try to remember."

"See that you do, and you'll be fine," Emi said.

"Hypothetically, if Kai and I had a heated argument about this very issue, how would you recommend I make amends?" Hiro asked.

"Groveling. Profuse apologies. Admitting your foolishness. More groveling. Honeycakes. She loves those."

"Honeycakes, eh?"

"The honeycakes are the least important part, man. Groveling, profuse apologies, admitting your foolishness." Emi ticked them off on her fingers.

"I appreciate your counsel," Hiro said with a chuckle.

"You're welcome. I imagine it won't be the last time you need my sage wisdom. Now, I came here to talk to you."

"You didn't stop by just to berate me for being a foolish man?"

"That was for fun. This is business. I'm here because Daarco is gone."

Hiro's eyebrows shot up. "What?" he said. "How do you know?"

"I went to see him," she said. "I went in the back way because I didn't want the guards hassling me."

Back way? he thought. *Emi sneaking in to see Daarco?* He filed the information away.

"He wasn't in the room. The window was open. I think he climbed out."

Hiro sat down heavily on the bed. "Gods. This doesn't look good! If he ran away, he looks even more guilty."

"You don't think he did it, do you?" Emi demanded.

"I...don't want to believe it," Hiro said. "But I hardly know him anymore. He did a lot better when life was just about killing moonburners. No offense."

"None taken," Emi said. "But I think... I think I saw something in him. In the forest. He might be able to find a new path."

"Why do you care?" Hiro asked, honestly curious. "Daarco's never been anything but an ass to you."

Emi sat down next to him, wringing her long, silver hair in an unconscious gesture. "Our whole generation—on both sides—grew up thinking that all we could ever do was kill. We were weapons with a single purpose. I lost my best friend because of that kind of thinking. Because she dared hope that her life could be about more than death."

"Maaya," Hiro said, the memory of her red blood pooling on dark stones surfacing in his mind's eye.

"Yes," Emi said, her jaw set. "We're not weapons. We're people. No one should think that all they have to live for is death. There's more in each of us. I owe it to Maaya to help others see that. Others like Daarco."

"I hope you're right," Hiro said heavily.

"We have to at least try. If we bring him back before Kai knows he's gone, it'll be like it never happened. Plus, he's a good sunburner, and we'll need all the soldiers we can get in the days to come."

Emi had carefully schooled her face for nonchalance, but he could see something there. A crack. Concern. Worry. She truly cared about him.

"I'm not sure Daarco deserves you," he said, standing up, "in fact, I know he doesn't. But if anyone can help him find his humanity again, you can. I'm in."

"Good," she said, ignoring his comment. "Do you have some water? I'll scry for him and see if we can find where he went."

He brought his washbasin over to the small table in the corner of his room and poured the pitcherful of water out.

Emi closed her eyes and pulled in moonlight. He couldn't see it, but he could feel the charge of energy in the air. She began tracing designs across the surface of the water as he watched, fascinated by the symbols she used. He had seen moonburners scry a handful of times, but the silver on the water still seemed strange and foreign. Sunburners could scry in flames, but the result was unpredictable, not nearly as effective as scrying with moonlight. The connection between the moonburner, the water, and the earth was steadier than a sunburner's tenuous control over the wild flames.

An image of Daarco appeared on the surface of the water and Hiro breathed a sigh of relief. He wasn't galloping away on horseback with Geisa at his side. In fact, the scene was a sad one. Daarco sat, hooded and alone, at a dingy bar, nursing a glass of what looked like sun whiskey. From the way his head hung, he had been there a while.

"Oh, Daarco," Hiro said softly.

"See," said Emi, tracing a squiggle of silver across the water, making the picture zoom out to show the front of the bar. "If he had freed Geisa, he would have fled, not stopped at some bar in the Meadows to get drunk."

Hiro had to admit the logic in that. "Let's go get him."

Emi assured him that it would be quicker to move through the city on foot, and so Hiro found himself stooping through the low door of the citadel crypt, stumbling in the darkness.

"You don't think we can just…walk out the front gates?" Hiro asked.

"Sure." Emi looked back at him, rolling her eyes. "If you want Kai to know exactly where we're going and why."

He followed silently, content to let her lead the way. It was fortunate this area hadn't collapsed completely from the earthquake. It must have been sturdily made.

Ryu had grudgingly agreed to stay behind after a significant amount of cajoling. He was too conspicuous. Hiro had dressed in nondescript clothing and had loaned Emi a cloak. It wouldn't be the end of the world if they were recognized as burners, but it was better if they went without notice.

As they made their way through the dark crypt, Hiro reveled in the cool air on his skin, despite the musty smell. It was still unnaturally hot outside. As they reached the corner of the crypt, Emi whispered a word while pressing on a stone statute of a sleeping woman. With a grinding noise, a piece of the wall slid back obediently.

"Afraid to give away all your secrets?" he joked.

"We have to keep some mystery," she retorted smoothly, but her cheeks had colored under the light of her moon orb. Old prejudices were hard to kill.

The dark tunnel from the crypt opened into a stone courtyard nestled in the shadow of the citadel's white walls.

Hiro fought down his growing sense of unease as he followed Emi out of the tunnel. Kyuden had never been a utopia, even in the best of times. But now, it seemed degraded, its civilization unraveling even in the few days since the earthquake.

Many of the oldest buildings had been shaken off their foundations, crumbling into the streets. People had moved the rubble to open narrow paths through the mess, but Emi and Hiro found themselves clambering over fallen stones, mortar and wood. There was no way a horse, let alone a cart, could get through the city, and they were trying to follow a once-busy road.

They passed through a market square and the scene was even more troubling. Many of the stalls sat empty and hollow, others smashed or upended. Those vendors that remained offered no more than limp vegetables or small bags of grain. Burly bodyguards bristling with steel were necessary to keep the hungry masses from even these meager offerings.

As Hiro watched, a young boy darted past one guard and managed to grab a small, sickly crab apple. Retribution was swift. The guard neatly bludgeoned the boy with a stout stick the length of his meaty forearm, and the boy crumpled to the ground like a paper doll.

Hiro halted, eying the bodyguard, who now stooped to retrieve the apple. Hiro could take him.

Emi grabbed Hiro by the arm and tried to pull him along. "We can't get involved in every sob story," she said. "The boy should have known better than to try something with the guard right there."

"He's hungry," Hiro said. "He's only a boy."

"They're all hungry," Emi said. "The kid won't last five minutes on the street if he doesn't learn to use his brain. He's probably new hungry. He'll either learn or die, whether we help him or not."

Hiro raised an eyebrow at Emi as she dropped his arm and continued up the street. Her cold regard for the boy's foolish gamble gave him new insight into her past. With a final guilty glance at the boy moaning on the cobblestones, he jogged after Emi.

As they passed through the Meadows, the normal foul smell of the area was compounded. For now there was not just human waste in the street, but bodies.

He covered his mouth, feeling the bile rise in his throat.

"Spotted fever," Emi said. "They're supposed to be burning the bodies. I'll have moonburners sent in here to move them."

As they continued walking, Hiro grew numb to the suffering around him. Hungry. Homeless. Dying. Displaced. Angry. He saw sorrow and weariness in many eyes, but in others he saw violence. Outrage. Those emotions always found an outlet.

And it seemed they had found it as they rounded a corner into a large square filled with a torch-wielding mob. A dirty man was standing on a chair at the far side of the square addressing the crowd.

Emi pulled her hood lower over her silver hair. "The bar Daarco's at is right through here."

"Let's stick to the shadows," Hiro said. He took her hand. "Stay close."

As they wove along the edges of the crowd, Hiro caught snippets of the speech.

"These natural disasters, the hunger, the heat—they are a divine judgment against us! Tsuki has turned her back on us because we have displeased her! We have abandoned our divine calling to kill the sunburners! Tsuki commanded us to destroy them and instead we lay with them!"

Hiro glanced at Emi, whose look of disgust mirrored his own. "This guy knows nothing," she growled. "He's riling everybody up for no good reason."

"People grasp for power where they can," Hiro whispered.

They passed through the crowd unmolested and slipped through the thick tavern door of the bar.

Hiro's eyes adjusted to the dim light of the tavern after a moment, but he couldn't say the same about his nose. Smells of stale beer and urine, unwashed bodies and pipe smoke assailed his senses.

"There," Emi said, seemingly unfazed by the dingy bar or its even dingier patrons.

Hiro followed her finger and saw Daarco, his cloak dark in the grimy candlelight.

They wove through the tables, boots crunching on nutshells and gods-only-knew-what-else.

They sidled up to the bar on either side of Daarco. His eyes were closed and his head hung.

Hiro placed a gentle hand on his shoulder. "Daarco."

Daarco whirled upright, laying a wicked-looking blade against Hiro's throat in a blink.

182

CHAPTER 26

Hiro held his hands aloft, not daring to move. "Easy, friend. We come in peace." The sour smell of whiskey lingered on Daarco's breath, exuded from his very pores.

Daarco's bloodshot eyes registered recognition, and he returned the knife to a sheath hidden in his sleeve. When he turned around and saw Emi, he grunted in surprise, smoothing a hand over his greasy hair.

"What're you doing here?" Daarco said.

"We're here to bring you back to the citadel before anyone realizes you're missing," Hiro said.

"Back?" Daarco said. "Why would I go back? They think I freed that moonburner general. They'll string me up."

"By disappearing, you look doubly guilty," Emi said with an exasperated sigh. "We were ready to plead your case, find out who really did it, and now you go running off, making it seem like you have something to hide."

"Nothing to hide," he said. "Just done. Besides. If I got anywhere near that general, I wouldn't have freed her. I woulda killed her."

"There's truth to that," Hiro muttered.

"What do you plan to do?" Emi asked, forging ahead. "Where will you go? You don't even have money to buy your own whiskey."

Daarco shrugged. "I've got a sword. There's always work for a man who can kill."

"Come back with us," Hiro pleaded. "Kai has a necklace that tells truth from lies. If you truly didn't free Geisa, she'll believe you."

"Even if she did believe me, what's the point? Nothing for me there. I'm a liability. The forest showed me that. Had to be rescued by women."

"The forest kicked all of our asses," Emi said. "I almost died. You don't see me slinking off."

Daarco rounded on her, his voice steely. "All I'm good at is killing moonburners. And if I can't do that, it's time for me to go." Their noses almost touched now, but Emi didn't back down. Hiro found he had his hand on the dagger at his waist.

"Just because you've never done something else doesn't mean you can't," Emi said, her voice strangely kind, considering the menace in her posture. "Doesn't mean you couldn't find something new to live for."

"I'm a soldier without a war," Daarco said. "It's better I leave."

"There's a war left to fight," Hiro said, his voice low and hard. "The war that's been waged against us for centuries, but we were too ignorant to see it. You didn't see the seishen elder, but it explained everything to us. The tengu have been pitting the sun and moonburners against each other for generations. The very reason we were at war, that we hated each other, was because of them. They're trying to destroy our world, and we're the only thing that can stop them. So they turned us against each other. The reason your father was killed by a moonburner...was because of them. Because they desired our suffering, our destruction," Hiro said. "And now they mean to finish the job. Unless we stop them."

"We were enemies," Emi said. "But only because we were too blind to see who the real enemy was. No longer."

"Help us kill the tengu," Hiro said. "If you truly believe that all you can do is kill, then you were born for this. This will be the most important battle we ever fight."

Daarco looked back and forth between Emi and Hiro. He took a deep breath. "It's true what you say? About why we fight?"

"Yes," Hiro said. "I swear it on my honor."

"You're not going to give me a choice in this, are you?"

"No," Emi said, her eyes dark. "We aren't."

Hiro downed the whiskey remaining in Daarco's glass. "Let's head back, my friend, and clear your name."

Emi threw a coin down on the bar and headed for the door. Hiro and Daarco followed her, Daarco unsteady on his feet.

As Emi pulled open the door, a cacophony washed over them.

"The crowd's getting out of control," Emi remarked, trying to wind her way through men shouting and lofting torches and weapons in the air.

The man at the front of the crowd had reached a fever pitch. "The sunburners are an abomination! If our queen will not destroy them, she is not fit to rule!"

The crowd roared in agreement, the people pumping their fists in the air, pounding their chests and makeshift shields with fists and weapons.

"Men," Emi said in disgust, but Hiro barely heard her as her comment was borne away by the sounds of the crowd.

"Outta my way," Daarco's slurred voice said from behind him. Hiro whirled around, just in time to see Daarco's fist connect with a man's jaw. The man dropped like a stone. But the damage was done. The movement had caused Daarco's hood to fall back.

"Here's a sunburner right here!" a man exclaimed. Daarco was now standing in a semi-circle of hostile men, looking in shock upon their fallen companion. The man who had shouted was thin and pale, but his hand looked strong enough as it tightened on the handle of his carving knife.

Hiro tried to push back through the crowd but couldn't make it through before Daarco, with a look of withering disgust, punched the man in the gut. The weight and power of Daarco's blow toppled the man like a tree, and he stumbled over the other fallen man, crumpling to the ground.

"Who's next?" Daarco asked, cracking his knuckles.

Hiro took advantage of the stunned silence of the crowd to leap into the opening and grab Daarco's arm. "Time to go," he said.

They plunged through the crowd as the men behind them came to life with a roar. Daarco and Hiro slipped through the press of bodies while their pursuers tangled with the masses.

Emi, who was waiting with wide eyes, took off as they reached her, elbowing her way through the crowd. She cut into an alley at the side of the square and they fled at full speed, the voices of the crowd biting at their heels. "Burner spies amongst us! Don't let them get to the citadel!"

Emi seemed to have a sixth sense for the twists and turns of the Meadows. Though the back streets all looked the same to Hiro, he could tell they were steadily approaching the white walls of the citadel.

To their left, the sounds of the roiling mass of people echoed—shouts, stomping feet, and even sporadic screams as an unfortunate bystander got in their way.

Just when Hiro thought his lungs would burst, Emi came to an abrupt stop in a doorway behind a pile of trash. Daarco stopped behind them and vomited wetly onto the cobblestones. He gasped for breath, his hands on his knees and his head hanging.

"The tunnel is past the mob," Emi said, biting her lip. "Maybe we can go over. I'm going to scout."

She shimmied up the side of the building, making handholds of the jutting pieces of brick and mortar. Daarco had righted himself and wiped his mouth, not taking his eyes from Emi's retreating form.

Emi's face peeked over the roof. "Come on," she said. "I think I can get us across."

"I think I'll stay here and let them kill me," Daarco muttered, eying the climb.

"Come on," Hiro said, pulling Daarco to the wall.

Hiro climbed up the side of the building with less agility than Emi. Daarco barely made it up, losing his footing and dangling for a precarious moment before he regained it.

Emi and Hiro reached over the roof and hauled him over the side.

The three of them lay there for a moment, panting. Emi popped up first. "Come on. No time for rest."

She led them across several uneven rooftops until they reached a point where two old buildings leaned towards each other.

Emi got a running start and leaped across the gap, stumbling to her knees. She stood and dusted herself off, motioning for them to follow.

Hiro wiped his brow and took a deep breath, following her. The gap looked farther than it was, but he made it across with room to spare.

He looked back at Daarco, who looked even more green than he had after vomiting.

"Come on," Emi said. "It's not that far."

"I don't think I can make it," he said flatly.

Hiro looked down. The street below them was filled with a roiling mass of people holding aloft torches and makeshift weapons.

"You can't go down," Hiro hissed. "It'll be just like the palace back in Kistana! Remember the jump to the cherry tree?"

"I was fifteen years younger and several stone lighter back then," Daarco said, shaking his head.

"You going to let a moonburner show you up?" Emi taunted.

Daarco growled and backed up.

Fifteen years older but just as easily goaded, Hiro thought with a smile.

Daarco ran towards the edge and leaped, but his foot slipped as he took off. He thudded against the other edge, his arms grasping at the dusty rooftop. Hiro and Emi lunged forward, grabbing his arms before he slipped over the edge. He was heavy, but they managed to pull him onto the roof.

They crossed the roof and made their way down a pile of rubble, dropping into a courtyard. In the center of the courtyard stood a fountain of a woman pouring water into the mouth of a kneeling man. It was where the passage from the crypt connected. He breathed a sigh of relief. They were safe.

They hurried back through the passageway and burst out of the crypt onto the citadel grounds.

Emi sprinted towards the front gate. The sounds of the mob were swelling outside the walls.

"Close the gates!"

CHAPTER 27

K ai had tossed and turned for hours in frustration after discovering that not only had Daarco vanished from his rooms, but Hiro was missing as well. But it seemed that she had eventually fallen asleep, for when she woke, there was moonlight streaming through the windows. Quitsu was nowhere to be found.

She crawled out of bed, feeling just as groggy as when she had laid down. How long had she slept? She padded out of her room into the hallway, looking for one of her maids. The hallway was deserted, the moon orbs dark.

Her senses fired in alarm. This was not her hallway. She was in the spirit world.

Kai's heart hammered as a scraping noise sounded down the corridor. In the pool of moonlight coming through the window at the far end of the hall, a black shadow stretched across the floor. A taloned hand curled around the corner, followed by a tall black shape.

Kai's scream caught in her throat and she fled towards the stairs, flying down them two at a time. An inhuman scream roared behind her as the tengu took up the chase, its taloned feet scratching and scrambling for purchase on the polished wood floor.

Kai burst out the front door of her quarters in a blind panic, her head whipping around, searching for a safe place. A hard hand clamped down on her face from behind and another hand pulled her backwards into the tall bushes to the left of the building. She screamed into the hand and struggled like a wild thing, all reason fleeing in her panic. Her burning, her weapons training, all of it had given way to the primal urge to free herself.

"Quiet," hissed a feminine voice. "It's me!"

Kai looked over her shoulder to the welcome sight of Hamaio. Kai relaxed and nodded in response to the woman's questioning look.

"You scared—" Kai began, but the woman hissed softly and pointed.

They both fell silent in the bushes, sinking down as low as they could, stilling their breathing. The tengu had emerged from the building and was sniffing the air with its misshapen snout. Perhaps it had once been a large cat, but now it was a twisted black thing of bone and membrane hulking on two legs, its padded paws split into ghastly toes.

It turned towards them as it continued to snuffle, its red eyes shining with a perverse intelligence. Kai held her breath, wishing she could stop her heart from beating. Its tempo droned so loud in her ears that she feared the tengu could hear the very blood pumping in her veins.

It took a step towards them and Hamaio tensed.

Another tengu across the courtyard barked, somehow communicating with its brethren. The tengu near them yowled in response, and their would-be attacker dropped onto all fours and ambled across the courtyard.

Both women let out sighs of relief.

"Come on," Hamaio whispered.

They kept to the shadows as they crept through the darkened citadel.

"There are so many of them," Kai whispered. "I thought you said the citadel was protected. That I shouldn't be able to come to the spirit world when I'm here."

"You shouldn't," Hamaio said. "The barriers between the world must be breaking down further. We have little time before they make their move."

Kai shuddered and slipped inside the familiar doors of the library behind Hamaio.

The other woman shook herself a bit and straightened. "We should be safe in here for a few moments."

"Thank you," Kai said gratefully. "You saved me from that thing."

Hamaio whirled, her porcelain face angry. "You can't keep bumbling in here. You're like a babe in the woods!"

"I know," Kai said, her face heating. She felt like a child being scolded by her mother. "I lost your charm in the lake, and I didn't make another. I didn't think I would need it here."

Hamaio huffed. "Now that you are back at the citadel, you can get something better. In the treasury is a ring made of three linked circles. One of gold, one of silver, and one of iron. If you wear it, it should prevent you from traveling over."

"It could take me hours to find it," Kai lamented. "We need to leave shortly."

"Make time. Unless you'd like to be eaten by a tengu!" the other woman said.

"Of course not." Kai sighed. "I'll find it. If...I got eaten by a tengu in the spirit world, would I die in the mortal world?"

"A burner cannot live without their spirit," Hamaio said. "No human can."

Kai nodded. It was as she suspected. "I have so many questions for you. Will you tell me how you sealed the walls between the realms?"

"It was a desperate, cobbled-together thing," Hamaio said. "The tengu had broken through the final barrier and were under the direction of their leaders, two greater tengu."

"Yukina and Hiei?"

"I see you've heard of them."

"They're the ones pretending to be Tsuki and Taiyo. They have incited war between the burners for hundreds of years."

Hamaio set her jaw. "They are very old and very powerful. They have been waiting for many thousands of years, testing the defenses of this world. They had driven us back to the castle at Yoshai, and we were fighting a desperate battle."

"Yoshai?" Kai asked.

"It was our capital," Hamaio said. "A beautiful city of courtyards and terraces. You could see all the way to the sea from its upper courtyard."

Kai furrowed her brow. Her words struck a chord somehow, as if a memory had been plucked, but only the ringing afterglow lingered in her mind. Was it the place she had seen in her fever dream?

"We linked together. Sun and moonburners, and their seishen. Through the seishen, we were able to draw the raw power of the creator.

My husband and I did the burning together, but it was intuitive… We pulled the power of the creator and wove it back into the barrier between the worlds, knitting together the hole the tengu had created. As it closed, the rest of our burners pushed the tengu back into the spirit world. We drained so much power from the earth that it scorched the land, forming what you call the Tottori. Thousands died and our city fell into the desert. Most of the burners lost their lives."

Kai grew paler and paler as Hamaio told her tale. The only way to defeat the tengu was to destroy Kyuden and everyone she had ever known? Was she willing to pay that price?

"I am sorry I do not have better news. If there was an easier way, I would gladly share it."

"It's all right," Kai said slowly.

"Perhaps because the creator has touched you, you will be able to seal the barrier without such a loss of life."

"Perhaps," Kai said, rubbing the mark on her chest. *If I knew how to use this power,* she thought. "What about the gods? The seishen elder showed us the box, the map. Surely the gods can help?"

The spirit realm reeled slightly around Kai and she stumbled, grabbing a nearby chair for support.

"Someone is trying to wake you," Hamaio said. "You should go."

The room reeled again. "What about the gods?" Kai said.

"Forget the box. It should not be used. That's why I sent it to the elder. I knew it would keep it safe and free them only when the tengu threat was neutralized."

Kai felt a stab of guilt, which was quickly overcome by a wave of nausea. She was waking. She reached out a hand to Hamaio, and then the woman was gone.

☾

Kai awoke to find Chiya in her chamber, shaking her.

"What is it?" Kai asked, unable to keep the grumpiness from her voice.

"You've got to get up. There's a mob at the gates."

"A mob?" Kai asked, her sleepy mind not comprehending.

"An angry mob. They seem to want…your head."

"An angry mob?" Kai squealed. She cleared her throat and took a deep breath to calm her frayed nerves. *I can do this. Whatever comes my way,*

I will handle it. "Let me put some clothes on."

Chiya led them to the guard-tower on the western wall. Nanase stood examining the scene, a grim expression on her face and her seishen, Iska, on her shoulder.

"What do we have here?" Kai asked, stepping forward and looking down. Thankfully, someone had had the wherewithal to close and bar the gate before the mob arrived. The citadel's walls were high and strong—no match for the axes and clubs she saw in the grubby hands below. But having a mob at her gate meant that her moonburners and guards would be stuck here, guarding the citadel, rather than out in the city helping people. This couldn't stand.

"It's more of what we've been hearing for months," Chiya said, her ponytail flapping in the breeze. "They think the natural disasters are Tsuki's wrath for our alliance and peace with the sunburners. It seems they have grown tired of complaining."

"It's madness!" Kai said. "And now we know the truth, but I cannot tell it, for fear our enemies will learn our plans. We need to stall. I need a few more weeks to free the real gods."

"You should address them," Nanase said. "We can't have this kind of discord at our gates and not say something."

"What would you have me say?" Kai asked. "It's all a trick by tengu masquerading as gods? Only the reappearance of the real gods will convince these fools of the truth."

"I don't know," Nanase said. "But underneath their anger, these people are scared. We have to try to reason with them before it turns to violence."

Kai sighed. Nanase was right. She had to try diplomacy before she sent her moonburners to disperse and probably kill her own people.

"Very well. I will try to reason with them." She looked at the roiling mob below. The people were chanting something about Kai's head. They didn't seem particularly amenable to reason. "Will you announce me, Nanase?"

Nanase stepped to the edge of the wall and sent up a shot of moonlight into the sky. "Fall silent to hear the words of the queen of Miina, Kailani Shigetsu."

The crowd quieted but for the shuffling of bodies and weapons. Sporadic curses and slurs burst forth from those bold or foolish enough to draw attention, words that drew an angry flush to Kai's face and twisted her insides.

Kai stepped forward and took a deep breath. "I know you fear for your families, your livelihoods. In this time of troubles, any sane man would fear. I understand that fear curdles into anger, and anger into hate. It is natural that your hate would fall upon the sunburners, who have been our enemy for so long."

"But your hate is misplaced. We are at war, yes. But not with the sunburners. Our great nation has had war declared upon it by a force that until now went unseen and unknown. Demons."

The crowd stirred with expressions of disbelief and outrage.

"I understand you may find it hard to believe. But if you believe in the goodness of the gods, is it so hard to believe that evil might oppose them? This evil feeds on our fears, our angers, our suffering. And it is hungry."

"We have a plan to defeat them and to right the world. But we cannot be distracted by talk of war or by mobs at our front doors. Do not play into their hands! Go home, care for your families, your neighbors. Give us the chance to fight this battle and win."

"Lies!" someone shouted.

"Sunburner whore!" another voice said.

Kai ground her teeth, looking back at Nanase and Chiya. Her anger flared. She had enough problems without these men trying to foil her plans. Her attention was needed elsewhere.

"It was a good speech," Nanase said, stepping forward behind her. "They're too far gone. The mob knows no reason."

"What would you have me do?"

"You have two choices. Let them be, or fire upon them."

The crowd rumbled, angry voices growing louder now. Someone threw a rock, which bounced harmlessly off the wall ten feet below where Kai stood.

Kai's anger boiled as she looked at her subjects, people she had bled for, that she would gladly die for. Angry at the injustice of it. Angry at the drought, the hunger, the spotted sickness. The shriveled husk that had once been the plentiful land of Miina. Her anger raged within her at what the tengu had reduced them to in so few months.

The mob was chanting now, savage words calling for Kai's head, her

193

death. But Kai didn't hear it amongst the inferno of rage within her. Somewhere that felt very far away, she knew Nanase and Chiya spoke to her in urgent tones, that Quitsu pressed against her foot to comfort her and bring her back to herself. She didn't care. What she felt was anger and sorrow at her own impotence. The need to do *something* that would make a difference.

A violent wind rose and whipped around Kai, tossing her silver hair about her face. The handprint on Kai's chest flared to life, glowing white through the fabric of her dress.

The air crackled with energy as clouds began to gather, dark and thick, filling a sky that had hung limp and dry for months.

The tenor of the mob changed from anger to fear. Venomous shouts dissolved into nervous murmurs.

Thunder rumbled across the citadel as more black clouds materialized. Kai wasn't sure what she was doing, not exactly. It was instinctive. The creator's power sang to her, called out to her. It wasn't like burning, where she pulled moonlight, or even this strange light of life, into her qi. It was more as if she spoke to the clouds themselves, to the lightning, to the raindrops in the sky.

Kai's voice rang out over the crowd, sounding foreign in her ears. "We are at war. But not for superiority of our nation. For our survival. We fight on the side of light! Against an enemy that would plunge our world into darkness. Our creator has not abandoned us. But he will not abide petty bickering! Return to your homes and ready yourself for the battle to come!"

Lightning forked across the sky, punctuating the final words of Kai's strange speech. As the afterglow of the lightning stung her retinas, the heavens opened. Rain poured from the dark clouds in sheets, the monsoon drenching the mob, snuffing their torches with a sizzle.

Shouts of awe and rejoicing sounded from below as men upturned their faces and opened their mouths to let the cool rainwater wash over them. The first rain in months.

Kai stumbled back, her rage doused by the water. She was suddenly chilled and shivering. Nanase and Chiya caught her, leading her towards the stairs, their eyes wide with wonder.

CHAPTER 28

K ai walked down the stairs of the tower into the courtyard below,
careful not to slip on the slick stone steps. She was suddenly weary
to her very bones. Though she had just awoken, she needed rest.

Hiro and Emi were waiting in the muddy courtyard, their faces
impassive. Daarco slouched behind them, refusing to make eye contact.
Water dripped down his crooked nose.

"It looks like you all have a story to tell," Kai remarked, blinking the
water from her eyes.

"Yes, though not such a story as you," Hiro said, taking her hands in
his own. His shook slightly, but not from the cold. She could see the
apology written across his face. Her heart softened. So he had gone to
retrieve Daarco. To bring him back.

"Let's get you inside," Hiro said. "Then we need to plead Daarco's
case to you. Emi and I believe he is innocent."

"Innocent men don't run," Kai said.

"I knew this was pointless," Daarco said, turning to go, his boots
squelching in the mud.

"No." Emi pointed at him. "You stay."

And surprisingly enough, he did, turning back around with a glower.

"I know he slipped his guards," Emi said, "but he returned. If he was
guilty, would he have come back?"

"I'm not sure if it speaks to his innocence or his stupidity," Kai grumbled. "But tell me. Do you vouch for him? Are you certain he did not free Geisa?"

"Yes," Hiro and Emi said.

"Let's see if you're right." Kai stepped before Daarco. She examined him, remembering the twisted hatred in his face the night of their first meeting when he had bound her hands and savagely kicked her. Was this really the best they could do for allies?

"Did you free Geisa?" she asked, weariness filling her voice.

"No," he said.

Her necklace lay cool on her slick chest. Truth.

"Do you still hate all moonburners?" she asked.

He was silent for a moment. His eyes flicked to Emi, an almost imperceptible movement.

"Not all," he said. Truth.

"Will you try to kill me again?"

"No," he said. Truth.

"Why did you return?" she asked.

His cheeks colored. "I'm just here to kill tengu." His eyes flicked to Emi again.

Her necklace warmed on her chest, but not with the full burn of a lie. A half-truth then. Well. His secret was safe with her. For the time being.

"If you're here to kill tengu," Kai said, "you've come to the right place."

☾

A hot bath and a plate of food awaited Kai when she returned to her room. The sight of it nearly made her weep for joy. She snagged a hot fluffy bun stuffed with spiced chicken and took a bite, savoring the flavors that played across her tongue.

Next to the tray of food lay a soft emerald cloth bearing a ring—three interlocking circles of sparkling metal. Kai had dispatched a servant on her way up to the citadel walls with Chiya, and it looked like the woman had been able to find it amongst the jumble of the treasury. Kai slipped it on, praying that the ring truly had the power to keep her in the mortal world while she slept. She didn't need another run-in with the spirit world or its tengu inhabitants. What she needed was a good night's sleep.

Kai's servants had drawn the thick curtains and her moon orbs had been dimmed, leaving her room cast in maudlin shadows. She undressed and stepped into the steaming bath water lightly scented with orange blossoms. The temperature was perfect. As soon as she settled on the tub's porcelain bottom, the heat of the water began to soothe her weary body and soul. The chill of the rain leeched out of her, replaced with pleasant warmth.

Kai tried to slow her racing mind, pulling back the many threads of herself into a coherent whole. She felt as if she was stretched thin, a piece leather over a tanner's tool. Another inch might break her. The questions swirled in her mind, whipped about by the wind of her worries. What was she becoming? She couldn't moonburn anymore—but she could access the creator's light instead. But that didn't explain how she'd done what she had done with the rain and the clouds. And in the Misty Forest, when the trees attacked. She touched the handprint on her chest, her nerves jangling. She remembered only glimpses of what she had seen when she lay dying from spotted fever. She needed to understand how to use these powers if she was going to defeat the tengu or seal the barrier between the worlds.

She closed her eyes and tried to remember, to draw the memories into her mind's eye. A tan castle. A view of the sea. Talk of guardians. Of the tengu. And falling. Anything beyond those memories seemed too far out of reach.

She splashed the surface of the water in frustration, huffing.

"What did the bath do to you?"

She turned towards the door and found Hiro standing there, his deep green eyes shining in the low light. His tone was friendly, but he stood stiffly. Warily.

"Spying on me in my bath?" she asked.

"Just jealous. I need one myself," he said, his boots squelching on the floor. He was still soaked through from the monsoon that had doused them at the citadel wall.

"Hand me that towel," she said. "I'll pour another bath for you. You're going to catch a cold in those wet clothes."

He walked to the chair that sat against the wall of the bathing chamber and picked up the fluffy white towel. "This towel?" he said, holding it just out of reach, a smile cracking across his face.

"Give it to me, you scoundrel," Kai said, grabbing at it, patently aware that the water of the bath left little to the imagination.

Hiro relented and gave it to her, turning his back as she stepped out of the bath.

Kai toweled herself dry and retrieved a colorful silken robe from the corner of her dressing screen. When she emerged, Hiro had removed his boots and was stripping off his sodden shirt.

She swallowed thickly, thoughts of the creator and tengu slipping from her mind like water down a drain. The firm muscles of Hiro's back were slick from the rain, and his wet pants hung low across his hips and taut stomach as he turned.

Their eyes locked and she forgot to breathe, molten energy crackling between them. "Hiro," she said huskily, hardly recognizing her own voice. "I'm sorry."

"I'm sorry too." In two steps he crossed the distance between them, enveloping her in his arms.

She shivered as he kissed her, simultaneously flushed with the heat of her own body and chilled by the rain on his skin.

He tangled his fingers in her wet hair and her head arched back, her mouth eager for more of him, her body pressing to his with a will of its own.

Her hands traced the hard planes of his arms, the curve at the small of his back, and she found them slipping around to the front, fumbling with the clasp of his belt.

"Wait," he gasped, pulling away from her kiss, shuddering under her touch.

But Kai had waited long enough. Nothing was certain anymore. Not her future, her kingdom, not even their very existence. If their world was plunged into darkness tomorrow, she was damn well going to experience its joys tonight.

"No more waiting," she said, tracing her fingers through his flaxen hair, down his temple, lingering on the sweet flesh of his lips.

"Are you sure?" His eyes smoldered as he held himself back from her, searching her face for her honest answer.

Kai was struck by how profoundly she had come to rely on Hiro, to trust him. He was the firm foundation among the storm of circumstance raging around her. But tonight, he was the storm that raged inside her. And she wanted nothing so much as to be lost.

"Yes," she said, standing on her tiptoes and crushing his lips with a kiss.

Hiro swung her up into his arms as effortlessly as if he were lifting a doll. He strode to the bed and placed her gently upon it, settling down next to her, moving the trailing heat of his kisses past her ear and down her neck. As his calloused hand stroked up her leg and found the opening of her robe, her thoughts dissolved completely, giving way to the enveloping pleasure of his body against hers, his hands tracing paths of fire across her skin.

They needed no words as the last line between them dissolved, demolished by their mutual need for comfort, for connection, to remember the beauty of love and life and what they fought for. Whatever came in the morning, for one night at least, they would know each other fully.

☾

Hiro ran his hand though Kai's silver hair as they lay tangled in each other's arms.

"What are you smiling about?" he asked, running a finger across her freckled cheek. Kai couldn't keep the grin off her face.

"I wish I could freeze this moment." Kai sighed. "For the first time in weeks, I don't feel completely overwhelmed." Her smile slipped as she thought of the angry mob that had swarmed her gates only hours ago.

"You're losing it," cried Hiro. "Don't think about it! I thought you were freezing the moment!"

She laughed. "I'm hopeless."

Hiro's stomach rumbled and he swung out of bed, walking to the table. "If the moment is gone, then I'm going to get something to eat. I'm starving."

Kai's cheeks flushed as she took in his naked form. He was the first naked man she had seen…in the flesh. Paintings and such didn't count. Although Hiro looked like he could have stepped right out of a painting, all tan skin and lean muscle.

He slipped back into the bed with a plate of food in one hand and a bottle of sake and two cups clasped in the other.

"You were peeking," he said as he set them down on the bedside table. He lifted up the cover to take in Kai's own naked body.

"Hey," she cried.

"If I'm to marry you, it's only fair to know what I'm getting into," he said with a laugh.

"I think you just found out," she said, suddenly unsure. The experience had been wonderful for her, but had Hiro enjoyed it as much as she had?

"If I wake up with you beside me every morning, I will count myself the luckiest man in the world," he said, kissing her gently. Hiro reclined on the pillows and grabbed one of the cold buns off his plate, popping it in his mouth.

She grabbed the indigo bottle of sake and poured them each a cup. "Here's to hoping there's still food to cook a month from now," she said.

"No," Hiro said, his green eyes locked on hers. "Here's to the best queen in a century, and the smartest and most determined woman I know."

The words washed over her, soaking into her weary soul. Her lip started to quiver, and before she could stop herself, tears welled in her eyes.

"Oh boy," Hiro said, setting down his cup and pulling her close. "What'd I say? What's wrong?"

Kai wiped her eyes, trying to stop the flow. "Sometimes I don't feel like any of those things. This is so big. How can I have the fate of Miina, of the very world, on my shoulders? I don't think I'm even supposed to be queen if I can't moonburn. And then there's Chiya…"

Hiro looked at her, sympathy written across his face. "We know this light is extremely powerful. More powerful than burning." He reached out and touched the scar on her chest gingerly. "I still think it's a gift."

"Some gift! I don't know how to use it! I can't sleep without waking up in the spirit world and almost being devoured by tengu!"

"Yes, but you will figure out how to use it. How to master it. And this Hamaio has been helpful, right? Given you valuable information?"

"I suppose," Kai said. "Mostly she's helped me not get killed."

"Think about it. You know more about the tengu and the breakdown of the seals between the worlds because of this. Any insight is valuable."

"I don't like having something inside of me that I can't control," Kai admitted.

"I understand," he said. "But some of the best parts of life are the parts we don't control. Things will work out how they're supposed to."

"I don't know how you can be so damn optimistic," she said. "But I guess I'll take it."

"You're not alone in any of this. I'm right beside you. And so are Emi, and Nanase, and Chiya, and all the rest. Whatever you ask of us, we'll be there."

Beside her. She liked the sound of that.

Kai stroked his face, his stubble scratchy on her palm. "I couldn't do this without you."

"You won't have to," he said. And then he kissed her again, the taste of sake sweet on his lips, and thoughts of war and demons fled from her mind.

CHAPTER 29

Kai woke that morning to a brief moment of bliss. Snuggled under her warm goosedown covers, Hiro's serene face on the pillow next to her, everything felt right.

Hiro stirred next to her, brushing away strands of golden hair. "Hello, lovely," he said, reaching out to stroke her cheek with his thumb.

She smiled and looked at him, trying to memorize the contours of the moment. "Hello," she said. "Back to reality."

"Not yet," he grumbled, wrapping his arms around her and pulling her to his warm body. As his lips met hers, the door to her bedchamber burst open. Ryu and Quitsu bounded across the room and onto the bed. The frame creaked as Ryu landed by their feet.

"Woah!" Kai exclaimed.

"Rise and shine, lovebirds," Quitsu said, bouncing a little.

They laughed, and Hiro ruffled Ryu's mane. "Feeling neglected?"

"I don't value private time with this one," Ryu said, tossing his head towards Quitsu, "as much as you do with that one."

"I'm a kind and gentle lover!" Quitsu said, waving his bushy tail in Ryu's face.

Ryu snarled at him and Quitsu jumped away, chuffing in laughter.

"This place is going to the seishen," Hiro said, throwing back the covers. "We're up."

Kai had asked her allies to meet in the library at the first bell to discuss their travel plans. Hiro went back to his room to change and Kai dressed in a simple white tunic and gray leggings. Quitsu sat on the table and looked at her with what could only be described as a smirk on his face.

"What?" she finally said, trying to keep the smile from playing across her face. "Am I not entitled to one minute of happiness before I'm killed by tengu and the world as we know it ends?"

"Just one minute?" he asked. "I would have expected better from Hiro."

"Quitsu!" she said with a scandalized laugh.

He cackled as he jumped off the table and trotted out the door.

Kai reached the library a few minutes early. Master Vita was sitting at the large table, studying the illustrated scroll.

She kissed the top of his head and sat down. "I've hardly gotten a moment to see you," she said, feeling guilty.

"Don't trouble yourself, my dear. You're busy running a country and saving the world. I understand that you don't have time to visit like you did when you were a novice," he said. "Besides, your mother visits all the time. And having her back is a better gift than I could ever hope for." Master Vita had been Kai's mother's tutor when she was a young princess at the citadel. He had helped her fake her own death and escape with Kai's father. Kai knew Master Vita considered Hanae a daughter.

"I know. We both thought we had lost her," Kai said. "And I thought I was going to lose you," she added softly. Since Kai's mother had returned, she had been able to treat Master Vita's consumption. He wasn't the picture of health, but he was no longer living on borrowed time.

"We do have much to be fortunate for," Master Vita said.

Kai nodded and was surprised to find she agreed. At times, her situation felt hopeless, but she was still surrounded by people she loved and who loved her. They could do this.

"Did someone say, 'fortunate'?" a voice called from the end of the library. "Because it's fortunate your two best moonburners are back to bail you out!"

Two women in moonburner blues strode into the library, their silver hair glinting in the moon orb light. "Stela! Leilu!" Kai cried, leaping up to embrace them both. "What are you doing here?"

"You didn't think we would miss all the excitement?" Stela asked, her striking eyes glittering.

"Demons to kill? Sign me up," Leilu said.

"I'm glad you're here," Kai said. "But...I don't understand." Stela and Leilu had been assigned to the palace in Kistana as the Miinan ambassadors to Kita. While Kai was happy to see them, she hadn't called them back.

Stela grinned. "Nanase contacted us and asked us to return. She said you needed some help for your...secret mission." She arched an eyebrow. "And she can't spare any burners from the citadel with the spotted fever in the city."

Kai squeezed Stela's and Leilu's hands. "It's so good to have you home."

"It's good to be home!" Leilu said. "We've missed so much. Demons. Lost gods. Earthquakes. And...we hear you're engaged? Does he know that if he hurts you, he'll have a long line of moonburners waiting to kill him?"

"Trust me, he knows," Hiro said, striding in with Ryu at his side. He hugged Stela and Leilu, winking at Kai over their shoulders.

Emi and Daarco arrived next, Emi greeting Stela and Leilu with hugs and squeals.

"Is this a meeting or a slumber party?" Daarco remarked to Hiro.

"Who's your surly friend?" Leilu asked, linking her arm with Emi's.

Emi made the introductions, and the rest of their group arrived. Hanae, Nanase, Chiya, Jurou. Colum strode in last to the questioning looks of the others.

"I asked him to come," Kai said. "He was the only one who didn't almost die on the last mission. He's a part of this if he's willing."

"As long as you're still paying, Queenie," he said, flipping the coin he always played with.

"I'm paying," she said.

"Are we getting paid now?" Stela asked, laughing as Kai rolled her eyes.

☾

They filled the chairs surrounding the huge table and talked through the details. Kai and Hiro would lead the two missions. Hiro to the north to find Taiyo, Kai to the south to Tsuki's rescue.

On Hiro's team was Daarco, Emi, Stela and Leilu. Chiya, Colum and Jurou would accompany Kai.

"You need at least one sunburner with you during the day in case the tengu attack in the light," Jurou had argued. "Unless you want to take Daarco on your team."

Kai had looked skeptically at Jurou's thin, bookish form, and then glanced to Daarco. She didn't like either option. Perhaps she didn't need a sunburner since she could use her new powers in day or night.

"You wouldn't deprive a historian of a chance to see history in the making, would you?" Jurou had finally said, and Kai relented. Colum had surprised her after all. Perhaps Jurou would prove helpful.

The teams would leave at sunup, as soon as Nanase gathered their provisions and weapons.

When Kai and Quitsu walked into the armory after dinner to retrieve their supplies, Stela and Leilu greeted them swathed in thick fur coats.

"Is it too late to switch to the tropical island expedition?" Leilu asked ruefully, her face framed by the fur trim of her hood.

Kai laughed and pulled Leilu's huge form into a hug. "You're a moonburner, remember? Every night can be a tropical beach for you. Keep yourself wrapped in warm air."

"What about the days?" Leilu pouted.

"You tell Hiro and Daarco to take good care of you during the days, and you take care of them at night. Everyone comes home with all their fingers and toes, all right?"

"I have to say"—Stela lowered her voice, taking her massive coat off—"I am curious to learn more about Emi's fellow." She nodded her head towards Daarco, who was examining his own furs with a scowl.

"Keep an eye on him," Kai said. "I think Emi will keep him in line...but he's unpredictable. Just make sure he remembers that the tengu are the enemies, not us."

When the rest of the teams arrived, Nanase went over the weapons, supplies, and food that she had gathered for their expeditions. Master Vita had come through on his research and had located precise coordinates for both groups. Hiro's team was heading to the high northeast pass of the Akashi Mountains. Kai's team would fly over the Tottori to the southwestern shore of Kita.

Kai approached Nanase. "Thank you for getting all of this ready so quickly. You've given us every chance. It's up to us to take it from here."

Nanase turned her intense hawk's gaze on Kai. "Remember your training, listen to your gut, and you will be fine," she said.

"Take care of my city while I'm gone," Kai said. "And my people."

"I'll do my best," Nanase said.

"And that will be enough," Kai said. "I trust your judgment. Make the hard calls if you need to."

Nanase nodded, and Kai knew she understood. The decision to use moonburners and citadel forces against Kyuden citizens was a heavy one. Kai hoped it didn't come to that, but if it did, she knew that Nanase would use the appropriate amount of force. She felt a moment of profound appreciation for the other woman. She left her country in good hands.

As Nanase turned to distribute the rest of the supplies, Hiro slipped his hand into Kai's, pulling her to the side of the room. "I feel like we were just here," he joked.

"Let's hope this mission goes better than the last," she said.

"We got the information we needed and everyone came home alive. It could've been worse."

"True," she said, linking her arms around his waist and laying her head on his broad chest for a moment. "Be safe. Don't take unnecessary risks."

"Don't be a hero?" he asked, stroking her hair.

"Exactly," she said. He looked down at her, his vibrant green eyes roving over her face, as if he was trying to memorize what he saw. She pushed down the lump in her throat that threatened to choke her. This wouldn't be the last time she saw Hiro. This wasn't where their story ended.

"I love you, Kailani Shigetsu," he said, kissing her gently. She let her world tilt for a moment in his embrace, breathing in the faint taste of mint on his lips, the spicy smell of leather and soap. And then, she broke off the kiss, pulling herself back to the task at hand.

"I love you too," she whispered.

"We'll see each other before we know it."

"Promise?"

"Promise," he said, taking her face in his hand and tracing his thumb across her cheek.

"Well, I guess…that's it," she said, pulling back with more than a little regret. "Time to go."

"You've got to give a speech," Hiro said.

"A speech?"

"Motivational. Rally the troops."

She sighed. The constant expected speeches were one of her least favorite parts of being a monarch. "Honestly," she said, "who has inspirational words ready at a moment's notice?"

"I'm confident you'll think of something," he said.

She harrumphed but turned to face the rest of the room.

"Listen up," Kai said, raising her voice. The others quieted down immediately.

"We do this to restore balance to this world. To free allies who will help rid our world of an evil that tries to destroy us. The tengu won't go down without a fight. Expect attacks. Stay on your guard, trust each other, and we will see this done. I can think of no group of people who I would rather have at my side and trust on the other side of the world than you all." Her voice wavered. "Come back safe, because you're all going to have to be in the wedding!"

Stela and Leilu whooped, and a ripple of laughter passed through her friends.

"Let's kick some tengu ass," Emi said.

INTERLUDE

Geisa sat unmoving. The pitiful fire before her had long since died away. Outside the cave in which she sat, the northern sun shone weakly, barely warming the frigid landscape. The cave stank from the fetid breath and musk of her creation, which sat stupefied across from her. Before she had smeared the mark on its face and called forth the dark magic of the tengu, it had been an ice bear, a majestic creature with thick snowy fur and sharp ebony eyes. The creature had fought until the end as the dark tendrils twisted into its flesh, transforming it from a free creature into this sad automaton.

Geisa used to love animals. As a child, she had swum every day with the iridescent fishes in the cove behind her house, diving in the clear water for crabs or oysters. When her seishen had arrived, a beautiful silver otter, they had frolicked in the waves, splashing through the surf and swimming out to the smaller islands to sleep the afternoons away in the shade of leafy palm trees.

She shoved the memory down, carefully replacing it in the mental box where she kept all her thoughts of her seishen. They were too painful to be remembered but too formative to be forgotten. She wasn't sure how the memory had come free; she was normally so careful with her mental discipline. She had to be. The memory of the happy times always led to the blackest moment of her life—when her seishen had been killed, slaughtered in that hell-hole beneath the sunburner palace. That day she had lost her soul. She should have sacrificed her pride, her body, her sanity. Those unimportant trivialities she had been clinging to.

Anything to save her soul.

A lump grew in her throat and a tear froze in the corner of her eye. She focused on the discomfort of it, the ice crystal tugging at her eyelash, scraping the lid. When had she last let a tear fall? Years. Not even for Airi. She was unraveling. She could sense somehow that the glue that had held the pieces of her together was melting away. So she focused on the remaining task before her.

She had already been waiting twenty-four hours, but had to stay until the fool sunburner prince and his band of misfits made their bumbling attempt to free Taiyo. It could be days more. At least once the moon rose again, she could burn for warmth.

She had been cautioned to wait, to let the burners release Taiyo of their own free will. But Geisa knew that with the right motivation, she could mold a will to her own. She was tired of waiting. Tired of careful political maneuvering, of being used, of sitting in cells, in caves. She was ready to burn this world to the ground—every face, every bit she recognized—until there was nothing but oblivion. She eyed her twisted tengu, waiting glassy-eyed for her instructions. She wasn't a safe pet anymore. She had gone feral.

"Bear," she called, her eyes gleaming in the pale light of the cave mouth. "Go find Prince Hiro. He will land below the pass. Bring him here to me, and we will use his blood to free his precious god."

CHAPTER 30

After two days of flying, Kai caught her first glimpse of the Adesta Islands. She sighed with relief. Her legs and back ached from the hours in the saddle, and her koumori's movements were sluggish beneath her.

Lights clustered on the north side of the largest island, evidence of the island's small fishing hamlet. They landed their koumori on the island's southern beach.

With rubbery legs, Kai walked down to the shore, where the waves washed up on the beach. Quitsu trailed behind her.

"I've never seen the ocean," she whispered into a cool breeze that tousled her hair and caressed her skin.

"Me either," Quitsu said, similarly awed.

The wind brought new smells—salt from the sea, seaweed washed onto the shore and dried in the sun. The sand beneath her boots was unlike anything she had ever felt—slippery, yet firm. The waves crashed into the beach in a rhythmic pattern that soothed her spirit and reminded her of her earliest lessons in moonburning. She knelt down and let a wave lap over her hand, burying her fingers in the cold, wet sand.

Colum joined her, looking out at the ocean, gray in the faint morning light. The other islands were shadows in the distance.

Colum's curly hair rustled in the breeze, and when he turned to Kai, there was a gleam in his eyes. There was a calm about him Kai had never seen before. As if the mask he wore had been washed away by the salt air. "I forgot how much I missed it," he said.

"It's incredible," Kai said. "I never knew what I was missing." She laughed ruefully. "Is this close to where you grew up?"

Colum pointed southwest. "A few days sailing that direction will get you there," he said.

"You should go visit," Kai said. "After all of this is done."

Colum was silent for a moment before he said, "This is your goddess's domain too."

"The ocean?" Kai asked. "I hadn't thought about it."

"It is," Colum said. "My people believe that Tsuki rules the waves, the tides. Taiyo rules the land, but Tsuki the sea. It makes sense that we'll find her here."

"I hope we do," Kai said.

They stared into the crashing waves for a time before Kai reluctantly turned and trudged up the beach to join the others.

☾

Chiya and Jurou set off at dawn to scout the neighboring islands, looking for the beach from the vision.

It took them less than an hour to find it.

"We didn't find Tsuki," Chiya said, springing off her koumori, "but we did find the beach where the vision begins. In the image, the viewer gets into a boat and rows towards the next island. So we figured we should start our search on that next island."

"Sounds good," Colum said, approaching from the water's edge. A strange, red-shelled creature squirmed in his hand, and a bag looped around his shoulder bulged with more.

"What is that?" Kai wrinkled her nose, bending over and looking at the creature. It snapped at her with a sharp pincer.

"Crab," Colum said, smacking his lips. "Tastes amazing roasted with butter."

Kai eyed the creature skeptically. "I might have to take your word for it," she said.

☾

They packed up camp quickly and headed for the next island, landing on its northern beach.

"See that little blue boat?" Chiya pointed across the channel to the next island.

Kai shielded her eyes from the sun and squinted. "Yes, I can just make it out."

"It's the boat from the vision. I can't believe it's really here."

"Good work, Chiya," Kai said, pondering the right time to tell Chiya the other part of her role. Why the box had only worked when held in her hand. The part where they needed her blood to open Tsuki's prison.

"Where should we look?" Kai mused out loud.

"Everywhere," Jurou said, wringing his hands in excitement.

Kai stifled a smile. He reminded her so much of Master Vita. His excitement for their adventure seemed undampened by the terrible future that would face them if they failed.

"Let's fan out," Kai said. "Each pick a path and walk it from one side of the island to the other. It's not a big place; we should find her before too long."

"What're we lookin' for, Queenie?" Colum asked, his hat low over his eyes.

"You'll know it when you see it. Quitsu, Tanu," Kai called, before the seishen had a chance to scamper off. "See if there are any animals on the island you can talk to. Ask about anything out of place. Buildings, sculptures…anything manmade, really."

"On it," Quitsu said and was gone with a flash of white. With a nod from Chiya, Tanu followed.

Kai walked through the island's lush foliage, unable to stop herself from gawking at the island's vibrant flowers, tiny cerulean frogs, and giant palm fronds. Her sense of wonder buoyed her spirits for a time until she emerged from the green center of the island onto the southern beach, where the rest of the group waited.

"Anything?" Kai asked.

They shook their heads. Kai took a swig of water from her canteen, wiping sweat from her brow. The heat of the midday sun was stifling despite the breeze that ruffled her hair. The air felt heavier here, more tangible.

"I found fresh water," Colum said. "So we won't die of thirst."

"That's something," Kai said. "Let's do one more pass before we rest.

When the moon comes up we can scry for her."

Their second search was as fruitless as the first. There was no sign that humans or tengu had ever been on the island, let alone buried a hidden goddess waiting to be set free.

Despite the setback, Colum's bounty from the sea raised their spirits at dinner. He roasted lemon-yellow fish on sticks over the fire and dropped the hard-shelled crabs right into the flames to crackle and warm.

They laughed at each other as they tried to break into the shells, squirting hot juices down their fronts. The flavor of the meat was salty and rich despite the creatures' tough exterior. Jurou examined the crustaceans with a puzzled expression before discovering the perfect way to twist the joints to be rewarded with a whole delectable piece of meat.

They fed the bonfire with dried palm fronds, and the sweet hazy smoke soothed Kai's restless mind. She reclined on her elbows, her belly full and happy. Colum produced a small flask of sun whiskey, and they passed it from hand to hand.

The warmth of the fire mingled with the cool salt air, and for a time, Kai forgot her troubles.

When the fire had died down to embers, Kai and Chiya walked down to the ocean to scry for the goddess. Kai scooped sea water into a shallow wooden bowl and handed it to Chiya. "Why don't you do the honors?" She wasn't quite ready to disclose to Chiya that she couldn't moonburn.

Chiya traced the symbols on the surface of the water, waiting for the water to reveal its prize.

Nothing appeared. It shimmered, as if trying to show something, but it stayed murky and dark.

"Crap," Kai said.

"Maybe it's the salt water?" Chiya ventured.

Kai hadn't thought of that.

They dumped the seawater and Chiya poured fresh water from her canteen into the bowl. They tried again. Nothing.

They walked back to the fire and sat down on the sand, dejected.

"Nothing," Kai told the rest.

Quitsu and Tanu emerged from the forest, revealed by the glow of the fire.

"We spoke with some wild koumidi who live here," Quitsu said. "They've never seen any sign of man on the island."

"We have to find her," Jurou said with a strange fervor, firelight glinting in his eyes. "We must have missed something."

Kai massaged the bridge of her nose, trying to think of what to try next.

"Sometimes it's best to start at the beginning," Colum said.

"What do you mean?" Kai asked.

"The box. A detail we've missed."

"We didn't bring it," Jurou said. "Kai made us leave it behind."

She recoiled slightly at the weight of his accusation but pushed down her frustration. After the seishen elder's warning, she had been adamant about leaving the box in the safety of the treasury. Jurou had argued long and hard that they should bring it with them.

"Queenie was right not to bring it," Colum said. "Who knows what could happen to it out here. Besides. We don't need it. We've all seen the image. Use your memories."

"Eyewitness recollection is notoriously faulty," Jurou grumbled.

"It can't hurt," Kai said. "We aren't going anywhere until we figure this out. Chiya, why don't you tell us what you remember?" Perhaps Chiya's connection as Tsuki's true heir would give her some edge—some ability to see what the rest of them had missed.

Chiya sighed but recited the vision, including every image in painstaking detail. "It ends with rowing the boat to this island. We know it's this island. I recognize it. Even the boat is right over there," she said, pointing to the other island across the dark stretch of water.

"Did you ever get to this island?" Colum asked, looking thoughtful. "In the vision. You didn't reach it, did you?"

"No," Chiya said. "It cut out right before the viewer gets here. With the phosphorescence."

"We've assumed that Tsuki is on this island. But what if she isn't?" Colum asked.

Kai's mind whirled. "Tsuki is connected to the sea. You think...she's underwater?"

"Why not?" Jurou chimed in, his excitement growing. "It's the perfect place to hide her. No one would happen upon her. And it's not like she has to breathe. She's a goddess."

"The phosphorescence," Chiya said. "In the vision. Maybe...I don't think it led across the whole stretch of water. What if it's a marker?"

"Let's get a koumori and check it out," Kai said.

"Aren't we getting ahead of ourselves?" Colum asked. "If she's truly underwater, how in the gods' names are we going to free her?"

"One problem at a time," Kai said. "We find her first. Then we can worry about how we free her."

Kai walked into the trees and whistled for the koumori. One of the females swept down onto the soft sand. Kai made quick work of harnessing her up and hopped on.

As soon as she was airborne, Kai saw what they had been missing. Of course Tsuki would reveal herself at night. The phosphorescence stood out below Kai in stark contrast to the dark waters of the ocean. A circle of shimmering white light pulsed towards a central point.

A veritable bullseye showing them their target.

CHAPTER 31

The flight to the Akashi Mountains was long and dark. As they neared the mountains, the cool air of the foothills washed over them, a relief after the hot and sticky city night. But as they traveled farther and higher into the mountains, Hiro began to shiver.

He let out a teeth-chattering sigh of relief when the two peaks came into view. They cut a forbidding figure in the moonlight—guarding the pass with twin faces of jagged rock and ice. Hiro directed his koumori to land near the top of the pass, but it refused, fighting his commands and twisting at the reins. With a grunt of frustration, he allowed it to sweep down and land on a flat spot below the two peaks.

The others landed around him, dismounting and rifling through their packs to pull out hats, gloves, and coats. One of the moonburners wrapped him in heat and he sighed as the tension in his body unraveled.

"Thank you," he said.

"You're very welcome," Stela said.

Hiro unstrapped Ryu from the golden eagle harness and his seishen leaped to the ground, letting out a huge teeth-baring yawn.

"We're headed up between those peaks." He pointed. The rugged crags looked even more imposing from below, the way up more treacherous. "It's going to be tough going, but we'll take it nice and slow. Let me know if you need a break. Now let's eat a little something and get moving."

They crouched in the snow, pulling out packets of dried meat and cheese. Everything was cold and hard; Hiro had to let a bite thaw in his mouth before he could chew it. He tried not to think of the idyllic tropical island from Chiya's half of the box.

When they were finished, they took out the rest of their gear, proceeding with much trial and error to strap sets of sharp spikes onto their boots.

"What's all this stuff for?" Leilu muttered, examining a fine-pointed axe that Nanase had insisted they would need.

"I reckon we're going to find out," Hiro said.

The air was thin; Hiro's team couldn't move for more than thirty minutes before resting. Hiro pushed his frustration down and concentrated on setting one foot in front of the other. He thanked Taiyo that the sky was clear and that they didn't have snow or bad weather to contend with. This was tough enough. They walked in silence. No one had extra breath left for talking.

As the sun rose, the landscape changed dramatically. Hiro and Daarco took over the job of warming their group, keeping protective layers of heat wrapped around each of the moonburners as they moved. The sun shone powerfully against the white snow, turning the landscape into a blinding mirror.

☾

The day passed at a glacial pace. Just after the sun set, Hiro's team reached a cluster of boulders. The stark gray monoliths were the most defensible position he'd seen all day and would shield them from the wind.

"Let's make camp here," he said, resting his hands on his knees to catch his breath.

The group trailed in, dropping packs and collapsing in the snow. No one moved for a few moments, relishing the brief reprieve for heaving lungs and aching legs. Only Ryu seemed unbothered by the day's exertions.

"Emi," Hiro called. "Will you get a fire going and start cooking some food?"

"Why me?" Emi snorted. "Because I'm a woman and belong in the kitchen?"

Hiro rolled his eyes. "No, because you're a moonburner, and you have most of the food in your pack."

"I don't know," Emi said. "Still seems a little sexist."

"I'll help you," Daarco growled, getting up with a groan and dusting the snow from his pants.

Hiro raised an eyebrow but said nothing.

"What would you like us to do?" Stela asked.

"Gather some snow to boil for water," Hiro said. "I'll work on setting up the tent."

"Snow?" Leilu asked, hands on her hips. "You sure we'll be able to find any?"

Hiro stifled a sigh. He supposed sarcasm was a good sign. He would need to worry when they lost their spirit entirely.

Despite her comment, Leilu walked over and helped Hiro set up the tent.

"Will you hand me that stake?" Hiro asked. "Leilu?"

She started, looking at him, mouth open. "Look," she said, pointing up the mountain.

Up the darkened face of the snowy slope, above where the two peaks touched the sky, danced the ribbon of light the box had shown them. It undulated and flickered in shades of green woven with streaks of indigo and gold.

"It's beautiful," Emi breathed. They all stared, eyes wide like children at their first solstice festival.

"Taiyo is up there," Hiro said, a sureness settling into his bones.

"And it looks like he wants to be found," Leilu said.

They ate quickly and in silence, methodically chewing hard slices of dried meat and stale crackers before washing them down with metallic-tasting snow-melt. They collapsed into their bedrolls minutes later. Hiro heard snores before he could even assign Stela the first watch.

Though Hiro's body was exhausted from the demands of the day, he couldn't quiet his mind enough to sink into sleep. It seemed he was not the only one. He heard Emi's whispered voice.

"Are you glad you came?" she asked Daarco, whose bedroll lay next to hers under the low tent.

"When I'm hours into trudging up a blinding, icy hill, I begin to doubt," Daarco said quietly with a low chuckle. "But yes. Hiro's had my back since we were kids. I owe him the same."

"Loyalty," she said. "It's a good trait. But it can be a shackle. Do you feel disloyal because you are allying yourself with moonburners?"

Pause. "Yes," Daarco said quietly.

Hiro thought about saying something to reveal to his friends that he was still awake, but his curiosity won out. He had been wondering what was going on in Daarco's head for weeks now. Perhaps this would be his chance to understand.

"You still feel disloyal, even knowing that the tengu are the ones who started the war? That we were being manipulated to hate each other? That makes me want to come together even stronger. To thwart them."

"Every time I think about putting it behind me, I see my father's face. A moonburner murdered him. Robbed me of him. How can I let that go?"

A pause. "You know the scars on my face? I've lived with them for over a year. I was in the hospital for weeks after I was injured. The pain was unbearable while they healed. I lost my ear. Do you think I should forgive the man who did that?"

"No," Daarco growled. "When I think about someone doing that to you...I want to rip them apart with my bare hands. Of course you shouldn't forgive him."

"But I have," she said softly. "Because it was you."

"What?" came the strangled word from Daarco.

"The sunburner attack on the citadel. I was in the dormitories, trying to get the younger novices to safety. I looked out the window and saw a golden eagle swooping towards us. I saw the rider throwing a ball of fire at the building. It was you."

"I...I..." Daarco stumbled over his words. "I'm so sorry. How can you even look to me? Talk to me?"

"There's something I learned a long time ago. Hatred and regret...these things choke the life from you. Sometimes slowly, sometimes fast. But you wither and die. Forgiveness...breathes life back in. It allows for something to grow in hatred's place. Love. Purpose."

Daarco was silent, but a sniff told Hiro that there were tears in his friend's eyes.

"I didn't tell you that to make you feel guilty or hate yourself, or to earn an apology. I told you to show you that it's possible to forgive. To forgive your enemies, but also to forgive yourself. It takes more courage than hatred, but it's worth it. I hope you discover that for yourself."

"I hope so too," Daarco whispered, barely loud enough to hear.

As Hiro drifted off to sleep, he found that his own cheeks were wet with tears, turning to ice in the cold.

"Hiro," a female voice said. He tried to shove the voice away, to descend once again into the comfortable black of sleep.

"Hiro." It was more insistent. Someone was shaking him.

"Hmm?" he said, opening his eyes groggily.

A heart-shaped face swam into view before him. "Hiro, wake up."

"Stela?" he asked, sitting up and rubbing his eyes. As soon as he sat up, he regretted it, as the cold of the night rushed against his exposed skin. He shivered.

"I heard something," she said. "I think there's something out there."

A surge of adrenaline coursed through him, washing away the remnants of sleep. He wriggled out from under the low tent, pulling his gear with him. He quickly hopped into his boots and coat, strapping on his sword and scabbard.

Stela pulled her hood back up, its white fur framing her face in the moonlight.

"Human or animal?" Hiro asked.

"I think…" she said. "Animal. It sounded like footsteps in the snow, but I heard snuffling too."

Ryu padded out of the tent to sit in the snow beside him. "I sense…wrongness."

They stood very still to listen, their breath fogging the icy air.

He heard it. A crunch of snow, faint but unmistakable. "It's moving slowly," he said. "It could be the Order of Deshi tracking us."

"Should we wake the others?"

Hiro hesitated. The other burners needed their sleep, and if he was wrong, he'd be dealing with four cold, grouchy people. But if he was right…

Hiro never got to make his choice. Because a white horror exploded out of the snow in front of them, leaping at him with jaws bared.

CHAPTER 32

T he creature's huge paws hit him first, knocking Hiro backwards. Hiro and the creature tumbled into the snow, rolling end over end, tangling with the canvas tent, and finally breaking apart against one of the nearby boulders.

Hiro's body was numb as he rose to one knee, gasping for breath. He pulled his sword from its scabbard and got his first real glimpse of his enemy.

It was on its feet before him, shaking the snow from its yellow-white fur. Once, it must have been a bear, like General Ipan's seishen, Kuma—perhaps an icy northern cousin. Now, it was monster, a bloody symbol smudged onto its forehead. Mindless red eyes burned with hatred above a slavering maw.

Anger bubbled up from Hiro's core at the idea of someone creating this monstrosity, perverting this once-proud creature into something evil.

Instinct took over as the massive beast leaped at him with club-like paws. He dropped to the ground just in time and the tengu overshot its target, scrambling on the boulder behind him, claws screeching.

As the tengu pulled itself to its feet and rebounded for another leap, Stela shot a blast of fire at it. It twisted to the side, out of the path of the flames, roaring in fury at being attacked. It bounded on all four legs across the snow towards her, its spiny vertebrae protruding from its hunched back.

"Stela!" Hiro cried out in warning.

As it leaped for her, Ryu intercepted it with a massive leap, barreling it sideways in the snow. The two creatures scrambled apart and faced off against each other with snarls and flashing teeth.

A blast of lightning struck the tengu from above, sending it stumbling to its knees. Emi had untangled herself from the mangled tent and stood on the hillside, her chest heaving.

The blow had dazed the tengu but hadn't killed it. It stumbled to its feet. Stela scrambled back in the snow as it lashed out at her, hissing and snapping.

Emi sent another blast of white hot heat into the creature, joined by one from Leilu, who had emerged next to her.

The tengu snarled and snapped, thrashing and shuddering in the snow.

"You need to behead it!" Hiro called.

With a grimace, Emi burned a slice of moonlight that severed through the tengu's neck. It gave a final shake and lay still.

Daarco finally threw the remains of the tent to the side, emerging from the canvas with an angry cry. Hiro couldn't help but chuckle, his relief palpable. "Everyone all right?"

Stela stood unsteadily, giving the creature a wide berth. "What was that?" she asked.

"Tengu," Emi said. "We had the pleasure of making their acquaintance on our last trip."

"The Order of Deshi knows we're here," Hiro said. "This likely won't be the only one."

"Great," Leilu said. "At least we won't freeze to death."

"Remind me to stop taking trips with you boys," Emi said icily.

Hiro smiled grimly. The sky was lightening in the east, painting an ombre palate of blues over the horizon. "Anyone need more sleep tonight?" he asked.

"Suddenly feeling alert," Leilu said. "Let's get moving. Might as well make some progress."

☾

The next day passed in an expanse of white. With the thin air and the thick snow, they moved slowly. But they moved. By nightfall, they were within a stone's throw of the pass between the two boulders.

"How are you all feeling?" Hiro asked. The group was sprawled about the snow, resting after their latest push. "Should we try to make it over the pass?"

"That pass will be more defensible than this open face," Daarco said.

"I agree," Emi said, looking warmly at Daarco. Those two had grown closer the farther they climbed. "If more tengu are headed our way tonight, I'd like to have the high ground. I'm up for a few more hours."

"What do you guys think?" Hiro turned to Leilu and Stela.

"My head agrees with Daarco, but my legs say this is as good a place as any," Leilu said with a chuckle. "I think I can keep my head in charge for a few more hours."

"Let's keep moving," Stela said. "We have to get there one way or the other."

A chorus of grunts and groans rang out as they stood on aching feet and shouldered their packs. As they resumed the trudge up the steep slope, even Emi and Leilu's sarcastic banter died down to sullen, tired silence. Hiro's muscles ached, quivering with each new step. He couldn't remember being so tired in his life.

The monotony of the steps numbed his mind until all he could think of was the fire in his lungs and his legs. When he looked up and realized he had crested the top of the pass, Hiro felt like weeping with relief.

Atop the pass, they were rewarded by a fantastic panorama—just as the box had displayed. A narrow angling slope leading down into a wide, shallow, snow-covered glacial basin. Cradling the basin was a row of stern peaks majestically clad in granite rock, downy white snow, and turquoise ice. Somewhere under there, Taiyo was waiting for them.

"Thank the gods," Stela said with ragged breath as she reached the top behind him.

"Let's get to a flat spot," Hiro said, "and we can make camp."

Making camp took all of about four minutes. The tent had been destroyed in the tengu's attack the night before, so they unrolled their bedrolls in a haphazard circle and flopped onto them, taking off boots and reaching into packs for hard food that could be munched on while horizontal.

"I'll take first watch," Stela said. She was dead on her feet, swaying slightly on exhausted legs.

"You had first watch last night," Hiro said. "You should get some rest. I'll take first, then I'll tap Emi in."

"You had a pretty exciting night yourself," Stela protested. "You need sleep too."

"I'll take a short watch," he said. "I've got Ryu to stay up with me. I'll be fine."

She clearly didn't have the energy to protest because she crawled into her bedroll without another word.

Silence descended over the frozen valley as his friends succumbed to sleep. The heat bubble that Leilu had been burning around each of them began to dissipate. A cold breeze blew across the snow. He shivered and walked for a few minutes towards the center of the valley, trying to warm himself.

"Never thought we'd be all the way out here," Hiro said to Ryu.

The ascent and the cold hadn't seemed to bother Ryu. He was a creature of spirit, after all. Hiro couldn't help feeling a pang of jealousy. To be mortal was very inconvenient at times.

"The life of a burner and seishen is never dull," Ryu said.

"That's the truth," Hiro chuckled, looking up at the stars. They were so bright and clear here, it was as if he could reach out and touch them. He could see all of the constellations he had learned about as a child: The black tortoise that guarded the northern star. The phoenix standing in the south with the winking red star as its eye.

"Do the seishen have stories about the stars?" Hiro asked.

"Of course," Ryu said. "See that one up there? It looks like a cross, but then two little stars hang down from the bottom star?"

Hiro searched the multitude of pinpricks in the sky until he saw the cluster Ryu referred to. "I see it. What is it?"

"It's the seishen elder," Ryu said. "The stars in the horizontal line of the cross are his wings, the other his head and body and the two little stars are his legs."

"The elder taught you a constellation that looked like him? Why am I not surprised?"

"He was here for the making of the world," Ryu said.

"I wonder what it was like," Hiro mused.

"You can ask him from hell," a quiet voice said behind him.

Hiro whirled around, almost losing his footing in the thick snow.

Before him stood Geisa, wearing a look of hatred that chilled him more than the arctic air ever could.

Hiro tried to shout for the others, but he found he couldn't speak. His throat was hot and angry. He grasped at his neck, trying to scream, but nothing came out.

Ryu dove for Geisa with a powerful leap, but a bolt of lightning snaked from the clear sky and hit him, tossing him into the snow. He scrambled to his feet and she hit him with another bolt, and then another.

Hiro barreled into her, desperate to draw her attention from Ryu. They tumbled together into the snow, but before he could strike another blow, a strange fever fill his body and his mind, turning his vision red.

She rolled him off her into the snow, kneeling over him so her face hovered above his. "Cooperate, my Hiro," she whispered, "and I won't kill your seishen. Try to wake the others, and he dies. Do you understand?"

He nodded.

"Now," Geisa said, pulling him to his feet. "Let's go meet your god."

☾⋆

Hiro walked in front of Geisa as if in a feverish dream. She rested the blade of a sword across his shoulder, kissing his neck with the cold steel. Not that she needed the weapon. At this time of night, he was as helpless as a lamb. He schooled himself not to panic and tried to think, his thoughts moving sluggishly through his fevered mind. Was Ryu all right? They had left him lying motionless in the cold snow. And why did Geisa want to free Taiyo? She had no love for the sunburners, or their god. When he thought about the things she had suffered at the hands of the sunburners, in their prisons...he knew her treatment of him would not be gentle.

"Why do you want to free Taiyo?" he finally asked. His voice was hoarse.

"I thought I should meet the god who taught his followers such respect for women," she said. "He's a model for the rest of us."

Hiro pushed down his frustration. "Tell me the real reason. I know you worship the tengu, that you're a part of the Order of Deshi. Why do you want him free?"

"So I can kill him, of course."

"You can't kill a god," Hiro said, his eyes widening in alarm.

"Are you sure?" she asked, drawing closer to him, taunting him.

Hiro said nothing. He wasn't sure. He didn't even know exactly how he was supposed to free Taiyo. Explanation and facts were Kai's business. He traded on instinct. Action. Two things that were doing him no good at the moment.

Geisa chuckled softly. "To come all this way, only to realize that you were the key to the destruction of your god. How delightfully ironic."

"Even if you think you could kill Taiyo, which you can't," Hiro said, "Kai is still freeing Tsuki while we speak. Tsuki will stop you."

"You still don't see, do you? This has been in motion for a very long time. It has been my task to follow your desperate little mission up this mountain, just as it has been my companion's task to follow Kai."

"You won't catch her by surprise. She'll be ready," Hiro said.

"Not even your clever Kai will be ready for a threat from the inside."

Hiro missed a step, stumbling in the snow. The cold of her blade nicked his neck. One of Kai's companions was a traitor? Fear for Kai blossomed inside him, and his fevered heart began to hammer. He had to warn her somehow.

"That's the thing about flying too close to the sun," Geisa said, her eyes shining in the moonlight. "You're likely to get burned."

CHAPTER 33

When the tropical sun rose that morning, fierce and bold over the horizon, Chiya flew to the neighboring island and rowed the little boat back to their shore. Colum, boasting of the impressive volume of his lungs, volunteered to dive into the warm water to confirm that Tsuki was in fact waiting for them below.

After several dives, he emerged from the sparkling sea, gasping that he had found her. Though a welcome development, it didn't solve the larger problem—namely, how to get Tsuki off the sea floor.

They had been arguing for hours when Jurou emerged from the forest and sat down, joining their circle.

"Where have you been?" Kai asked crossly.

He smiled pleasantly, picking a rosy fruit off the pile that lay on the canvas of Kai's flattened pack. "I think better when I'm moving."

"Uh huh," Kai said, watching in strange fascination as he dug his long fingernails into the flesh of the fruit.

"It looked like she was in a stone burial box," Colum said. "It had a carving on the top of some sort of figure, though she was tough to see under several hundred years of barnacles. The coral reef has grown around it. It might take hours to break the coral and free the box."

"And even then, we haven't a clue how to retrieve a stone box from the bottom of the sea," Jurou said.

"So basically we're back to square one," Chiya said, leaning back on her elbows in the sand.

"We know she's down there," Colum said. "That's something."

"Anyone have any ideas?" Kai asked.

Jurou muttered to himself, as if working through options, but Chiya and Colum said nothing. Eyes averted, hands drawing circles in the sand. Kai didn't have any ideas either.

"Let's take a break," Colum finally said.

Kai rolled her eyes, but it wasn't a half-bad idea. Her brain had been spinning in circles for hours.

"Fine," she said. Kai walked down to the shore and sat in the sand, looking out over the waves at the spot where Tsuki lay.

"Mind if I join you?" Chiya asked, standing uncertainly on the sand behind Kai.

"Please," Kai said.

Chiya sat down next to her, hugging her knees against her chest. She looked vulnerable for a moment, despite her muscled form. "She's so close," Chiya said. "I can almost feel her."

"Me too," Kai said. "I wish I could figure out how to get her up here."

"We will," Chiya said. "It'll come to us."

"I'm glad you're here," Kai said, wishing she could explain to Chiya the camaraderie she had begun to feel for the other woman.

"Me too," Chiya said. "This is the sort of mission I imagined I was signing up for when...well, you know. Last time."

Kai remembered the fateful day in the citadel courtyard when Chiya had signed up for Geisa's special "mission." She shuddered at the truth of it, that the women had been used as part of an experimental burner breeding facility.

"That was unforgivable," Kai said quietly. It wasn't until she learned about the facility that she had known that former Queen Airi was well and truly mad.

"I never believed that you could defeat Airi," Chiya admitted.

"I'm not sure I did either," Kai said ruefully. "But it seemed like someone needed to try."

"That's..." Chiya paused for a moment. "That's what I respect about you. You try, even when it's not easy or certain. In fact, when it seems impossible."

"So I'm completely impractical," Kai said with a chuckle.

"Basically." Chiya laughed too.

"I couldn't have done it alone," Kai said. "You played a big part in defeating Airi. Nanase too. And Hiro and Quitsu. A ruler is only as good as the people supporting her."

Chiya nodded. "I don't envy you. Being queen."

Kai's heart thudded. They were so close to the truth. Was now the time to tell Chiya? "You've never thought about being queen?"

"I always daydreamed about being Nanase as a kid," Chiya said. "Not Airi."

"Nanase is pretty inspiring," Kai said.

"Agreed. And she…took me under her wing. There were a few of us at the citadel who had been rescued from the desert," Chiya said. "She made sure we were taken care of. She was the closest thing I had to a mother."

Kai looked at the other woman, studying the profile of her face. Kai could see her father, Raiden, in that face—the strong jaw, the bright eyes. It was so unfair that they had never known each other and never would. She saw Hanae too, the arc of Chiya's eyebrows, the fine strands of her hair. It wasn't too late for Hanae and Chiya. Kai couldn't keep this secret from Chiya any longer.

"Chiya…" Kai said.

But she didn't get to finish her sentence because Chiya leaped up. "I've got it!"

Kai blinked, her curiosity overcoming the momentum she had gained towards revealing Chiya's heritage. "Tell me."

"Do you remember in Nanase's class when she talked about using the world around you in your burning?"

"I had the shortened 'we're going to war' curriculum," Kai said. "I'm not sure if we actually covered that."

"Oh," Chiya said, disappointed. "Well, she always said a fighter or burner shouldn't look inward for their power but should look outward, to their surroundings."

"Okay…" Kai said, restraining herself from shaking Chiya and telling her to get to the point.

"I was exploring our surroundings with my burning. Delving into the land under the island, the sea floor. I think this island chain was created by a volcano."

Kai's ears perked up. Volcano meant heat, which meant something they could control with burning.

Chiya went on. "There's a network of undersea vents along the island. If we could heat one to boiling, if we were controlled about it, we could send a jet of hot water up through the surface right under Tsuki, and sort of shoot her up to the surface."

"Heat rises," Kai said, working through the scenario in her head. "But once she was on the surface, how would we move her to the shore?"

"If we could keep her buoyant, perhaps we could snag her with a rope and tow her to shore?"

"Wouldn't the boat boil in the hot water?" Kai asked, trying to work through the problems.

"We could have one burner in the boat, cooling the water underneath it, while the other works the vents," Chiya suggested.

"It...it could work," Kai said. Excitement flooded her before quickly dampening. It was time to share the bitter truth. "Only...I...can't moonburn anymore."

"What?" Chiya's voice was low.

"This handprint," Kai said. "Ever since I woke up with it, I haven't been able to access moonlight. Instead, I'm able to burn the white light, like what you get when moon and sunlight are combined."

"That light seems vastly more powerful than moonlight," Chiya said. "Couldn't you use it on the vents?"

"It's also vastly harder to control. I'm not sure it works on the same principles as moonlight."

"It's still worth a try, right?"

"Agreed," Kai said. It was the only plan they had.

Chiya rose and offered Kai her hand. Kai took it, and they headed back towards the fire pit, where it looked like Colum and Jurou had dozed off.

"Wake up," Kai said, clapping her hands. "Chiya has an idea."

Kai and Chiya excitedly explained the plan. When they were done, the two men stared at them with wide eyes.

Colum recovered first. "You expect me to stand in a leaky ol' rowboat over boiling water, lasso a god in a stone box with a bit of rope, and tow her to shore? Without dying?"

Kai nodded. "That sums it up."

He pondered this for a moment, before he shrugged. "I'm in."

"Maybe we should wait until sunrise," Jurou said. "We will be better able to see what we are working with."

"We need multiple burners to make this work," Kai said, shaking her head. "Chiya's familiar with the vents. We do it now. This can work. Right, Chiya?"

"It can work," Chiya said, though Kai wished it was with a bit more confidence.

☾

And so Kai found herself with Colum in the little wooden boat, floating just shy of the glowing spot that marked Tsuki's resting place. Chiya stood on shore, preparing to superheat the vents.

"Ready?" Chiya called from the shore.

"Ready!" Kai called, exchanging a look with Colum.

"I've done a lot of stupid things in my day," Colum said, "but this might be the dumbest."

"We'll find out," Kai said.

The water began to roil as Chiya poured heat into the undersea vents.

"Maybe we should back up a bit," Kai said nervously, but Colum was already rowing them farther from the disturbance.

Kai opened herself to the raging torrent of alabaster light, wishing that it was moonlight's sweet calming essence. *Please, creator,* Kai prayed, *you gave me this power; help me use it to save Tsuki.* She filled her qi with light in a strained effort, opening her senses to the ocean around her, to the grains of wood on the boat, to the sweat beading Colum's brow. She burned the light beneath the boat, wrapping it in a protective cocoon between them and the ocean as a jet of superheated water and steam blasted up a stone's throw away.

Kai hastily split her focus, wrapping the cocoon over them so the boiling water pattered harmlessly against a roof of pure energy. She hardly understood what she was doing, but her instincts seemed to know the right approach.

The water continued to churn and boil. Kai's heart hammered and her breath came gasping in her throat as she struggled to maintain her focus, grappling with the strength of the light to keep their little boat safe amongst the chaos.

"She's up," Chiya screamed, barely audible over the roar of the water and steam. Amongst the roiling sea, a dark gray mass surfaced, churning about in the waves.

Colum, bathed in brilliant light, screamed over the roar of the boiling sea, "Get rid of this blasted roof! I can't throw the rope!"

Kai hastily pulled at the power, but it was like trying to trap a thunderstorm in a teapot. She silently cursed the creator for giving her power but no direction for how to use it. Finally, after precious seconds ticked by, through sheer force of will, Kai successfully moved the white light protecting them above, joining it with the light below.

Colum, squinting against the brilliant glow beneath them, took a rope and circled it over his head, preparing to throw at the mass of coral and stone. Kai prayed that the rope would catch on something so they could tow Tsuki to shore.

He let the loop of rope go, and it soared into the boiling water, flying true. He pulled it tight, but it recoiled, coming back to them. He hadn't caught anything.

As Colum hauled the rope back up, he hissed and dropped it, cradling his hand. It had been superheated in the water. He grabbed a piece of burlap from the bottom of the boat and used it as a rudimentary glove to gather and coil the rope again.

Colum circled the rope again and tossed it. Again, it looked to be on target, but it failed to snag on anything amidst the roiling water.

He pulled it back. "It's not working! We'll need to go get her ourselves."

"I'm not strong enough," Kai said. Sweat poured from her and her heart thundered in her chest. She couldn't keep this up much longer. "We'd boil to death. You have to make the rope work."

"Kai," Chiya called. Her voice held a tinge of desperation. "Hurry!"

"You can do it," Kai said.

Colum stood in the rocking boat, circled the rope over his head, and let it go. This time, it snagged on a knob of coral sticking off the gray stone slab. "Yes!" he said.

He tossed the end of the rope to Kai, who tied it off quickly, while Colum sat back down at the oars and began rowing towards the shore.

"We've got her!" Kai hollered, feeling her strength waning. Chiya was supposed to keep the pressure of the vent under their location, slowly allowing Tsuki to move along the surface of the water. It was complex burning, and Kai knew Chiya must be as exhausted as she.

As they neared the shore, the bubbling in the water subsided. The rope went taught as the weight of the stone coffin began to sink back into the water. The stern of the rowboat dipped lower in the water.

"I'm out of vents," Chiya yelled, her voice strangled.

She and Jurou were down at the waterline now.

"Row, Colum!" Kai said, letting the rope out a little bit, relieving the weight on the boat.

Colum strained against the oars with each stroke, sweat beading his brow, the muscles in his arms straining in the early morning light. Kai tried to divert a piece of the white light to support the box, but her focus trembled and almost broke. She was too weak, too drained from the effort of keeping their little boat safe.

The bow of the boat hit the sand of the shore and Kai leaped out into the waist-deep water.

"Come on," she cried.

The others splashed through the surf, grabbing the four corners of the stone crypt that bore their goddess. The tumult of the waves helped them bear her towards the shore, but they strained with quivering muscles against the pull when the rhythmic waves rushed out to sea.

Slowly, inch over inch, they heaved and pulled the stone up onto the beach. Finally, at long last, they collapsed, panting onto the sand. They had done it.

CHAPTER 34

As Hiro and Geisa walked, a crystalline structure took shape in the moonlight: a raised dais of ice—tapered square platforms placed on top of each other. Hiro scrambled for an idea, a play. If he could knock Geisa out, he might be able to escape. Or kill her. He couldn't leave her out there, free to wreak whatever havoc she planned. If he could get the sword and knock her out before she had time to boil him alive with her moonburning, he might be able to get the upper hand.

"I see you, Hiro, thinking, tensing those thick neck muscles of yours," Geisa said. "Do you think you're faster than me? Personally, I don't. But I'm curious to find out."

Maybe he was faster than her with the element of surprise, but it was clear he didn't have it. But he had to try something.

"Up," she said, prodding him with the sword.

He took a step up the first stair. Taiyo was on the platform above, an icy crypt illuminated by the moonlight. It was now or never. He needed to make his move. Hiro tensed and whirled, knocking the sword away. As he did, Ryu exploded out of the darkness behind Geisa, flattening her against the stairs with a sickening thud.

Geisa lay still. Blood trickled down her face and her silver hair spread across the ice like a halo beneath her. Her chest still rose and fell with breath. Unconscious, not dead. Hiro realized with a sinking feeling that he had to kill her, and that he only had seconds to do it. He didn't relish the idea of killing a helpless woman, even one as twisted as Geisa. But he knew it had to be done. The chance of her waking up and boiling his blood in an instant was too great.

He drew his sword and approached Geisa's prone form with more confidence than he felt. She looked peaceful. With a deep breath, he lifted his sword and plunged it towards her heart.

Her eyes flew open and she spun to the side. His blade pierced the ice where she had lain a second before.

She sprang to her feet, her eyes rolling like a wild animal. Hiro and Ryu circled her warily, placing their feet carefully on the thick ice.

Hiro lunged at her and she danced out of the way of his blade. The handle of his sword grew warm and then hot until he was forced to drop it, cradling his burned hand. She smiled. She was toying with him.

"What do you think is the most painful way to die? I want Kai to know that you suffered."

"I'm not afraid to die," Hiro said.

"You may not be," Geisa said. "But there are some fates worse than death. Believe me, I know." She whirled and burned a jet of fire directly at Ryu.

"No!" Hiro cried.

Ryu was tossed from the icy platform onto the snow below. He lay still, his blackened fur smoking.

Hiro grabbed his knife from his belt and ran at her with a howl of grief and rage. She was ready. An arc of lightning coursed through his body, lancing white hot pain through his very soul. He collapsed to his knees and she stood over him, a sick smile on her face.

I'm so sorry, Kai, Hiro thought, closing his eyes.

Another blast of heat warmed his face, but then passed. He opened his eyes.

Emi was striding up the stairs, a look of unearthly fury on her face. Leilu and Stela flanked her. Daarco trailed behind, his sword drawn.

Geisa stumbled to her feet and shot gouts of flame in quick succession at the other women.

And then the real fireworks began. Geisa and the other moonburners threw fireball after fireball at one another. Emi and the other burners enjoyed the benefit of superior numbers, and they slowly pushed Geisa back over the platform. But Geisa was tricky and fast. She used heat to melt the ice under Leilu's feet and the woman fell into a well of frigid water, slipping into the darkness before surfacing again with a shuddering gasp. Daarco pulled her out; she was shivering and blue before she flooded heat through herself and the water dried from her clothes.

Geisa sent a jet of boiling steam at Emi, but Emi diffused the heat with a motion, letting the water vapor flow around her like she was opening a set of curtains. She was now a few paces from Geisa, who backed onto the snow, her face strained.

"Time to go," Geisa said, and a flash of light blinded them. When Hiro regained his vision she was fleeing, sprinting away from the platform with Emi on her tail.

"The platform!" Stela shouted. "She melted it!"

Hiro backed up as a spider web of cracks sped through the surface of the ice. The heavy weight of the icy tomb was too much, and the platform cracked underneath, one half of it beginning to tilt and slide into the water beneath.

"Freeze it back!" Hiro shouted. "If it sinks, we'll lose him!"

Leilu and Stela focused on pulling heat from the mass of water and ice before them, and Hiro sighed with relief as the ice grew cloudy and firmed.

Hiro ran to where Ryu lay smoking in the snow. His golden flank was charred and his eyes were closed, but he was still breathing. Still warm.

Stela ran to his side and began delving Ryu with moonlight. "He's stunned," she said. "But he should live. I can speed the healing process by applying heat to the right areas."

"Do it," Hiro whispered.

Hiro watched with his heart in his throat as she worked, moving her hands over Ryu's still body. He breathed out a huge sigh of relief when Ryu opened his great amber eyes. Hiro leaned forward, resting his head on his seishen's shoulder. *Thank you, Taiyo, for sparing him,* Hiro thought.

Ryu stood unsteadily and followed Hiro back to the platform.

The icy tomb was carved in the image of a man lying down, his eyes closed. He held a cup in his hands, the base resting on his chest, as if offering whatever liquid it contained to the heavens. The detail of the man's fine face and rich clothing was exquisite. Beneath the ice, it was just possible to make out a darkness, a form.

Emi climbed the steps slowly, approaching from behind him. She drew in a shaky breath, resting her hands on her knees. "I didn't catch her. She tripped me up and was gone in a mass of wind and snow. I'm sorry."

Hiro shook his head. "You saved my life. We stopped whatever Geisa was planning. We should consider it a victory."

"What was she trying to do?" Daarco asked.

"She seemed to think…that she could kill Taiyo. If we released him."

"That's disconcerting," Leilu said, her arms crossed. "Is she mad?"

"Maybe," Hiro said. "But somehow…I don't think so."

"She could be trying to throw us off our mission," Emi said. "Nothing's changed. We're here to free Taiyo, so I say we do it."

The others nodded. "If we don't do this," Stela said, "the tengu win. It's a risk we have to take."

Hiro nodded. He still clutched his knife in his right hand. He loosened his fingers on the grip and stepped up next to the icy visage of Taiyo.

"The cup," Ryu rumbled. "Put it in the cup."

Hiro drew a thin line across the meat of his left palm, wincing slightly as the knife cut into his skin. He held his fist over the cup, letting the blood drain into the icy chalice. As the drops of red blood slid into the clear cup, a light burst from inside the coffin.

Taiyo was waking.

☽⁺

Golden light poured from the block of ice where Taiyo lay. Cracks ran along the sides, growing and snaking until the top cracked into pieces, showering them with bits of ice and snow. They stood in silence as a man sat up, looking around in apparent confusion.

The man was…remarkably un-god-like. He was undeniably handsome with smooth bronzed skin, strong cheekbones and a defined jawline. But as for the rest—he wasn't impossibly tall, or well-muscled, or radiant. The only thing that set him apart was a thick shock of fire-red hair, which swooped down over his brow.

Hiro revised his assessment as Taiyo met Hiro's gaze. His eyes were strange as well. Glowing and bright, like two tiny suns.

The god vaulted out of the icy coffin, nimble as a deer. His carriage was proud and regal.

"What a strange place you've brought me to," he said, peering around the icy bowl. His voice was deep and reverberated through Hiro's body as he spoke. "So much frozen water. This must be my lady's creation."

Even in the moonlight, Taiyo's clothes stood out in a rainbow of color against the dull frozen landscape. The garments were old-fashioned; he wore wide crimson pants topped by a rich bronze tunic wrapped in an obi sash of golden braid.

Hiro wasn't sure how to proceed, so he decided to dive right in.

"I am Hiro, crown prince of Kita, and a captain in the sunburner army," Hiro said, bowing low. "We have freed you from your prison where the tengu trapped you."

Taiyo frowned, stroking his chin. "Trapped, you say?"

"Do you…not remember?" Hiro ventured. "Do you remember the tengu? They have been masquerading as you for many years. They have found a way to travel from the demon world to our own."

"The tengu vexed us for many years. Never satisfied with their realm. Wanted to have ours as well," Taiyo said. "But I must admit, I don't recall being trapped. We fled the spirit world when those awful tengu and their followers broke through. They were halfway through the barrier to the mortal realm too. The burners and Tsuki and I agreed that it would be best if they hid us."

"Hid you?" Emi asked, her voice flat.

"Yes. The demons wanted to kill me and my love because if we are lost, the sun and moon will disappear. And they are quite fond of darkness. They are born and bred in the dark. So Queen Hamaio, King Samsua, and their guardians hid us away until such time as the danger passed. Has the danger passed?"

"No," Hiro said weakly.

"Then why have you freed me?" Taiyo asked.

"We…thought…you could help us. To defeat the tengu."

Taiyo recoiled. "Fight? Oh, no. The creator made Tsuki and me to shine light into this world. The burners and the guardians were created to protect us."

Hiro closed his eyes, breathing in deeply and letting it out in a slow exhale. Geisa's mocking words replayed in his head. *How delightfully ironic.* They had been played.

"If you can't help us fight, what good are you?" Daarco asked, stepping up beside Hiro.

"I shine the light upon the world, without which all living things would shrivel and die," Taiyo snapped. "So there is that."

Hiro laid a calming hand on Daarco's shoulder, though what he really wanted to do was punch something. "You understand these tengu better than we do. You have a history. What do you think our next course of action should be?"

Taiyo stared at them blankly. "Put me back to sleep. It is the best solution the burners came up with."

"We...don't know how to do that," Hiro admitted.

Taiyo frowned. "I'm afraid it is a lost cause. They are too powerful. They have been striving towards this end for a millennium."

"Surely, you sell yourself too short," Stela said. "You command great power, and we know the burners of old had much wisdom. Otherwise, they couldn't have held back the tengu for so long. Are you able to remember something that could help us fight them? Tactics the burners used? Tengu weaknesses?"

Taiyo brightened, like the clouds had cleared before him. "They *are* weakest in daylight, under the direct light of my sun. The burners and their guardians had weapons they used to shine light on the tengu to weaken them. Mirrored shields...and little devices that would explode inside the tengu's gullets." He chuckled. "Very crafty, actually."

"Do any of these weapons still exist?" Emi stepped up, an edge of excitement in her voice.

"Perhaps," he said. "In the armory at Yoshai. Many such things were kept there."

"Where?" Hiro said.

"Yoshai, the capital of all the lands. The grandest city ever built. Our stronghold."

Hiro looked to the others, who met his glance with shrugs or blank faces.

"I'm not familiar with this city. Perhaps its name has changed?" Hiro said. "Can you take us there?"

"Yes," Taiyo said. "Once the sun truly rises."

The morning light was filtering over the tops of the twin peaks, just minutes from shining into the glacial bowl where they stood.

Hiro sent Leilu and Stela back to camp to retrieve the rest of their gear. He turned back to Taiyo to find him standing with Ryu.

"A fine guardian," Taiyo said. "Your connection to the earth is strong."

"Thank you," Hiro said.

Leilu and Stela returned ladened with backpacks and weapons as the sun's rays peeked over the mountaintops.

When the sun hit Taiyo, golden light exploded from his skin and hair—even his eyes and ears. For a moment, he was a smaller twin sun, reflecting the rays back towards his mammoth brother. After a few seconds, Taiyo's light winked out, but his countenance was much changed. It was hard to look at the god without squinting, and when he moved, he left a golden afterglow, a brilliant shadow that confused the mind.

"The sun and I are one," he said. "Being kept from its rays for so long left me weak. Now, we may go."

He stood, raising his arms above him. Nothing happened. One minute stretched to two. The burners exchanged confused glances, each silently daring the others to be the first to disturb the god.

Leilu twirled her finger about her ear, mouthing the word "crazy."

Stela put her hand over her mouth, her shoulders shaking in silent laughter.

Hiro couldn't help his surge of annoyance. Taiyo had been their one hope of defeating the tengu, and it turned out that they were actually doing the demons a favor by freeing the god. This was no laughing matter.

Abruptly, Taiyo lowered his arms and opened his eyes.

"Ah. Here they come."

Sinuous shapes appeared in the clear northern sky.

Hiro squinted to make out the creatures, and then his eyes widened like saucers. Dragons. Real live dragons. With flashing teeth and ice-white scales and curving wind-swept wings. And they were coming in for a landing.

"This day just got more interesting," Emi said.

CHAPTER 35

As the sun rose they cleaned the pieces of coral off of the stone tomb, prying years of growth away with their knives and fingers. An image appeared as they worked—a woman lying on her back, carved in relief on top of the stone slab. A thin circlet sat atop her intricately carved head, the face below serene. Her hands were clasped beneath her bosom, holding a stone cup.

"She's one lady I wouldn't mind meeting in person, if you get my drift," Colum said with a wink.

Kai rolled her eyes. "You're lucky she doesn't smite you where you stand."

"Better get all my admirin' in before she wakes up, then," he said.

"What next?" Chiya asked. "How do we wake her?"

This was the part Kai was dreading. "We need your blood," she said.

"What?" Chiya started. "My blood? Why? You're the queen."

Kai shook her head. "The seishen elder said…whoever reveals the visions inside the box is the one to wake her. It's got to be you."

"It doesn't make sense." Chiya furrowed her brow. "Why me?"

"The box worked for you, so does it matter?" Kai asked. "We can puzzle it out later. Right now, we need to get Tsuki awake and see if she can defeat the tengu. Every minute counts."

Chiya crossed her arms over her chest. "What aren't you telling me? We'll talk about it now. Before my blood gets involved."

Kai ground her teeth. "This really isn't the time."

"Make time."

Clearly, Chiya was beyond reasoning. But Kai didn't want to explain it here in front of these others when she was racing against time to prevent the destruction of her people.

"Chiya, we need your blood right now. That's an order." Kai put her hands on her hips and drew herself up to her full height. "Are you disobeying a direct order from your queen?"

Doubt flickered across Chiya's face.

"Oh for gods' sakes," Colum said, throwing up his hands. "Chiya, you're Kai's long-lost sister, and so you're the true heir of Tsuki and so on and so forth. She didn't tell you because the world is ending and there hasn't really been a good time for a succession challenge. She was going to tell you eventually etcetera."

Kai's mouth fell open and she glared daggers at Colum. "How could you?" she hissed at him. She should have been the one to explain everything to Chiya when the time was right. How dare he take that from her!

"Is this true?" Chiya asked quietly, her eyes blazing.

"I've only know for a few weeks," Kai said. "We were going to tell you once this was all over."

"We?" Chiya asked, her voice still low.

"Me and my mother. Our...mother," Kai said.

"I had a mother...and a sister...and you didn't tell me? You used me all this time, lied to me?"

"Please, Chiya. I will tell you everything you want to know, but right now, we need to free Tsuki."

"That's all I'm here for, isn't it. My blood. Well, here you go." She pulled out a dagger and sliced her forearm, stepping up to the stone box and letting the blood drip into the open cup. "Are you happy? Now will you tell me the truth?" Chiya rounded on her, the knife still in her hand.

A silver light emanated from the stone tomb, running its way along the edges of the lid. But Kai couldn't look away from Chiya, from the look of betrayal and anger on her sister's face.

"I'm so sorry I kept this from you, you must believe that it ate me up inside. It was necessary," Kai said lamely. "I wanted to tell you, but I was worried that it would destabilize everything when things were already going to hell. We needed to defeat the tengu before we could process this and decide what to do."

"Decide what to do?"

The top of the stone crypt cracked in two with a loud snap, and the two pieces fell to the earth with a thud.

Kai glanced at the box for a moment, but her gaze was pulled back to Chiya at the chill in her next words.

"Oh, yes, *decide*. Because I am the rightful heir, aren't I? You're an...impostor."

"We didn't know you were royal, Chiya. My mother thought her first child had died. It wasn't like I set out to take your throne!" Kai said. "I never wanted to be queen. Do you think I wanted all of this responsibility at eighteen?"

"Uh...Kai," Colum said.

"What?" Kai exploded, turning to face the other man.

Then she realized that a young woman was sitting up in the stone box, rubbing her face. Tsuki had awoken. Kai had been so intent on Chiya she had missed it. Double curse Colum!

As she moved towards the goddess to bow low and welcome her back to the world, Kai realized that the air around her was crackling with energy, the strange sensation of a sunburner burning.

"Jurou?" Kai said. "What are you doing?"

The man had been silent during this exchange, hovering near the stone box. Now, his face was radiant, his eyes alight with happiness at the sight of the goddess. But the laugh that bubbled forth from his unassuming throat chilled her.

His hands twitched and a blast of fire roared straight at Tsuki.

Colum moved faster than Kai would have thought possible. He leaped in front of the flames, taking the full brunt of the heat to his shoulder. He fell to the sand, smoke curling from his torso.

Kai and Chiya dove out of the way as Jurou burned again, sending flames shooting in each of their directions. But Kai wasn't quick enough.

A blast of heat hit her in the chest, and with a flash of pain, her vision turned red. Then black.

☾

Kai opened her eyes to find them gritty with sand. The world was tilting strangely, and each rocking movement sent shudders of pain through her body, leaving her breathless.

The rocking stopped and Kai felt her body lowered into the sand. She struggled to move, her ears ringing, her eyes blurred with tears. "What...?" she croaked.

Chiya's face swam into view. The look she bore was angry but concerned. "Good," she said. "You're awake. That blasted scar seems to have saved your life."

Kai touched her chest with trembling fingers and hissed as her fingers made contact with puckered, blistered flesh. A circle of angry burns surrounded the handprint. But that was preferable to being dead.

A groan escaped as Kai rolled onto her stomach in the sand. Chiya had dragged her into the protection of the forest, away from the intensity of the fire that Jurou shot at them.

"He herded us," Chiya said. "Away from Tsuki."

Kai tried to think, her mind searching for a way to get Tsuki away from Jurou, but her thoughts felt like honey on a winter day. Chiya was all but defenseless against a sunburner in daytime. Colum was down. But Kai had the white light. She could stop him.

Kai opened her qi to the light to pull the power into herself. The raging torrent ripped through her mind, blasting her head with a searing pain that turned her stomach and blinded her vision. Kai retched into the soft sand, a cold sweat pricking across her body. She slammed her mental doors with a gasp, closing herself off from the light. The pain subsided.

"I can't...burn." Kai gasped, too shaky to even hold her head up.

"Screw this," Chiya said, drawing her sword. "I'm going for it."

She rose and darted forward to take Jurou from behind.

But he must have sensed her. He sent a jet of white hot flame in an arc around him and Tsuki, melting the sand into a bubbling line of molten glass.

Chiya fell back into the sand, scrambling away from the inferno. There was no jumping over that arc. Not if she meant to live.

Tears rose in Kai's eyes unbidden, not from the heat or smoke of the flames. They were so close. They had found the goddess. And freed her. And now this?

Kai dragged herself to her knees, wiping the sand and sick from her face.

"Jurou!" she shouted, her voice hoarse. "Whatever you think you're doing, don't! Help us save this world! Give Tsuki back to us!"

He sneered as he tightened the final strap of his koumori's harness. The beast was clicking nervously at the flames, huddling close to the sea waves. He strode to stand across the line of fire from her. Gone were his shaky hands, his nervous mannerisms, his hunched scholar's shoulders. This man stood tall as he looked down on her.

"I'm not interested in saving this world," he said. "I will remake it into a world of darkness and fire. No more burners or *seishen*"—he spit the word—"no more kings or queens. The tengu have promised me that."

"The tengu are using you," Kai managed. "They'll discard you as soon as you've outlived your usefulness."

"Even now, your ignorance astounds me," he said. "I am using them! Just as I used you! The scroll, the blood of the heir, you never would have gotten this far without me leading you by the nose. It wasn't the tengu who trapped the god and goddess, it was your precious burners! They hid them to protect them. And now you've uncovered them for me once again. I must thank you. Without your assistance, I never would have made it this far. You have the privilege of knowing that you played an integral part in the unmaking of this world."

Kai's mind reeled. Had she truly undone what Hamaio and her followers had died hundreds of years ago for?

"What will you do?" Kai asked, afraid of the answer.

"I will kill your precious goddess and use her silver blood to rip open the seal between this world and the spirit world." He smiled grimly. "I was going to kill you. But I wouldn't deprive you of the moment when the moon goes dark for all eternity. And then the sun." He strode back to his koumori, picking Tsuki up and throwing the goddess over his shoulder like a sack of grain. He trussed her in front of the saddle, tying her down. Tsuki looked faint, eyes blinking in confusion as Jurou bound her to the saddle. Why didn't she do something...god-like to defend herself?

Hiro. Emi. Kai's heart twanged painfully. Were they under attack too? Already dead? She looked at the sun hanging over the horizon in the east. Taiyo wasn't dead yet. Maybe Kai could stop it somehow...but she couldn't even stand.

Kai knelt in the sand numbly as Jurou's koumori took flight. Through the shimmering heat and flames, she vaguely registered Chiya moving around the arc of fire to fall to her knees beside Colum, feeling his pulse. At her side, Quitsu called out to her.

But her eyes were locked with Jurou's own—black and cruel in the firelight. As his koumori rose in the air, he burned a blast of fire, engulfing the island's lush forest in flames.

It was all going up in flames.

CHAPTER 36

Riding a dragon was nothing like flying on a golden eagle. The ride was smooth and fast; the wind chilled Hiro's face, whistled in his ears. In front of him flew Taiyo, the sun god. His god. That he had worshipped all his life.

The god was nothing like he'd expected. He had expected someone powerful and forbidding, like the legendary warriors of sunburner lore. Instead, the god seemed almost...absentminded. Hiro wondered if hundreds of years frozen in ice had...damaged him somehow. He shook the thought aside. Clearly the god still had some power, or he wouldn't have been able to summon these dragons. Hopefully, these weapons he spoke of would be enough. They had to be enough.

After several hours of riding, they began to descend into the burnt expanse of the Tottori Desert. The air was clear and dry and the sun scorched Hiro's back, thawing his frozen appendages.

They landed with a flurry of sand underneath alabaster dragon wings. Taiyo hopped off the back of his dragon and stood before its reptilian face, communicating with it in a language totally unknown to Hiro. The others dismounted as well, bodies stiff from hours clutching dragon hide.

"What is he doing?" Emi asked in a loud whisper.

"He seems to be...talking to it," Hiro said.

"Why?" Emi asked, mirroring the question in Hiro's own mind.

Hiro sighed and approached where the god and dragon were carrying on their conversation.

"Excuse me," he interjected, leaning forward apologetically. "Is...is there some sort of problem?"

"I think this dragon has a mental deficiency," Taiyo said, putting his hands on his hips. The dragon reared back slightly and growled at the comment. Perhaps the beast couldn't speak their language, but it could clearly understand it.

Taiyo continued. "I asked it to bring me to Yoshai, but it has brought me to this wasteland instead. Is this some kind of joke, dragon?" he demanded.

"What does the dragon say?" Hiro asked, wanting to apologize to it for Taiyo's rudeness.

"He says we are here," Taiyo said, looking around. "But how could we be here? There is nothing but sand!"

"You've been gone for hundreds of years," Hiro said. "And according to the histories, this desert wasn't always here. Is it possible your city is...gone?"

Taiyo stroked his chin, considering this possibility. He closed his eyes and outstretched his hands. His body began to vibrate, humming slightly. Hiro took a step back.

Taiyo's golden eyes popped open. "It is as you say. Yoshai has fallen into the earth. No doubt these tengu are to blame for burying our glorious city in this wasteland."

Hiro's shoulders sagged. His own dismay was mirrored on his friends' faces. They had flown into the middle of the Tottori Desert for a promise of ancient weapons that were now buried under hundreds of years of sand.

Taiyo clenched his fists, his eyes flashing. "I'll show them." The god closed his eyes again, taking a deep breath. Golden light began to pour out of him like it had before. But it grew brighter, so bright that Hiro was forced to shield his eyes. The dragons took to the air in a flurry of wings and mirrored scales.

Hiro backed up, joining the others. The ground underneath them began to shake. Emi grabbed Daarco's arm, steadying herself.

"What's happening?" Stela asked, linking hands with Leilu.

"I don't know," Hiro said, "but I don't like it."

The shaking intensified, tossing Hiro forward to his knees. The sand shook around them like rain droplets falling on the surface of the ocean.

"I think we're…rising," Daarco said, awe in his voice.

Hiro saw that it was true, as the ground where they stood now seemed to tower above the desert floor. Shapes were forming—walls, windows, the contours of roofs and buildings beyond them.

"Is he building a city?" Emi asked in disbelief.

"I think he's raising it," Hiro said, realization dawning on him. "I think it was here…before."

Minutes passed before the shaking stopped. Taiyo dropped his arms and opened his eyes. The light emanating from him faded and died away.

Hiro's jaw dropped as he surveyed what Taiyo had unearthed. They were standing in the courtyard of a palace. A long line of steps descended before them into a tiered city of tan and red sandstone interspersed with pink-veined marble. Behind them, there were sweeping round towers reaching skyward, topped with glittering blue- and green-tiled domes. The city below held graceful arching bridges, sturdy streets, orderly homes and shops. It was magnificent.

Taiyo walked over to the edge, surveying the scene below. He moved stiffly and his face was drawn. Raising the city had taken a toll. "It's a magnificent city," he said. "Of course, we'll have to wait for Tsuki to bring the water and grow the plants. That sort of thing was always her forte."

"How many people lived here?" Emi marveled.

"Thousands," Taiyo said. "It was our palace and home. This is where they will come for us."

"When?" Hiro asked.

"Soon," Taiyo said, pointing to the east. In the far distance, a tiny black dot was barely visible, marring the perfect apricot expanse of the desert.

"What's that?" Daarco asked.

"Tengu," Taiyo said grimly. "They must have sensed my work here. Ready yourselves for a battle, my brave burners."

Hiro shielded his eyes from the sun and squinted. He couldn't tell from this distance how many shapes made up that dot.

"Let's get inside," Hiro said. "Emi." He pulled her aside. "Have Taiyo summon one of the dragons again. Fly to Kistana as fast as possible. Tell my father to send every sunburner in his army as quickly as possible."

"You'll need every fighter here," Emi protested.

"It's daytime. You're a valiant warrior, but less help here than a sunburner. Even if you can bring five or ten, it could mean the difference…" He looked at the horizon. "Between us making it or not."

"How will I convince him to believe me? I could be leading him into a trap."

Hiro took off his signet ring. "He knows you from the Battle at the Gate. And give him this. Convince him. You must."

"I'm going with her," Daarco said, stepping up.

"You know you can't," Hiro said, at the same time that Emi said, "No."

"I need you here. You're my only other sunburner," Hiro said.

Daarco ground his teeth but nodded sharply. He turned and swooped Emi into his arms, locking his lips with hers in a fervent kiss.

Emi twined her fingers in Daarco's hair, leaning into him.

Hiro raised an eyebrow and caught Leilu's eye. She was smirking.

"Ahem," Hiro said, after what felt like long enough.

Emi broke off the kiss and grabbed the ring from Hiro's outstretched hand. "I'll come back," she said breathlessly. "Just stay alive until I do."

"You can count on it," Daarco said.

"Let's get inside," Hiro said to the rest, and they jogged towards the entrance to the palace. The dark speck was growing nearer.

The inside of the palace was intricately crafted. Hiro wished he had time to take in the carvings on the mahogany shutters, the images rendered in mosaic tile, the richly-woven carpets and tapestries. To think that their history and culture had been sitting under the Tottori Desert all this time.

Taiyo led them through a set of sumptuous redwood doors, which opened to reveal a vast chamber lined along one wall with high arched windows.

"This is where we will make our stand," Taiyo said.

Hiro looked around skeptically. "This room isn't very defensible."

"I need sunlight to be at my strongest," Taiyo said. "As do you. Besides"—Taiyo opened the double doors to the next room, revealing walls filled with glittering weapons—"we're close to the armory."

The huge armory bristled like the inside of a giant porcupine. Bows and arrows, spears, swords, knives, maces, and more lay neatly on racks and wall hooks. Several suits of practice armor formed of padded leather plates stood in the corner.

"Many of the weapons in this room are specially designed to fight tengu," Taiyo said. "I infused them with light myself. Tengu are creatures of darkness. The weapons don't stop them completely, but they weaken them."

They flocked to the walls and racks to pick out weapons, giving them test swings and jabs to get a feel for their balance and weight. Hiro was drawn to a set of double swords that hung in an X on the wall. The hilts were wrapped in sturdy red leather and their pommels were formed of twin nuggets of unfinished amber.

"Fine choice," Taiyo said, startling Hiro.

Hiro turned, circling his wrists, feeling the heft of the blades. "They'll do."

"Might I recommend adding a few of these to your arsenal?" Taiyo said, opening his hand to reveal two innocent-looking glass vials.

"What are they?" Hiro asked, taking one of the vials and holding it up to the light. It was two vials in one, Hiro realized, sealed on each end, with a division of glass in between. The liquid in one chamber was a murky silver, while the other was a liquid gold.

"A concoction dreamed up by one of my old allies." Taiyo said, a wistful look in his eye. "An extraordinary burner—and an innovative fighter. When the glass breaks, the sun and moonlight combine into quite an explosion. Pure white light. Just throw it at an enemy, and it will break."

Hiro's eyes widened as he regarded the vial with newfound respect.

"These vials contain light? From a burner? How is that possible?" He recalled when his and Kai's powers had merged in the Battle at the Gate last year, forming a powerful shield of white light.

"No idea." Taiyo shrugged. "Like I said, he was innovative. There are more over there." He motioned to a table in the corner of the room.

"Thank you," Hiro said, putting the precious vials in his shirt pocket. Once again he was struck by how little they knew about burning. About their world. If the burners who had created such fantastic weapons hadn't been able to defeat the tengu, what hope did he have?

The hours quickly passed, full of nervous energy and sharpening of blades. The burners had emerged from the armory bristling with weapons. Stela had slung a bow and a quiver of arrows over her shoulders, while Leilu bore a yari staff with a wicked curved blade. Daarco held a double-headed masakari axe as tall as he was and had shoved four daggers into his belt.

Hiro sent Leilu and Daarco to search the palace for any signs of water or food, after their restless pacing across the great hall began to drive him mad. Hiro suspected it was a futile effort, but it gave them a task and got them out of his hair, which Hiro counted as a small victory.

Stela seemed content to sit with Taiyo, asking him quiet questions about his former life and the movement of the stars and seasons.

As for Hiro, he sat with Ryu's head on his lap, stroking his seishen's thick mane. Ryu's wound from Geisa's blow had healed into a neat red line, and Hiro didn't think it would trouble him during the battle. The seishen's close ties with the spirit world lent added benefits to their mortal bodies. Hiro was a bit envious, but grateful, for Ryu's quick healing abilities.

☾

Daarco and Leilu jogged back into the great hall, their waterskins empty. Daarco leaned against the two huge doors, closing them with an ominous thud.

"They're almost here," Leilu said, breathless from their rapid return.

"No," Taiyo said, standing and walking to one of the tall arched windows. "They have arrived."

A flock of black creatures streaked past the window, descending into the courtyard outside with thuds and screeches.

Hiro motioned the others to him. "We keep Taiyo safe no matter what. Hopefully, Emi will return with reinforcements. But until she does, we're all he has."

"He *is* a god," Leilu said in a low tone. "Don't you think he could take some...you know...ownership over his own safety?"

"I'm sure he will join us in the fight," Hiro said. "He did raise this place so we could access the weapons."

"Do you think..." Stela began. She pursed her lips. "Never mind."

"Out with it," Hiro said.

"I'm sorry. I'm just wondering if it was a mistake to make our stand here. Should we have fled, gotten Taiyo to somewhere safer?"

"I wondered that too," Hiro said. "But as far as we know, wherever we go, there could be tengu and Order of the Deshi there. Better to make a stand where we can defend ourselves. And hope reinforcements come."

"We hold out as long as we can," Daarco said.

"Do you think they'll tell stories about this day?" Leilu asked with a grim smile.

"We woke a god, rode on dragons and saw a city rise out of the desert," Hiro said. "And it's only the afternoon. I'd say this is a day for the storybooks."

As the words left Hiro's mouth, the heavy doors at the far end of the hall burst open.

A nightmare flooded in.

CHAPTER 37

K ai stumbled forward through the sand, falling to her knees beside Colum's prone body.

Chiya was already evaluating his condition. She held her fingers to his neck, feeling for a pulse.

Kai bit her lip, watching with wide eyes. How could he have survived a blow like that?

"I feel something," Chiya said, her shoulders sagging in relief.

Kai closed her eyes briefly, gratitude welling through her.

"Colum." Chiya shook his shoulders gently. "Colum, wake up."

He moaned, but his eyes remained closed.

Chiya narrowed her eyes, and in one swift motion, she unstopped her canteen and dumped the contents over his face.

Colum's eyes flew open and he gasped for air, his hands clutching his chest.

Tears sprang to Kai's eyes as she and Chiya exchanged a look of relief. Then they quickly looked away from each other, realizing that they had unfinished business between them.

"Colum," Kai said. "It's a miracle you're alive. Jurou got you with a fireball."

"You don't think…" He coughed weakly. "I'd die without getting paid?"

Kai laughed out loud. "Of course not. You wouldn't let me off that easy."

"Exactly. Now help me up."

Kai and Chiya helped Colum into a seated position in the sand.

The three humans and two seishen looked back at the island in dismay. Every living thing was on fire, the flames burning tall and hot behind them, palm leaves curling and smoking in the heat. Their koumori had fled; Kai could see their dark forms in the distance headed to the next island.

"We're trapped," Chiya said.

"Can we swim for the next island?" Colum asked.

"Not in your condition. Or mine," Kai said, struggling to take a deep breath. "Quitsu, can you reach the koumori? Or another seishen?"

"I can't speak to koumori telepathically, and we're too far from other burners to reach any seishen," he said. "I'm sorry."

"Could you try your fancy new power?" Colum asked, pointing to the handprint on Kai's chest.

"I don't know what it could do to help us," Kai lamented. "It doesn't cooperate when I ask it to."

Kai looked back at the flaming island and swallowed, her dry throat sticking. Maybe this island would be all of their graves.

Chiya stood in a fit of rage, her hands balled into fists at her side. "How could you let this happen, Kai? I thought we were freeing the goddess so she could help us! Not so we could deliver her to the tengu wrapped with a bow!"

"I…" Kai faltered. "I missed it. I wanted so badly to believe we had found a solution…I missed the signs. I should have realized there was something off about Jurou."

She should have seen it. How he'd showed up unannounced. How he had conveniently discovered the scroll that started them on this whole wretched course. Geisa's escape, still unexplained. She should have seen through him. But he was so helpful, so unassuming. And she had been desperate for a way to fight the tengu. "Do you think the others…?" She thought of Hiro, Emi and their team. Were they under attack as well?

"Probably!" Chiya said. "If they've freed Taiyo, it's only a matter of time until the Order swoops in to kill him. It's inexcusable. You had a responsibility to all of us! And here you were harboring secrets, lying, making plans that would mean our downfall! You're no different than Airi."

Chiya's words were like a slap in the face. But a slap that Kai had been waiting for. That she almost welcomed. Finally, someone had spoken aloud what the silent voice inside her had whispered all along. She wasn't fit to be queen. She was no different than Airi.

"Now, now," Colum said. "No need to twist the knife. I've worked for several Miinan queens now, and I can say without a doubt that Kai is nothing like Airi, or your grandmother, Isia."

Kai felt ridiculously grateful for Colum's kindness, a small bloom in a barren wasteland of fear and shame and disappointment.

"Let's not take it out on each other. We know who our enemy is, and we aren't done fighting. It's always darkest before the dawn," Colum said.

"It's midmorning," Chiya said flatly.

"It's a metaphor," Colum said. "Things get worse before they get better. For instance. Take us at this moment. Stranded on this burning island with no water, no transport, grievous wounds... With only two powerless moonburners, two over-important rodents, and one daring adventurer to save the day."

Quitsu and Tanu growled, and Chiya crossed her arms menacingly.

Colum held up his hand. "But take us now, thirty seconds later, when the same ragtag group has discovered a boat."

"We have?" Kai asked.

Colum pointed behind them, where the little teal boat lay forgotten, swamped in the surf, pushed up onto the sand of the beach with each beating wave.

"Colum, you're a genius!" Kai said, springing at him with a fierce hug.

As they rowed through the surf, Kai found herself looking back at the burning wreck of what had once been a tiny paradise. It had gone all wrong.

They hopped out as the boat scraped onto the sandy shore of the nearest island. Colum pulled the teal boat out of the water.

"Now what?" he asked.

Kai let out a sharp whistle to call their koumori. Kai said a silent prayer to Tsuki that they hadn't flown too far. Then she laughed, a harsh sound escaping her.

"What?" Colum asked.

"I just prayed. Force of habit. I guess it's time to stop doing that, now that we've doomed Tsuki to death."

"I was never much for prayer," Colum said. "I've always found it more effective to trust in no one but myself. Harder to be let down. Though not impossible," he amended.

"I'm the one who messed everything up," Kai said. "I'll have to try another philosophy."

"Kai—" Colum began but cut off as black shapes emerged from above the green foliage of the island. Their koumori.

Kai heaved a sigh of relief.

"How will we find Jurou and Tsuki?" Kai wondered.

"I can find them," Chiya said. Her eyes remained fixed on the approaching koumori, her face stormy. "I can feel her. Ever since she woke up. Like a tug inside me."

Because you're the true heir, Kai thought.

Kai's stomach twisted. Every time she thought she felt as low as she could feel, another weight piled on, burying her further.

At the head of the horde was an impossibly tall creature in the shape of a man. Corded muscle bulged from beneath its robes of charcoal and navy. In one massive hand it held a broadsword as long as Hiro was tall. But its face was the most chilling part of the strange countenance; its features were distorted, as if hidden behind a slab of ice.

"Taiyo," the creature said, its deep voice reverberating through the hall and setting Hiro's very bones on edge. "So kind of you to deliver yourself for execution."

"Hiei," Taiyo said, examining his fingernails. He looked up. "To find that you have spent all these years impersonating me? How disappointing. On your best day, you could never be more than a second-rate god."

Hiei snarled, taking a threatening step forward.

Hiro nervously eyed the tengu arrayed behind Hiei. Black twisted shapes, snarling and slathering, clicking and scratching long claws on the polished floor. He tightened his grip on his swords.

"You always did talk too much," Hiei said. "It's all you're good at.

Talk. Talk and hiding. But you can't hide any longer. Your foolish burners made sure of that. They fell right into our trap."

Hiro's face burned at the truth of Hiei's taunt.

"My burners could take you and your mongrel demons blindfolded," Taiyo said with distain.

"You're welcome to try." Hiei's voice lowered to a threatening whisper. "But I've been waiting a long time for this day."

Hiei swung its sword in a wicked arc towards Taiyo, who sidestepped at the last minute. The force of the sword hitting the floor shook the room, obliterating the tiles beneath.

Hiei came at Taiyo again, surging forward. Taiyo ducked out of the way, diverting a ray of sunlight into the demon's eyes.

The tengu roared in frustration, swinging its sword in a wide arc.

Taiyo evaded the tengu's blows but made no attacks of his own. He was a god of creation, not destruction.

Hiro's attention snapped to a snarling tengu coming right at him. He swung his sword and made contact with a sickening crunch, slicing the creature's neck down the spine.

Stela leaped in front of him and shot two arrows in rapid succession into the face of a wolflike tengu racing for them. The tengu crashed to the ground before them, skidding to a halt at their feet. She pulled a knife and tidily slit its throat, opening its neck. Hiro had always admired moonburner fighting prowess.

Hiro slashed at a birdlike tengu that came at them next, its sharp beak headed straight for his face. It knocked him back with one of its wings, but he kept his footing and dove forward, plunging his sword into its soft belly. It fell to the floor with a squelch of black blood. With another swing he lopped its head off.

Hiro took advantage of the brief reprieve to survey the scene. Hiei and Taiyo were still locked in a deadly dance. Black, masked figures at the back of the room directed the lesser tengu, who attacked his friends in relentless waves. Hiro growled. Order of the Deshi. Traitors to humanity.

One of the black-clad figures spun to send two feline tengu towards Daarco and Leilu on the far side of the room. Stela had seen them and sent arrows into them before they could reach their target.

"Save some for us!" Leilu called.

Hiro directed his attention back to the Deshi operative and saw a flash of silver hair beneath her mask.

"Geisa," he growled. That woman had plagued them for long enough.

He pulled sunlight into his qi and burned it into a ball of flame, sending it towards Geisa with all the force he could muster.

She dove to the floor at the last minute, and the ball of fire exploded against the wall behind her.

As Hiro reached for more sunlight to send another volley, something changed. The sunlight slipped from his grasp like water draining out a bathtub.

The light in the room dimmed, as if someone had pulled a curtain across the windows. But the glass windows were unobstructed.

It was the sun. It had darkened.

Hiro looked frantically around the room for the cause of the dramatic change. Taiyo. He was staggering, clutching his stomach. Golden blood spilled over his fingers.

Hiro took in the god's look of surprise a split second before he saw Hiei towering above Taiyo. Its broadsword was raised, swinging down to take the killing blow.

Hiro launching into action, sprinting towards the god while desperately grasping at sunlight. It felt foreign to his mind, far away. He would be too late. Hiei would kill Taiyo. And their world would go dark.

But Hiro wasn't the only one who saw the flash of Hiei's blade, who understood what was at stake if it found its mark. Leilu dove towards Taiyo and shoved him out of the way an instant before the sword stroke fell.

It fell instead across her back, slicing her body in half.

CHAPTER 38

As Kai stretched out her hand to greet her koumori, a strange phenomenon occurred. The bright tropical morning sun darkened, as if a cloud had passed over it. But the azure blue sky was cloudless. The sun had...dimmed.

"Taiyo." Quitsu said the word like a groan. He stumbled against Kai's leg.

Kai swooped him up into her arms, holding him to her to hide her shaking hands.

"He's hurt," Kai said, realization dawning. "Hiro's team is under attack. We have to go to them."

"We have to follow Tsuki," Chiya said, rounding on Kai. "Your boyfriend doesn't matter. He's got other burners with him, while Tsuki is completely undefended. Plus, we don't know if Hiro is still in the mountains. We know where Tsuki is."

Kai opened and closed her mouth, trying to find the hole in Chiya's reasoning. She held Quitsu before her like a shield, a barrier between her and the force of Chiya's distain. She couldn't abandon Hiro...could she? But she didn't trust herself anymore. It seemed every decision she made had been wrong. Maybe it was time to let someone else decide.

"You're right," Kai said, finally. "Let's go after Tsuki."

Their koumori harnesses had been incinerated on the island, so they swung onto their koumori bareback, Kai and Chiya holding Quitsu and

Tanu tight to their chests.

"Be gentle," Kai whispered to her koumori, her thighs gripped like iron vises, her fingers twined in the wiry hair at her koumori's neck.

"Appu!"

☾

The next minutes were a blur.

Hiro threw a vial at Hiei, shattering it at the demon's feet in an explosion of white light.

Hiei roared with anger, backpedaling away from the burst of energy, away from the wounded god and Leilu's mangled body.

"Retreat!" Hiro screamed, and the stunned burners leaped into action. Daarco shuffled forward and heaved Taiyo over his shoulder, while Hiro grabbed a berserk Stela around the waist, dragging her away from Leilu. They scrambled back through the doors to the armory, barricading the opening behind them with a huge iron-reinforced beam.

"She could still be alive!" Stela screamed at him, pummeling him with her fists as tears streamed down her cheeks.

Hiro stood and let her flail at him until one of her blows nailed him across the chin, sending his head snapping to the side. He grabbed her wrists in his hands, pulling her to him.

"Stop," he said, as gently as he could with adrenaline surging through his blood. "I saw the blow. There's no way she made it. I'm sorry."

Stela struggled for a moment longer before collapsing against him with shuddering sob.

Hiro wrapped his arms around her and let her cry into his chest, trying to keep the tears from his own eyes. Leilu had saved them. Had saved Taiyo. But her sacrifice might not be enough.

Daarco had torn a piece of his shirt off and was trying to staunch the golden blood pouring from Taiyo's wound. "I thought gods were immortal," Daarco growled.

Taiyo coughed, blood dribbling from his mouth. "Not...totally," he choked out. "Men cannot kill me, but demons like Hiei are not men. They are not even of this world. Against them...I am vulnerable."

Hiro released Stela gently and knelt by Taiyo's side. Hiro examined Taiyo's wound—Hiei's blade had cut a deep slash across the flesh of Taiyo's stomach. Whenever Daarco took pressure off the area to let Hiro examine it, golden blood spurted anew. Hiro knew enough to know that a man likely wouldn't survive a wound like that. Would a god?

Hiro pulled in what weakened sunlight he could and delved into Taiyo's form, sending heat and light into the wound to heal it. It was like trying to patch a river with a bucket of water. It all flowed together.

"There's nothing I can do," Hiro said, wiping a spatter of black tengu blood from his face with the back of his hand.

Their brief reprieve was shattered as tengu bodies hit the other side of the door, scratching and snuffling and growling. Worse was the great laugh that echoed through the wood, setting Hiro's teeth on edge. The explosion had only stunned Hiei.

Hiro caught Ryu's eyes and silent understanding passed between them. They were still alive only because Hiei was content to toy with its prey for a few minutes. But soon it would tire of the game and would blow the doors off their hinges. And then it would be over.

Another crash against the doors made Hiro jump. He gripped his swords and stood, bracing himself for the horror that would come through those doors.

A blur outside the window caught his eye. He squinted, peering into the darkened sky. Another streak. A golden eagle!

Hiro laughed incredulously. "Reinforcements!" he shouted. "The sunburners are here! Emi did it!"

The doors shuddered and splinters of wood exploded towards him. One of the doors had been breached, and a black snout with snapping white teeth shoved through. The tengu scraped frantically at the opening with fangs and claws, diving and plunging to get through. The wood bent and splintered beneath its frantic assault.

Hiro darted forward and slashed it across the face.

The tengu yelped and pulled back from the hole with a spray of black blood. No new tengu moved forward to take its place.

Shouts of men sounded behind the doors, met with beastly snarls and hisses. The sunburners had landed.

"Daarco, I'm going out to see what kind of reinforcements Emi brought," Hiro said. "And to see if there is a better healer among them."

"Let me go," Daarco said, striding to meet him at the doors. "I'm here to kill tengu. Let me do my job. You're more valuable than me."

Hiro considered this. Daarco was probably right, but Hiro didn't know if he could sit in the safety of the armory while his friends fought and died.

"Hey!" Daarco exclaimed.

While they had been debating, Stela had lifted the beam blocking the doors and was slipping out through a narrow opening between them, bow in hand.

Ryu leaped between Hiro and Daarco after Stela, and Hiro darted after. "Stay here and block the door! I'll send someone!" he shouted before slipping into the fray.

"Damn it, Hiro!" Daarco said before slamming the door closed.

The grand hall was a melee of burners and tengu. Twenty sunburners had answered Emi's plea, including General Ipan and his seishen, Kuma. The general, clad in full battle armor, tossed a tengu through a window with a swing of his great axe. Stela was lost in the action, her silver hair flashing as arrows flew true, finding their targets. Four sunburners focused on Hiei, pummeling the tengu with blow after blow of fire and lightning. Hiei roared with anger, throwing fire back at its attackers.

The sunburners were driving the demon and his followers back towards the door one step at a time. Hiro caught a glimpse of Emi, her swords spinning in a whirling arc, taking a tengu down before her.

Hiro fought his way to General Ipan's side, cutting down a tengu who darted into his path, its jaws bared.

"Quite a mess you've gotten yourself into, my boy," General Ipan said as he sank the blade of his axe into the skull of a black-clad member of the Order who had darted at him with needle-thin swords.

"Thank you for coming," Hiro said. "Do you have a healer? Taiyo is wounded."

"That explains a lot," General Ipan said. "Sadayo!" he called to a sunburner on the far side of the room. "To me!"

Hiro and General Ipan fell into a rhythm, swinging and parrying, ducking and cutting. They each felled two more opponents by the time the sunburner reached them.

"See what you can do for our wounded god," Ipan said.

"Through those doors." Hiro pointed. "Daarco is guarding them. Give him some warning before busting in."

The burner nodded and sprinted past them.

"I think it's time for a final push," General Ipan said, surveying the remaining fighting at the end of the hall. Hiei was backed against the far wall.

But before the General could make the order, the great hall shook, as if a giant had taken a step.

Hiei began to laugh and ducked through the far doors, its remaining tengu and Order followers trailing behind.

The sunburners lowered their weapons, looking to the general for guidance.

"What are you waiting for?" he roared. "Finish them!"

The men cheered and headed for the door—Ryu, Kuma, Hiro and the general bringing up the rear. They piled out the door into the sandstone courtyard illuminated by the eerie light of the darkened sun. The sun was setting as it was, and the strange dusk cast harsh shadows across the land.

Hiro was barely out the door when the men in front of him came up short.

In front of them stood Hiei and the tengu masquerading as Tsuki. Yukina. This demon was taller than Hiei and wore dark robes flowing in an unnatural breeze. It shared the strange illusion that was set before Hiei's face, but its face had a different cast, like looking through rain on a windowpane.

But it wasn't the demon's form in all its strangeness that drew Hiro's eyes. Flanked on either side of the two tengu were four massive black beasts. They stood three times as tall as a man on sinewy legs and with long arms ending in curved talons. Their faces were sick corruptions of the visages of different beasts—a falcon, a wolf, a bull, a bear. Massive wings covered with sickly black skin protruded from their shoulders. They were truly demons from hell.

But then, Hiro saw something that filled his mouth with bile, a sight more horrible to him than these demons could ever be.

"Jurou?" Hiro whispered.

Strolling between the two demons came Jurou, his father's historian. Jurou, who had taught him history when he was no taller than the man's waist. Jurou, who'd brought books to the dinner table when everyone else had feasted and danced in the throne room. Jurou, who had been intimately involved in every aspect of his father's kingdom and military campaigns for the last two decades. He didn't look meek or bookish now. He looked triumphant, his head high, his eyes burning in the red light of the sickly sun. An unconscious woman was cradled in his arms. Not a woman. A goddess. Tsuki.

"Jurou, you traitor!" Ipan shouted. "What in Taiyo's name do you think you're doing?"

"Retreat," Hiro hissed at the fighters before him. "Retreat now!" They began to slip behind Hiro and Ipan through the doors. If Ipan could keep talking long enough for them to retreat, they could barricade the doors and regroup.

"It looks like I picked the winning side this time, Ipan," Jurou sneered.

"You're a burner! You must know what they plan! Why would you agree to help destroy the source of your own power?" Ipan said, genuinely lost.

"I've never been more than a second-class citizen to you and Ozora!" Jurou shouted. "Not good enough for a seishen, not good enough to be a warrior. In the new order, I will be first! You will bow to me! If you live long enough."

Most of the men were inside now. "Go," Hiro whispered to Emi with a twitch of his head towards the door. She grimaced, clearly torn about abandoning him. But she relented, disappearing inside.

"Where's Kai?" Hiro asked, his voice low.

"Never fear. I left her quite safe and sound. Although without food or water, she won't be safe for long—"

"Enough," Yukina bellowed, its voice reverberating through his body. "Give us Taiyo, little burners, and perhaps we will spare you. You are clearly outmatched."

"I sent for backup from the citadel," Ipan whispered to Hiro.

"So we need to stall," Hiro breathed.

"Yes," the General said.

"What about Tsuki?" Hiro asked.

"Triage," Ipan murmured back. Hiro understood. Sometimes, a sunburner had to make impossible choices on the battlefield. To abandon a gravely-injured soldier to save one that could be kept alive. They had little hope of rescuing and saving Tsuki out here in the open with dozens of foes set against them. But Taiyo... Perhaps they could still save him.

"We will consider your proposal," Hiro said loudly with a curt nod to

Ipan. The two men and their seishen turned and darted through the great hall doors, slamming them closed against the monsters in the courtyard. They heaved a massive hewn beam down across the door, barricading it before retreating farther into the armory.

"We have minutes before they break through," Hiro said to the others. "If we're lucky."

Daarco knelt by Taiyo and shook his head gravely. The light coming through the windows was dull and watery.

"Orders?" one of the men asked, eying the door nervously.

"They want to kill Taiyo," Hiro said. "We can't let them."

"We have reinforcements coming," General Ipan said. "We hold here and protect Taiyo. If we can't, we do as much damage as possible on our way out of this world."

The men straightened, their courage bolstered by his words.

Until the unthinkable happened. Taiyo took a shuddering breath and fell still. The remaining sunlight winked out, plunging the room into darkness.

Hiro's heart sank. His breath came in shallow bursts in the darkness. They had lost.

The dark room devolved into chaos as the men shouted and moaned in fear, and the demons outside rejoiced with otherworldly howls and screams.

A white orb shot into the air, illuminating the room with moonlight. Emi stood by the body of their god, her face grim.

"Quiet," General Ipan shouted, and the men fell into an uneasy silence. "New plan. We attack and try to rescue Tsuki before they can kill her," he said. "Protect her as long as possible."

"But, General," one burner said, "Taiyo is dead. The sun is dark!"

"You have a sword, don't you?" General Ipan barked.

"Yes, General," the man said, his cheeks coloring under his golden hair.

"Have you forgotten how to use it?"

"No, General."

"Then we fight."

CHAPTER 39

The flight felt like an absolute eternity. They had been flying over the Tottori Desert for several hours but hadn't yet caught up to Tsuki. The sun still glowed mutely in the sky. The fact that it still shined told Kai that all hope wasn't lost. She held on to that hope like a lifeline.

"Is that a city?" Chiya shouted from her koumori.

Kai shrugged, peering through the twilight.

"Yoshai," Quitsu said. "It's supposed to be a legend."

"So were gods and demons," Kai muttered.

As they neared the city, a white shape swooped past Kai in the twilight. She peered into the dim, trying to make it out.

"It's Iska!" Quitsu said.

Nanase's seishen? What was it doing all the way out here?

The bird banked hard to the right, apparently realizing Kai had spotted it.

"It says to follow!" Quitsu said.

"Chiya, Colum, follow me!" Kai shouted.

They landed with a terrifying thud, Kai and Quitsu sliding halfway over the koumori's neck. They stumbled to the ground amongst two dozen other koumori.

"Nanase?" Kai said, squinting in the gloom.

Nanase strode to Kai. "We received word from General Ipan that they're under attack. We thought they could use reinforcements come nightfall."

Kai grabbed Nanase in a hug, the impulse overcoming her.

Nanase stood stiffly for a moment but finally patted Kai on the back.

"Thank you for coming for them," Kai said.

"This is our world too," Nanase said. "And they are our allies now. We fight together. Where's Tsuki?"

Kai bit her lip. "Jurou took her. He's in the Order."

"Damn it," Nanase cursed.

"How are things in Kyuden?" Kai asked.

"Barely holding together," Nanase said grimly. "No doubt this strange darkness will lead to full spread rioting. Even if we are successful here, who knows what we will return to."

Kai drew in a shaky breath. "One problem at a time. We need to get in there—now."

As Kai said the words, the dim light of the sun winked out completely, plunging them into darkness. But it wasn't the darkness of night, full of cheerful stars and the moon's comforting presence. It was emptiness. A black void where something should be.

"Taiyo," Kai whispered.

"We're already too late," Nanase said.

"Maybe not for Tsuki," Kai said. "We go now."

Nanase nodded. Kai darted back to her koumori and hopped on, scooping Quitsu up.

Their koumori climbed up over the wall of the desert city and to the palace that perched at its top. As they neared, a strange feeling overcame Kai. A memory. She had seen this city before. Been here.

They descended towards a courtyard filled with dark figures. Kai squinted, trying to count their numbers. Many. Too many.

Her koumori screeched and lurched sideways, almost sending Kai tumbling from her back. Quitsu was jerked from her fingertips. She managed to grab his tail before he tumbled into the night sky. He yowled with pain as she hauled him up in front of her.

"What was that?" she said shakily, her heart hammering in her chest.

Kai's question was answered as a huge shape banked beside her, approaching Nanase's koumori from behind. It was a massive black beast with wings like a koumori's. A tengu far larger than she had ever seen.

"Look out!" Kai screamed at Nanase.

Nanase reined her koumori in, dropping sharply. The tengu shot past, inches from Nanase.

The ground was rapidly approaching and Kai yanked up on the reins. Her koumori pulled out of her dive just in time, but Kai and Quitsu were torn from her back by the force. They hit the stones of the palace courtyard hard, tumbling in a ball of limbs and fur.

With her head spinning, Kai pulled herself to her knees and then her feet. A line of snarling tengu greeted her. Behind them were Hiei and Yukina flanked by three impossibly-tall and fearsome-looking tengu. Jurou stood between Hiei and Yukina, Tsuki on the ground at his feet. Kai swallowed and drew her sword.

The other moonburners were landing now, jumping off their koumori and drawing weapons, facing off in a line against the tengu. The doors behind them burst open and the sunburners poured out, joining the moonburners' ranks. Hiro and Emi stood on either side of Kai, Ryu at Hiro's side. General Ipan carried Taiyo's body in his arms and laid it gently on the stones behind them before pulling his great golden axe from the strap on his back.

Kai's heart felt as if it would burst in her chest at the gravity of the moment, as her despair over Taiyo's broken body mingled with her profound gratitude for her friends. They could still save Tsuki. They had to.

"Give Tsuki to us," Kai called to the tengu.

"No," Yukina said petulantly, and nodded to Jurou.

Jurou drew a thin dagger from his belt and raised it for the killing blow. But before his blade found its mark, true night fell, and a thin sliver of moon appeared on the horizon.

Tsuki's eyes flew open, filled with shining quicksilver energy. The moonlight pooled and pulsed around her, filling her, pouring from her in blinding rays.

Jurou stumbled back, shielding his eyes from the brilliance.

When the light dimmed, Tsuki stood tall before the tengu in a billowing white gown and bare feet. Her hair was not the silver of most moonburners, but an icy blue, the blue of pale dawn on a clear winter morning. Tsuki surveyed the scene with slate gray eyes topped with thick white lashes, a look of fury on her flawless face.

"You!" Tsuki pointed at Yukina. "What have you done to this world? To my husband?" A bolt of white lightning snaked down from the clear sky, striking the stones as Yukina leaped clear.

And then the battle began in earnest.

The demon horde met the burners in a clash of animal fury against steel and moonlight. Hiei and Yukina launched themselves at Tsuki, who flitted away in darting movements, sending fire and lightning at them with punishing ferocity.

Kai found herself fighting for her life with as fearsome tengu and lightning-quick Order members flew at her in wave after wave.

She lost sight of Hiro and Quitsu and anyone else as her universe narrowed to the fight before her, the next blow, the next foe.

"We have to get the big ones down." Chiya appeared through the crowd as she sliced the head off a bird-like tengu in one swift movement.

"Ideas?" Kai asked, her arm swinging, her chest heaving.

"I…think so," Chiya said. "Follow my lead?"

Kai nodded, skewering a tengu that came at her with gnashing black fangs.

"Come on," Chiya said. She darted into the fight, heading towards the huge black tengu with the head like a wolf. It was tossing moonburners aside like leaves in the wind with smacks of its massive tail and fearsome claws.

Chiya ran under its legs, jerking back at the last minute, narrowly missing being crushed by its huge foot. Kai harried the tengu from the front, slicing at its belly as Chiya circled around behind it.

Chiya slashed out with a vicious blade of light, severing the tendons in both of the demon's hind legs. It reared back and roared with pain, toppling forward first onto its knees, and then to the ground.

Its flailing tail caught Chiya in the chest and threw her across the courtyard, where she rolled to a stop with a crunch against the hard stone wall.

"Chiya!" Kai screamed, launching herself towards her fallen sister. The injured demon scrambled around, roaring its fury at Kai, blocking her path.

Kai felt for the creator's power, the raging river that waited for her. As if the light itself was eager to take part in the fray, it poured itself into her qi as soon as she opened her mind to it. Burning the light in a swift movement, she slit the creature's throat with a blow powerful enough to sink through to its spine.

"Chiya," she screamed again, half-running, half-crawling around the tengu as it thrashed in the throes of death.

Chiya hadn't gotten to her feet. When Kai reached her side, having to fight her way through two tengu on the way, Chiya's face was pale and there was blood on her lips. *Broken ribs*, Kai thought. *Perhaps a punctured lung.*

Chiya's seishen, Tanu, had found his mistress's side and was burying his furry silver face in the crook of Chiya's neck.

Kai knew she shouldn't move her, but Chiya couldn't stay here, exposed. "I'm going to get you somewhere safe," Kai said, sheathing her sword and heaving Chiya up by her armpits. Tanu backed up to give her room. The woman was heavy.

"Let me," a voice said, and Kai turned as Hiro knelt beside her, his face streaked with blood, both black and red. Gratitude blossomed in Kai's chest as she quickly moved to Chiya's feet, lifting her together with Hiro. They carried Chiya though the doors of the great hall before lowering her gently to the floor.

Chiya's eyes fluttered and opened as they settled her down. She reached out one hand to Tanu, who pressed against her hip, whimpering softly.

As Kai knelt down beside Chiya, her eye caught sight of a broken body across the great hall, still in a pool of dark blood. Silver hair stained red.

"Who is that?" Kai whispered.

"Leilu," Hiro said, the word an apology.

Kai squeezed her eyes closed, images of the first night she had met her friend swimming into view. Sitting at a table in the Fox and Fiddle with Maaya and Emi and Stela and Leilu. Leilu's mischievous smile as she ordered another plate of noodles and a second bottle of sake. Flirting with Stela's friends and feeling carefree and alive and welcomed amongst these women, who'd taken her in as one of their own.

"Oh, Leilu." Kai keened, her heart splintering at the loss of another friend.

Chiya coughed and Kai opened her eyes, struggling to shift from one sorrow to another.

"Don't move," Kai said. "I think your ribs are broken. We'll send a burner to guard you."

Chiya gripped her hand as Kai turned to stand. "On the island," Chiya said. She coughed, and blood flecked on her lips.

"Don't try to talk," Kai said.

Chiya's grip tightened as she ignored Kai's instructions. "On the island...I was hurt. I said things I didn't mean."

"You'll have plenty of time to tell me this after the battle," Kai said. "When you've healed."

"There may be no...after the battle." Chiya coughed again.

Kai looked at Hiro and saw her reluctant assessment mirrored on his face. Chiya's condition was grave.

"...Proud to be your sister."

"I'm proud to be your sister, too," Kai said. Chiya's words were a balm to her wounded spirit, her grief, her anger and disappointment at herself. "There's no one I'd rather have as part of my family. After this is all over, I'll tell you everything about our father, all his annoying traits. He would whistle this horrible song..." Kai trailed off as Chiya smiled, her teeth coated in crimson blood.

"He would have loved you so much," Kai said, tears pricking in her eyes. "You would have driven each other crazy, of course. Stubborn as mules, the both of you."

"You're...one to talk," Chiya managed as a triumphant demon cry sounded from the courtyard outside.

"Kai." Hiro laid a hand on her shoulder and squeezed. "We have to go. I think something's happening. I've found a burner to guard Chiya."

A burner Kai recognized from the citadel stood behind him, two short swords bloody in her hands.

"We'll talk about all of this after the battle," Kai said to Chiya, trying to stand. "Catch up on everything."

Chiya pulled at Kai's hand, not letting her go. "You're...a good queen. I've always...thought so."

"Thank you," Kai whispered.

She stood as Chiya's hand fell from her grip.

Hiro ushered her out through the doors, and as Kai looked back at her sister, she couldn't help the feeling that she was seeing her for the last time.

CHAPTER 40

Though the battle was still raging fiercely, it had taken a turn. Somehow, Yukina had wounded Tsuki, and blood now poured from a wound in the goddess's shoulder.

Yukina howled in triumph and redoubled its efforts, slashing at Tsuki with a long, thin dagger in one hand and gouts of flame from the other.

The goddess stumbled backwards and looked as if she would fall.

"Tsuki!" Kai screamed, pulling white light into her qi to burn Yukina out of this world.

But it was too late. Yukina's blade buried itself in the goddess's chest to the hilt. When the tengu pulled the sword out, the goddess fell to the stones in a shower of silver blood.

The moon, hanging low in the sky, winked out.

Kai stood still as a statue, the life drained out of her. Leilu was dead. Chiya was dying. And the moon was gone. Gone.

It was Nanase who broke first from the daze and disbelief that had struck the moonburners. "Keep fighting," she screamed, felling an Order member who ventured too close to the arc of her swinging sword.

The others followed suit, throwing themselves back into the fray, weapons slashing, hacking at tengu and masked Order members. Hiro dashed across the courtyard to take on one of the huge tengu that was being harried by multiple burners and was ripe for attack.

But Kai couldn't move. They had lost. Tsuki and Taiyo were dead. All light and life in this world was gone. What was the point of going on?

"Kai!" Quitsu screamed at her from below, appearing through the mass of booted feet and scratching claws.

Yukina, freed from its fight with the goddess, was now prowling the battlefield. The massive demon stalked towards Kai, the dagger in its hand, still dripping with Tsuki's blood.

Kai looked on, soaking in the violence and bloodshed that she had caused like salt rubbed in a wound. Chiya may have said Kai was a good queen, but it was a lie. Kai had set them on this path. It had been her idea to free Tsuki and Taiyo. She had caused this. Let the Order fool her into handing over the gods. Handing over her world. Her people. It was time she paid for what she did.

Yukina stopped before Kai, a deep chuckle emanating from the demon's throat.

Kai didn't care that the demon was mocking her. None of it mattered anymore. She had been a child playing at being queen. And she had destroyed everything.

As Yukina drew back to strike, a flash of white crashed into her, toppling the tengu onto her back. The tengu fell with a thunderous boom and an immense white form clawed at it, ripping its face and body with sharp talons.

It was the seishen elder, pure white against the blackness.

It leaped from Yukina's prone form and landed in front of Kai, a fearsome sight with red eyes and glorious outstretched wings. "I told you to let them be," it shouted at Kai.

Tears sprang to her eyes as shame welled up inside of her. She hadn't listened. She deserved whatever punishment it had come to bestow upon her. "I'm sorry," she whispered. "For everything."

"Don't be sorry," it said. "Make it right."

It reached out an eagle-like arm and pinned her against the wall. It was going to kill her. And she probably deserved it. She had destroyed its world.

But when its talons made contact with the handprint on Kai's chest, they didn't dig into her flesh. Instead, a white light burst out from her chest and enveloped her and the elder.

Kai gasped in surprise, and with a swift motion, the elder reached out with its other arm and poured a vial of liquid down her throat. Pure sweet water. From the lake that had healed Emi. It had to be.

For as soon as the water passed her lips, Kai's vision exploded into bright white. Images and memories flashed before her. The creator. Sitting with him on this very rooftop, looking at the sea. And then she was him, seeing through his eyes. The beginning of the world. How he'd formed the universe into three realms, banishing the tengu to the demon realm, sealing it off. Then the spirit realm. Creating the sun and the moon, setting them in the sky, bright and cheerful to give life and light to the world he had created. And then the mortal world, shaping mountains, dotting the land with green, washing the earth with blue seas. The first seishen, guardians of the mortal realm, colossal majestic beings that walked the earth and soared through the sky and swam the seas with their burners at their sides. She saw all of it. Knew all of it.

The world she saw when she opened her eyes was painful, wrong. Discordant. It grieved her. Burners bleeding and dying under a moonless sky. Tengu feasting on their flesh.

The tears in her eyes now fell for a different reason. Anger. She met the eye of the seishen elder, and understanding passed between them. Make it right.

The roar of the battle was quiet around her as time seemed to slow. Kai stooped down and caressed Quitsu's soft head, filling him with the magic she had seen, the magic of creation that held the seed of what his ancestors had once been.

Quitsu burst with brilliant radiance and grew in size, transforming before her eyes into a creature of alabaster white that stood taller than she. His teeth and claws shone wickedly, and hard muscle rippled under his snowy fur.

Quitsu adjusted to his new form quickly, diving at a tengu and ripping its head from its body with one jerk of his powerful jaws.

Iska swooped past Kai's outstretched hand and with a touch burgeoned into the size of a roc, a massive mythical bird of old.

The seishen ran to her, understanding though not understanding the power that had transformed Quitsu and Iska. First Ryu, then Kuma, the seishen swelled into beautiful, fearsome versions of themselves that turned on the tengu with a powerful fury.

☾

Blood poured from a slice in Hiro's thigh where a tengu had slipped through his guard. But he wasn't done fighting. In one hand, he gripped his sword and in the other, the tiny vial of light Taiyo had given him. This could be the only sunlight left in the world.

He had seen so many impossible sights that day that he felt little shock when a strange light began to pour from the handprint on Kai's chest, casting a luminous white across the carnage of the courtyard.

The light pulsed from her, filling her, pouring out of her ears and mouth and fingertips. Her eyes were two fissures of glowing white. And then—she did the impossible. He watched as she transformed Quitsu with a touch into a creature of legend, towering and deadly. He watched as the other seishen flocked to her, his voice sticking in his throat as his Ryu went too. Hiro wanted to call him back, to selfishly protect him from this strange transformation he didn't understand.

But it was Kai. Even if he didn't understand what had changed or understand this mystical power she seemed to wield...he trusted her. Loved her. And her power was helping their cause. As long as she stayed alive. Which she seemed utterly unconcerned with. Her sword had fallen from her outstretched hand. Were her eyes even open?

"Protect Kai," Hiro shouted, dashing towards her, taking out a tengu with horns like a bull on his way.

Colum fell in on the other side of Kai, his tanned face smeared with blood, his curly hair wild in Kai's light. Hiro nodded at him gratefully.

As the newly transformed seishen attacked, Yukina and Hiei snarled in rage, sending their tengu into the fray.

The mythical seishen clashed with the massive black demons, meeting with fearsome screams and flashing teeth and claws. Iska grappled with one in the air while Kuma and Quitsu snarled and snapped at the bull-headed beast, sending it to the ground. The burners fought furiously against the smaller tengu, Emi and Daarco standing back to back, weapons swinging deadly glory. Even the elder joined in, ripping and rending tengu flesh with his beak and talons.

But Kai continued to stand still, staring through luminous eyes at Tsuki's crumpled form.

Hiro slashed at a tengu that came slavering towards Kai, taking its jaw off with his sword, as Colum speared one coming from the right. She moved forward towards Tsuki's body.

"Kai, what are you doing?" Hiro said, gripping her arm. She shrugged him off without looking at him.

"Look out," Colum shouted.

Hiro whirled around to meet the newest threat. Geisa stood behind them, her face twisted in hatred, her sword whistling down towards Kai's head.

But Geisa's blade didn't find its target. Colum managed to get the staff of his spear up in time, parrying her blow at the last second.

As her steel glanced off his wooden stave, Colum shoved in front of Kai, facing off against Geisa.

"Mesilla?" Colum said, his voice choked. He lowered his weapon, reaching out a hand towards her, the blood draining from his face.

"Colum!" Hiro cried.

Geisa made to swing, taking advantage of Colum's open guard, but faltered. Her face transformed. Shock, confusion, recognition. "Colum?" she asked.

"Mesilla! It's really you!" he said. "I never stopped lookin' for you...I never gave up hope!"

What? Hiro thought.

"That's not my name anymore," Geisa said, shaking her head in disbelief. Her sword dropped from her outstretched hand and clattered to the stones. She backed up slowly. "Mesilla is dead." She turned and ran. Sprinted away from Colum, away from the battle.

He ran after her. "Mesilla!"

Hiro turned from the strange scene to find that Kai had fallen to her knees beside Tsuki. He drew close and stood over her in a defensive stance. *What the hell was she doing?* She still glowed with an unnatural light.

Kai closed her eyes and put her hands on Tsuki's wound.

Hiro squinted as her form grew brighter, casting white light across the garish scene of the courtyard. Was she trying to heal Tsuki?

Hiro turned his head from the glare and surveyed the courtyard, trying to identify who was still standing. Daarco and Emi. Ipan. He couldn't see Stela or Nanase. Bodies littered the ground.

With a heavy sigh, Kai lifted her hands from Tsuki's still body, the light around her dimming once again.

The moon burst back into existence, hanging low and bright in the sky as if wanting to embrace its weary children.

Tsuki's eyes fluttered open.

Hiro's jaw dropped. Kai had healed the goddess. She had set the moon back in the sky.

The moonburners let out raucous cheers and sobs of relief as they threw themselves back into the battle, burning lightning and fire into the attacking tengu, driving them back. He thought the burners outnumbered the tengu now, three of the largest tengu laying still, their bodies broken on the stones. The seishen harried the fourth. It wouldn't last long. Hiei and Yukina still stood.

Hiei launched himself at Kai, his sword held in both huge hands, but he was knocked sideways by a powerful blow from Quitsu.

Kai stood and turned, gliding like a sleepwalker towards Taiyo. Hiro pulled Tsuki up, supporting her with one arm as he flanked Kai. More burners fell in around Kai now as they realized what she was doing, protecting her as she moved. She stepped over dead and dying on her way to kneel before Taiyo's body and turned to her task of restoring the sun.

When Taiyo's eyes snapped open, Hiro let out a shuddering breath of relief. The feeling of sunlight, liquid heat and fire raging over the next horizon, flooded back into him. He wanted to weep with joy, to pull Kai into his arms and kiss her for the miracle.

But Kai wasn't herself. She stood and turned back to Yukina and Hiei. The two had drawn together, backing up slowly against the far wall of the courtyard. Their robes were torn and Yukina had long, raking wounds down her face and chest. The rest of their tengu army had been dispatched, black bodies lying broken and mangled on the stones.

"You do not belong here," Kai shouted, her voice echoing through the night with the force of eons.

Yukina turned and seemed to tear the air behind them, ripping the fabric of the mortal world to form a yawning opening. The air around the demons crackled with energy.

"This is not the end, burner," Hiei snarled. The two demons turned and leaped into the blackness of the rift, disappearing.

Kai started forward after them. *Was she crazy?*

"Wait!" Hiro grabbed her hand. "What are you doing? You don't know what's in there. It could be a trap!"

Kai turned back and shook her head sadly, her eyes glowing with the raw magic of creation. "It's my path. You have to let me go."

Hiro hesitated…and dropped her hand.

She leaped into the darkness.

She was gone.

CHAPTER 41

Kai found herself in the upper courtyard at Yoshai, a cool breeze rustling her hair. The courtyard was empty of burners and tengu and bodies. She was in the spirit world. Alone.

She turned back to the rift the tengu had torn, using the creator's fingers to feel the torn fabric of the seal between worlds. She summoned the pure white power of creation, the sweet nectar that she had come to understand through her visions. She had watched as the creator built the first walls between the realms. She had seen it. She had done it herself. She knew the magic by heart. And so she pulled the threads of the universe together, binding them into a barrier so secure and indestructible that the tengu could never pass. Stronger than last time.

"Kai!" a voice screamed at her.

Kai opened her eyes to see Hiei's sword swinging at her neck. Kai flickered out of existence as it swung through where she stood, rematerializing a step away. Thanks to the knowledge the seishen elder had imparted, she finally understood the rules of this place. She was the master of this world.

The warning had come from Hamaio, who stood at the far side of the courtyard, her lovely features tight with worry.

Hiei and Yukina faced off against Kai now, bellowing. They attacked in tandem, striking at her with deadly weapons and savage fists.

Each blow, Kai simply avoided, flitting about the courtyard like a hummingbird, too fast for them to catch.

The demons howled in frustration.

"You don't belong here," Kai said, furrowing her brow. "You have terrorized this realm for too long."

She took a breath, and with it seemed to grow until she stood even with the two tengu, tall and strong, looking into their strange faces. She reared back and with a mighty blow, hammered the heel of her hands directly into their chests.

As she pushed, she opened a rift into the demon realm, sending them through into the eternal darkness beyond, the empty void that was their home. And just as fast, she sealed the opening behind them, strengthening and fortifying the walls between the spirit world and the demon realm until no demon would ever be able to pass through, no matter what cruel magic sought to aid them.

When her task was complete, Kai stumbled, fatigue washing over her. The sky lightened in the east, the sun dawning. Time had always been strange in the spirit world.

Kai found her way to a chair by the small table at the back of the courtyard, collapsing into it.

Hamaio sat down next to her in the chair Kai herself had once sat in.

"You did it, Kai," Hamaio said warmly. "He's very proud of you."

Kai laughed ruefully, blowing a lock of unruly hair off her forehead. "All I did was clean up my own mess."

"This mess was fated, even before my time. The tengu had set out on this path many centuries ago. All he could do was hold back the tide until he found someone strong enough to finish it. To make it right again."

Exhaustion was overtaking Kai as the creator's intoxicating power drained from her. "Why didn't he tell me? Explain everything in the beginning? Why put us through all of this?"

"He's not allowed to directly interfere once the creating is done. It's one of the immutable laws of this universe."

"Lending me his power isn't interfering?"

"He sent you back to the mortal world when it wasn't your time to die. It's not his fault if you borrowed a little power on your way back."

"Borrowed? I didn't do anything…" Kai began in disbelief but then relaxed as Hamaio winked.

"I wish he would have told me what he wanted of me. So I didn't have to muddle through and make such a mess of things."

"He gave you what aid he could and trusted that you would the find the rest of the puzzle pieces when the time was right. The fact that we are sitting here shows that his trust was not misplaced."

Kai looked down at the handprint. It glowed faintly, strangely warm against her skin.

"It's ready to find its way back," Hamaio said.

"What?"

"His power." Hamaio nodded at the handprint. "It was never yours to keep. I suspect you know that."

Kai nodded, relief coiling through her. She missed moonlight, silvery sweet and simple and familiar. "How do I…?"

"Just release it. It will do the rest."

Unsure what Hamaio meant, but trusting the magic to find its way home, Kai closed her eyes, imagining herself standing beside the whitewater rapids of the creator's power. *Thank you,* she thought. *But it's time to go now.*

The river churned and bubbled in farewell before it vanished, leaving the afterimage of its brilliant course burned in her mind's eye.

Kai opened her eyes. Between her and Hamaio flapped a soft iridescent moth the size of her palm. It flitted for a moment around Hamaio before rising into the air and flapping into the distance, leaving a trail of light in its wake.

Looking down confirmed what she already knew. The handprint was gone. She sighed with relief. "What now?" Kai asked.

"It's still not your time," Hamaio said.

Kai pulled her knees up to her chest and wrapped her arms around them, laying her cheek to rest on them. "I don't know if I can go back," she whispered. "Everything that happened…so many people died because of me. I led them astray."

"This is true. But you saved them too. Being a leader doesn't mean being perfect. There is wisdom in admitting your imperfections and learning from your mistakes."

"I'm tired of learning," Kai said. "I'm just tired. I don't know if I want to do it anymore. I wasn't even Tsuki's true heir. What right do I have to rule Miina?"

Hamaio laughed. "Of course you're not the heir. You're the queen."

"What?" Kai asked. "No, Chiya is older; she was supposed to be queen."

Hamaio pursed her lips as if suppressing a smile. "My husband and I tied the gods' hiding places and the clue box to our heirs, the sunburner and moonburner next in line for the throne. We knew we might be lost in the battle against the tengu, and we wanted someone who would remain. You are the current queen, the wearer of the lunar crown, so it was *your* heir whose blood was necessary. The sunburner king, what's his name, Ozora? He couldn't have opened it either—only his son, his heir, could."

A scarlet flush colored Kai's cheeks. She hadn't even thought about the fact that Hiro, not his father Ozora, could open the box and Taiyo's tomb.

"See?" Kai said weakly. "I couldn't even interpret your riddle correctly."

Hamaio leaned forward and took Kai's hands in her own. "He saw something in you, Kai. When you appeared in the spirit world near death but full of light, clinging so hard to life. He saw a chance for this world. Is that woman gone? That spirit?"

Kai didn't respond. That woman was before Leilu. And Chiya. And bodies crushed by earthquakes and wasted by famine. And mobs at the gate and being tricked by the Order. Before the misery and despair of looking up into a moonless sky and knowing the sun would never rise.

"I suppose you could stay if you truly wished it." Hamaio frowned. "I will let you think on it. But in the meantime, the creator would like to give you a gift. As a token of his appreciation."

"A gift?"

"I'll send it up." Hamaio stood and left Kai, disappearing down the steps at the far end of the courtyard.

Kai stood and walked to the edge, surveying the shining line of the sea as the sun warmed her face. It felt good to be alone. No worries. No obligations.

But she wasn't without worry, without obligation. Her mind flashed to the people she loved, their faces conjured up before her. Had others been lost in the battle? What had happened to the seishen when she'd vanished? Did she really want to stay here? Never return? What would happen to Quitsu? What would Hiro think?

"There you are, my little fox."

Kai whirled around at the deep voice, a tight knot forming in her throat.

"Father?" she said, her voice a whisper.

He stood before her, tall and as strong as the last day she had seen him. His short hair was burnished gold now, shimmering in the morning light. He grinned, his white teeth flashing.

She ran to him and threw herself against him, her face buried in the muscles of his chest. Tears sprang to her eyes and she sobbed, wetting the linen of his shirt.

"Shhh," he said, rocking her in his arms.

She pulled back. "I'm so sorry I couldn't save you. I'm so sorry I didn't listen and I was exposed as a moonburner and everything is my fault." She buried her face again, sobbing as two years of guilt bubbled forth, a shallow wound that had never healed.

He laughed his deep barrel laugh, and the sound of it was so wonderful that her tears doubled, a waterfall of emotion pouring from her. Gods, the world wasn't right without that laugh.

When Kai's tears finally began to subside, her father, Raiden, cupped her blotchy face in his hands and looked into her eyes. "You saved our people from destruction twice over, once from a war where we destroyed each other, and now from an enemy that would have devoured us all. This world owes you a debt of gratitude."

"But so many have died," she said. "Because of me."

"No." He shook his head vehemently. "People live because of you. This world is safe because of you. Everyone who has died fighting this evil did so because they chose to. When you take the blame for their deaths, you diminish their sacrifice. You didn't force anyone to fight."

She hadn't thought of it that way.

"I was sentenced to die twenty years before the sentence was ever carried out. Those twenty years were a blessing from the gods. They were the best of my life because of your mother—and you. I have no regrets."

His deep chocolate eyes soothed her. "You must put your regrets aside too. Do not let what has passed before cripple the life you have left to live. Every wrong decision was the right one in the end. The creator knew he could trust you. And I'm sure as hell glad he did, or I'd be a tengu sandwich right now. Even the spirit world was overrun."

Kai cracked a smile, wiping her eyes.

She thought of the storms she had weathered with her friends, the scrapes they had avoided. She didn't bear all the praise for saving their land, and perhaps she didn't bear all the blame for its downfall either. In truth, did she not want to see Miina bloom again, to ruffle Quitsu's soft fur, to feel her body warm under Hiro's touch? She began to smile as the memories flashed by one by one.

But her smile faltered. "I don't want to leave you. Won't you be lonely?"

Her father looked over his shoulder towards the staircase, where a woman stood, silhouetted against the sky.

A sob ripped anew from Kai's chest as she recognized Chiya, her strong arms crossed before her, her silver hair pulled back in a ponytail. She wore her navy moonburner uniform and Tanu sat beside her booted feet, his striped tail swishing.

"I have your sister with me now," Raiden continued. "We have a lot of catching up to do. We'll be waiting for you when it's your time. Just not yet."

Chiya nodded from across the courtyard, a sad smile on her face.

"Okay," Kai whispered, pulling him into another hug, trying to memorize every bit of him.

They pulled apart, and he took her hand, walking with her to the edge of the courtyard, where the creator had once pushed her off.

Kai looked back at Chiya and raised her hand in a solemn wave.

Her sister waved back.

"Ready?" Raiden asked.

"I think so," she said.

Kai stepped up on the low ledge, not letting go of his hand.

She turned.

"I love you," Kai said. "Tell Chiya…I love her too."

"I love you too, my little fox," Raiden said. "And she knows."

Then she jumped.

CHAPTER 42

The first rays of a new day's sun were stretching over the desert horizon.

The exhausted burners had piled the tengu bodies against the far wall and had laid their own dead in a line. Hiro examined the faces, memorizing each one. Leilu. Chiya and Tanu, side by side. Sunburners he had grown up with, sparred with, commanded in battle. The broken golden body of Kuma, General Ipan's seishen, lay at the end of the line, his throat ripped out by the falcon-headed giant tengu. Ryu, who had returned to his original size upon Kai's disappearance, lay quietly by his brother, mourning him.

Nanase was gravely wounded—the gash to her thigh gaped angry and wide. The general sat by her side numbly as Tsuki bent over the wound, weaving moonlight to reknit the flesh and blood vessels.

Hiro put his hand on the general's shoulder.

The general looked up, tears streaking his face. "It should have been me. Kuma had no right to go and die on me."

"He went out how he would have wanted," Hiro said. "A warrior's death."

The general smiled. "It was an epic end to his story. He took down that other big one, you know, before the bastard got him."

"I know," Hiro said. "We'd all be lost without him."

"Proud of him," Ipan said. "It was good to see him like that. It's not often you see a thing's soul from the inside out, but we got to. Our seishen. They're extraordinary beasts."

Hiro nodded. "Kuma was one of the best."

Hiro looked around the courtyard at the moonburners tending wounded, at the light rising in the east. At the pile of tengu carcasses, Jurou's broken body thrown on top of them. He looked everywhere but the spot where Kai had disappeared. The spot where Quitsu now sat, still as a statue, keeping silent vigil until his friend returned.

The lump in Hiro's throat grew.

Emi and Daarco approached, studying Quitsu's lonely form. "He won't move?" she asked.

Daarco placed a comforting hand on Hiro's shoulder.

"No," Hiro said. "He insisted that Kai will return. And that he'll be waiting for her."

"Maybe he's right," Daarco said.

Hiro let out a bitter laugh. "You never were a very good liar."

"I think..." Emi said. "Her time came when she had the fever. And the last few weeks we had with her... It was borrowed time."

Hiro shook his head. "There must have been something I could've done. A fork in the road. If we hadn't freed Tsuki and Taiyo... If we had discovered the tengu's plan sooner, before the fever spread. Some way we could have seen her through this."

"You could drive yourself mad thinking that way. You did exactly what you were supposed to do," Emi said. "What the world needed you to do. What Kai needed."

"How do you figure?" Hiro asked.

Emi took his hand and squeezed. "You let her go."

Hiro nodded, not trusting his voice to speak. "I'm going to miss her," he finally managed, barely more than a whisper.

They turned away together, unable to look at the solitary seishen any longer.

A loud thud sounded behind them, followed by a groan.

"You landed right on me!" Quitsu's voice exclaimed.

Hiro whirled around. A figure lay on the ground, tangled up with Quitsu. It...it couldn't be. But it was!

Hiro whooped with joy and dashed over to where Kai and Quitsu lay.

He swooped Kai up in his arms, spinning her around, crushing her to him. His heart soared with the sight of her, the feel of her in his arms, warm and real.

"I think…I'm gonna be sick," she croaked, and he stopped his mad twirl, setting her down.

He pulled back only slightly, refusing to break contact, needing to feel her solid presence. He took her face in his hands and looked her over. Flowing silver hair, warm hazel eyes, playful freckles dotting her nose. She looked like herself.

"I thought I lost you," he said.

"You almost did," she said. "But I had some help remembering what I have to live for."

"How—?"

His question was cut off as she kissed him, wrapping her arms around him in an embrace full of promises.

"Enough of the kissy stuff," Emi said, trotting over to peer at the two of them from an uncomfortably close vantage. "Spare some for the rest of us!"

Hiro and Kai broke apart with a laugh and Emi wrapped Kai in a bear hug. And then the burners were whooping and laughing and hugging and congratulating Kai in swirls of silver and gold hair.

The excited chatter died away as Tsuki and Taiyo approached hand in hand, the seishen elder behind them.

The god and goddess glowed with life and health. Gone were their disheveled, blood-stained clothes. They wore fine silks—Tsuki a fitted dress of navy covered with stars, Taiyo a handsome tunic of emerald, embroidered with gold.

As they neared, Kai ran her fingers through her wild and tangled hair and tugged at her torn and dirty shirt.

"You look beautiful," Hiro murmured in her ear, and she blushed, allowing her hands to fall still.

"Kai and Hiro, together with your loyal burners and seishen, you have saved us and this world from a dark future."

"It was our pleasure," Kai said, looking sideways at Hiro. He suppressed a grin. Just a walk in the park.

The elder walked between the two gods, and bowed low before Kai. Her eyes widened in surprise at the gesture.

"Kailani Shigetsu, I fear I owe you an apology," the elder said, rising from its bow and sitting on its haunches. "When you came to me in the Misty Forest, I should have let you drink from the lake. Its pure essence would have given you the knowledge you needed to truly wield the creator's life light. But I feared you were not worthy of such power, and so I kept it from you. I see now that I was wrong. I could have made your journey, your fight, much easier. I regret that I did not."

Pain flashed across Kai's face as her eyes flicked to the line of bodies lying on the stones, those friends lost. But Hiro found he didn't have the energy to be angry at the seishen. How could it have known what was to come?

Apparently, Kai reached the same conclusion. "Someone wise told me that every wrong decision was the right one in the end. What matters is that you came when we needed you, and without you, all would have been lost. You have my thanks," Kai said.

The elder bowed again. "I see the creator showed much wisdom in his choice. I am glad to have known you. You and my dear Quitsu are well-matched."

"The elder is right," Tsuki said. "We owe you a great debt of gratitude. How can we repay you? Ask anything of us, and it shall be yours."

"Heal our land," Kai said without a second's thought. "And our people. The tengu wreaked havoc on us…disease, famine, earthquakes. Please set it right."

"It is a wise ruler who thinks of her subjects before herself. It will be done," Taiyo said. "And for you?" He turned to Hiro.

Hiro's arms remained firmly fixed around Kai's waist, and he was unable to tear his gaze from her profile. "I already have everything I want."

Kai's blush deepened.

"If there is nothing you desire other than your beloved," Tsuki said, "perhaps a wedding present is appropriate."

She stood back from Taiyo and closed her eyes, opening her hands to the heavens. The ground beneath them rumbled and water gushed out of the empty fountain in the courtyard below them, the sound of rushing water and tinkling droplets rising like a symphony throughout the city. Plants exploded out of the dry ground to the left and right of the courtyard, vines crawling along window frames, palm trees springing up tall outside of doorways, fruit trees blossoming to shade tidy courtyards. Tsuki's power swept over the city and life sprang up wherever it touched. The music of chirping birds and buzzing honeybees joined the city's vibrant timbre.

When Tsuki opened her eyes and let her hands down, the city was transformed, full of life and color. Over the city walls, the verdant green stretched as far as the eye could see—all the way to the distant sea. The Tottori Desert was no more.

Taiyo put his arm around Tsuki. "Yoshai is a city fit for gods. But it needs a king and queen to rule it."

"Thank you," Hiro said. "I've never seen such a fine city." He turned to Kai with a smile. "I guess we won't need to fight over where we're going to live anymore."

Kai grinned. "Or where to get married."

EPILOGUE

Flurries of activity bustled around her, but Kai was at peace. Quitsu sat on her lap, though Hanae tried to shoo him off.

"He's the same color as the dress, mother," Kai said, rolling her eyes. "Let him be."

Though her aides had insisted that a dress for a royal wedding had to be outlandish, Kai had won that fight. The dress she wore was simple. A fine white fabric, high at the neck with a keyhole back. Crystal buttons ran down the dress's front from her neck to the floor.

She wore the lunar crown woven into her hair in such an elaborate fashion that she didn't think it would ever come out. So maybe she hadn't won every fight.

In the months since the tengu attack, Miina had flourished, and so had she. She still had moments where she felt fragile and full of self-doubt, especially when she went to visit the graves of the burners who had lost their lives in the past year. But she had saved lives too. She would learn from her mistakes and be a good queen, even if it took her a lifetime to learn how. She thought she was headed down the right road.

As Kai walked into the great hall at the palace in Yoshai, her heart swelled at the sight. The room was filled with shining faces with hair of gold and silver. Former enemies, now friends, bonds of friendship and love forged strong in the fire of the tengu attacks. Emi and Daarco, hands clasped and happy smiles on their faces. Daarco had a nice smile.

She had never noticed. Nanase sitting with General Ipan, looking gruff and mirthful, respectively. Nanase was still recovering from near death at the hands of the tengu and was being grudgingly nursed back to health by Ipan, who seemed to appreciate the distraction from the sorrow of his seishen's loss.

There were faces missing. Leilu and Chiya. Sweet Maaya, whose absence still haunted her. Colum, who had left days after the battle in search of Geisa, his long-lost love. He was sure that he could bring her back to herself if he could find her. Kai's father—though somehow, she felt he was watching over her with a smile on his face.

And there was Hiro. Looking so handsome it made Kai want to weep, standing at the end of the hall in a suit of white trimmed with gold. Ryu stood witness for Hiro, Quitsu for Kai. When she reached the end of the aisle and put her hands in Hiro's, her world clicked into place.

They said the vows that would bind them together for a lifetime, and Kai's heart took flight. This day, there was no dire prophecy, no lurking enemy to defeat. Just the ordinary adventure of living each day as the woman she was meant to be.

FROM THE AUTHOR

Dear Readers:

Thank you so much for taking the time to read *Sunburner*!

Reader reviews are incredibly important to indie authors like me, and so it would mean the world to me if you took a few minutes to leave an honest review wherever you buy books online. It doesn't have to be much; a few words can make the difference in helping a future reader give the book a chance.

If you're interested in receiving updates, giveaways, and advanced copies of upcoming books, sign up for my mailing list at www.claireluana.com. As a thank you for signing up, you will receive a free eBook copy of *Burning Fate*, the prequel to *Moonburner!*

ABOUT THE AUTHOR

Claire Luana grew up reading everything she could get her hands on and writing every chance she could. Eventually, adulthood won out, and she turned her writing talents to more scholarly pursuits, going to work as a commercial litigation attorney at a mid-sized law firm. While continuing to practice law, Claire decided to return to her roots and try her hand once again at creative writing. She has written and published the Moonburner Cycle and is currently working on a new trilogy about magical food. She lives in Seattle, Washington with her husband and two dogs. In her (little) remaining spare time, she loves to hike, travel, binge-watch CW shows, and of course, fall into a good book.

Connect with Claire Luana online at:
Website & Blog: www.claireluana.com
Facebook: www.facebook.com/claireluana
Twitter: www.twitter.com/clairedeluana
Goodreads:
www.goodreads.com/author/show/15207082.Claire_Luana

CPSIA information can be obtained
at www.ICGtesting.com
Printed in the USA
FFOW03n1742291117
43832189-42775FF